CW00642278

Pl
on

To
or c

You

COL
CAN

The Girls Who Dared To Love

DINEY COSTELOE

An Aria Book

First published in the UK in 2024 by Head of Zeus,
part of Bloomsbury Publishing Plc

9 7 5 3 1 2 4 6 8

A catalogue record for this book is available from the British Library.

ISBN (HB): 9781801109857
ISBN (E): 9781801109833

Cover design: Simon Michele

Printed and bound in Great Britain by
CPI Group (UK) Ltd, Croydon CR0 4YY

Head of Zeus Ltd
First Floor East
5–8 Hardwick Street
London EC1R 4RG

WWW.HEADOFZEUS.COM

For my beloved family - so strong for
me through difficult times

Chapter One

Lucinda McFarlane stared at herself in the cheval glass, a slim, elegant creature dressed in white silk and lace. Her shining auburn hair, swept back off her face to emphasise her delicate bone structure and artfully arranged in shining folds by Denby, her mother's personal maid, was crowned with a headdress of white feathers, the height of fashion and *de rigueur* for a debutante to be presented at court at Queen Charlotte's Ball. Could this really be her? She smiled at the mirror and her reflection smiled back.

Turning to her maid, Clara, she said, 'Is this really me?'

'Oh Miss Lucinda,' cried Clara, 'You'll be the belle of the ball!'

Both Clara and Denby had been hired by Lady McFarlane when her own personal maid had left under a cloud, earlier in the year. Denby, an experienced lady's maid, had agreed to train Clara, much younger and less experienced, in all she needed to know.

'If you work hard and listen to what Miss Denby tells you,' Lady McFarlane said to her, 'there is no reason why you shouldn't, in time, become a proficient lady's maid. One day Miss Lucinda will be getting married and setting up her own establishment, and you could take a senior position in that household.' With a serious look at Clara her ladyship went on. 'You understand what I am proposing, Clara?'

Clara, who certainly did understand, bobbed a curtsey and said, 'Yes, my lady. Thank you, my lady.'

The plan had been a success. Clara was quick to learn, and though on this very special evening it would be Denby who styled

Miss Lucinda's hair, it was Clara who had helped her put on her silk stockings, her silk chemise, and at last her court evening gown and evening gloves. Denby had been summoned to dress Lucinda's abundant auburn hair and at last to attach the short train that trailed behind her.

Turning from the mirror, Lucinda rested her hand lightly on the back of a chair and swept the curtsey she had been practising for weeks.

'There'll be no chair to hand when you make your curtsey to the king!' Lady McFarlane had come into the room to approve her daughter's appearance. 'Do it again, properly.'

Lucinda did as she was told, her mother watching her in the mirror; the curtsey was perfect.

'Suppose I fall over, Mama?' Lucinda said. It was something that had been giving her nightmares these last few nights.

'You won't, Lucinda, of course you won't!' Her mother sounded more sympathetic now. 'You just take a deep breath as you move forward to the face the king and queen, remember to smile and just two curtseys later, no more than a moment, it'll all be over and you can relax.'

Lucinda was being sponsored for her presentation by her mother's school friend, Amelia FitzGiles, now Lady Charlton, wife of George, fifth Viscount Charlton. Amelia was also bringing out her own daughter, Muriel, and the two mothers had spent the last few weeks making lists of eligible bachelors, prospective husbands for their daughters, guest lists for their coming out ball, and lists of the invitations already received. The girls had known each other from childhood and were eagerly anticipating their joint entry into adult society. Their mothers had done everything they could to ensure that the two girls would shine among the coming season's debutantes. Each of them only had one daughter to launch into society, so no expense was to be spared.

Lady Charlton had favoured Maison Olivier Vaubon for Muriel's wardrobe, whereas Lady McFarlane remained faithful to Couturier Chantal and Madame Chantal, who had, for some years, dressed Lady McFarlane. She was now given the job of producing the numerous evening gowns, day dresses, afternoon gowns, hats and gloves and shoes required for the attire of an elegant young girl about to step into the limelight in search of a husband.

'How can you possibly need all those clothes, Lucy?' demanded her brother, Iain, when she told him about her new wardrobe. 'You'll spend your whole day changing from one to another!'

'A girl making her debut,' said his mother, who had overheard his remarks, 'must be properly dressed for every occasion.'

Over the previous months the two girls had been attended by Luigi Bartoli, an Italian dancing master, who taught them how to make their court curtsey...

'No, no, Miss Charlton... with the right leg forward, so...'

... how to manage their trains...

'Simply slide it a little to the side, Miss McFarlane, as you rise, thus...'

The girls had practised and practised their curtseys, anxious lest their trains should trip them up.

Lady Charlton had invited her dear friend Isabella and daughter Lucinda to travel to Buckingham Palace with her and Muriel in Lord Charlton's carriage.

'But my dear,' said Sir Keir when he heard of this arrangement, 'Croxton can drive you in the Rolls.'

'Yes, I know,' agreed his wife, 'but for the look of things, you know, it would be far more...' She seemed at a loss for the word.

'Impressive?' Sir Keir suggested helpfully.

'Far more *gracious*,' said his lady. Sir Keir gave a snort of laughter and Lady McFarlane pursed her lips. 'We don't want to appear "nouveau".'

'Of course we don't,' agreed Sir Keir, with difficulty suppressing a smile. 'And so much more fun for Lucy to arrive with her friend.'

On arrival at the palace, they had had to wait in a line of similar conveyances before it was their turn to disembark, but at last they were walking in through the doors and up the red-carpeted stairs to the ante chamber where they would wait their turn to be announced.

The ante room was crowded with girls, nearly all of them in white or cream court gowns. Lucy looked round the room. There were several they knew already, girls who had attended the same exclusive school to be 'finished'.

'Completely finished?' Iain had asked innocently. 'Or will there be something left?' A question which had earned him a thump on the arm from his sister and a rebuke from their mother.

'Lucinda's learning the etiquette she needs to take her place in polite society,' retorted his mother. 'And it wouldn't hurt *you* to learn some society manners, either.'

Iain, in his last year at Cambridge, saw little of Lucy and when he came down, he was surprised at the alteration in her, the transformation from schoolgirl to young lady.

'Well,' he said when he had given her a hug, 'you're definitely finished now.'

Now, they were all awaiting the arrival of the king and queen and their entourage in the royal drawing room.

'Isn't this unbelievable, Lucy?' whispered Muriel. 'Us at Buckingham Palace!'

'Being presented to the king himself,' replied Lucy. 'I just pray I don't wobble, or trip over my train.'

''Course you won't,' Muriel assured her, with far more assurance than she felt herself. 'Our curtseys will be perfect and Signore Bartoli will be very proud of us.'

'Aren't you nervous?'

'Of course I am, who wouldn't be? But that part of the evening will be over in a minute or two and then we can relax and enjoy ourselves. We'll have been launched into London society, and,' added Muriel with a grin, 'we shall take them by storm.'

'It's all right for you,' Lucy said. 'You know so many more people than I do. You'll be asked everywhere.'

'So will you, silly,' answered Muriel. 'You'll see.'

The moment they had all been waiting for, prepared for during the previous months, came upon them. The king and queen entered the royal drawing room and took up their positions on a dais, the king standing, his queen seated beside him, surrounded by an entourage of ladies and gentlemen of the court.

As each debutante's name was announced, she entered the room and with practised steps approached the king.

'Your Majesty, may I present Miss Muriel Charlton, daughter of Lord and Lady Charlton...'

'Your Majesty, may I present Miss Lucinda McFarlane, daughter of Sir Keir and Lady McFarlane...'

Lucinda stepped forward and, managing her train with an apparent assurance, which she certainly did not feel, swept her curtsey, remembering to raise her eyes to the king and smile before bowing her head again as she rose and moved on to make her curtsey to the queen; Miss Lucinda McFarlane, a marriageable young lady with a summer of delights before her.

When she had said she knew fewer people than Muriel, it wasn't really true. Her parents had a busy social life themselves and an extensive circle of friends, many of whom had sons and daughters of a similar age to Iain and Lucy, and with Lady Charlton's sponsorship there were already invitations gracing the mantelpiece in the Chanynge Place drawing room, invitations to balls, musical evenings, picnics in the country, theatre visits and soirées.

Lucy joined her mother in a mood of exhilaration. She had made her curtsey, the serious part of the evening was over, now the ball and the rest of her life could begin. They waited together, chatting with Muriel and her mother for the presentations to be concluded so they could all could go down to partake of the supper before the ball began.

And that's when Major Sir David Melcome, Baronet, first saw her.

Chapter Two

Major Sir David Melcome had inherited his baronetcy at the age of fourteen when his father, Colonel Sir Randall Melcome, Baronet, an officer in the Dragoon Guards, had been killed in the battle for Ladysmith in Natal, South Africa. A second war with the Dutch settlers, the Boers, had broken out and his regiment of the Dragoon Guards had been despatched to reinforce the British troops already stationed there. After several skirmishes, and some heavy fighting with losses on both sides, the British troops had retreated and taken refuge in the army fort in the garrison town of Ladysmith, where they were besieged by the Boer Commandant, De Wet, with a superior army. It was one hundred and eighteen days before General Buller broke through the Boers' siege-lines to relieve the Ladysmith garrison, and in that battle, Sir Randall Melcome took a bullet in the neck and died within twenty-four hours. He had been buried at once in the small cemetery outside the town, but the war was not yet won and it was a month before the news of his demise reached his wife Joan, who was left to bring up their fourteen-year-old son, David, as best she could.

Having no other immediate family, mother and son inevitably turned to each other for comfort. Lady Melcome did her best, determined that David should be grow up a fitting heir to his father's title. Eton was followed by Oxford, where he graduated with a second-class classics degree. It wasn't until he had come down from Oxford aged twenty-one that he got up the courage to tell his mother that he intended to follow his father's footsteps and apply for a commission in the army.

'In Father's regiment, of course,' he said, the dark blue eyes inherited from his father glowing with enthusiasm.

'Of course,' replied his mother. She wasn't surprised. She had seen it coming. David idolised his father and was fascinated by everything military. His mother had only the faintest hope it might be a passing phase. It was not, and within weeks of telling her, he was off to Sandhurst. She had known he would go, long before he broached the subject. She wouldn't stand in his way, but her heart ached at the very thought. She had lost her beloved husband to the army, and was terrified she might lose her son as well. David had no such worries. He was welcomed into the regiment as his father's son, the son of a hero, and he had now attained the rank of major.

'You should be very proud of him, Lady Melcome,' his commanding officer said when they met on Derby Day at Epsom racecourse. 'Youngest major in the regiment.'

Joan Melcome assured him she was, thinking even as she said so that she would be proud of David whatever he did. Her only disappointment was that he showed absolutely no sign of settling down and getting himself an heir. It wasn't as if he couldn't attract a suitable, well-bred girl if he wanted to. As an eligible bachelor, with a hereditary title and sufficient fortune, David was at the top of every guest list for those mamas with single daughters looking for husbands. He had enjoyed light flirtations with several hopeful girls but, to the despair of his widowed mother, never with serious intent. He seemed too caught up in army life, too restless, to be thinking of marriage.

'It's high time you settled down, David!' Lady Melcome admonished. 'Time you were starting a family, providing yourself with an heir.'

'Plenty of time for that, Mama,' he had smiled. 'I'm not yet thirty.'

'You should be presenting me with grandchildren by now!' replied his mother stiffly. 'You were ten years old by the time I was thirty.'

'Ah, Mama, that's an entirely different thing,' teased David. 'You were a child bride! It's always different for men, you know that, but I promise you there'll be time enough for grandchildren.'

However, to please his mother, he once more, rather reluctantly, attended Queen Charlotte's Ball, where this year's crop of hopeful debutantes would be on display. It was the usual crush of the great and the good, an evening which he thought little better than a cattle market, and this year seemed no different. Until, that was, he saw, standing in an alcove with another debutante and their mothers, the most beautiful girl he'd ever laid eyes on. David Melcome froze. Who was she? Tall and slim, her auburn hair like a burnished crown beneath her headdress, her movement graceful as she inclined her head in conversation, with sparkling eyes and laughter lighting up her countenance, she was, David knew without a shadow of doubt, the girl he'd been waiting for; the girl he wanted for his own, now and for ever. Farewell to the hope of any mother regarding him as a possible suitor. She must cross him off her list.

He watched as a young man came up and made a bow to the assembled ladies, took the beauty's hand, and said something to her that made her smile.

Such a smile! But who was she? And who was the young man who was so familiar with her? David did not know the beauty or her mother, and though he recognised Lady Charlton, she was not an acquaintance. He was sure his mother would know her, but his mother was not here to effect an introduction. He saw a group of old friends and moved through the crowd to join them, but always aware of the girl.

When the assembled party went downstairs for supper, David saw another young man come up beside her, saw her lay a hand on his arm, allowing him to take her into the table.

As the evening wore on, David discovered her name.

'The redhead?' asked his friend and brother officer Freddie Chambers. 'That's Lucinda McFarlane, I was at school with her brother, Iain. Do you know him?'

David shook his head.

'That's him, with her now.' Freddie nodded towards where Lucinda was seated with the man who had taken her hand. Only her brother.

When they all returned to the ballroom and the dancing began, he managed to effect an introduction to Lady McFarlane through the good offices of one of the chaperones and thus, an introduction to Lucinda herself.

Lucinda had not noticed him before. There was such a crush in the room and her attention had been, naturally enough, on her own curtsey to the king. Now she looked at him with interest. He was a handsome young man, standing a head taller than most of the others in the room, with broad shoulders and an athletic build, at present resplendent in a Dragoon Guard's dress uniform. His dark blond hair was smoothed back from a high forehead, his moustache neatly trimmed above a generous mouth, and the set of his jaw warned of determination. His manners were impeccable and his address charming, but what Lucinda found stayed with her most was the expression in his deep-set, navy blue eyes. Her grandmother had once told her the eyes were the window on the soul, and her words came back to Lucy as she looked into David Melcome's eyes. They danced with humour and glowed with affection, looking at Lucinda McFarlane with an expression she had never encountered before, with a tenderness he had never felt before. Colour flooded her cheeks and she lowered her own eyes as she murmured, 'How do you do, sir?'

'Very well, thank you, Miss McFarlane,' he said with a smile. 'Now that I've met you. May I presume to ask you for a dance?'

Lady McFarlane, hearing the request, answered before Lucinda could reply.

'I regret, sir, that my daughter's dance card is already full.'

'Then that is indeed my regret as well,' he answered. However, turning again to Lucinda, he went on, 'I look forward to our becoming better acquainted in the future, Miss McFarlane.' And with a bow to both ladies, he turned away and melted into the crowd.

'Mama,' murmured Lucinda with an edge of frustration, 'I *could* have danced with him.'

'Not on such a brief acquaintance,' replied her mother firmly. She knew of Sir David by reputation and did not want Lucinda wasting her time with a man who would pay attention, flirt even, but never come up to scratch.

At that moment, Lucinda's next partner, young Gerald Bloom, an old school friend of Iain's, came up to claim her, twirling her onto the already crowded dance floor. Lucinda had known Gerald from the nursery and it was as if she were dancing with another brother, but even as they danced she found herself aware of the tall, attractive gentleman in military dress uniform who had been introduced to her. He was standing with a group of his friends, but with his eyes on the dancers. She would have allowed him to sign her dance card if her mother had not precluded it. She had a dance pencilled in for Iain, and she could have given that to the Dragoon Guard's officer, David Melcome, whoever he was. Her mother seemed to know and did not approve, which, Lucinda thought as Gerald guided her easily about the ballroom, somehow made him all the more interesting.

'I've just been introduced to Sir David Melcome,' she said to Gerald. 'Do you know him?'

'Yes, but not well. We aren't in the same set.'

'So Iain won't know him?'

'I'm sure he knows who he is,' answered Gerald, 'but he's not an acquaintance. He's a major in the Dragoons; not one of us.'

That night, when she finally got into bed, exhausted from the exhilaration of her presentation and first society ball, she thought once more of the tall major with the smooth fair hair and the dark blue eyes, and hoped their paths might cross again at some of the parties to which she had already had invitations.

Lucinda need not have worried. Sir David was asked everywhere by hopeful mothers, and he sought her out at any social gathering to which they had both been invited. On the few occasions when he was not present, Lucinda found herself searching the room for his tall figure and was unaccountably disappointed if he did not appear.

After her own presentation ball, held at the Waldorf Hotel since the house in Chanynge Place had no ballroom, Lucinda had received a severe reprimand from her mama for allowing Sir David two dances on her card, one of which was the supper dance.

'That was most unseemly, Lucinda,' reproved her mother. 'As the hostess you should have ensured no gentleman be allowed that privilege.'

'But, Mama,' protested an unrepentant Lucinda, 'he was the only one who asked me twice,' adding with a faint blush colouring her cheek, 'and he *is* very handsome!'

'What has that to say to anything?' snapped her mother. 'It was most unbecomingly forward of you.'

Following that evening, Lady McFarlane took more careful note of the attention Sir David was paying her daughter. His name appearing twice on Lucinda's dance card might be a sign of serious interest. She knew Lady Melcome was a widow, and that David had inherited the baronetcy when his father had been killed in South Africa.

Would he be acceptable as a husband for Lucinda? she wondered. More than one hopeful young lady had been left disappointed in the past.

'I suppose Melcome might do, if he comes up to scratch,' she said to her husband when he joined her in the bedroom after the select evening party given to celebrate the engagement of Muriel Charlton. 'He spent almost all this evening at her side; far too much to be seemly unless he has serious intent and your blessing on an engagement. Will you allow him to pay his addresses if he asks for her?'

'My dear Bella,' Keir said with a sigh. 'This is Lucy's first season. She's not quite eighteen, hardly more than a child. Surely she must be allowed to consider several young men before being asked to make a choice.'

'Not so much her choice, but his,' replied his wife. 'Once she is provided for, and has an establishment of her own, she will grow into her place as his wife.'

'If he asks to address her, I will consider the matter, but,' Sir Keir added firmly, 'I won't rush her into any such decisions. What does it matter if she isn't engaged to be married by the end of her first season?'

'It will matter to her,' remarked Isabella.

And to you! Sir Keir thought, but did not say. He knew his wife's social aspirations.

'Look at Muriel, already engaged to Lord Frain,' went on Isabella. 'You know he's the Duke of Allerton's heir?'

'Yes, I know. He's also a widower, twice her age, with two motherless daughters.'

'Well, no doubt he's hoping for a son this time,' answered Isabella, pragmatic as always. 'And Muriel will live in comfort for the rest of her life, ending up as a duchess.'

'Is that the sort of marriage you want for Lucy?' asked Keir. 'Surely young Melcome would be far more suitable; a good family, a hereditary title and closer to her in age. Lucinda's very young; she could wait another year, even two or three for the right husband, before being considered on the shelf.'

'I was only just eighteen when we got married,' Isabella reminded him as he climbed into bed beside her. 'And you were twenty-four.'

'So I was,' agreed Sir Keir as he drew her close. 'A difference of six years, not twenty-five. Perfectly proper. And I had to make sure no one else stole you first.'

'Hmm,' sighed his wife as she nestled against him, warm in his arms. 'So you did!' And for the next while, neither of them gave a thought to their daughter.

Lucinda herself could hardly be unaware of David's serious attention, and she had already made up her mind. From their first real encounter at Lady Belston's musical evening, when they had to sit through an evening of chamber music, she felt entirely comfortable in his company. Neither of them enjoyed the music, and with David she found she didn't have to pretend. When the interval came and the guests were invited to the supper table, David was accosted by his hostess and said, 'Beautiful music, Lady Belston.' As they passed on into the dining room he murmured, 'Didn't you think so, Miss McFarlane?'

'No, not really,' confessed Lucinda. 'It was a bit dreary, didn't you think?'

'I did,' he said trying to suppress a laugh at the naivety of her answer. 'But not a sentiment I shall share with my hostess.'

As Lucinda got to know him better, she found she could talk to him about anything, without being anxious about his reaction. It was the way he looked at her from the depths of those dark blue eyes that had captured Lucinda's heart, making it beat faster and filling her with an inexplicable joy.

David longed to speak to Lucinda of his feelings, but she was so young he hesitated. Certainly, he should speak to her father first, but he needed to be sure she felt as he did.

At last he suggested to his mother that she should take a box at the opera for a party of no more than eight, followed by a private supper; a select evening to which Lady McFarlane and Lucinda would be invited. Having finally seen her son interested in a suitable young girl, Lady Melcome immediately agreed.

When the invitation came, Lady McFarlane was doubtful about accepting it.

'I have only recently met Lady Melcome,' she said. 'At Lady Ware's card party, but we've neither of us left cards.'

'Does it matter if you are not yet on visiting terms?'

'It's unusual,' answered his wife. 'Perhaps it is a declaration of intent.'

'Well, so it may be,' Sir Keir agreed. 'But I thought that was what you wanted, to know the man's true intentions.'

'Well, of course, I do,' his lady answered cautiously, 'but...'

'Have you asked Lucy if she wants to go?'

'I know she would *like* to accept,' replied Lady McFarlane, 'But of course it isn't her decision.'

'Who else makes up the party?'

'Sir David's cousin, Maria Helford, and, I hear from Lady Charlton, she and Muriel, escorted by Lord Frain.'

'Then it sounds quite unexceptionable, and of course you should accept,' said Sir Keir. 'It will commit you... or rather Lucinda, to nothing, but it would be a definite snub to Lady Melcome if you refused such an intimate invitation.'

Following the conversation with his wife, Sir Keir took time to seek out David Melcome and finding him at his club, discovered him to be not only pleasant company, but a man who had a great deal of common sense, able to speak intelligently on aspects of the news that Sir Keir would never have discussed with his wife, or even Iain, recently graduated from Cambridge with a first class law degree.

Thus it was, when Sir David asked to speak with Sir Keir on a private matter, he suggested that he come and visit him in his chambers where there would be no interruptions.

When David was shown into Sir Keir's office, he found him seated behind a large desk, with a pile of documents at his elbow. Sir Keir immediately got to his feet and the two men shook hands.

Sir Keir waved David to an armchair beside the fireplace and then took up his own seat, opposite.

'Will you take a drink?' offered Sir Keir.

'No, thank you, sir, no.' For a moment David seemed absorbed by the arrangement of brilliantly coloured dahlias filling the summer fireplace. Sir Keir said nothing, simply waited, and the silence lengthened

'Sir,' began David and then paused again. He had decided exactly what he was going to ask before he came into the room. But now, suddenly faced with Lucinda's father, a judge of renown, his planned words deserted him.

For a long moment there was a silence between them and then Sir Keir took pity on the young man before him. He remembered too well having to ask Isabella's father for permission to address her; and her father had given him no encouragement at all. 'Yes?' he now said encouragingly.

David got to his feet and took a step away. 'I wanted to ask you... to ask you if I might address Lucinda. If I might ask her to marry me!' There he'd said it, and it was greeted with silence.

Then Sir Keir said, 'Sit down again, man. Don't tower over me.'

David resumed his seat, perching awkwardly on the edge of the chair.

'Why?' asked Sir Keir. 'Why do you want to marry Lucinda? You could take your pick of the debutantes.'

'Because I love her,' answered David, 'And I've never seen another girl that I wanted to marry, to spend the rest of my life with.'

'And does my daughter feel the same way?' enquired Sir Keir.

'I think she does,' replied David carefully, 'but I haven't asked her.'

'And if I give you permission to ask her, what then? She's very young. Not yet eighteen.'

'If she accepts my proposal, we shall be betrothed, but need not rush into a hasty marriage. I have waited long enough to find the right woman, I can always wait a little longer.'

Woman! thought Sir Keir. He had never thought of Lucinda as a woman. A girl, obviously, but a woman? Isabella had been eighteen when they had married and she'd certainly been all woman then, but his Lucy?

'Certainly not before she's eighteen,' he declared, before adding, 'And if you are mistaken? If she doesn't want to marry you?'

'Then I shall withdraw my suit,' David mildly, 'and trouble her no more.'

The two men held each other's gaze for a long moment until

finally Sir Keir said, 'You may speak to Lucinda and make your feelings known to her. When you have her answer, and if it is agreeable,' said Sir Keir, 'we can discuss practicalities, her dowry...'

'I have no need of a dowry, sir,' put in David. 'I have the house in Sloane Square where at present I live with my mother and a house in Crayne Abbas, a village near Buckingham. I have plenty of money for us both and will settle her with an independence for her lifetime. Let us make no mention of money again.'

This time it was Sir Keir who got to his feet, followed immediately by David. He extended his hand and the younger man took it.

'I am very happy to allow you to speak to Lucinda on those terms,' Sir Keir said. 'I think you will make her a good husband, but I won't put pressure on her if she refuses you, or if she wants to take her time giving you an answer.'

'Did you *know* he was going to visit you?' demanded Isabella when came Keir home that evening.

'He asked to speak with me, yes, but of course I had no idea what he was going to say.'

'Oh don't be ridiculous, Keir,' cried Isabella. 'You must have guessed. Why else would he have asked to speak to you?'

'He might have needed legal advice about something?' suggested Keir with a smile.

Ignoring this answer entirely, Isabella asked, 'Well, so, what *did* he say?'

'What did he say?' mused Sir Keir. 'He asked if he might speak to her.'

'And?'

'And after some discussion, I said that he might, but if she refused there would be no pressing her to change her mind.'

'So, you have given him permission to come and see her?'

'Yes,' he replied patiently. 'With certain provisos.'

'But when is he coming?' demanded Isabella. 'When have you invited him to come?'

'He will call at three-thirty tomorrow afternoon…' began Sir Keir.

'Tomorrow?' cried his wife.

'Why not tomorrow, my dear?' asked Sir Keir, his eyes twinkling with amusement. 'I assumed you'd want Lucinda's betrothal to be in *The Times* by the weekend. Only Muriel will be ahead of her, you know!'

For a moment Isabella's expression was one of irritation, but seeing his smile, she returned a rueful one of her own and said, 'Well, of course, I should have hoped for a duke, but since you have allowed a mere baronet to address our daughter, we shall have to make do with him!'

'We shall indeed,' agreed her husband mildly, 'and when you get to know him, I think you will discover he is an admirable young man, an officer and a gentleman, intelligent as well as charming.'

Chapter Three

The following afternoon David Melcome presented himself at 11 Chanynge Place and was greeted by Felstead, who took his hat and cane and passed them to William, the footman, before saying, 'Her ladyship is in the drawing room, sir.'

So, thought David as he followed the butler upstairs, at least I am expected. Felstead opened the drawing room door, and standing aside, announced, 'Sir David Melcome, my lady.'

As David stepped forward, he saw that Lady McFarlane was not alone in the room. Lucinda was seated in a chair by the window, a piece of embroidery in her lap.

Lady McFarlane rose to welcome their guest. 'Sir David, how good of you to call,' she said, but she did not cross the room or extend her hand.

'Good afternoon, Lady McFarlane,' replied David with a slight bow, before turning to Lucinda and inclining his head, murmuring, 'Miss McFarlane.'

Lucinda set aside the embroidery in which she had not set a stitch the entire afternoon, and stood up. 'Good afternoon, sir.'

Her mother had mentioned Sir David Melcome might be calling, and Lucinda had spent every minute since wondering why her mother had invited him. Now, here he was.

'Tea,' said Lady McFarlane briskly, adding almost as an afterthought, 'you'll take some refreshment, Sir David?'

'Thank you, yes.'

'Send William up with tea, Felstead,' she said to the waiting butler.

The tea was poured, the cakes were served, and Lady Charlton's dinner party from two days earlier was discussed, before Lady McFarlane turned to their guest and said, 'It is a beautiful afternoon, is it not, Sir David.'

'It is, ma'am,' he replied.

'A pity to be indoors on such a day,' went on his hostess. 'Perhaps you would like to take a turn in the garden when you have finished your tea. I'm sure Lucinda would be happy to show you our roses. I always think a garden should be viewed in the sunshine, don't you? Winter gardens are so dreary, no colour and grey sky.'

'I do so agree,' maintained David, though he had never paid gardens that much attention. 'And I would very much like to see your rose garden.' He glanced across at Lucinda, but though her pale cheeks coloured becomingly, she kept her eyes fixed on her plate.

'Then Lucinda shall show you,' stated Lady McFarlane.

From that moment, time seemed to stand still. David drank his tea, refused a second cup and then had to contain his impatience as Lady McFarlane refilled her own cup and took another of Mrs Bellman's tiny chocolate and cream éclairs.

At last, after what seemed to David an eternity, she suggested that Lucinda ring for William to clear away the tea things. As soon as he had done so and returned below stairs, David rose to his feet and said, 'If you will excuse us, Lady McFarlane, it would give me great pleasure for Miss McFarlane to show me your rose garden.'

'She may if she wishes,' answered her ladyship. 'Don't forget your parasol, Lucinda. The sun is still quite hot, and you want no more freckles.'

Thus dismissed, David followed Lucinda downstairs to the small sitting room on the ground floor, which had French windows opening onto the small London garden, a mere acre or so fenced by the two neighbouring houses.

Dutifully Lucinda picked up the parasol from a stand by the

doors and, followed by David Melcome, stepped out into the warm summer afternoon.

'It's not a very big garden,' she said. 'The one at Haverford is much bigger, with a kitchen garden and a greenhouse where Paston grows peaches and apricots.'

Lucinda had taken very little part in the teatime conversation, but now, released from the constraint of her mother's presence, she relaxed a little, and found she could speak to Sir David with her usual freedom, the freedom of friends.

In one corner of the garden there was a circular, wooden summerhouse, a folly, set to catch the afternoon sun, but sheltered by a lilac tree and affording a modicum of privacy. Once he had admired Lady McFarlane's roses, planted in a circle around a statue of Pan playing his pipes, and aware that they could be seen from the house, David suggested they might enter the folly and sit for a while.

Lucinda glanced anxiously back at the drawing room windows, but as there was no sign that her mother was watching them, she allowed herself to be led into the summerhouse.

'I don't know what Mama will say when she realises I am alone with you in here with no chaperone, not even a maid.'

David laughed at that. 'My dearest girl,' he said gently, 'you can always say you were avoiding getting more freckles.'

'I've got far too many already,' Lucinda said ruefully.

'You wouldn't be as beautiful without them,' David said, 'and I love every one of them.'

'Oh, don't be silly, David,' Lucinda laughed. 'You can't love freckles.'

It was the first time she'd addressed him by his Christian name. Despite their growing friendship, the necessary social formality had always been maintained. In her mind she had used his given name for some time, and now as she spoke it aloud, it seemed so natural that she hardly noticed.

David had noticed, and taking her hands in his, raised them to his lips. 'I can if they're yours, Lucy.'

Uncertain how to react now that she was without a chaperone, Lucinda felt herself blush, and seeing the colour flood her cheeks, his grip tightened on her hands and he said, 'Oh Lucy, oh my darling girl, how I do love you!'

'Do you?' She looked up at him under her lashes and her smile made his heart miss a beat.

'My dearest girl, ever since the night of Queen Charlotte's Ball, I have thought of no one but you, the girl I've been waiting for all my life.'

'But you didn't know me,' objected Lucinda.

'Even so, I fell in love with you, there and then, and that hasn't changed. Every day I've come to love you more. My darling Lucy, dare I ask you? Do you feel the same? And if so, will you do me the honour of becoming my wife?'

Lucinda looked at him, the man who had haunted her dreams for the past weeks. Did he really love her as much as she loved him? His gaze held hers as he waited for her reply and at last, she gave him her answer. 'Yes,' she said, with a tremulous smile. 'Yes, David, to both questions.'

For a long moment they looked at each other and then David pulled her gently towards him and, slipping his arms round her, drew her close. She raised her face to his and he lowered his lips to hers; he kissed her, at first very gently, but as he felt her response, more deeply.

'So, are we engaged, now?' Lucinda asked him when, a little breathless, they finally drew apart.

'We certainly are,' David assured her, 'and with your father's blessing.'

'Papa? Did you ask him?'

'Of course I did,' replied David. 'It would have been wrong to speak to you first.'

'But you knew, anyway.'

David laughed and hugged her closely, murmuring into her hair, 'Well, I hoped anyway.'

Putting his hand in his pocket, he pulled out a small leather box. 'And this will make it official, if you'll wear it,' he said. Opening the box, he took out the ring it contained, a glowing ruby set within an oval of diamonds.

'Oh David,' breathed Lucinda. 'It's beautiful!'

'It was my grandmother's,' he said. 'Her engagement ring left to me, but if you don't like it I will buy you something else.'

'No, no,' cried Lucinda. 'I should be honoured to wear your grandmother's ring,' and she held out her left hand. Gently he slipped the ring onto her third finger and, raising her hand to his lips, kissed her fingers. 'It's a little bit loose,' he said as he admired it on her hand, 'but we can soon get that rectified.'

Returning to the house they found Lucy's parents waiting for them in the drawing room. One look at Lucinda's face gave them the answer to David's question.

'I think this calls for champagne,' said Sir Keir and rang the bell for Felstead.

While they were waiting, Iain appeared, and when he heard the news he gave his sister a quick hug, before shaking hands with Sir David.

'We shall put a notice in *The Times*,' Sir Keir told them.

'Thank you, sir,' David said. 'But if you could wait a couple of days so I can tell my mother. She's in the country at present, but I wouldn't want her to read of it in the newspaper. I shall travel down to see her tomorrow and tell her the news.' Turning to Lucinda, he went on, 'I'm sure she'll come straight back to town, and then I can take you to meet her properly, as my fiancée. I know she'll be delighted.'

Early next morning David took the train to Crayne, arriving while his mother was still having breakfast.

'David,' she cried getting up from the table. 'What a lovely surprise!' And then suddenly anxious at his unexpected appearance, 'Is everything all right?'

'Couldn't be better, Mama. I've come to give you some news.'

'News? What's happened?'

'I'm getting married,' he replied. 'I've proposed to Miss Lucinda McFarlane and she's done me the honour of accepting!'

David was surprised that his mother didn't react in the way he had been expecting.

'Lucinda McFarlane,' she said. She had seen her son had a partiality for the young McFarlane girl, but she had not recognised the seriousness of his intent.

'Yes, Lucy McFarlane,' answered David. 'Who else?'

'She's very young, David,' she replied. 'Are you quite sure?'

'My dearest Mama, you have been telling me it's time I settled down and now you're asking me if I'm sure. Well, I can assure you, I have never been as sure of anything in my life. So, give me your hand and wish me happy.'

'Of course I wish you happy,' cried his mother. 'It just seems to have happened very quickly. I mean, I could see you were interested in her, that you liked her and found her good company, but marriage? It's only been a few weeks.'

'Don't worry, Mama,' David said, 'A few weeks was plenty of time. After all, *I* knew the minute I saw her.' He smiled across at her and was pleased to see she gave him a smile of real pleasure. 'I'll bring her to see you. Sir Keir is announcing our engagement in *The Times* but I'll bring her before he does.'

Lucinda was nervous when David had taken her to meet his mother as his future bride. She and Lady Melcome had already met at the opera, but meeting her as her future mother-in-law was quite different.

'Mama will love you,' David promised when she admitted her worry to him.

'But she doesn't really know me, does she?'

'She will very soon,' he said, 'and when she does, she'll know I have chosen the perfect girl for me.'

Back in London, Lady Melcome, greeted her future daughter-in-law warmly and said she was sure Lucinda would make David an excellent wife.

'I shall do my best,' Lucy replied shyly. 'I shall be proud to be his wife.'

She couldn't have chosen better words: it was exactly what Lady Melcome thought an appropriate reply.

'Where will you choose to live?' Lady Melcome asked David. 'Here in London, or in Crayne?'

'We haven't discussed that,' David replied. 'But I plan to take Lucinda down to show her the house, and then she can decide. Whichever she chooses, Mama, you won't be turned out of your home.'

As soon as the news of their engagement had been officially announced in the society columns, Sir Keir called the servants together in the entrance hall and told them that Miss Lucinda had become engaged to Major Sir David Melcome; and with that news, wedding fever overtook the entire household.

Chapter Four

The day the Oakley family moved from their rented home in Cockspur Lane to the house Mabel owned in Barnbury Street was on the August bank holiday.

Mabel had first heard that Thomas Clarke, the elderly printer who had employed her as his assistant, had made her the sole legatee in his will some months earlier. The bequest included some money, and the freeholds and contents of both his small print workshop by the railway bridge and his home, a three-storey semi-detached house in Barnbury Street. At first it was only the immediate family who were told the unbelievable news, but realising that it would soon become obvious something had changed, Mabel's father Andrew suggested the fact, though not the extent of the bequest, should be shared with the wider family.

Inevitably there had been amazement at her good fortune, closely followed by great discussion about what Mabel should be doing with her unexpected wealth.

'How much has he left her?' wondered Aunt Susan to her husband, James. 'She shouldn't keep it all for herself! She should share her good fortune with all of us.'

Mabel's mother, Alice, who always found her sister-in-law extremely difficult, especially when she offered unsolicited advice, overheard, and for once could not contain her anger.

'How much he's left to Mabel is nobody's business but hers, and certainly none of yours!' she snapped.

'How dare you speak to me like that?' retorted Susan, angry colour flooding her cheeks.

'And,' continued Alice as if Susan had not spoken, 'if Mr Clarke had wanted *you* to have his money, he would have left it to you!'

'Well, at least I suppose it means you won't have to work for that dreadful man any more,' replied Susan spitefully.

'At least what I do is good honest work,' answered Alice. 'Whereas you've never lifted a finger to earn your bread! You're a parasite, Susan, and always have been!'

This last comment brought Susan to her feet. Casting a withering look at Alice, she raised her chin and said, 'Come along, James. We're obviously not wanted here!'

There was no truce and Alice and Susan had not spoken a word to each other in all the months since.

Mabel's money had been left to her in trust, the trustees being her father, Andrew, and Mr Clarke's solicitor, Hugh Morrell.

The first time Mabel met Mr Morrell she was on edge, afraid he might prove difficult about how she wanted to spend her money. In fact he seemed more lenient than her father. Andrew Oakley knew Mabel wanted to take care of the family's financial problems, but he was determined that her inheritance should be as much or more when she came into her own on her twenty-first birthday as it had been the day Mr Clarke had died.

'Let us make no decisions without considerable thought,' said Hugh Morrell as the three of them sat round the table to discuss the provisions in Mr Clarke's will. 'You have the annual allowance of fifty pounds mentioned in the will, which you may spend as you choose, but any other expenditure will have to be agreed by your father and me.'

One thing to be considered was whether the family should continue to live in the rented house in Cockspur Lane, the family home ever since Andrew and Alice had married, or in the larger Barnbury Street house.

'If we move to Barnbury Street,' Mabel pointed out, 'there'll be no rent to pay. Think of the saving that will be.'

'Is the house suitable?' wondered Andrew anxiously.

Paralysed from the waist down and confined to a wheelchair, he had established a routine in the familiar home where he and Alice had brought up their children, and the thought of moving to a new, unfamiliar house filled him with dread.

'Perhaps we could go on living here, and rent out the Barnbury Street house,' he suggested.

'Perhaps,' agreed Hugh Morrell, 'but then you'd be paying rent when you don't have to. A larger house of your own in Barnbury Street would give you more space.'

Alice, Eddie and Mabel went to look the place over, to work out if Andrew could manage living in a house with a basement and three other floors.

It was Eddie, ever the practical one, who saw the possibilities, and explained how his father might be able to manage. After much discussion the decision to move was made, and August bank holiday was designated as moving day.

Mabel awoke early and, unable to sleep, she got out of bed and crossed to the bedroom window. The view was the one she had known throughout her childhood: the back of a terrace of dirty brick houses in the next street, their windows staring back at her over the wall at the end of their own small yard. The usual view, but this morning everything was different; this morning she was staring at those houses squatting in the early morning sun for the very last time.

As she turned away from the window to get washed and dressed, Mabel knew a sudden stab of uncertainty. Had they made the right decision? Should they have remained in the familiarity of Cockspur Lane?

Too late now! she told herself. Tonight they would be sleeping in the Barnbury Street house where Tom Clarke had lived. Surely that's what he'd meant her to do, wasn't it? Pushing her doubts aside, she finished getting dressed.

Before she went downstairs, Mabel stripped her bed and folded the bedclothes into a waiting trunk on the landing, The last of her personal belongings she packed in the old canvas bag she had used when working as a maid in the McFarlane household the previous year. With a final glance round her old room, she descended the stairs, ready to move on. The street outside was bathed in sunshine, the sky clear and blue, promising a warm summer day.

At least, she thought, we shan't be trying to move in the pouring rain, but it's going to be a long day.

The bank holiday had been carefully chosen because the two businesses that employed Eddie and Stephen, Mabel's brothers, would be closed and they would be free to come home and help.

'Are you sure Mr Carter will let you come?' Alice had asked anxiously. 'I'm not sure we can do it without you, even with Mr Holman's cart and driver.'

'Of course,' Eddie assured her. 'What else would I be doing with the factory shut up for the holiday? Mr Carter told me to wish you all the best.'

'Same for me,' said Stephen. 'Mr Solomon's staying closed for the holiday, so he don't need me.' He didn't add that Mr Solomon would be working on his clock and watch repairs despite the official holiday.

'You must go,' the old man had insisted. 'Your mother needs you.'

Mr Holman, the butcher who employed Andrew's older sister, Jane, had offered to lend them his cart and driver, an offer Alice had accepted with relief.

Andrew watched from his bedroom window as Eddie and Stephen began carrying the family's furniture out of the house, to be stacked as the first load onto the cart.

'The last time I saw that cart,' Andrew remarked to Mrs Finch, who had nursed him since his accident, 'was when I was strapped to a stretcher and loaded onto it myself.'

'Best move you ever made,' she replied, holding the mirror for him as he shaved. 'You couldn't stay in that place when you had your wife waiting for you at home.'

'Yes... and no.' Andrew sounded less than enthusiastic. 'But later today they'll load me up again and take me to this... this new place.' He looked round his room and said bitterly, 'I haven't even seen the house yet. Eddie says it has two staircases. How am I going to manage two sets of stairs?'

'Don't you worry, Mr Oakley,' soothed Mrs Finch. 'Your Eddie's got things sorted and I'll still be coming to help you in the mornings, don't you fret!'

Andrew's room was the last to be emptied. He sat in his wheelchair and watched as his own small suitcase and the final boxes of the family's possessions were loaded onto the waggon and driven away. Mrs Finch had departed, promising to come to see him at the new house. There was nothing left in the Cockspur Lane house. Andrew could hear Alice's feet echoing through the empty rooms upstairs as she checked that nothing had been forgotten and he sighed. The moment he had been dreading had arrived.

When Eddie brings the cart back next time, he thought, I'll be hoisted onto it like so much baggage and taken to this new place.

'Now then, Dad.' Eddie's voice from the hall made him jump. 'It's just you, Mum and me.'

'But where's the cart?' asked Andrew, looking out into the empty street.

'Gone back to Mr Holman, with our thanks. We don't need it to move you. I'll push you in your chair and Mum'll walk alongside. It's only a mile or so, it won't take us long.'

'But where are Mabel and Stephen?' Andrew looked round, as if he expected to see them hiding.

'They're busy sorting things out at home.'

'At home?' echoed Andrew faintly.

'At our new home, Andrew,' murmured Alice, coming down the stairs to stand at his side. She took his hand in hers. 'Your room will be all ready and waiting for you.'

'Come on, Dad,' Eddie encouraged him, tucking a small blanket round his father's useless legs. 'I got some beer in and we'll drink to our new home.' Eddie pushed his father out of the front door, down the small ramp they'd had built when he'd first come home from the hospital and across the cobbles to the smoother pavement that edged the main road. With Alice walking beside the wheelchair, Eddie pushed his father the mile or so to Barnbury Street.

Mabel had been right, it had been a long day, but somehow they were in the house with the front door closed behind them. Andrew had been wheeled into his new room. It was larger than the one he had inhabited in Cockspur Lane and looked out over the garden below. It was on the same level as the kitchen and the living room, so that he was always part of the household. He had to admit as he looked round it that it was larger and more comfortable than the Cockspur Lane front room. Besides the bed and small table, there was a comfortable armchair set by the window and a table where he could eat if he wanted to, or set up the draughts board, and in one corner of the room behind a screen was a small wash basin and the commode. Someone had put a bunch of sweet peas, tied with a ribbon, in a vase on the mantelpiece and the room was pervaded by their sweet scent.

Mabel, thought her father, and smiled at her thoughtfulness.

Later that evening, the whole family sat down to eat the cottage pie which Mrs Finch had brought round for their supper. 'Thanks to Stephen and Mabel, everyone's got a bed,' announced Alice when they had finished. 'We can leave everything else until the morning.'

As she and Mabel helped Andrew to settle down in his new bedroom, he said, 'Thank you for my sweet peas, Mabel. They smell lovely.'

Mabel glanced at the vase and felt the colour rise in her cheeks. 'They came from Mrs Finch, Dada,' she confessed, wishing with all her heart she had thought of the idea. 'There are some growing at the bottom of the garden and she went out and picked them for you before she went home.'

'Did she? That was very kind,' Andrew said. 'I must remember to thank her when she comes in the morning.'

As she drifted off to sleep, Mabel remembered the sweet peas and wished again that she had picked them.

Chapter Five

Mabel awoke early the next morning and for a brief moment, as she stared at the unfamiliar curtains across the window, she couldn't remember where she was; then everything flooded back. Of course, Barnbury Street. At once she got out of bed and padded to the window to throw back the curtains and look out at the day. Like her father's room on the floor below, her window looked out onto the garden, but today it was a garden drenched with steady rain. Gusts of wind tossed the branches of the trees next door. It looked more like a grey November day than summer. Where had yesterday's blue sky gone?

Thank goodness it wasn't doing this yesterday, Mabel thought as she stared at the rain. It would have been a nightmare moving everything from Cockspur Lane with an open waggon.

Still, it wasn't a day for staying indoors and doing nothing. It was time to be up and doing. Now the business of moving house was done, she needed to pick up the reins of her fledgling business and get back to work.

This morning she had an appointment at Mr Clarke's erstwhile printshop to hand over the keys to shoemaker Cecil Baker, who was moving in as her tenant.

'I'm sorry, Mam,' she said to her mother as she hastily ate a bowl of cornflakes, 'but I have to meet Mr Baker in half an hour to give him the key to the workshop.'

'Never mind,' said her mother with a sigh. Eddie and Stephen had already left to return to their work, and Alice had hoped Mabel would stay at home that day to help with the settling in.

'There'll still be plenty of unpacking and organising to do when you get home again.'

'I'll be back to help you as soon as I can,' promised Mabel. She picked up her bag and gave her mother a peck on the cheek.

'Don't forget it's your William's night off,' Alice reminded her. 'He'll be coming for his tea, won't he?'

''Course he will,' cried Mabel. 'I hadn't forgotten.' Though if she were completely honest, with so much on her mind, it had indeed slipped her memory. 'You know I'm dying to show him the house properly.'

At that moment, Mrs Finch arrived to help Andrew start his day, and Mabel took the chance to slip out of the house and head for the workshop by the railway bridge. As she hurried through the damp and windy streets, she thought the move couldn't really have gone any better. Mam was right, there were lots of things still to be done, but at least after today, she could leave the workshop in Mr Baker's hands and simply collect the rent once a week.

As she turned the corner and walked towards the end of the bridge, she saw Albert Flood standing outside his news kiosk, shouting something.

What's the matter with him? she wondered as she approached. While she had been working with Mr Clarke, Mabel had come to know the little news vendor well enough to realise it would take a great deal to bring him out into the rain. Even now, in the height of summer, he spent most of his time on a stool at the door of his kiosk, and yet here he was, out in the street.

'Extra! Extra! Read all about it! Britain declares war on Germany. Read all about it! Britain at war with Germany!'

In his excitement, Albert was doing a brisk trade, his piles of newspapers diminishing rapidly as people heard the overnight news for the first time: Britain was at war with Germany.

What with the upheaval of the move yesterday, Mabel's mind was far from the affairs of the nation, but she paused beside

Albert and found the coins she needed to buy his last copy of the *Daily Mail* for her father.

'Is it really war?' she wondered as she read the headline.

'Yes, looks like it,' confirmed Albert excitedly. 'We'll teach them a lesson they won't forget. Always too big for their boots, the Hun.' He gave a toothy grin. 'Sent their ambassador packin' an' all! See, says so here in the *Mail*.'

'Haven't got time to read it now,' Mabel said, folding the newspaper and tucking it into her bag. 'But I'll take it home for my dad. He'll want to read all about it.'

She smiled at him as she turned away and he began calling his headline again. She was fond of the old man and she would never forget it was Albert who had raised the alarm when she'd been attacked earlier in the year.

Mabel could tell he was thrilled with today's news, but as far as she could see it would have little impact on her life. A war, to be fought on foreign soil, in defence of a foreign country? There had been rumblings over the last month, ever since that Archduke somebody or other and his wife had been shot in Sarajevo, but Mabel had given them very little thought. She had been coming to terms with the change in her own life; the legacy from Tom Clarke had given her a level of independence she could never have imagined.

When she reached the little workshop by the bridge, she unlocked the door and went inside. Today would be the last day she was able to simply to walk in. From tomorrow the new tenant, shoemaker Mr Cecil Baker, would have moved in and set up shop. The printing press that had belonged to Thomas Clarke, Printer, and his chair, had been moved into the basement of the house in Barnbury Street. The room, bereft of the press, seemed far bigger than before. Mabel paused for a moment to look round. The shelves lining the walls were empty, awaiting the tools of the shoemaker's trade. She peered out through the dusty glass of the window onto the railway lines below, stepping back as an express roared along the track, clouding the windows with smoke. Mabel turned back to the tiny sink and picked up the two mugs from which she and Mr Clarke had drunk their tea together and put them into her bag. Now there was nothing left of him, not here, but he would always be with her for the rest of her life.

At that moment there came a knock on the door and Mabel opened it to Mr Baker.

Mabel greeted him with a smile and said, 'Good morning, sir.'

'Good morning... er... Miss err...' began Cecil Baker awkwardly.

When Mr Baker had answered the advertisement he'd been astonished to find he was dealing with a teenage girl. He had seen the ad on a printed post card in his local shop, 'PREMISES FOR RENT! APPLY THOS. CLARKE', and made a note of the address. The landlord of his current premises on the far side of the railway bridge had given him notice to quit and he had less than a month in which to get out.

He had been surprised to find that not only was he dealing with a young girl, but she had her own solicitor ready to draw up the agreement. A small, rotund man of nearly sixty, Cecil Baker was not used to dealing with women, let alone girls as young as Mabel. Discussing business with her made him feel awkward, but, he told himself, beggars couldn't be choosers. He needed new premises, and he needed them soon. The old printing workshop was just the right size. So, he had swallowed his pride and agreed the very reasonable terms that were being offered. If the solicitor, Mr Morrell, partner in a respectable local firm, had not been party to the whole thing, Cecil Baker might still have backed off, feeling there was something shady about the deal, but satisfied with the written agreement, Mr Baker had signed. Today he had come to collect the key so he could remove his equipment before the notice to quit expired.

His wasn't the only property that had been repossessed at short notice. Several of his neighbours were in the same position.

'Out by the end of the month, or the bailiffs will be round to turn you out!'

'It's not even as if we know the landlord anymore,' Cecil had moaned to his greengrocer neighbour, Bert Smith. 'Some company or other seems to have bought the whole street. Even them old cottages in Noah's Path, what was built nigh on a hundred years ago.'

'Well,' said Bert, 'I did hear as they was building a new bridge over the railway and need to clear the land. Or I read it. Yes, that would be it. I'm sure I read it in the paper somewhere.'

'But there's a perfectly good bridge already,' pointed out Cecil.

'Not a road bridge there ain't,' said Bert. 'And knowing the council, they'll likely knock down the old footbridge an' call it progress. Anyhow,' he continued, unaware of the effect his words were having on his neighbour, 'if they do, they do, nuffink we can do about it, is there?'

'Well, I 'spect, that won't happen any time soon,' Cecil said, clinging to this hope. It was no good worrying about the future; the future would have to take care of itself.

Now, Mabel handed over the key to the stout padlock that secured the front door.

'It's only a padlock,' she said. 'I expect you'll get a new one of your own. If you do, I'll need a spare key, but I promise I won't be bothering you with unexpected visits. Just to collect the rent on a Friday evening.'

It was Hugh Morrell who had suggested that she keep the little workshop by the bridge and rent it out.

'Gives you added income on a regular basis, and you still have the value of the property should you ever need an injection of capital.'

When Mr Baker answered her advertisement, his seemed an ideal business for the small workshop, and with her trustees' agreement, Mabel agreed the rent and signed the required papers.

The deal had been for a week's rent in advance, and anxious to see the back of his unlikely landlord... or should he say landlady… (though that conjured up pictures of fearsome women who ran boarding houses in Stepney) Cecil Baker put his hand in his pocket and pulled out the required cash.

Mabel thanked him, marked the amount and the date in his rent book, and handed it back.

She put the money into her bag, but as she was turning to leave, he asked, 'You hear the news?'

'The news?'

'You know, that we're at war with Germany?'

'Yes,' Mabel replied. 'I heard that. Not sure why.'

'Put the Hun in his place,' answered Cecil.

Albert had said the same, but she wasn't any the wiser. Never mind, Dada would know. He had become an avid reader of the *Daily Mail* since his accident, and when Mabel had asked him why, he replied, 'I like to keep in touch with the world outside.' He gave her no further explanation, but it was those few words that brought home to Mabel just how restricted her dad's life had become.

How dreadfully awful, she thought, to be confined to the house, unable to leave of your own accord. How frustrating it must be, not to be able to say, 'I'll just go down the pub for a pint,' or, 'I'm off to work now, see you this evening.' The accident he'd had in the street had cut him off from a life beyond the front door. Unless someone took him out in his chair, reading the paper to bring him up to date with whatever was going on in the wider world was his only means of escape. Once Mabel had come to realise this, she had brought home a *Daily Mail* every day, and he read it from front page to back. She would ask Dada about this latest news when she got home again.

As soon as she got in, Mabel hurried to his room and found him sitting at his window staring at the dismal day outside. Shedding her coat as she came in, she pulled out the slightly damp newspaper.

'Important news, Dada,' she said as she handed it to him.

Her father scanned the front page before resting the paper

on his knee and saying, 'I'm not surprised, not really, not since the archduke and his wife were murdered by some Serbian revolutionary back in June.'

'But who *were* they?' asked Mabel. 'I'd never heard of them before they were killed.'

'He was heir to the Emperor of Austria. He'd have been the next emperor.'

'Well, very dreadful,' agreed Mabel, pulling up a chair to sit beside him. 'But what has that to do with us? The British, I mean?'

'It started off a chain of fighting, with Serbia and Russia on one side and Austria and Germany on the other.'

'But that's still nothing to do with us,' pointed out Mabel.

'Well, it is,' replied her father. 'Britain has guaranteed neutrality for Belgium.'

'What does that mean?'

'It means, Mabel, that if Belgium is invaded, our government says we will fight beside the Belgians.'

'And is that what's happened?'

'That's what's happened. German troops are already marching through Belgium to attack France and have refused to withdraw.'

'So now we have to fight the Germans?'

'So now we have to fight the Germans. They're becoming too powerful... getting too big for their boots if you like... and must be stopped before they go any further.'

'That's what Albert said,' remarked Mabel.

'Well, I don't know who Albert is, but that just about sums up the situation,' agreed her father with a slight smile.

'How do you know all this, Dada?' Mabel asked. 'All this stuff about other countries?'

'Because I read the papers,' answered her father, adding in a matter-of-fact tone, 'after all, I've plenty of time and nothing much else to do.'

'But will the Germans come here?' wondered Mabel.

'Most unlikely,' replied her father. 'We shall send our army over to France to deal with the situation. They're well-trained and will soon see the Germans off. Don't forget, we also have the best navy in the world; it wouldn't surprise me if it was all over before Christmas.' Andrew took his daughter's hands in his and gave them a squeeze.

'Now don't you worry your head about it anymore,' he said. 'Did I hear your mother say that William will be coming here this evening?'

'Yes,' answered Mabel. 'He's finally been given his evening off. I wonder what he'll make of the news.'

'Just be waiting to see what's going to happen, like the rest of us, I suppose,' said Andrew. 'Now, be a good girl and find which box your mother packed the draughts board in, so we can set it up ready. I've missed my games with William.'

It was Mabel who had packed up the draughts set, and she knew exactly where to put her hand on it. Five minutes later she had pulled a small table up beside her father's chair and left him setting out the pieces as she went to find her mother and help with the last of the unpacking.

William Gale, footman to the McFarlane family in Chanynge Place, arrived at the Barnbury Street house that evening soon after six o'clock. He looked at the house with interest. He had seen it before from the street, of course, but had never been inside. As he stepped up to the front door he thought, fancy Mabel actually owning a house like this!

It hadn't surprised her parents that Mabel had let William into the secret of her legacy; they had become close friends and she didn't mind him knowing, but she had not disclosed the extent of the inheritance. When Mabel opened the door to him, he stepped inside, put his arms round her, and gave her a hug.

'Oh, Mabel, I've missed you,' he said as she returned his hug.

'I've missed you, too, Will.'

It was some time since he had been able to visit, and he took both Mabel's hands in his for a long moment, and smiled down into her eyes.

'Is that William at the door?' Alice called from the kitchen. 'What are you doing, standing about in the hall? Bring him on through.'

Alice had every hope that when Mabel was a little older, she and William might marry. Both she and Andrew approved of him, steady and well-mannered and obviously devoted to Mabel.

Mabel was clearly fond of him, but she had given no real sign that she had marriage in mind. Of course she wasn't quite seventeen, but she was mature for her years and had gained immensely in confidence since she had left the McFarlanes and begun working for Thomas Clarke.

'Come on,' Mabel said now, and led the way into the kitchen, where her parents were sitting. The kitchen was bigger than the one in Cockspur Lane and aside from the table in the window, there was an armchair for Andrew.

Mabel's parents greeted William warmly and he knew with sudden pleasure that he was truly welcome.

'We haven't seen you for a while, William,' said Alice, as he sat down and she poured him a cup of tea.

'No, well, since Miss Lucinda got herself engaged to be married, the whole place has been like a madhouse.'

'Have they set the date?' asked Mabel. She'd already heard news of the wedding from her cousin Lizzie, a parlour maid in Chanynge Place, and she herself knew Miss Lucinda from when she worked there too.

'Twenty-third of September,' William answered. 'More than a month away, too early to fuss if you ask me.'

'Not all that long to arrange a large, society wedding,' remarked Alice. 'I expect Lady McFarlane wants everything to be perfect. How many guests, I wonder?'

'I don't know,' said William with a shrug. 'Too many to fit into the house, anyhow, so the wedding breakfast ain't going to be in Chanynge Place.'

'That must be a relief to the Killer-bee and Mrs Bellman,' remarked Mabel.

'You'd think so, wouldn't you,' replied William, 'with all the upheaval it'd cause if it was. But no, both of them are annoyed. They think Lady M doesn't think they are up to the job.'

'And is that what she does think?' suggested Alice.

William shrugged. 'I don't know, maybe. I'm glad it's somewhere else. It's bad enough preparing for the people who are staying with us.

'Where will it be?' mused Mabel. 'Lizzie didn't know.'

'The Waldorf,' answered William. 'I heard sir and her ladyship discussing it while I was clearing the breakfast table.'

That made Mabel smile. She knew only too well that those in the servants' hall knew the family's business almost before the family did. Titbits overheard during the course of their work in the house were swiftly relayed below stairs, discussed and dissected at length for what import it might have for the household in general. Felstead pretended to be above such gossip and little was said in front of him, but Mrs Kilby was another thing altogether. Although she pretended no interest, she had her finger on the pulse of the household and seldom missed a beat.

'I bet Lizzie is relieved it isn't at home,' Mabel remarked. 'I would be!'

'Lizzie is coping very well,' William said, 'though there's so much to-ing and fro-ing. Lady M is writing lists. Dressmakers coming and going. Posh photographers come to take a studio portrait of the bride for *The Tatler*.'

'With the groom?' asked Mabel.

'No, that would bring bad luck, so the Killer-bee says.'

Mabel pulled a face; she had never got on with the McFarlanes' housekeeper, Mrs Kilby, and hadn't forgiven her for assuming that, when a valuable brooch watch had gone missing, it was Mabel who had stolen it.

'She would,' retorted Mabel but then smiled, adding, 'but, is he handsome?'

'Who?'

'The groom of course,' laughed Mabel. 'Oh, come on, Will. What's he like?'

'He's a soldier,' answered William, 'in the Dragoons.'

'Yes, I know that, too, but is he handsome? I bet Lucinda wouldn't agree to marry anyone who wasn't.'

William shrugged. 'I suppose,' he said vaguely. 'He's a good catch, I will say that for him; rich enough and with a title. Miss Lucinda seems happy enough.'

'And Lady McFarlane?'

''Spect she was looking for a duke.'

'Maybe, but Lucinda being engaged at the end of her first London season is something.'

'Enough of weddings,' said Andrew, who had contributed nothing to the conversation. 'What do you think about the news?'

'About the war? Well, don't suppose it'll affect me much,' replied William. 'I still got my job to do.'

'You won't think about joining the army?' suggested Andrew.

'No, they wouldn't want the likes of me.

'They might,' answered Andrew. 'What about Mr Iain?'

'Not likely. He's only just joined his father's chambers as a junior clerk.'

'No more talk of war,' said Alice sharply. 'Help me dish up, Mabel. I expect we're all hungry.'

After supper, William and Andrew played their usual game of draughts, and despite their new surroundings, it felt as comfortable as it had in Cockspur Lane. When William had to leave, Mabel went with him to the front door.

'You got a lovely new home here, Mabel,' William said. 'And your dad seems to have settled all right.'

'I think so,' Mabel replied. 'It's early days yet, but I think he'll be all right. Eddie's built ramps so we can push him everywhere, even up from the basement round the outside of the house.'

'He's a clever one, your Eddie,' said William.

'I know,' said Mabel. 'Don't know what we'd do without him.'

'An' I don't know what I'd do without you.' William reached for her and pulled her into his arms.

For a moment she rested her head on his chest and then she pulled away, saying, 'You'd better go, Will, or Felstead will lock you out!'

For a moment she watched him as he walked down the street, but by the time he reached the corner and turned for a final wave, she had gone inside and closed the door.

Chapter Six

Once Lady McFarlane had accepted that Lucinda was going to marry a simple baronet and not the heir to a dukedom she had hoped for, she set about arranging the wedding of the season. Only Muriel Charlton would be married before Lucinda, and soon the preparations for Lucinda's wedding were in full swing. When her father had said he would give them his blessing, he had forbidden them to marry until she was eighteen.

Lucinda and her mother agreed to this stipulation and the date was set for twenty-third September, Lucinda's eighteenth birthday.

Sir Keir knew that he had been out-manoeuvred by his women folk and gave in.

The Waldorf hotel was chosen for the wedding breakfast, guest lists were prepared, invitations were printed and most importantly Lucinda's trousseau was placed in the hands of Madame Chantal.

'The place has become a madhouse,' William had told Mabel when he visited on his evening off. 'You'd think no one never got married before. It's a relief to get out of the house, I can tell you.'

William was not the only member of the McFarlane household to be relieved when he left Chanynge Place. Sir Keir felt the same as he was driven by Croxton to his chambers in Lincoln's Inn. He was delighted to see his daughter's happiness, but apart from giving her away on the day, he had very little to do with the organisation of the wedding. That he left to his wife. She was determined Lucinda's wedding should be the social event of the year. It wasn't going to be the first of this year's crop of debutantes, but it was going to rival Muriel Charlton's marriage to Lord Frain at St Margaret's, Westminster and no expense was spared.

It's a good thing I've only got one daughter, Sir Keir thought ruefully, when his wife let slip the cost of the wedding breakfast at the Waldorf. He didn't begrudge the money, he too wanted Lucinda's wedding to be perfect, but even so, having already stumped up the required cash for her London season, he was glad that there would not be another one next year.

He had escaped to his chambers one morning, and just settled down to write a judgement on a case he had heard earlier, when his clerk, Martin Mayhew, knocked on his door.

Sir Keir looked up as he came in and saw that Mayhew's expression was one of barely suppressed excitement. Sir Keir laid down his pen and said mildly, 'Well, Mayhew, you look about to burst. What news?'

'Telephone call for you, sir,' he replied rather breathlessly, 'from Number 10, sir!'

Sir Keir raised an eyebrow. 'Number 10?'

'Number 10 Downing Street, sir. The Prime Minister's office.'

'Indeed,' said Sir Keir, cautiously, thinking of a current case which involved a junior MP. 'Was there a message?'

'No sir!' exclaimed Mayhew. 'They want to speak to you.'

'Speak to me?' Sir Keir almost leaped to his feet. 'You mean they are still on the line?'

Mayhew shrugged. 'I suppose so,' he replied. 'They said to fetch you to the telephone.'

'Well, why didn't you say so, man?'

Seconds later he was grasping the receiver. 'Keir McFarlane speaking. Good morning.'

'Good morning, sir,' came the calm reply. 'This is Arthur Edwards from the PM's office. Mr Asquith would like you to meet with him here in Downing Street at four-thirty this afternoon. I assume that's convenient?'

Not really a question Keir thought. One didn't say 'no' to a summons like that.

Keir heard the caller say, 'We'll see you then, sir,' before the line went dead.

When Sir Keir returned to his chambers, Mayhew was still waiting.

'Anything I can help with?' he asked hopefully.

'No, thank you, Mayhew. Except, well, I shall be out this afternoon. Perhaps you'd see to cancelling my engagements for the rest of the day.'

Once he was by himself, Keir sat down in his armchair and considered the matter. He knew Herbert Henry Asquith slightly. They were both old boys of the City of London School. Though Asquith was older and their time at the school had not coincided, as practising lawyers, they had occasionally crossed swords across a court room. Much of Asquith's life had been devoted to politics and law-making, while Keir McFarlane had concentrated on dispensing justice when those laws were broken, but each had great respect for the other. Asquith had reached the pinnacle of his political life and McFarlane had acquired a reputation for strict but fair judgements on the bench at the Old Bailey, but the two men had not actually met each other for more than three years, and Keir could not think what the Prime Minister could want with him now.

Three forty-five found him being driven by Croxton from Lincoln's Inn to Downing Street. As he reached the corner, Sir Keir stopped the car, saying, 'I'll get out here, Croxton.'

'Very good, sir,' answered Croxton and drew up at the kerb.

'You can wait for me here,' Sir Keir said. 'I won't be long.'

Actually, he had no idea how long he would be, but he had decided he would approach the Prime Minister's residence on foot. He paused for a moment outside the wrought iron railings and admired the gleaming paint and shining brass of the famous front door. A solitary policeman standing at the gate touched his helmet in salute.

'Good afternoon, sir.'

'Good afternoon, officer,' replied Sir Keir and, drawing a deep breath, stepped forward to ply the knocker.

Immediately the front door swung open and Sir Keir was greeted by an aide. 'Good afternoon, sir. The Prime Minister is expecting you. If you'll come this way?'

He led Sir Keir up an elegant sweep of shallow stairs to the floor above. Even as he followed his guide, Keir couldn't help pausing to look at the portraits of earlier prime ministers lining the staircase. The aide waited for him at the top of the stairs and led him through an office, where a secretary sat typing.

He knocked on a door on the opposite side and announced, 'Sir Keir McFarlane, sir.'

Sir Keir found himself in an office where the Prime Minister was seated behind a large mahogany desk. He stood up as Sir Keir walked into the room, extended his hand and said, 'Good of you to come, McFarlane!'

'My pleasure, sir.'

Asquith led the way to some easy chairs and a sofa that were grouped round an empty fireplace, and sitting down himself, waved Sir Keir to a chair opposite to him.

'I hear your boy has just come down from Cambridge,' he said. 'Joining you in chambers, is he?'

Sir Keir was surprised. Surely he had not been invited to Number 10 to talk about Iain. But he answered easily enough, saying, 'Yes sir, as a very junior clerk!' and waited for Asquith to come to the real reason for his summons.

'The thing is, Mac...' began Asquith.

Keir McFarlane had not been addressed as Mac since he'd left school.

'The thing is... Well, I'll come straight to the point... With this damned war, I'm going to need some more support in Parliament.'

Keir nodded, but said nothing, wondering where this was

going. He was in no position to help with parliamentary decisions.

'We have to act quickly, before the Germans get a hold in France. Our first troops are leaving tomorrow, but though the country seems to be behind us, we need to ensure that Parliament remains firm.' The Prime Minister paused and a moment's silence stretched between them, before he went on and said, 'I was wondering if I have your support?'

'For the war?' queried Sir Keir. 'Indeed you do. We are bound by treaty to come to Belgium's aid. Germany has no right to march her army through a neutral country and Britain must stand by her given guarantee of protecting that neutrality.'

'In which case,' said the Prime Minister, coming straight to his point, 'I was wondering if you would accept a peerage? A barony, to allow you to sit in the House of Lords? That way I could rely on your support in the difficult days to come.'

Sir Keir stared at the Prime Minister in amazement, unable to find words to express his surprise. In the past there had been several cases of prime ministers filling the benches of the House of Lords with their own supporters to get difficult legislation through, but not that often.

'Of course,' Asquith went on, 'it would be a new peerage, but your son would inherit the title in due course.' He paused for a moment before continuing. 'I need more support in the Lords to prosecute this war and the only way I can get it is to appoint more peers who see things as I do.'

Finally Sir Keir spoke. 'I know we have to fight this war and difficult decisions need to be taken. I am happy to support you in those, but we have to realise that elevation to the House of Lords will almost certainly give rise to accusations of, well, of payment for votes.'

'No, I don't think so,' said Asquith. 'You are already a senior judge with a distinguished record in court.'

'Of course I would support you as far as I could, but you have to accept that if I think you are making wrong decisions, I will have to vote as my conscience prompts me. I cannot guarantee my support would be automatic. If that is not acceptable, I will have to decline the honour.'

'Mac, I know you to be a man of integrity, and that's why I need you at my back. I also have to admit that you are not the only man I've approached. One voice may not be enough.'

'Then on the understanding of those terms, Prime Minister, I should be delighted to accept your offer.'

'In which case, we shall put things in hand and have you in the Lords sometime in November.' Asquith got to his feet and held out his hand. 'Congratulations, Baron McFarlane of...'

'Haverford,' answered Sir Keir.

'Haverford,' confirmed Asquith. 'Of course, this is entirely between ourselves. No hint of it must leak out before the announcements are made. You understand, I am sure.' The interview was over.

Still unable to believe the turn the meeting with H.H. had taken, Keir now followed Asquith's aide downstairs.

Baron McFarlane of Haverford. He could hardly credit it. He thought of Isabella's reaction and knew he shouldn't risk telling her until it was all official. With the best will in the world he knew she would never be able to keep silent, and he couldn't risk the news being circulated in advance. With these thoughts racing through his brain, Sir Keir walked out of Downing Street to where Croxton was waiting with the car. He had only been away for half an hour, and in those thirty minutes his whole prospects and those of his family had changed.

Chapter Seven

Within days of the declaration of war, a British Expeditionary Force had been despatched across the Channel to Le Havre to help the French army stem the tide of German troops now pushing through neutral Belgium on their way towards Paris. The British army was made up of regular, professional soldiers and, as such, was the first to be deployed. David's regiment, the King's Own Dragoons, were stationed in Lucknow in India, but he'd returned to England in the spring on extended furlough, and had yet to rejoin them. He was, of course, still a serving officer and, in the days since war had been declared, he realised every trained man would be needed. There was no conscription. That wasn't government policy, but the call for volunteers had already gone out and within a week over 100,000 men had queued up to enlist; untrained young men, eager to fight for king and country.

David had been half expecting a call to arms, and was not surprised when Watson, the butler, brought him a telegram instructing him to report to the War Office the following day.

There, he was met by Brigadier Marsh, one of his regimental senior officers, who had also been home on leave.

'Good to see you, Melcome,' said the brigadier. 'You'll be glad to hear the regiment will be leaving Lucknow and on its way home. Expected to land in Marseilles in a few weeks' time. From there they'll head straight up to the front where we shall catch up with them.

'In the meantime you and I will be seconded to the 2nd, the Queen's Bays. They are already in France, and incurred some casualties in action. We leave to reinforce them in a couple of weeks.'

For a moment David stared blankly at his senior officer, and seeing his reaction, so different from the enthusiasm he'd been expecting, Brigadier Marsh snapped, 'You've nothing more important to do, have you, Melcome?'

David swallowed hard and said, 'No, sir, of course not.'

'Good. Tell your man to be prepared to leave on twelfth of September. He did come home with you, didn't he?'

'Corporal Fenton? Yes, sir. He's with me now.'

'Good. Carry on. Definite embarkation orders will follow.'

David returned home to warn his soldier servant that they were soon to be back in the field. Fenton had been his servant all the time they had been in India and knew what preparations would need to be made for their departure. He had travelled with David on his return to England and continued to look after him in London.

When Lady Melcome had suggested that David look for a 'proper gentleman's gentleman', he had laughed. 'Don't worry, Mama, Fenton suits me fine. I don't need anyone fussing about me. Fenton knows what's needed and we're used to each other.'

Far more worrying was that he had to break the news of his departure not only to his mother this time but to his beloved Lucy. Their wedding day was set for twenty-third of September, by which time, as things now stood, he would be in France.

He tackled his mother first. She was used to the army dictating her life, but even so she stared at him in dismay.

'But, David, Lucinda? Your wedding! What will you do?'

'I don't know, Mama,' he replied miserably. 'I don't know. I'll have to call to Chanynge Place this afternoon and break the news.'

He went almost immediately, leaving his mother to her thoughts. She was desperately sorry for young Lucinda, a girl about to be married and now, to be left, unmarried, until her soldier fiancé came home to her. She knew the constant ache of worry that would be with the girl, goodness knows she had lived with that herself for long enough, but Lucy was so young. Would *she* have the strength?

When David arrived at Chanynge Place he was told that Miss Lucinda and her mother were out, but expected back within the hour.

'However, Sir Keir is at home, sir,' Felstead said.

'Thank you, Felstead,' David replied, 'Perhaps you would ask him if he will see me.'

Moments later David was being shown into the library, where Sir Keir was working at his desk.

'Sir David,' he said, at once getting to his feet. 'It's good to see you. I'm sure Lucy and her mother will be back directly. Will you take a drink?'

'No, sir, I thank you. I'm quite pleased that Lucy is out. I need a chance to speak to you before I see her.'

'Dear me,' responded Sir Keir, waving him to a chair and taking a seat opposite. 'That sounds serious.'

'I'm afraid it is,' David answered, and explained the situation. 'I realised I would be recalled to my regiment when they returned from India, but had no idea I might be sent to France ahead of their arrival.'

'And there is no way you can refuse to leave on the twelfth?'

David gave a mirthless laugh. 'Hardly, without deserting, sir.'

'No, of course not. Stupid question. So what do you propose?'

'It appears to me that there are three options. The first is to postpone the wedding until I return from the front.'

'Which would be when?'

'Impossible to tell at the moment, sir. I know everyone is saying that the whole thing will be over by Christmas, but I have to say I am not that optimistic. The news coming back from France is not very encouraging. Our troops have been retreating for some days now.'

'I see.'

'Until we get more troops across the Channel, life is going to be quite difficult.'

'There've been plenty of volunteers,' said Sir Keir. 'Have you seen the queues lining up outside the Central London Recruiting Depot at New Scotland Yard?'

'No, sir, I haven't, but I believe it's the same all over the country. The trouble is that these men are no use to the army until at least they've had some basic training. It will all take time.'

'And your second option?'

'To release Lucinda from our engagement, leaving her free to move back into society. When I return, if she is still of the same mind, I will return the ring and we can be married then.'

Sir Keir nodded. On the face of it, that seemed the more sensible, the more honourable way forward. After all, it was possible that someone as young as Lucy might well change her mind when her beau was not close at hand to dance attendance on her.

'And the third option?'

'The third option, sir, would be to cancel the wedding as it is currently being organised and have a small, quiet affair before I leave in two weeks' time.'

'I doubt her mother will be in favour of that,' remarked Sir Keir. 'The arrangements are too far advanced.'

'As to that, sir, whichever way we decide, the wedding being arranged as it is now will have to be cancelled,' pointed out David.

Sir Keir sighed. He knew that Isabella had her heart set on a big society wedding. She would surely want to postpone the big day until David returned. And Lucy, what would she choose? Would she be guided by her parents? As for David himself, about to leave the woman he loved, indefinitely, what would he choose?

'I think I'll have that drink now,' Sir Keir said. 'Change your mind?'

At that moment they heard Lady McFarlane and Lucy coming

back home, the rumble of Felstead's voice telling them of Sir David's arrival.

Almost immediately the library door flew open and Lucinda erupted into the room.

'David! Why didn't you let me know you were coming? I'd have stayed at home. I only went out with Mama to look at some of the new fabrics Madame Chantal has in.' She hurried to his side and he raised her hands to his lips. Seeing the joy on her face twisted his heart. How could he tell her that their wedding was going to be cancelled?

Sir Keir knew that Lucinda and her mother needed to hear the news separately. Their reactions would be so different. David had to be alone with Lucinda when he broke the dreadful news and so Keir turned to his wife and said, 'My dear, I'm glad you're back early. Something's come up and I need to have a word with you.' Turning back to the young couple he went on, 'It's a beautiful afternoon. Why don't you two take a turn in the garden?'

Relieved at this suggestion, David agreed at once. He wanted to explain to Lucy privately, to be alone with her and comfort her.

Lady McFarlane was surprised and wondered what could be so important, but she made no comment. Lucy was engaged to David and it was perfectly proper that they should walk together in the garden unchaperoned, and she was intrigued to know what Keir wanted to discuss with her. Something important about the wedding, of course, but some secret idea he'd had?

'Sit down, my dear,' he said once they were alone. 'I was about to have a drink,' he said as she sat in an armchair, 'would you like something?'

'No, thank you.' She watched as he poured himself a whisky and added, 'I'd have thought it was a bit early for you, too.'

Keir added a splash of water to his glass and then sat down opposite to her.

'It's the war,' he began.

'The war!' exclaimed Isabella. That was the last thing she'd been expecting.

'Yes, well, the war, indirectly.' There was no easy way to explain what had changed, so he said, 'David is going to France with his regiment.'

'Yes,' said Isabella. 'But surely his regiment is still in India, isn't it? It'll take weeks for them to come back to England, won't it? Too late for them to be involved with any fighting. It's all going to be over by Christmas.'

'So they say,' replied Keir, 'but David has been seconded to a different Guards' regiment and has to leave England on the twelfth of September.'

'The twelfth?' echoed Isabella. 'But he can't! What about the wedding?'

'I'm afraid we'll have to cancel that for now,' answered Keir.

'But we can't!' cried his wife. 'The invitations have all gone out. We've been receiving acceptances. There have even been some presents.'

'Everyone will understand, my dear,' soothed Keir. 'He's a soldier after all, and it's his patriotic duty to go. We should all be proud of him.'

'But Lucy? What will Lucy say? She'll be heartbroken.'

'She will be extremely upset,' agreed Keir, 'but she's chosen to be an army officer's wife, and this is something she'll have to get used to.'

'But surely he can defer his departure. He can tell them he's getting married and...'

'And they'll say "Never mind, Major, come and join us when you're ready"?' Hardly, my dear.'

'So, when does he propose to tell her there isn't going to be a wedding?' demanded Isabella.

'He's telling her now,' replied Keir.

'I must go to her at once,' cried Isabella. 'The poor child will be distraught!'

'Almost certainly she is,' said Keir, putting out a hand to stop her. 'But I think we should leave them alone together. He'll be able to comfort her better than either of us.'

'But I'm her mother,' protested Isabella. 'She needs me!'

'Of course she does,' soothed Keir, 'but just at present she needs David more, don't you think?'

'Well, if there's really nothing we can do about it, we must draft an announcement for *The Times* to explain the change of plans. I only hope people don't think that this army story is to cover up the fact that he's jilted her! We all knew he was seldom serious in his flirtations. Do you think he's changed his mind? That he's grown tired of her already and is looking for a way out?'

'No, indeed I don't,' retorted Keir. 'You didn't see his face when he was telling me what had happened and was suggesting various solutions.'

'What do you mean? What was he suggesting we can do about it?'

Keir explained the three options David had suggested.

'None of those seem particularly helpful,' said Isabella. 'I mean, we can put off the wedding until he comes home again, but when's that going to be? And what does poor Lucinda do in the meantime?'

'They remain engaged and when the war is over, well, then they can get married.'

'And suppose, after all that time, he's changed his mind? Then what?'

'I think that would be a problem to be dealt with as and when it arises,' Keir replied.

'During which time she may miss the chance of finding another husband.'

'Isabella, listen to me.' Keir very rarely spoke to his wife in that tone of voice, but when he did, she knew she must be silent and let him speak. 'I know you want our daughter to be suitably married and settled with an establishment of her own, but that is not the be-all and end-all of a London Season. Far more important is that she finds a man she loves and respects to be her husband, a man who loves her... loves her as much as I love you.'

'But...' began Isabella, but Keir held up his hand to silence her.

'It's not a matter of when she gets married, or even *if* she gets married. It's Lucinda's happiness that should concern us most, don't you agree? So we can make suggestions, but it must be they who decide. It's their future. We may not agree with their decision and we are at liberty to say so and point out why we don't agree, but the actual decision isn't ours to make.'

'Have you thought that he might not come back from the war?' said Isabella. 'He might be killed.'

'So he might,' answered Keir, 'but there is no need for you to press that point. They will certainly have considered the fact, and included it in their decision-making.'

Keir reached for Isabella's hand and gave it a squeeze. 'How would you have felt in the same situation?' he asked gently.

'I don't know,' admitted Isabella, 'but I wouldn't, necessarily, have taken my parents' advice.'

'Like mother, like daughter,' Keir responded, and leaned forward to kiss his wife, 'and I love you both! Now, why don't you ring for some tea while we wait for them to come back in?'

'You haven't finished your whisky yet,' Isabella countered, anxious to hide her pleasure at his declaration.

Keir laughed and tipped his head back, downing the last of his drink before William appeared in answer to the bell.

'Tea, please, William,' he said. 'And we'll take it in the drawing room.'

Chapter Eight

Once again, David and Lucinda let themselves out into the garden through the small sitting room's French windows. This time they spent no time admiring the roses or even pretending to do so. David took Lucinda's hand and led her straight to the little summerhouse hidden among the lilacs.

As before Lucinda glanced back at the house, but there was no face at the window, no one watching them in the garden. Noticing, David smiled and said, 'We're engaged, my dear girl, we're allowed to be alone together in your parents' garden.' But immediately he wished he could take back the words. How much longer would they continue to be engaged?

Once they were seated in the little round house, with David's arm about her shoulders, Lucy sighed and said, 'I can't believe that in nearly four weeks' time we shall be married.' As she spoke she nestled against him, her head tucked in beneath his chin, and he held her close.

I must tell her, he thought as he felt her body respond to his embrace, and I must tell her now.

'Lucy, dearest,' David began and then stopped. He mustn't blurt it out. He drew another deep breath and started again. 'Lucy, I have something to tell you.'

'Have you?' Lucinda smiled. 'I hope it's something nice.'

'Not particularly,' David admitted. He knew he ought to get on and stop procrastinating, but he was loath to spoil the moment: Lucy in his arms on a glorious summer's afternoon. The war in France seemed a world away.

'Well, what is it?' Lucy demanded pulling free of his arms and looking up into his face. What she saw there was so dejected an expression, she said, 'David, is something wrong? What's wrong? Tell me.'

'Lucy, you know I love you more than life itself, that I wouldn't willingly do anything to hurt you.'

'But you're going to.' Lucy was suddenly all prescience. 'You're going to tell me something you think will hurt me. What is it? Tell me now.'

'I have been recalled to join my regiment,' he said softly, as if that would lessen the hurt.

For a moment she said nothing, and the silence lasted so long that David was beginning to wonder if she had actually heard what he'd said. He looked down at her face, but she wasn't looking at him. She was staring, unseeing now, at the garden still basking in the afternoon sun.

'Sweetheart, did you hear me?'

'Yes, I heard. You're going to fight... in France. When do you have to go?' Her voice was flat, emotionless, and if he hadn't been looking down into her face, he might have thought the news was of no consequence to her, but already the tears were streaming down her cheeks.

His arms tightened round her and with his cheek against her hair, he rocked her gently as if she were a child who'd awoken from a nightmare.

'Soon,' he said. 'Before your birthday.' He couldn't bring himself to say 'before our wedding day'.

But Lucinda, dashing the tears from her face, said it for him. 'Before we're married.'

'Yes,' he murmured. 'Oh my darling, I'm so sorry.'

Lucy held on to the rags of her pride now and said, 'It must happen to lots of people when everything is changed by the war.'

'If you're a soldier, your life is governed by the decisions the army makes.'

'Then, as a soldier's wife, *your* wife, it's something I shall have to get used to, isn't it?'

David made no reply, loving her for what she'd just said, but knowing it would not be as easy as she'd made it sound.

Lucy said nothing for a long moment and they sat together tightly embracing before she was suddenly all action.

'So,' she said, 'what are we going to do? Have you told my father? Is that why he sent us out here, for you to tell me and for him to have time to tell Mama?'

'Yes,' answered David. 'I wanted to tell you myself, when we were alone, just the two of us. I wanted to hold you in my arms as I told you, so you'd know how much I love you.'

Silence enfolded them again, before David said, 'I know your mother will be very upset, but she's going to have to cancel the wedding arrangements.'

'When do you have to leave?'

'I have to embark on a transport ship on the twelfth of September.'

'But you told me your regiment was out in India. That you're on extended leave. Are you going there first?'

'No.' David explained about being seconded to a different regiment until his own arrived from India.

'Then we have just two weeks,' Lucinda said. 'Have you thought what we might do?'

'Yes, I think there are three different things we must consider.'

'And they are?'

David outlined the suggestions he had already made to Sir Keir.

'That's the answer, then,' Lucy said once he had finished. 'It's as easy as that!'

'What is?' David asked with a smile. 'What's "as easy as that"?' He loved the way Lucy always knew and spoke her own mind, even if what she actually said wasn't quite what she thought she was saying.

'Mama will have to cancel the wedding...'

'Yes,' agreed David with a sigh.

'And then we'll just get married before you go?'

'Darling, that's a wonderful idea… in theory, but I'm not sure it's possible.'

'David,' Lucy said severely. 'We can make it possible. And once we've decided that's what we're going to do, well, Mama will make it happen somehow.

'David.' Lucy got to her feet and turned back to face him, 'David, do you want to marry me?'

'Oh, come on Lucy,' he replied in anguish, 'do you have to ask? You know I want us to get married more than anything else in the world.'

'Good,' said Lucy. 'Then that's what we'll do.'

'We can't just suddenly change the date,' answered David. 'Everything has been arranged for the twenty-third.'

'So, we just *un-arrange* that and arrange a different wedding… on a different day. Sooner.'

'But it was to be your big day, you the blushing bride at the centre of the celebrations.'

'It will still be *our* big day!' Lucy told him. 'It'll be our special day, yours and mine.' She gave him a dimpling smile. 'I might even manage to blush, if you think that's important.'

That made David laugh. 'Lucinda McFarlane, you're impossible!'

'I may be impossible,' Lucy agreed cheerfully, 'but our getting married before you go isn't.'

'I think you may have difficulty in convincing your parents, particularly your mother,' David remarked.'

'Oh, I'll talk her round. We don't need hundreds of guests and a huge reception. What if we got married at Haverford in the village church, with a wedding breakfast at Haverford Court? We don't even have to spend all day there.'

David gave a shout of laughter at that. 'Lucy, Lucy! What *am* I going to do with you?'

'Well, marry me, I hope!' she replied.

David shook his head in mock despair, but then, suddenly extremely serious, he said, 'You do realise this is a war I've been called on to fight. There will be battles and skirmishes and casualties.' He took hold of Lucy's shoulders and looked down, his dark blue eyes searching her face. 'You do understand that I shan't be playing at soldiers. That there will be casualties and not everyone comes home again. Suppose I'm killed and don't come home to you?'

'David,' Lucy said, her expression as serious as his. 'I want to be married to you. I want to have as long together as possible. If that turns out to be short, at least we shall have had our time together as husband and wife. The fact that you might not come home again is all the more reason to seize the time we have on offer now.'

'Or if I'm badly injured,' went on David relentlessly. 'You could be tied to a cripple for the rest of my life.'

'I know that could happen,' said Lucinda. 'I'm not stupid, but my argument remains the same. I'd still want to have memories of our life together, husband and wife. I want to be your wife in every way, David, even though I may not know yet quite what that entails; you will show me and I will learn. Please don't leave me alone, not knowing what it is to be your wife.'

'Oh my darling!' David gathered her into his arms and kissed her hard and long.

At last, a little breathless, Lucy pulled away and said, 'The sooner we tell my parents the new plan, the better, don't you think?'

'Only if you're certain-sure.'

'I am certain-sure,' responded Lucy. 'Now, how do I look? Are my eyes all red from crying?'

'You look as beautiful as always,' David assured her, 'though perhaps your cheeks have a little more colour that usual.'

'That'll have to do,' she said and taking his hand, she drew him out of the summerhouse and led him back indoors. As they went inside she paused and said, 'Leave the talking to me. I'll explain.'

They found Sir Keir and Lady McFarlane in the drawing room

with a tea tray between them. Both looked up anxiously as their daughter came into the room and were surprised and relieved that Lucinda did not seem in the grip of extreme emotion.

Rather at a loss, Lady McFarlane said, 'Would you like some tea? William has just brought us a fresh pot. Ring and ask for two more cups and another plate of cakes... that is, if you're hungry.'

In answer to the bell, William was sent for the extra cups, but they both turned down the cake.

Once these were brought and the tea was poured, an awkward silence fell until Lucy broke it by saying, 'You know David has been recalled to his regiment unexpectedly...'

'Yes,' answered her father. 'He told me and I've been discussing it with your mother.'

'We'll have to give thought as to what you're going to do,' put in her mother.

'Don't worry about that, Mama,' said Lucinda. 'David and I have already decided.'

'Have you now?' said Sir Keir, sounding serious, but with a twinkle in his eye.

'Without reference to us?' Lady McFarlane spoke sharply. 'Your parents?' She turned to David and said, 'I'm surprised at you, Sir David. Have you told your mother?'

'Yes, Lady McFarlane. She was there when the telegram arrived.'

'I see.'

Lady McFarlane was clearly not mollified and Sir Keir said, 'Why don't we hear what they would like to do? It may be exactly what we'd been considering ourselves and we'll simply have to work out the details.'

'Well, whatever happens we shall have to cancel the wedding. We can hardly go ahead without the bridegroom!'

Lucinda drank the last of her tea and put down the cup. 'Of course the wedding, as it stands, will have to be cancelled, Mama,' she said.

'What do you mean, "as it stands"?' You mean you want to postpone it until Sir David is home again? I think that is the best way forward. Everyone will know that he has to put king and country before everything else and…'

'No, Mama,' interrupted Lucinda. 'That isn't what we plan to do.'

Lady McFarlane's lips tightened and she said, 'So, perhaps you'd care to enlighten us.'

'Yes,' agreed Lucinda. 'As you say, Mama, the big society wedding you've been planning won't be able to take place. Certainly not before David has to leave for France, so we've decided to get married in the country. Just a quiet wedding in Haverford village church followed by the wedding breakfast back at the house.'

'But my dear girl,' protested her mother. 'Haverford Court isn't large enough to accommodate even a reduced number of guests.'

'Just family, Mama,' said Lucinda. 'A very small and quiet affair.'

'It's impossible,' said Lady McFarlane flatly. 'Quite impossible to arrange in the time. No time for the banns to be called.'

'I already have a special licence, Lady McFarlane,' David said, 'so the question of banns doesn't come into the matter.'

'And what does your mother say to all these ideas? She must think the whole thing very "hole in the corner". I'm afraid I can't countenance such a hasty wedding. I shudder to think what people will say.'

'My mother will understand the reason,' David spoke firmly. 'She of all people understands what it is to be an army wife. I'm sure she will give us her blessing.'

'Whether she does or not is hardly the point here,' maintained Lady McFarlane. 'Lucinda is not yet of age and she may not marry without her father's permission, which I can assure you will not be given, no matter what the circumstances.'

'Papa!' Lucinda turned immediately to her father. 'You won't say we can't get married before David has to leave, I know you won't.'

'I've already stipulated that you may not marry until you are at least eighteen,' came Sir Keir's reply. 'If that is to change, it will only be after due consideration.'

Chapter Nine

Now that the printing press had been set up in the basement of 27 Barnbury Street, Mabel had to advertise her change of address. Eddie had built an elegant archway over the side gate that led from the street to the back garden. It was painted the same glossy dark green as the front door, and inscribed with THOMAS CLARKE, PRINTER in bright, white paint.

Several of the local schools had accepted the cut-price offers she made to print registration cards and report cards, and the word had got round that Mabel Oakley at Thomas Clarke, Printer was reliable and gave good value for money.

However, afraid she might lose some of her regular customers, Mabel had printed and distributed flyers advertising the fact that the business had moved to new premises. These she spent a weekend pushing through letterboxes, pinning on corner shop noticeboards and leaving with newsagents for distribution with their papers.

It was as she visited one such corner shop that Saturday morning that she met up again with her old school friend Annie Ford. They had been close friends when in the same class at Walton Street Elementary School, but when Mabel had had to leave unexpectedly and go straight into service as a maid, they had seen nothing more of each other. Mabel's life had ceased to be her own with very little free time to come home and visit her family. Annie had had to stay at school until the end of the summer term and then had several menial jobs in the market and so their paths never crossed. Indeed, they lived in entirely different worlds, and though Mabel might have been able to imagine Annie's situation, Annie could have had no concept of the life of a between-maid in a Belgravia household like the McFarlanes'.

As it was, when Mabel first walked into the small newsagent's and general store not far from Noah's Path where Mrs Finch lived she didn't immediately recognise Annie. It was a shop she hadn't visited before and she was hoping to persuade the proprietor to display some of her flyers on his counter. As it was, the girl at the till greeted her with a cautious smile of recognition.

'Mabel? Mabel Oakley, is that you?'

Startled, Mabel stared at her for a moment before saying, 'Annie Ford!' and her own expression creased into a smile of pleasure to match Annie's.

'Yes, it's me,' beamed Annie. 'Though I ain't Annie Ford no more!' She held out her left hand to display the ring that nestled on her third finger. 'Annie Granger, I am now.'

'You're married?' cried Mabel.

'Just a month ago! Me and Ron got hitched at the registry.'

'Well,' Mabel managed to say, 'congratulations to you both. Fancy you, married! Where do you live?'

'Here,' replied Annie.

'In this shop?' Mabel glanced around at the small shop, its shelves stacked with far more than the newspapers and magazines she had expected to see.

'Yes,' Annie said, glancing a little nervously over her shoulder to a curtain that cut off the back of the shop. 'Ron's a postman, but his parents have this shop and there's a flat upstairs. We all live here, over the shop.'

'That's convenient,' was all that Mabel could think of to say.

After a moment's awkward silence, Annie said, 'What about you, Mabel? You still in service in that posh house up west?'

'No,' replied Mabel. 'I left there two years ago.'

'Did you? Why?' Annie looked at her old friend somewhat suspiciously. 'You wasn't turned off, was you?'

'No, I wasn't,' Mabel said firmly. 'I left of my own accord. I got another job, much better!'

'Oh! Well, so where d'you work now, then? Still up west?'

'No, I'm not in service at all,' Mabel answered. 'I got a job with a printer.' She held out the flyers she had brought in with her. 'Thomas Clarke, Printer,' she said. 'I was hoping that you might let me leave some of these with you. On your counter, perhaps? For people to pick up?'

Annie looked doubtful and, casting another nervous glance over her shoulder, said, 'People what want to advertise stuff put cards up over there.' She pointed to a small noticeboard on the wall. 'But you have to pay Mrs Granger to do that... so much a week, an' yours are bigger than the usual cards.'

'I see.' Mabel was disappointed although she had half expected it. 'What I was hoping was that you might keep some on the counter or behind it and when someone comes in and buys something, you could just slip one of these into the bag as well.'

'What sort of thing?' Annie asked, looking a little puzzled.

'A paper, anything,' replied Mabel. 'Anything they're buying. You just put one of these into the same bag and they take it home with them.'

'You'd have to ask Mrs Granger,' Annie said.

At that moment the curtain beyond the counter was swept aside and a stout woman dressed in a wrap-around overall with her hair tied up in a yellow duster came through to the shop.

'Ask me what?' she demanded.

Annie looked at her with frightened eyes, but made no reply and so Mabel, unintimidated by Annie's mother-in-law, spoke up.

'Good afternoon, Mrs Granger. How do you do? My name's Mabel Oakley. Annie and I used to be good friends at school but we lost touch.'

'Did you now?' Mrs Granger was a round, dumpy woman with rather bulging eyes set into a round, pudgy face. Her ample bosom strained at the overall that tried to constrain it and her arms, bare from above the elbows, would not have looked out of place on an all-in wrestler. The only thing small about her was her mouth, thin-lipped, pursed, and angry. Definitely not a woman you'd want to cross, Mabel decided; nor to have as a mother-in-law you had to live with. 'So you got her chatting,' Mrs Granger was saying, 'and wasting her time when she's got work to do!'

'I was hoping to do a little business with you,' Mabel said smoothly, 'and Annie was about to ask you to come through so we could talk.'

'Business? What sort of business?'

'I work for Thomas Clarke, Printer,' said Mabel. 'We are a local firm and we like to advertise our trade in our local area.'

'So what's that got to do with me? I don't want no printing done.'

Mabel explained her idea. 'Of course we would pay you for your trouble,' she said. 'And we wouldn't be taking up space on your noticeboard.'

'Your boss would pay us to put them leaflets in with our goods, would he?'

Now was not the time to be explaining that she was the boss, so Mabel simply agreed, 'Yes, he would.'

'Then he's got more money than sense,' stated Mrs Granger. 'I ain't got time for all that nonsense. Now, if you ain't come in here to buy something, I'll ask you to leave. We're busy. An' you, madam,' she turned on Annie, 'you should be going through them cards on the board and taking down the ones what are out of date. Get on with it.' And with that she turned on her heel and retreated behind the curtain.

Annie scurried round to the noticeboard as Mabel walked to the door.

'I'm still learning the job, see,' Annie said. 'She ain't always like that.'

I bet she is, Mabel thought, but managed not to say. She

handed Annie one of the flyers. 'Here,' she said. 'Keep this, it's got my new address on it. We've moved house not long ago, but now I know where you are too, we can stay in touch.'

Annie took the paper and stuffed it into her pocket. 'Yeah,' she said with yet another anxious glance at the back of the shop, 'maybe.'

And pigs might fly thought Mabel as she walked away down the street. Poor Annie! I hope her Ron is worth it.

'You should have seen her, Mam,' Mabel said when she got home and related her encounter with Annie and Mrs Granger.

'Can't be easy for her, sharing a flat above the shop with her in-laws,' pointed out Alice. 'That and working for them all day as well. Still, I suppose it puts a roof over their heads.'

'I know that shop, Grangers,' put in Mrs Finch. 'Old battle-axe, she is. Certainly wouldn't want her for my mother-in-law. Old man Granger ain't too bad, but he likes a quiet life and leaves everything to her.'

'Do you know Ron, Annie's husband?'

'Know him to see,' said Mrs Finch. 'Don't *know* him. Think he's a postman.'

'Yes,' agreed Mabel. 'Annie said.'

'Well, he's out all day, ain't he? No problem for him, living with his parents.'

'They've only been married a month,' Mabel said. 'I expect they'll move out as soon as they can get a place of their own.'

'Easier said than done,' said Alice. ''Specially when they're as young as that Annie.'

Mabel made no further comment, but she could have said, 'She's the same age as me, and you want me to settle down with William!'

Chapter Ten

The following Friday, when she went to collect the rent from Cecil Baker, Mabel took some more of her leaflets with her.

'I've brought these in case anyone comes to look for me,' she explained, holding the bundle out to him. 'I'm running my business from Barnbury Street now.'

Cecil looked doubtful. 'Nobody's been to ask,' he said.

Mabel didn't allow her disappointment to show, but replied cheerfully, 'Well, you never know. I'll leave them with you, just in case.'

Reluctantly Cecil took the flyers and set them aside. He really disliked doing his business with a girl young enough to be his daughter. However, when he held out the money for his rent, Mabel refused to take it.

'If you promise to pass on one of my flyers to anyone who comes asking,' she said, 'that'll be your rent for this week.' And taking his rent book, Mabel wrote the date and beside it 'Paid in full.'

Cecil stared at her incredulously and then when she nodded, he said, 'How do you know I'll do it?'

Mabel handed him back his rent book and said with a smile, 'Because I trust you, Mr Baker. Because I'm sure you're an honest man.'

When she'd left, Cecil Baker dumped the pile of printed flyers on a shelf. Unlikely anyone would come asking. They'd just see that it was now a shoemaker's and go away again. Not much of a businesswoman, that girl, he thought as he returned to the shoe he had been fitting with a new sole. She won't last long if

DINEY COSTELOE

she takes people on trust like that, they'll simply take her for a ride and she'll go bust.

However, to his surprise a young man turned up at the workshop the next day. He pushed the door open and stepped inside, before coming up short when he found himself looking at a cobbler's workshop rather than a printing works.

Cecil put down his knife and, wiping his hands on a piece of towelling, said, 'May I help you, sir? A pair of boots perhaps, for the winter?'

The young man shook his head. 'No, sorry, afraid not. I was looking for the printer.'

'Were you? I'm afraid she's moved away.'

'Oh!' The young man looked crestfallen. 'Don't suppose you know where, do you?'

Cecil almost said no. He couldn't be dealing with Mabel Oakley's customers, he needed customers of his own, and then Mabel's words echoed in his head. 'I'm sure you're an honest man... I trust you.'

Almost reluctantly he reached for a flyer and handed it to the young man. 'Here you are, sir, I believe this is where she works from now.'

The man ran his eye over the flyer and then stuffed it into his pocket. Glancing at the range of shoes displayed on a stand by the door he said, 'I might be in need of some new boots. I haven't time to stop today, but I'll come back.' And with that he hurried out of the door and disappeared.

'Harrumph,' said Cecil as he turned back to his last. 'Doubt if I'll be seeing him again!'

72

Chapter Eleven

Outside in the street, Iain McFarlane flagged down a taxi and directed it to 27 Barnbury Street. Why had Mabel moved from Mr Clarke's workshop? he wondered. Thank goodness the shoemaker had known where she had gone. It was clear from the flyer that she was still in business and he hoped she would be able to help him with a rush commission.

His father had finally agreed that Lucinda and David Melcome could be married before the major left to join the expeditionary force in France, and immediately Lady McFarlane swung into action. It wouldn't be the high society wedding she had hoped for, but neither would it be a hole in the corner affair, as if they were ashamed of the match; and so an announcement had already been sent to *The Times* explaining the change of plans. So far the war in France had hardly impinged on the upper echelons of London society. The season was over and many families had already moved to the clean air of the country to recover. The British army would take care of the Germans and the war would be over before Christmas. However, Sir David Melcome was an officer in the Dragoons, and it would be clear to anyone who might give thought to the matter that it was his duty to go and join the army at the front.

The wedding was now to take place in Haverford. The rector had been approached, and the wedding breakfast was to be at Haverford Court. Time was of the essence, and having new invitations printed for Lucinda's wedding was definitely a rush job. Iain had promised his mother that he'd get the new invitations delivered within a couple of days. He had already tried two well-established print firms, but neither had been able to meet his time frame. And then he had thought of Mabel and wondered. He often thought of Mabel, though that was something he didn't often admit even to himself, let alone anyone else.

The taxi deposited him outside number 27 and Iain looked up at the house. He was surprised to see that it seemed to be a normal semi-detached dwelling rather than the workshop he'd been expecting. Seeing the sign arching over the side gate, he ignored the front door, pushed the gate open and followed the path down the slope into the garden. There he found himself at the foot of an outside staircase leading up to what, at the front of the house, would be the ground floor. Beside him was a door above which was another green and white sign, THOMAS CLARKE, PRINTER. This door, standing ajar, led into a basement from which came the regular thud of a printing press. Iain looked in through the small window beside the door, and for a moment watched Mabel rhythmically feeding paper into the press and removing the prints.

'Are you looking for Mabel?' The woman's voice came from above and Iain looked up to see who had spoken. Alice Oakley was standing on a landing at the top of the outside steps. Seeing his face, she looked surprised and said, 'Oh! It's you.'

'Mrs Oakley, good afternoon,' said Iain, raising his hat.

'Mr Iain! Are you looking for Mabel?'

'I was, yes,' replied Iain, 'but I can hear her at work down here.'

'Just knock on the door and if she doesn't hear you, simply walk in.' And with that Alice Oakley went back indoors, leaving Iain standing in the garden.

Oh well, he thought. I might as well, now that I'm here. Turning back to the basement door, he gave a sharp rap with his knuckles. The rhythmic sound of the press continued unchanged, so Iain pushed the door wide and walked into the room.

At his sudden appearance, Mabel allowed the press to slow

down. Annoyed at being interrupted, she snapped, 'What are *you* doing here?'

'Looking for you,' replied Iain, his voice casual, even as his heart beat faster at the sight of her standing on a block before the printing press. 'Your mother told me to knock and if you didn't answer, just to walk in.'

'I see.' Mabel, stepping down from the block, looked suddenly smaller. 'Well, what do you want?'

'I was hoping you could do some work for me.'

'I'm very busy, as you can see,' remarked Mabel. 'What sort of work?'

'It's a bit of a rush job—' Iain began, but Mabel cut him off.

'Then sorry, but I doubt if I can help you. I have a full order book for the next few weeks.'

'Things must be going well, then,' Iain said. 'Congratulations.'

Slightly mollified by his easy tone, Mabel said, 'What's the job?'

Despite stating that her order book was full, Mabel knew that the work marked up in her book was about to run out. She really couldn't afford to turn down a job, even if it did come from Iain McFarlane.

'Lucinda is getting married,' he replied.

'Yes,' answered Mabel. 'William told me.'

'And did he also tell you that her wedding has had to be cancelled?'

Mabel stared at him. 'No,' she said. 'He didn't. Why has it?'

'Her fiancé is a regular soldier, an officer in the Dragoon Guards, and he's been called to the front.'

'But William said they were getting married in a few weeks' time.'

'So they are, or rather, so they were,' agreed Iain, 'but he has to go to France before the date set. Now they are going to be married in the country, just a small affair, but my mother is determined to send out proper invitations for the few guests who will be invited.'

'Poor Lucinda,' Mabel said. She spoke sincerely. She was truly sorry for the bride-to-be. 'She must be very upset.'

'Very determined, more like,' said Iain with a grin. 'Still, she and my mother are *both* determined to make it a very special day.' Iain put his hand in his pocket and pulled out the draft of an invitation. Mabel took it, scanning it quickly before looking up at Iain again.

'And you want me to print this for you?'

'If you can do it straight away, yes,' Iain answered, 'but if you have too much work on, I'll be on my way.'

'How soon do you need them, and how many?'

'Forty should do it, and today if possible?'

'You don't want much, do you?' said Mabel.

'But you could do it?'

'It depends,' she said, 'whether I have the high-quality card necessary for such an invitation. I see you have it set out as it should be, but you'll have to tell me what font you require.'

For a moment Iain seemed at a loss. The Mabel he was dealing with now was brisk and efficient, not the rather shy maid-of-all-work who had served his mother. No longer the girl whose smile tugged at his heartstrings, but a young woman grown, able to face the world with confidence.

'What do you suggest?' he asked. 'You know more about these things than I do.'

Mabel crossed to the small desk in the corner of the room and, opening the top drawer, extracted a sheet of paper and handed it to him. Iain looked at it with interest. Printed on it were several lines of type, each with the same words, but with a different type face.

'Those are the most common ones,' Mabel told him. 'One of them might suit you.'

'And if I choose one now?'

'You don't give up, do you, Iain?'

'I just want everything to be arranged as soon as possible, so that Lucinda and David can be married before he has to leave.

My mother will have the invitations hand-delivered to the guests as soon as they are ready. If you think you can do it, well, the job's yours. If you can't, I'll leave you to what you were doing, and try elsewhere.'

The expression of resignation on his face made Mabel relent. She had printed invitations before, there was no reason why she couldn't do these.

'Of course I can do it,' she said. 'If you can choose the card from some I already have, I'll work on it this afternoon and pull off a proof. Come back this evening and take it to show your mother. If she approves it, I'll run them off straight away. I assume you'll want envelopes as well.'

Iain hadn't given any thought to envelopes, but he was so relieved that Mabel was going to produce the invitations, he said, 'Well, yes I suppose so.'

Twenty minutes later Iain left, having approved a plain cream card, a simple serif font and matching cream vellum envelopes.

'Only one condition, Iain,' Mabel said as he made ready to leave. 'These invitations will have been printed by Thomas Clarke, Printer. There is no need for your parents to know that they have anything to do with me. Thomas Clarke, Printer, is the name of my business and always will be, so there is no deception there.'

It suited Iain McFarlane very well not to reveal it was Mabel Oakley who was doing the work. Her dealings with the McFarlane family were at best strained. She had picked up a printed invoice and, after scrawling her terms, scribbled an indecipherable signature at the bottom.

'I'll see you later, then,' she said as she handed it over. 'About six. All right?'

'Yes, thank you, Mabel.' Iain was again at a loss for words. The amount on the invoice seemed very low. Could she really produce the high standard his mother would demand? 'Are you sure? About the price I mean?'

'I'm not charging you any more than I would anyone else for the same work,' said Mabel stiffly. 'Or less.'

'No, I'm sure you aren't,' agreed Iain hastily. 'I just thought it might cost more... for the rush job... you know?'

'Oh, Iain, for goodness' sake. Just go away and let me get on with it. I'll have the proof ready for you when you come back this evening.'

Pushing the invoice into his pocket, he raised a hand in salute and went out of the door. He could go back and tell his mother that Thomas Clarke the printer was producing the invitations and they would be ready for distribution tomorrow morning.

Chapter Twelve

While Lady McFarlane was organising and reorganising the wedding, David and Lucinda were thinking about the honeymoon. They would have six days between the actual wedding day and the morning when David would have to leave. Where should they spend those precious hours? When he consulted Lucinda, she laughed and said she didn't mind. First of all David suggested Crayne House but then he worried that Lucy might not want to be buried in the country.

'On the other hand, we could stay in town,' he suggested. 'Not in Sloane Square, of course, but somewhere special?'

When Lucinda didn't immediately reply he went on hurriedly, 'The Savoy perhaps, or the Dorchester? What do you think? Would you prefer a hotel in Mayfair? Just tell me. We could drive in the park, go to the theatre, dance the night away.' He reached over and took her hands in his. 'Of course,' he said, 'in normal times I'd have taken you on an extended wedding trip to the continent, France, Italy, Switzerland, but obviously that'll have to wait for the time being.'

'Oh, David,' Lucy scolded him, 'what could be more special than just being together... anywhere? As long as you're there with me, I don't want to share you with anyone else.' She looked up at him from under her lashes and a dimple peeped on her cheek. 'Unless of course *you'd* prefer the bright lights of London, surrounded by the world? I don't mind dancing, if that's what you'd choose?'

David groaned and, pulling her into his arms, kissed her

gently on the mouth before releasing her, murmuring, 'Minx! I want you all to myself, for every precious minute.'

'Good,' replied Lucy with satisfaction. 'I want the same.'

'Crayne? An excellent idea,' said Lady Melcome when David told her of their plans. 'What could be better than a few days together there? I shall go down at once and warn the Crofts to prepare for your arrival.'

Croft and Mrs Croft, the couple who looked after the Melcomes' country home and had known David from babyhood, were delighted to hear, not only of Sir David's approaching nuptials, but that he and his bride would be spending their short honeymoon in Crayne House.

'Don't you worry, my lady,' said Mrs Croft. 'Now our Ivy is away training to be a nurse, Janet Mead from the village comes in to help me keep the place up, and until Sir David employs his own staff, I'll bring in a couple of the village girls, temporary like, for while the happy couple are here. Carrie Ferney for one. You know Tam Ferney, the farrier? His daughter, she's fifteen now and ready to go into service, and perhaps Ethel Barnes, though she'll have to be watched. Flighty piece she is, but even so, a good worker with a good heart. The place'll be spotless when they arrive.' She glanced across at her mistress and added, 'And the new Lady Melcome will be bringing her own maid, I daresay?'

'I'm sure she will,' agreed Lady Melcome. Her ladyship had seen Clara on one occasion, and though she didn't think she was up to much as a lady's maid, she supposed she would do until David found Lucinda someone more suitable.

So it had been agreed and Crayne House was prepared: the furniture polished to within an inch of its life, the hangings washed, ironed and rehung. Polishing silver was Croft's forte, and every piece in the house gleamed, reflecting the light from the oil lamps and candles.

'You must get electricity put in,' Lady Melcome said to David when she came back from inspecting the house and discussing menus with Mrs Croft. 'We should have done it years ago. A pity it's too late now to do it before you get married, but when you come home again, you should certainly have it done. So much cleaner and more efficient, even than gas.'

'Well, Mother, you and Lucinda can find out what we need to do while I'm away, and then we can sort it all out as soon as I'm home again.'

David's man Fenton had been taking care of the arrangements for their departure for France, but there was the question of the horses. As an officer in a cavalry regiment David would be taking his own two hunters, Hector and Lysander, with him, and he was determined that it should be he himself who oversaw their departure.

'Can you spare a day to run down to Crayne and see the house?' David asked Lucinda. 'I need to go myself as there are some things I ought to see to before I go to France.'

'Of course,' replied Lucinda, even though she knew her mother would be horrified.

'David wants me to see the house before we arrive there on our wedding day and I want to meet the staff,' Lucinda explained when Lady McFarlane threw up her hands in despair, crying, 'It's impossible, Lucinda! I need you here!'

But Lucy stood her ground. 'I'm sorry, Mama. It's important for me to go. I at least need to know the names of the staff and what positions they hold, so I don't make any embarrassing mistakes when I get there.' She didn't give way, but simply said, 'David wants me to go, Mama.' And that was it. From the day they had met, David's preferences always took precedence.

They travelled to Crayne in the Melcomes' touring motor car, its hood folded down beneath a blue autumn sky. David drove with Lucy sitting beside him in the front seat. Her hair was tucked into a large hat held in place by several hat pins and a silk scarf tied under her chin.

'Tell me about Crayne?' Lucy said as she settled back to enjoy the drive. 'Has it always been in your family?'

'No, there was an older manor house on the site, but the present house was built by my great-grandfather, James Barton, when he returned from India.

'India?' echoed Lucy. 'Tell me more!'

'He went to India as a young man where he made himself a fortune. When he finally came home again, he was well into his forties and was determined to make a suitable marriage and take his place in society. His money came from trade of course, but that could be overlooked provided there was enough of it.'

'And was there?' asked Lucy.

'Oh yes,' laughed David. 'More than enough. He looked for somewhere to establish himself and found the manor house at Crayne Abbas. At the time it belonged to an impoverished viscount, Lord Exton. Mr Barton liked the position and he liked the view and the small estate that went with it. The rest of the land that had once been part of the Crayne estate had been sold off piecemeal to fund the noble lord's gambling habit. Mr Barton had it in mind to found a dynasty and he offered a deal to Lord Exton. He would marry the viscount's spinster daughter, the Honourable Eleanor Exton, thus buying his way into the aristocracy; he would pay off all Exton's debts once and for all; and Eleanor would bring him the house as her dowry. Unable to fend off his creditors in any other way, Lord Exton agreed the deal. Mr Barton married Eleanor, her father's debts were cleared and he took himself off to London where, we believe, he drank himself to an early death.'

'But didn't Eleanor mind being used like that by both of them?' cried Lucy. 'I bet she didn't have any say in the matter!'

'No,' agreed David, 'she probably didn't, but in fact, if you think about it, she had much to gain herself: for example, the status of a married woman instead of dwindling into an old maid. She would be mistress of her own household, a house she'd grown up in, and you must remember, Mr Barton wasn't used to moving in upper class circles. She could teach him the etiquette of his new status.'

'Hmm,' mused Lucy. 'I wouldn't want to be disposed of like that just because I was old and ugly.'

'Oh, I didn't say Eleanor was ugly,' said David. 'She certainly wasn't. Indeed, there's a portrait of her in the drawing room at Crayne, showing her as exceedingly pretty. I'll show it to you.'

'So what happened about the house?'

'Well, it needed a great deal of attention. Lord Exton hadn't spent anything on its upkeep since he'd inherited it from his father. Mr Barton, the wealthy businessman, decided the original house wasn't grand enough, so he set about the necessary repairs and at the same time extended it. He altered the front façade to a more modern style and added a wing on either side to make it far more impressive.'

'Didn't Eleanor mind her home being so changed?'

'I doubt it. Don't you think she'd be grateful for something more comfortable? But anyway, she didn't live there for very long.'

'Why not?' Lucy was intrigued by the story now.

'She died.'

'Died? How did she die?'

'She died giving birth to my grandmother, Marguerite.'

For a long moment Lucy said nothing and then in a very small voice said, 'That's really sad. She didn't have much of a life, did she?'

'Strangely enough,' said David, 'I think she and Mr Barton were happy in their marriage. He certainly didn't marry again, and he doted on his daughter.'

'He didn't blame Marguerite for killing his wife?' suggested Lucy quietly.

'No, I don't think so.' David sounded surprised. 'Is that the way you see it?'

'I don't know,' replied Lucy. 'I'm just sad for them both.'

'Well, he employed a nanny and then a governess, and he and Marguerite continued to live at Crayne. Mr Barton concentrated on his building works, but just as the finishing touches were made to the house, he died of a heart attack. Simply dropped dead in his library. Lucy, darling, why don't we talk about something more cheerful.'

'How old was Marguerite when he died?' asked Lucy as if she hadn't heard him.

'Sixteen. She inherited everything,' said David, really wishing he hadn't started on the story of Crayne House. 'As an heiress, she was very much sought after.'

'But who did she marry?' asked Lucy, intrigued.

'She married baronet Sir Geoffrey Melcome, my grandfather,' said David. 'It was a love match, leading to a long and happy marriage. However, my father was an only child. I have cousins on my mother's side, but as you know I'm an only child, so the baronetcy is hanging by a thread!'

'But were you brought up at Crayne?'

'Not exactly. We lived in Sloane Square as we do now, but before my father was killed, we spent a lot of time there. Crayne has always been there, always special.'

'Tell me who I'm going to meet now,' said Lucy. 'I need to know their names and what they do.'

'That's easy enough,' he assured her. 'Croft and Mrs Croft look after the house when we're living in London. They've been there forever. They have a daughter, Ivy, just older than you, who's training to be a nurse at St Thomas's Hospital, so not at home anymore. The others come in daily from the village. Out of doors there is Grey, the gardener, with a young lad, Joe, to help him. Then there's Farley, whose father was my father's coachman. He's getting on now, but he still looks after the stables and drives my mother when she's in the country. If we're going to use the house more often, we shall have to employ some more permanent staff, but in the meantime Mrs Croft can manage with the temporary maids she has organised from the village. Nothing for you to worry about, everything has been taken care of. You'll see in a minute or two: we're nearly there.'

Moments later David had turned off the main road and they

were driving through the small village of Crayne Abbas, past the church with its solid square tower at the edge of the small village green. A half-timbered village inn stood opposite, its painted sign declaring it to be The Bell. Lucinda looked eagerly from the car window, taking in the few shops which lined the single village street. There were several people going about their business, but more than one stopped to stare at the car as they drove by. One woman was standing outside the post office, a small boy at her side. He pointed and waved when he saw the car and shouted with delight when Lucinda waved back.

'Here we are,' announced David, as they swept between two tall stone gateposts and up a tree-lined drive that opened onto a circle of smooth gravel in front of the house.

Chapter Thirteen

Despite all David had told her about Crayne House, Lucy couldn't believe her eyes as the house came into view. It was far larger and more imposing than she'd imagined. She stared up at it as the car came to a halt and her heart sank. How could she possibly become the mistress of such a place?

The house was four storeys high, topped with a decorative stone parapet behind which was a mansard roof with a line of four dormer windows.

The frontage of the house was completely symmetrical, with four deep windows on either side of a pillared portico sheltering the front door. A similar line of matching windows crossed the façade on each of the three floors above.

'Welcome to Crayne House,' David said as he got out of the car and came round to open the passenger door for Lucy. 'And here's Croft and Mrs Croft come out to greet us.'

'Welcome, Sir David,' said Croft. 'It's good to see you before you go off to France.'

'Thank you, Croft. Good morning, Mrs Croft. This is my fiancée, Miss McFarlane. I've brought her to meet you and to see the house. I know you'll show her round while I'm outside with Farley.'

'Good morning, sir, Miss McFarlane,' said the housekeeper. 'May we offer you our congratulations on your engagement?'

'Thank you, Mrs Croft,' replied David, which Lucy echoed softly, 'Thank you, Mrs Croft.'

David turned back to Lucy. 'I'm going round to the stables to see Farley about the horses, Lucy. You go with Mrs Croft and have a look at the house. I'll come back indoors once I've seen them off. And then,' he turned again to the housekeeper, 'perhaps you can find us something to eat before we set off home again.'

'Certainly, sir. As soon as I heard you were coming, I asked Janet to lay out a cold collation in the dining room.'

'Splendid,' said David. 'I'll look forward to that. I suppose Farley is already in the stables?'

'Yes, sir,' answered Croft. 'He come up first thing this morning to make everything ready for when you arrived.'

'I may be a little while,' David said to Lucy, 'but I know you'll be in safe hands with Mrs Croft.' And with that he gave her a smile and disappeared round the side of the house.

'Come your ways in, Miss McFarlane,' said Mrs Croft. 'I'm sure you will want to make yourself comfortable after your journey. And perhaps some refreshment?' The housekeeper led the way up the steps and through the portico into a semi-circular double-height hall, lit by the window on either side of the door and the three from the floor above.

Lucy was indeed glad to make use of the small cloakroom tucked away at the back of the hall and for the tea and shortbread that Janet brought to her in the morning room. As she drank her tea, Lucy looked round the room. It was not that large, but comfortably furnished to be used either as a small dining room or a snug sitting room. The windows gave onto the front drive and Lucy could see the car parked outside, the hood now pulled up in case of rain.

Mrs Croft returned once Lucy had finished her tea and said, 'I'm sure you're looking forward to getting to know Crayne House, would you like to see round it now?'

'Yes, please,' said Lucy, getting to her feet.

'Well, this is the morning room,' began Mrs Croft. 'The family usually take their breakfast in here as it has the early sun.'

And so the tour began. There were several doors off the hallway and Lucy admired the dining room, the library, the billiard room, all of which looked out onto the garden from the east wing. Facing south was the drawing room.

'This is part of the original house,' Mrs Croft said. 'So much older than the other rooms downstairs.'

'It's a lovely room,' Lucy said, looking round. It was elegantly furnished with sofas on either side of a huge fireplace over which hung the portrait of a young lady.

Was that Eleanor? Lucy wondered, but didn't like to ask.

She crossed to the wide windows which gave onto a view across the flower garden, now dressed in its autumn colours, and to the meadows of the countryside beyond. The view was indeed beautiful and Lucy could quite understand old James Barton falling in love with it.

'The garden is looking lovely,' she said, turning back to Mrs Croft.

'Yes,' replied the housekeeper. 'Always does. He's a good gardener, Grey is. Always plenty of colour whatever the season, and a kitchen garden to supply the house with vegetables.'

From the drawing room they moved on to a parlour, clearly the preserve of the Lady Melcome, furnished with pretty chintz curtains and comfortable chairs grouped round an ornate fireplace. From this window Lucy could see what must be the stables, a separate building and a yard beyond a wall entered through an archway. She wished she'd gone there with David instead of trailing round after Mrs Croft.

'The kitchens are through this door,' Mrs Croft was saying and pointed to a door similar to the one that led to the kitchens in Chanynge Place. 'Perhaps we should look at those when you've seen the family rooms upstairs?'

How am I going to be mistress of a house like this? Lucinda wondered as she followed Mrs Croft, dutifully admiring. I'll never find my way around the house.

As if sensing her dismay, Mrs Croft paused at the bottom of the wide staircase that rose from the hallway in a graceful sweep to the gallery landing above and said, 'It's a big house,

Miss McFarlane, but you'll soon find your way about. There're eight bedrooms and two bathrooms up on the family's floor, four more and a bathroom on the nursery floor and then the indoor servants' rooms are on the top landing.' Here she indicated a door that emerged from a back staircase and twisted up an even narrower staircase to the top of the house.

'Croft and I have a sitting room off the kitchen,' she explained. 'When there's no family or guests, we're snug in there and there's a bedroom off.'

'It really is very big,' Lucinda said a little nervously. It was, indeed, far bigger than Haverford Court. Would she ever be able to live here as mistress of such a mansion?

Of course you will, she told herself. David will be here with you and you'll soon get used to it. And anyway, you'll be living in London most of the time, so you don't even have to come here much.

For a moment she had stopped listening to Mrs Croft and suddenly she realised the room the housekeeper was now showing her was the bedroom she would share with David.

There was a door at each side of the room which Lucy assumed were wardrobes until Mrs Croft opened one and said, 'And through here is your dressing room.' She stood aside to allow Lucy to see into the room beyond. 'And the opposite door connects to Sir David's.'

The bedchamber was a large, well-appointed room with tall windows offering the same view as the drawing room, comfortable furnishings, a fireplace and dominated by a large four-poster bed. As she surveyed the room all Lucy could think of was that next time she stood there, she would be married to David and would be going to share that huge bed with him. And then what?

'Of course,' the housekeeper was saying, 'the hangings in these rooms are old-fashioned now. I'm sure you'll be wanting to change them to suit your own taste.'

Lucy smiled and said, 'Perhaps, but not, I'm sure, straight

away,' and thought she saw a flicker of relief cross Mrs Croft's face.

What Lucy really wanted to ask was, 'Which is Lady Melcome's room?' Surely one of these rooms must be hers, and clearly I shan't be changing anything in her room. But it wasn't a question she felt she could ask one of the servants, even one as important and long-serving as Mrs Croft. Perhaps she'd pluck up the courage to ask David on the way home.

When David came in from the stables, having seen his beloved hunters set off on their long journey to France, he seemed very quiet. There was always the risk that they would not survive any action, but that wasn't something he wanted put into Lucy's mind and so he made no mention of the horses at all.

'Poor Lucy,' he said as he led her into the dining room where the promised collation had been laid out and the fire lit. 'You must be starving, I know I am.'

'I had tea and some delicious shortbread earlier to keep me going,' she replied, 'but I am hungry now.'

The long dining room table had not been used, but a smaller gate-leg table had been set up before the fire and the two of them sat companionably, tucking into cold ham, a pork pie with baked potatoes which, along with the tomatoes and lettuce, had come, Mrs Croft told them proudly, 'Straight from the kitchen garden, sir. Grey sent them in special like.'

David thanked her and when he smiled at her and said they would serve themselves, the housekeeper bobbed the suspicion of a curtsey and left them alone.

'So, you had a tour of the house?' David asked as he cut Lucy a slice of ham.

'Oh yes,' replied Lucy brightly, determined to conceal her misgivings. 'Mrs Croft showed me everything.'

'I'm sure she did,' David said with a smile. 'She's as proud of it as if it were her own, but if there is anything you want to change, just say. Some of it is very old-fashioned, and looking rather tired, but we can soon smarten the place up. It's our home now.'

The idea of altering anything in the big old house terrified Lucinda and she said, 'But not until you're home again. After all, I'll be living in Sloane Square while you're away.'

'Yes, of course you will,' agreed David, 'But there's nothing to stop you spending time at Crayne if ever you want a change of scene.'

It had been decided that when David left for France, Lucinda would live with his mother in Sloane Square. David had suggested that while he was away, she might like to return to live with her parents in Chanynge Place, but Lucinda knew once she had the status of a married lady, she would be loath to return to her father's house. She had been adamant she would not move back under her parents' roof.

'It's entirely up to you,' David had said when she had expressed this determination with some force. 'I just thought you might be more at home there with your own family than living with my mother, who you hardly know.'

'It will give me a chance to get to know her better,' Lucinda told him. 'I have to stand on my own two feet. If I moved back into Chanynge Place, my mother would treat me like a child, telling me what I am and amn't allowed to do!'

Thus, although Lady Melcome had privately expressed some reservations to her son about Lucinda moving into Sloane Square, once the decision was made, she appeared delighted with the idea.

'But on your return from France, David,' she said firmly, 'I think I shall remove to Crayne.'

'But, Mama, you shouldn't be turned out of your home, simply because I've got married,' said David. 'I've said that all along. You must live in Sloane Square as long as you wish.'

'Thank you,' replied his mother with a smile, 'that's generous of you, but by then it will be high time Lucinda became the true mistress of your home. As your wife, it's where she should be and I should not. Young as she is, Lucinda will soon assume her place as mistress of this house. Mrs Watson will help her to begin with, just until she finds her feet, but I don't think it'll take long. She's a sensible girl and I'm sure her mother runs a tight ship, so she will know how things should be done. I will not be needed and I shall, with your permission, remove to Crayne. I don't need London society anymore. I shall be perfectly happy living quietly in the country. I always have plenty to do when I'm down there, and the Crofts look after me wonderfully well.'

Thus the matter was decided and a bedchamber and private parlour were chosen in the Sloane Square house and prepared for Lucinda's arrival.

With her new home taken care of for the present, Lucinda turned her attention to her wardrobe. The only completely new gown she had was her wedding dress, elegantly simple, created for her by couturier Madame Chantal. Work had been begun on this as soon as she had become engaged, which meant it could be finished in time for the earlier wedding date. It hung now in her room in Chanynge Place, an exquisite gown of ivory lace over delicate cream silk, waiting, with its floor-length lace train, to be packed and taken to Haverford Court. Madame Chantal had already designed Lucinda an extensive wardrobe for her debut. With no time to create another, the seamstresses who had made the original gowns under the direction of the couturier herself now sewed and altered, matched and redesigned, so that only those with a particularly discerning eye would have recognised the resulting outfits as anything but new creations, with hats, gloves, shoes and reticules, all perfectly fitting for a bride's trousseau. All would be ready for transfer to Haverford Court two days before the wedding and on to Crayne House thereafter.

Chapter Fourteen

When Iain returned to Barnbury Street that evening, the relentless thump of the printing press was silent. Mabel was still in her printshop, and this time she heard his knock and called him to come in.

'That's good timing,' she said by way of welcome, 'I've just finished. Here.' She picked up an invitation card and passed it to him. 'I hope this is what you wanted. If not I can still alter it, this is only a proof.'

Iain looked at the card and then smiled at her.

'That looks perfect,' he said. 'My mother will be delighted. When can you print the rest?'

Mabel looked surprised. 'Well straight away, but won't Lady McFarlane want to approve it first?'

Iain shook his head. 'No,' he replied. 'She's left it to me.'

'Oh well,' said Mabel, 'if that's the case, I can run them off now, if you like. The press is all set up, but once they are printed that will be it. I shan't change anything. So look at the proof again to make sure. No spelling mistakes, nothing left out, no errors with names.'

Dutifully Iain looked at the card again:

Sir Keir and Lady McFarlane
request the pleasure of your company
at the marriage of their daughter
Lucinda Mary
to
Major Sir David Melcome Bart

of Sloane Square and Crayne Abbas, Buckinghamshire
on Saturday, 5th September at 12 o'clock
At St Michael and All Angels Church, Haverford, Berkshire
And afterwards at
Haverford Court
R.S.V.P
11 Chanynge Place, Mayfair

'No,' he said, 'it really looks fine to me.'

'Good,' Mabel said and stepped up to the press. 'Forty, was it?'

'Yes, please.'

'Sit down if you want to,' Mabel said as she spread more ink and set the huge flywheel turning.

Iain took a seat on a stool in the corner of the room and watched as Mabel pulled off two more proofs and inspected them with great care before she began to print.

Once, months ago, Iain had told Mabel that he would love to watch her working the printing press, to which she had snapped, 'Well, you can't!' But now here he was, watching her graceful movement as she removed each printed card with one hand and inserted the next with the other. He watched the deft movements and the look of concentration on her face as Mabel worked the press, apparently unaware of his scrutiny, and was struck anew at the confidence this young girl – a girl of far lower social standing than he – had in her own abilities. She had matured in the months since he had last seen her, and was now a beautiful young woman, but still, he knew, as unobtainable as she always had been.

'There,' she said, as she placed the last card onto the pile beside her. 'I've done fifty, just in case you should need a few extras. Tomorrow I shall need to get back to what I was doing before, so won't be able to set the press up again for any more of these.'

Iain watched her take down a box of envelopes from a shelf

and count out the fifty he would need, tying them into a neat bundle, before doing the same with the invitations themselves. Adding a compliments slip from *Thomas Clarke, Printer*, she parcelled them all together for Iain to take.

Iain drew out his pocket book and extracted her invoice and a five-pound note.

'Thank you,' she said, and having found him the required change, she took the invoice and wrote '*Paid in full*' and the date, before she again scrawled an illegible signature across the bottom.

Iain had nearly told her to keep the change, it wasn't that much after all, but caught himself in time. Mabel's pride would have been furiously offended at what would have looked like charity. Instead he put the money into his pocket and picked up the parcel.

'You will of course remember our agreement, Iain, won't you?' she said, her eyes searching his face. 'No mention of me to your family.'

'I'll remember,' promised Iain, and he extended his hand to her. For the briefest moment Mabel hesitated before accepting his handshake.

'Good luck, Mabel,' he said. 'You deserve to succeed.' And with that he turned and walked out of the room. Mabel heard his feet crunch on the gravel of the path, the click of the gate, and he was gone. With a sigh Mabel sat down in Mr Clarke's chair and for a long moment closed her eyes. The peaceful sounds of evening drifted in through the open door, bird song in the garden, a voice calling in the next garden and then, suddenly, the sound of the front doorbell.

Mabel jumped to her feet. William! It was William's night off and he was coming to the Oakleys' for supper.

'Mabel!' Her mother was at the top of the outside steps and calling. 'Mabel, William's here.'

Mabel stuck her head out of the door and called back, 'I'm just clearing up, Mam! I'll be up in five minutes.' She heard her mother go back inside. Will was always welcome in the Oakleys' house and wouldn't mind sitting with her parents until she'd left things shipshape in the print room.

By the time she joined them in the kitchen, William was sitting at the table with her father and Mam had already poured the tea.

Handing Mabel her cup, Alice said, 'You seem to have had a busy day, dear.'

'Yes, a rush job, but all done now. How are you, Will?'

William had not got to his feet to greet her as he normally would. He sat across the table from her, stirring his tea and eating a piece of cake, but somehow seemed to be avoiding her eye. 'All right,' he mumbled.

Sensing some sort of tension between them, Alice asked, 'How are the preparations going for Miss Lucinda's wedding, William? Everything going to plan?'

'No,' replied William. 'Everything's changed.' And he went on to explain what Iain had told Mabel earlier.

'Oh dear,' cried Alice. 'What are they going to do with all the arrangements made, I wonder?'

'They're getting married at Haverford before he goes,' William said. 'Bit of a rush if you ask me. They should wait until he comes back.'

Now was the time, Mabel knew, to tell William she already knew what was happening in the McFarlane family, that she had just produced the second batch of invitations, but something held her back. It was Iain McFarlane who had brought her the invitation job and there was history between the two men, which was better forgotten by all of them. Months ago, Iain, son of the house, and William, footman, had joined in an uneasy alliance to try to protect Mabel, and together they had come to her rescue when Alfred Everette, an erstwhile friend of Iain's, had attacked and tried to rape her. But after that, knowing he and Mabel could have no future together, Iain went back to Cambridge to finish his law degree. William had told Mabel he loved her and had talked of their future together, but Mabel had made it clear that she had no intention of marrying anyone for years yet, and William, prepared to wait, returned to being a footman in the McFarlane household. He was, however, still suspicious of the young master's intentions and the unlikely truce was over.

By common consent, after supper, Alice took Andrew back to his own room to set up the draughts board for his regular game with William, leaving the young couple together at the kitchen table. At first there was an awkward silence and then William asked abruptly, 'What was Iain McFarlane doing here?'

'Iain McFarlane?'

'Iain McFarlane. I saw him coming out of your gate as I was coming up the road.'

'He brought me a printing job,' Mabel said.

'Did he now?' William sounded sceptical. 'And what sort of job was that then?'

'If it's any of your business, William, it was to print some new invitations for Lucinda's wedding. Change of date and venue.'

'And why did he come to you, just a small printing works? Why not one of them big, posh firms? Why didn't he go to one of them?'

'I think he had tried, but they had to be ready for delivery tomorrow, and I was able to produce them within the time frame.'

'I bet Lady M won't be too happy when she hears who printed them.'

'She's not going to hear, unless you tell her,' remarked Mabel. 'But honestly I doubt if she'll mind as long as she has them on time.'

'A bit deceitful isn't it,' said William. 'Not telling her?'

'She'll know it was Thomas Clarke, Printer who produced them. That's the name of my business, after all.' Mabel scowled at him. 'Look, William, what's got into you? Are you trying to pick a fight?'

'No, of course not,' retorted William. 'It's just that I saw him coming out of your gate and wondered what he was doing.'

'Well, now you know,' Mabel replied and getting to her feet she continued, 'Are you going to play with Dada, or not? He's waiting for you.'

William gave her a sheepish look. 'Don't be cross, Mabel. I just worry about you when Iain McFarlane's about, that's all.'

'Well, you shouldn't,' answered Mabel. 'This was purely business and I'll do business with anyone who wants a job done and is prepared to pay for it.'

Chapter Fifteen

The morning of Saturday 5th September dawned bright and clear. Lucinda, waking early, lay in bed and listened to the dawn chorus greeting the new day… her wedding day. Today she would marry her beloved David. She could hardly believe the day had come at last. There had been so much reorganisation to advance the date, but now lying here she could see her wedding dress hanging on the wardrobe door, waiting for her, and she knew a shiver of anticipation.

This is the last morning I shall wake up as a girl, she thought. Tomorrow when I open my eyes, David will be beside me in that big bed in Crayne House and I shall be a married lady. I'll know then what actually happens between husband and wife.

She had asked her mother, but Lady McFarlane's answer was vague. All she would say was, 'You and David will share a bed, as man and wife, and you must allow him to lead you to further intimacy from there.'

It had been clear from her mother's tone of voice that this was all the information she was going to get, but Lucinda couldn't help wondering how different she might feel tomorrow.

The morning started quietly, her breakfast tray brought up to her and on it a gift, beautifully wrapped in gold silk.

'Where did this come from?' she asked Lizzie.

'Delivered by hand this morning, Miss Lucinda,' answered Lizzie. 'To be placed on your tray.'

Lucy picked it up and untied its gold silk bow to reveal a maroon leather jewellery case. Inside she found a necklace of beautifully matched pearls with a diamond clasp on a bed of white silk and a handwritten card with the message:

For my darling on her wedding day.

She lifted the necklace from the case and held it up to the light. Her wedding present from David.

When her mother came into her bedroom and found Lucinda had eaten almost nothing, she scolded her. 'Come along, Lucinda. You must eat something or you might faint in church.' Under her stern eye, Lucinda ate some toast and drank some tea before she got up and began to prepare for the day.

Clara had been relegated to under maid on this special day and it was Denby who dressed Lucinda's hair and brushed her nose with a dusting of powder. Clara had been allowed to ease on her silk stockings and then, all of a sudden it seemed, she was stepping into her ivory dress and Denby was doing up the numerous tiny pearl buttons that ran from below her waist to her shoulders. Her veil, attached to a spray of orange blossom on top of her auburn hair, floated behind her almost to the floor, and round her neck was David's pearl necklace.

Her mother came to her room as Lucinda finally stood ready in front of her mirror.

'You look beautiful, my dear,' she said. 'I only wish more people could be here with you on this special day.'

'I don't need them, Mama,' replied Lucinda. 'Just family and friends... and David.' She reached up and kissed her mother on the cheek. 'Shall we go down?'

Together they descended the stairs to where her father and her maid of honour, David's cousin, Maria Helford, were waiting for them.

Sir Keir greeted her with outstretched hands. 'Lucy, oh my Lucy,' he said. 'Our beautiful daughter!' Then turning to his wife, he said, 'Now then my dear, Croxton's outside waiting to take you and Maria to the church, and then he'll come straight back for us.'

While Croxton was driving Lady McFarlane to the church, Felstead appeared with two glasses of champagne on a tray.

Taking one of them and handing the other to Lucinda, Sir Keir said, 'I thought you and I together should salute the day.' He raised his glass. 'I wish you every happiness, my darling girl,' he said. 'If you're as happy in your marriage as I am in mine, all will be well.' They each took a sip and then Sir Keir said, with a burst of emotion, 'Be happy, Lucy. David is a lucky man.'

When Lucinda and her father finally got into the white-ribbon-bedecked car to be driven the half a mile or so to the church, they found that much of the village wanted a glimpse of the bride. Lucinda had spent almost every summer at Haverford Court and the main street was lined with people who had known her from childhood and wanted to wish her well.

When the car drew up at the church, Lady McFarlane and Maria were waiting in the porch to settle Lucinda's train and spread her veil. Beside them was Iain, the chief usher, and the rector, waiting to welcome the bride.

Lady Melcome and her cousin, the dowager countess of Staveley, were already in their pew when Iain escorted his mother into the church. The ladies acknowledged each other across the aisle and Lady McFarlane took her place on the opposite side of the church.

David was waiting at the altar steps with his best man, a brother officer, Captain Alexander Leighton, both resplendent in dress uniform.

'Don't look so nervous!' Alex admonished David, as yet again he glanced anxiously towards the back of the church. 'The bride is always late!'

'I'm not,' maintained David. But in truth he was. Had they actually got to this day when Lucinda would be his?

When Iain returned to the porch where Lucy and her father

were waiting to make their entrance, he took Lucinda's hand and murmured, 'You look truly beautiful, little sis. David's a lucky man!'

The rector, having greeted them at the door, now returned to the altar steps, the sign for the organist to play the arrival and the congregation fell silent.

Sir Keir, who had never seen his daughter look more beautiful, took her arm and, gently squeezing her hand, whispered, 'Ready?'

'Ready!' replied Lucinda and together they stepped into the church. For a moment they paused at the top of the aisle and David, turning, had first sight of his bride. His beloved, beautiful Lucy. He felt such an explosion of love for her as she came towards him that he was nearly unmanned. Never, ever had he experienced the happiness he felt now. Could never even have imagined it.

When they reached the altar steps and Maria had drawn back Lucinda's veil, Sir Keir placed his daughter's hand on David's arm and stepped aside. As David took her hand and Lucinda turned to face him, she saw that his deep blue eyes were bright with a joy that reflected her own.

An hour later, Sir David, with the new Lady Melcome on his arm, emerged from the church and entered the waiting car to be driven to Haverford Court.

For Lucy, the afternoon passed in a haze, all the guests wanting to congratulate the bride and groom. The wedding breakfast, overseen by the housekeeper, Mrs Scott, was a six-course banquet for the sixty guests, prepared by Mrs Bellman, served by Lizzie and William, yet Lucinda ate little. Seated at the head of the table next to David, she was conscious of his every move, and when they stood together to cut the wedding cake, each with a hand on the knife, she could feel the warmth of his skin against her own and her heart beat a little faster.

At last she was able to leave the reception and retire to her room to change. Clara, who was to accompany Lucinda as her personal maid, had already been despatched to Crayne House with her mistress's trunks, so it was Denby who came to undo the pearl buttons and help Lucinda divest herself of her wedding dress. Her travelling dress was of pale green silk worn with a neat jacket of a darker green, the colour chosen to complement her eyes. With it came kid gloves and matching hat. As she sat at the dressing table, Denby brushed out and rearranged her hair, sweeping its soft auburn curls into a smart chignon as befitted a married lady and placed her hat with its jaunty feather at a becoming angle to frame her face. Once Denby was satisfied, Lady McFarlane came up to see her before she made her appearance downstairs.

'You look beautiful, my dearest,' she said, reaching up to touch Lucinda's cheek. 'Your father and I are so proud of you.'

'Thank you, Mama,' murmured Lucinda. 'For everything.'

Croxton had brought the car to the front door, and the guests poured out onto the gravel sweep of the drive to wave the couple off on their honeymoon.

It had not been the society wedding Lucinda's parents had anticipated, but it had been a joyful day and would be remembered by everyone for its simplicity and elegance.

When David and Lucy finally reached Crayne House they found all the servants lined up in the hall to greet them.

Croft, as the most senior, spoke for them all. 'Welcome to your new home, my lady. We look forward to serving you in any way we can.'

Lucinda smiled at the assembled group. 'Thank you,' she said. 'I'm looking forward to getting to know you all.'

David stepped forward. 'Thank you for your welcome. It's been a long day, Mrs Croft. Perhaps you will take her ladyship up to her bedchamber and then bring some tea to the drawing room.' Turning to Lucinda, he continued, 'I'm sure you will want to remove your hat and make yourself comfortable, my dear. I shall do the same and then I'll be in the drawing room when you're ready to come down.'

'If you'll come this way, my lady,' said the housekeeper. 'Your maid is already up there and will have unpacked for you by now.'

Clara was waiting for her and Lucinda knew a moment's relief to see a familiar face.

'I've brought some hot water up for you, Miss Lucinda,' Clara said and then broke off awkwardly and stammered, '... sorry. My lady, I should say.'

'Don't worry, Clara,' smiled Lucinda. 'We'll both have to get used to it.'

A quarter of an hour later, she made her way back downstairs. Standing in the hall outside the drawing room door, Lucy felt suddenly shy. She wasn't Lucinda McFarlane anymore, she was somebody else, someone she didn't yet know, but would be always, from now on. As she waited, summoning her courage to walk into the drawing room and her new life, Croft came through from the kitchen, carrying a tea tray.

'Sir David ordered some fresh tea, my lady,' he said. 'He thought you'd be in need of refreshment when you came down.'

Taking a deep breath Lucinda said, 'Thank you, Croft. He was quite right.'

The butler opened the door and stood aside to let her precede him.

David was sitting in an armchair in the bay window, enjoying the last rays of the evening sun, a glass of whisky at his elbow.

At the sight of Lucy, his face creased into a smile of pleasure and getting to his feet he said, 'Just leave the tray on the table, Croft. We'll help ourselves.'

When Croft had withdrawn, David reached for Lucinda and drew her close.

'Are you happy, my darling?' he murmured into her hair. For a moment she felt stiff in his arms and then, as he continued to hold her, she relaxed against him. There was no need to be anxious. This was David after all. He had held her in his arms before, kissed her more than once on the mouth, but somehow, now, it was different.

Feeling the change in her, David held her away from him and said, 'I don't know about you, but I'm starving. Are you hungry? I don't think you ate much of that amazing banquet earlier. I certainly didn't, so I've asked Mrs Croft to lay out some bread and cheese and cold meats in the dining room. I thought we might take a turn in the garden first and then come in for a light supper. How does that sound?'

'It sounds lovely,' Lucy replied. And it did.

As the sun slipped below the horizon, leaving the September sky a blushing red streaked with shafts of orange, the evening took on an autumnal chill which brought them back into the house, where they found Croft had lit fires in the dining room and the drawing room. They ate the food Mrs Croft had set out in the dining room and David poured them each a glass of wine. Even so, Lucinda could not relax. It was nearly time to go to bed and she was becoming increasingly nervous. Suppose she got whatever it was she was supposed to do wrong? Suppose David was disappointed in her?

As dusk deepened into darkness, David said, 'Why don't you go up to bed now, Lucy? And I will come and say goodnight to you in a little while.'

Lucy managed a smile and said, 'Yes, I will. I am tired. It's been such a wonderful day.'

'I'll ring for Mrs Croft,' David said. 'She'll light your way up.'

Mrs Croft came immediately and, leading Lucinda out into the hall, lit one of the small oil lamps which stood on a table, ready to light the way upstairs.

Clara was waiting for Lucy in the dressing room which opened off the main bedroom. A fire had been lit in both rooms against the autumn night air, and a large lamp shed mellow light across the room. Lucy's wedding-night bedroom was beautifully warm and comfortable, and she found she was indeed tired after her long and exciting day. With Clara to help her, she was quickly undressed and made ready for bed. Attired in one of her new lace nightdresses, with her hair brushed out and her teeth cleaned, she slipped between the warmed sheets of the bed and pulled the bedclothes up to her chin. The fire still glowed in the fireplace, giving out a steady warmth. Clara lit two candles, which she placed on the mantelpiece before extinguishing the lamp and leaving the room.

Outside, she paused on the landing. Should she have warned Miss Lucinda what was going to happen when Sir David came and joined her? It seemed to Clara that her mistress was singularly unaware of what would occur in the marital bed. Clara, as the eldest of five children, four of which were daughters, had learned several years ago how babies were conceived. Living in a small cottage, she had heard many a coupling in her parents' bedroom.

Strange that the gentry don't teach their daughters the facts of life, she thought now, rather than leaving them to discover for themselves on their wedding night. And who could tell what way a man might take his pleasure? Sir David didn't look the violent type, but you never knew, did you? Should she have warned her ladyship? Should she do so even now? she wondered, but then, hearing the master's footsteps on the stairs, realised that it was too late, and hurried up the servants' staircase to her little room in the attic.

David had allowed nearly half an hour before he climbed the stairs and went into his dressing room on the other side of the bedroom. Fenton was not here at Crayne, he was in London preparing for their departure the following weekend, but Croft had left a lamp burning and filled the bowl and ewer with hot water. He undressed quickly and pulled on his dressing gown to cover his nakedness. Five minutes later he went to the adjoining door and tapped, before entering the room. The candles on the mantelpiece gave soft warm light, making shadows dance with the draught from the door. Silently he crossed the room and for a moment stood by the bed looking down at his wife, who lay still under the bedclothes, her glorious auburn hair fanned out on her pillow, her eyes shut… already asleep?

'Lucy?' He spoke gently. 'Lucy, my darling girl, are you awake?'

Lucy had wondered if she should pretend to be asleep when he came to her, but realised that would only put everything off, so she answered softly, 'Yes, David. Here I am.'

Her words, few as they were, sounded like an invitation… An offering. David cast off his dressing gown and, tossing it aside, slipped naked into the bed beside her.

'Don't be afraid, my love,' he murmured as he reached for her. 'It's only me and I love you more than life itself.'

While she had been lying alone, waiting for him to come to her, Lucy had made a decision. Drawing a deep breath she whispered, 'David, I don't know what I'm supposed to do.'

David smiled in the darkness. 'Just lie beside me,' he replied. 'Let me hold you close so your body's next to mine and I will teach you. I will show you what each of us can do to give and receive pleasure, and then I promise, you will discover what to do.'

When she made no reply, he said, 'Lucy, do you love me?'

'Oh David, you know I do!'

'And you know I love you?'

'Yes.' She sounded breathless.

'Then just relax, my love, and let me show you just how much.'

When Lucy awoke in the morning, she was still cradled in David's arms, his body moulded around hers. For a moment she lay completely still, remembering the gentleness with which he had soothed her fears, slipping his hands beneath the lace of her nightdress, caressing her skin with the lightest of touches, his fingers tracing her breasts and trailing across her quivering stomach until she moaned with pleasure, before he had claimed her for his own.

Now in the early light of morning she thought about what they had done, twice, a second time more slowly, and she sighed.

It had seemed an extraordinary thing to be doing at first, but even as she thought about the new sensations she had experienced, she felt David's lips on her neck once again and she gave an anticipatory shiver.

Chapter Sixteen

As the sun set on Lucinda's wedding day and the Haverford Court household retired for the night, Keir joined his wife in their bedroom. Wearing a silk dressing gown over his pyjamas, and with a glass of whisky in his hand, he paused in the doorway. He saw, as he had hoped, that Isabella was also ready for bed, sitting at her dressing table in a pale peach peignoir, brushing out her hair.

'On your own, Isabella?' queried Keir. 'Can I come in?'

'Yes, of course,' Isabella replied. 'I told Denby to take the rest of the evening off. It's been such a long day, I thought she was entitled to a free evening.'

'Certainly she is,' agreed Keir. 'I sent Blundell off, too.'

He crossed to the fireplace where a fire had been kindled against the autumnal chill of the September evening. Adding a log, he poked it into life, making the flames leap and shadows dance upon the walls.

For a moment Isabella put down the brush and looked at herself in the mirror. Staring back at her was the mother of a married daughter, a woman past the first flush of youth and with a sigh she said, 'She did look beautiful, didn't she?'

Sir Keir came up behind her and, resting his hand on her shoulder, regarded her reflection. 'So do you, Isabella,' he said, kissing the top of her head. 'She takes after her mother.'

He took a sip of his whisky, savouring its peaty flavour before placing the tumbler on her dressing table.

'Haven't you had enough alcohol, Keir?' Isabella scolded. 'You've been drinking all day.'

'Not a proper drink,' he replied defensively, 'this is to relax me after launching our beloved daughter into the arms of another man.'

'It won't stop her being our daughter,' pointed out Isabella.

'No of course it won't,' Keir agreed. 'But we have to accept that David will always come first. She doesn't really need us anymore.'

Leaning forward he reached for her hairbrush and, standing behind her, began to brush her hair. It was a ritual they both enjoyed and Isabella leaned in against him, allowing the steady sweep of the hairbrush to soothe her. Finally he set the brush aside, and put his arms round her from behind and, nuzzling her ear, murmured, 'Come to bed, my darling, and I'll tell you a secret.'

'A secret? What secret? Tell me now.'

'No, not yet,' teased Keir, and taking her hand he pulled her to her feet and led her to the bed. With great gentleness he removed her nightclothes, stroking the skin of her breasts as he did so, making her nipples harden and her heart beat faster. Isabella, languid now, lay back on the bed, watching him divest himself of his night clothes. Her husband, Keir. They had been married almost twenty-five years, and yet the sight of his naked body, tall and strong despite his fiftieth birthday on the horizon, still had the power to stir her own body in instant response.

He switched off the light, leaving the room lit only by the glowing embers of the fire, and slid into bed beside her. As his arms slipped round her, Isabella shuddered with desire, and they came together in a mutual passion that allowed no other thought.

Sometime later, lying in each other's arms in blissful fulfilment, Isabella murmured, 'What secret?'

Keir smiled in the darkness. 'It's a secret just for you and me,' he said.

'So, tell me.'

'If I do, you must absolutely promise not to tell anyone else, not until I say you may.'

'I promise,' cried Isabella. 'Oh, don't be so irritating, Keir!'

'Is it irritating when I do this?' he asked, trailing his fingers between her breasts. 'Or this?' He bent his head and took her right nipple in his mouth, making her gasp, before turning his attention to her left.

'Yes, very,' she muttered, breathing hard as his hand slipped between her legs.

'Would it be any less irritating if I were a noble baron, do you think?'

'Hmm,' she sighed, before taking in what he'd said. 'What!' she squeaked, jerking free to look into his face. 'What did you say?'

'Baron McFarlane of Haverford. Elevated to the House of Lords. Peer of the realm. Is he irritating do you think?'

Isabella gave a gurgle of laughter and said, 'Him? He's the most irritating man in the world, and I wouldn't exchange him for any other!'

Chapter Seventeen

Nurse Doreen Finch stepped down from the carriage onto the platform. There were few people leaving the train at Ashton St Anne that morning and as the guard blew his whistle and the train steamed out of the station, the platform had quickly emptied. The man who had been collecting tickets at the exit walked through to the platform and seeing Doreen, scowled.

'What you doin' here?' he demanded.

'Come to see Mavis of course,' replied Doreen. 'Why else would I be here, eh?'

Her daughter, Mavis, was married to Sidney Hughes, the station master of Ashton St Anne, a small station on a branch line off the main line from London to Southend-on-Sea. He was a hectoring, officious little man, with a pointed nose, wary, mistrustful eyes and prominent teeth. A face like a ferret, Doreen always thought privately; vicious and unpredictable. They did not get on, and though she made an effort for Mavis's sake, Sidney never did and was often gratuitously offensive. However, apart from the one porter who dealt with the few items of luggage that arrived, he was the only employee of the Great Eastern Railway on the Ashton St Anne branch line and thus it was he who had been granted the small railway cottage that went with the job.

'Just what I'm wonderin',' Sidney growled.

'Well, now you know, p'raps you'll get out of my way.'

For a moment Doreen thought that her son-in-law wasn't going to let her pass.

'Ticket?'

Without a word Doreen produced her ticket and, with a scowl, he stood aside.

Once outside the station, Doreen crossed the road to the cottage, but even as she knocked on the front door, she could feel Sidney's eyes boring into the back of her head.

'Mum!' exclaimed Mavis when she opened the door. 'What you doing here? I didn't know you was coming!'

'Nor did I Mavis,' replied her mother, 'but something's come up that I need to talk to you about.'

'What's that, then?'

'P'raps we could go inside?' suggested Doreen. 'So's I can tell you properly?'

Reluctantly Mavis stood aside, and as Doreen went into the house Mavis glanced over her mother's shoulder to see Sidney glowering at her from across the road, and sighed. Sidney and her mother had never got on, and now Mum, turning up uninvited and unannounced on the doorstep, almost certainly meant trouble.

'Sid'll be in for his tea just now,' Mavis said, as she lit the gas ring under the kettle, adding, 'you want tea, Mum?'

'Yes, please. I had to leave early this morning to catch the train and I'm parched.'

Without waiting to be asked, Doreen pulled out a chair at the table and sat down. 'Good to get the weight off my feet,' she said as she hooked her capacious bag onto the back of the chair. 'How you been Mavis? All right, are you? Not still being sick? Usually wears off after three months.'

Mavis, expecting her first baby, had been plagued with morning sickness, and even now, Doreen thought, she looked very washed out.

'A bit better, but I'm very tired.'

At that moment the front door opened and Sidney came into the kitchen. He was not a big man, but somehow he managed to fill the room.

'Well, Mother-in-law,' he said taking the only other chair and leaving Mavis standing at the sink. 'To what do we owe this pleasure? Come here for a free meal, have you?'

'Sid, don't,' protested Mavis weakly. 'Mum's come to see how I'm getting on with the baby and that.'

'Has she? Well now she's here, she can give a hand with all them chores you say are too much for you.'

At his words, Doreen saw Mavis's eyes flick across to the corner where a basket of ironing awaited her.

'Actually,' said Doreen evenly, determined not to rise to his rudeness. 'I've come to ask for some advice. A letter's come, and I don't know what to do about it.'

'A letter? Who from? Give it here?'

Doreen took the letter from her bag, meaning to give it to Mavis, but Sid reached over and snatched it from her hand. There were two sheets, and he scanned them both, before dropping them onto the table and saying, 'It's obvious, isn't it? You got to move out of your house.'

'What!' exclaimed Mavis. She picked up the letter and read it through. 'It's from some law firm?' she said glancing at her mother in surprise before looking at the letter again. 'Some solicitors. Do you know them, this Ferris, Beacon and Ferris Solicitors and Commissioners of Oaths?'

'No, 'course I don't,' answered her mother. 'But I don't know what to do about it? I mean, can they just kick me out like that after all the years I've lived there?'

Sid gave a shrug. 'Sounds like it,' and taking the letter back he read it aloud.

It was brief, very much to the point and dated the previous day, Friday 4th September 1914.

Dear Madam

The attached document is a formal notice to quit the property known as number 4 Noah's Path within 7 days from receipt of this

letter. As a tenant paying weekly rent,
please accept this formal notice to vacate
the said property before the stated date.
Provided said rent is paid up to date, and
as a gesture of goodwill, the landlord will
remit the final week's rent of 15 shillings
and 6 pence.

Signed:

It was signed with an unreadable scribble, beneath which was typed:

PP Martin Finlay.

'And who's he when he's at home?' demanded Doreen Finch fiercely.

'His name's at the top,' said Mavis. 'He's one of the partners.'

'Well,' said Sid cheerfully, 'sounds like you'll just have to go.'

'But where to?' said Doreen shakily. 'I've nowhere to go?'

'Well, we can't have you,' stated Sid. 'No room for you here. Not with the baby coming.'

'Perhaps we could, just for a little while,' ventured Mavis. 'Baby isn't due for at least another five months. Mum could stay for a little while, just until she's found somewhere else.'

'No, she couldn't,' Sid said firmly. 'We got to get the room ready. I'm going to do it up nice for the baby, so she can't stay here.'

It was the first time Mavis had heard that Sid was going to do up the tiny second bedroom for their child. She had been desperately hoping they might make that room into a nursery, but it had not been discussed between them yet. You had to pick your time for things like that with Sid, so for a moment too long she didn't say anything, giving Sid time to find other objections.

'An' if you was living here, how would go on with your job?'

he asked with a smirk. 'We ain't in a position to keep you, you know, another mouth to feed with nothing extra coming in. You wouldn't be able to pay your way.'

'I'll have to try and get a job round here,' Doreen said, at last showing her hand; making it clear she'd come looking for a roof over her head.

'Thought it all out, haven't you?' he said. 'Well, jobs don't grow on trees round here you know.'

'Mum, you know we'd love to help out,' said Mavis, though not quite able to meet her mother's eyes. 'But really it could only be for a few days. You'd be far better finding somewhere in London, permanent-like. It might be nice to have a change.'

Have a change! Doreen almost screamed at her. I don't want no change!

The previous night Doreen had lain in bed, tossing and turning, as she tried to decide what to do. What could she do? It would be nigh on impossible to find somewhere else she could afford and still be able to get to the Oakleys' every morning. They were her only source of income. As her thoughts churned in her tired brain, she kept coming back to the same thing: she would have to go and see Mavis and explain that she needed somewhere to stay for a few days... or weeks... or, added the tiny voice in her head which she tried to ignore... months! Resolutely she pushed that thought away. She would go to Ashton and see Mavis, preferably without Sid being there too. She would ask about the baby, just a friendly visit, until she had shown Mavis the letter.

Mavis's comment now hung between them in the air. Perhaps she could just stay tonight, she thought, remembering the nightdress and toothbrush she had shoved into her handbag. Perhaps over supper she would be able to talk them round.

Sidney had other ideas. 'Well, that's settled then,' he said, downing the last of his tea. 'If you're quick, Ma-in-law, you'll be able to take the train back to town, it'll be through in ten minutes.' He got to his feet and saying to Mavis, 'I got to meet the train,' he left the house with a slam of the front door.

For a moment mother and daughter looked at each other and then Doreen said, 'I don't know how you came to marry that man, Mavis.'

'He ain't always like that, Mum,' Mavis protested.

'Yeah, he is,' asserted Doreen, 'an' you know it.' She got to her feet and hitched her bag onto her shoulder. 'Better go, or I'll miss my train.' When Mavis reached out to give her a hug, Doreen returned it briefly. 'I'll let you know where I go,' she said, 'but don't you tell him where, then if you need to come to me, he won't know where to find you.'

Doreen left the house as the train appeared round the curve of the track, its brakes squealing as the wheels gripped the rails. Sidney was standing in the ticket office, expecting her to need a ticket, but she walked past him without a glance and boarded the train. She'd bought a return, knowing she would need to go back to Noah's Path to pack up her things and to warn the Oakleys that she would have to leave them.

As the train steamed back towards Liverpool Street station, Doreen sat staring, unseeing, out of the window. She knew that she would never go back to Ashton to see Mavis while she was still married to Sidney; she had never felt so alone in all her life.

Chapter Eighteen

As Doreen turned into Noah's Path, her next-door neighbour was leaving his house, and seeing her coming up the street, he hailed her.

'Hey, Dor, you had one of them letters? From a posh solicitor?'

Doreen stopped outside her door. 'Giving me notice to get out?'

'Yeah, that's the one. A week to be out!'

'Yes,' she replied. 'It come yesterday.'

'Thought you might. Reckon we've all had one, everyone living in Noah's Path.'

'Everyone?' echoed Doreen. 'But why?'

'Sounds like the whole street is going to be knocked down. I was talking to Cecil Baker, you know, the cobbler? An' he says they're going to build a new road bridge and have got to clear all the houses round here to make space for it.'

'Knock them all down!' Doreen exclaimed. So it wasn't just her. They were all going to lose their homes. 'Does the council know?'

'Reckon the council's behind it.'

'An' they're letting us be turned out of our homes?' Doreen was outraged.

'That's what he says. He and Bert Smith have already had to give up their shops, haven't they?'

'What we going to do about it?' she asked.

'Not much we can do about it,' he replied. 'If we ain't out by the time they come for the rent on Friday, I reckon the bailiffs'll put us out on the street.'

When Doreen was back in her own home, she looked round at what it contained, all her worldly goods, and very few they were. She could pack her belongings into two suitcases, including her two precious photos, one of her and Edwin on their wedding day and the other of the two of them with baby Mavis in his arms. The one or two sticks of furniture she owned were hardly worth taking. Her bed, her rocking chair with its embroidered cushions and the whatnot which stood in the corner of the room: they might all have to be left behind.

Tomorrow, she thought as she boiled the kettle and made herself some tea, tomorrow I'll go round all the corner shops and look at the cards in their windows.

Even though tomorrow was Sunday, corner shops might be open, selling the Sunday papers and all she wanted was the offer of accommodation that she could afford. She knew it was a forlorn hope, but you never knew, someone might be offering a room somewhere, and she couldn't afford to be fussy.

That's it, she decided, I got to find something, even if it has to be temporary. Once I've got somewhere, I can take my time finding something better.

Next morning she woke and for a split second she didn't remember the notice to quit, but then it all came rushing back, her need to move, the frosty reception from Sid and Mavis, the fact that she would probably have to give up her job with the Oakleys, which in turn meant that she had no income to support herself. All these things ambushed her, weighing her down so that she didn't know where to turn. 'It's not fair!' she shouted at the kitchen. 'It's not fair!'

Fighting tears, she got up and made herself a cup of tea and a piece of toast.

If I'm going hunting for somewhere to live, she thought with a sigh, I must have some food inside me.

At weekends Alice and Mabel usually managed Andrew's care between them, and as Doreen was not expected in Barnbury Street she spent the day trailing round her local area looking for accommodation, but it was a fruitless search and she was one day nearer to being evicted. Tomorrow, she thought, she would have to tell the Oakleys what had happened and warn them they would almost certainly have to find Andrew another nurse. Alice should be able to manage on her own for a short while, but in the long run they would have to find someone else. Alice was one of the breadwinners and she would find it very tiring to manage Andrew's care as well.

When Doreen arrived on Monday morning, Andrew could see immediately that something was wrong. She never entered his room without a smile on her face, but on this particular morning the smile was strained, lacking all spontaneity.

'Are you all right, Mrs Finch?' he asked a little diffidently. 'You look a bit glum.'

'Never better,' responded Doreen, 'but I need to have a chat with you and Mrs Oakley before I go home. Now then, let's get you washed and dressed. It's a beautiful day outside and you'll be able to go down into the garden later, when it's a bit warmer.'

Andrew was not convinced that Mrs Finch was 'never better', but he said nothing more and allowed her to help him get ready for the day.

When he was dressed, she pushed him into the kitchen, where Alice was making soup with the remains of the vegetables from the previous night's supper.

'Will you make us some tea, Alice?' Andrew said. 'Mrs Finch would like a word with us, and if Mabel is working downstairs, it would be a good idea to call her up here too.'

'She isn't,' replied Alice as she set the kettle to boil. 'She went out on a delivery run, but I don't suppose she'll be very long.'

The three of them shared the pot of tea, but when there was still no sign of Mabel, Doreen took the plunge and said, 'I'm afraid I've had some difficult news.'

'Oh, Mrs Finch,' cried Alice. 'What's happened?'

'This come on Friday.' Doreen took out the letter and the official notice to quit and passed them across to Andrew. He read them quickly and passed them over to Alice. 'You worked in a solicitor's office, didn't you, Mr Oakley?' asked Doreen. 'What I want to know is, can they do this to me? Can this solicitor simply throw me out into the street, with a week's notice?'

'Well, it's not the solicitor who's doing it,' Andrew said. 'He's simply acting as agent for the landlord. Who's your landlord?'

'I don't know,' sighed Doreen. 'Me and Edwin, we've lived in that cottage for nigh on thirty years, and since he passed away it's just been me. I don't know who the landlord is. I just pay my rent to the collector what comes every Friday evening. I never asked who he worked for.'

'Remind me again exactly where you live.'

Doreen explained where Noah's Path was. 'They're old cottages, ten of them, five on each side of the street. It's not even a street really, you can just about get a cart along it, but not some of them big waggons that come into London from the country. My neighbour says he's heard they're going to build a new road bridge across the railway and need the space.'

'Well, that is something we can find out,' Andrew said. 'If they're demolishing all the houses.'

'Still, that's not the important thing for poor Mrs Finch,' said Alice. 'How can they turn her out, with just seven days' notice?'

'You say you pay your rent once a week? Every Friday?'

Doreen nodded.

'Then that's probably why they don't have to give you more notice,' Andrew explained. 'I'm afraid it's the landlords that hold all the cards, Mrs Finch. They're the ones who actually own the property. The man who collects the rent may not even know who he's collecting it for.'

'Well, what I'm trying to explain,' Doreen said, 'is that I may have to move further away to find a place I can afford, up Shoreditch or somewhere, which means I won't be able to carry on helping you, Mr Oakley. At present, it's very convenient for both of us, me being just a short bus ride away. But maybe you can find someone else living close.'

'But don't I remember you've got a married daughter? asked Alice. 'Where does she live? Couldn't you stay with her for a bit, while you find something to suit you? We can manage without you for a little while and we'd keep your job open, rather than lose you.'

'That's very kind, Mrs Oakley,' Doreen fought the tears that threatened to overcome her and continued, 'Mavis, yes. She and her husband live at Ashton St Anne near Southend. I did think I might go and live with her for a while, but Essex?' Doreen pulled a face. 'I wouldn't want to live there, much too far away. Anyhow, she's expecting, and they really don't have room for me and the new baby.'

Resolutely she got to her feet and picked up her bag. 'I'd better be going,' she said. 'I'm sure I'll find somewhere before long and in the meantime, I'll come as long as I can. Still, if you do find someone else, I shall quite understand.' She swallowed hard at the lump in her throat and managed, 'I'll come tomorrow,' and hurried from the house.

It was twenty minutes later that Mabel came in and found her parents still sitting at the kitchen table. Dumping her now-empty satchel onto the floor, she flopped down on a chair and asked, 'Any tea left in that pot?'

'Needs topping up,' said her mother, reaching for the kettle.

'You're both looking very serious,' Mabel said. 'What's up?'

Andrew explained the situation in which Mrs Finch found herself.

'Well,' said Mabel after she'd taken a mouthful of tea. 'We can sort that out easily enough, can't we? She can come and live here.'

'Here?' echoed her mother. 'With us?'

'Well,' Mabel said, 'why not? Dada needs her. To be honest, we all need her. We don't use the top floor, do we? There's two rooms up there she could have.'

'Hold on a minute,' said Alice. 'Let's think this through. For a start, there's no bathroom or kitchen up there.'

'No, Mam, I know, but for the time being, so that Mrs Finch isn't out on the street, she could have those rooms, share the bathroom and eat with us... don't you think?'

'I don't know what I think,' retorted Alice. 'But I don't like being bounced into things.'

'I'm not bouncing you,' Mabel said, though in fact she knew she was. She could understand her mother's reservations, but she also knew that her father would be lost without Mrs Finch. It would take ages for him to get used to someone else and Mabel was prepared to do anything which enabled Mrs Finch to continue to care for him.

'What do you think, Dada?' asked Mabel. She knew that her father blamed himself for the situation he was in. Seeing the difficulties his moment's inattention had caused the rest of the family, he seldom put his wishes forward, just accepted what was decided by everyone else.

'I think it makes life easier for your mother to have Mrs Finch come here every day.'

'Not every day, Andrew,' Alice pointed out. 'We manage very well without her at weekends, don't we, Mabel?'

'We do,' agreed Mabel. 'But there are times when another pair of hands would be a blessing.' She smiled across at Alice, knowing how tired she was at the end of a normal day. 'And she gives Dada a chance to get out into the garden, or to go to the park. She has been an absolute godsend.

'It would only be temporary,' Mabel went on, 'until she can find somewhere else not too far away.'

'It's typical of you, this sudden spontaneous and generous offer, Mabel,' said her father. 'But it must be given serious consideration before we actually offer it to Mrs Finch. There are definitely questions that need to be answered. Would you, for instance, charge her rent?'

'No,' replied Mabel, 'but neither would I pay her for looking after you, at least nothing like we are at the moment. Obviously she'll need some money for other things, but I'm sure we can come to an arrangement on that. The important thing is to put a roof over her head, so that she can go on helping you as usual, Dada.'

For a moment there was silence as the three of them considered the idea of Mrs Finch moving into the two rooms on the top floor.

'Why don't we see what she says to the idea?' Mabel suggested. 'We could make it clear from the start that it would only be a temporary measure, just until she found somewhere.'

Alice was the one who needed to be convinced. Did she really want to share her kitchen with somebody else, another woman who would have different ways of doing things? To have a stranger's toothbrush by the basin in the bathroom? Well, not a stranger really, but someone who wasn't family? Another woman in the house when the boys were at home? Stephen didn't live there permanently, but he still had his room there, and Eddie helped Andrew at bedtime.

'What will the boys say,' Alice wondered, 'about you inviting someone else to live with us on a permanent basis?'

'That's the whole point, Mam,' said Mabel patiently. 'It won't be permanent, just until she finds somewhere to live nearby. I expect the boys will be glad you've got extra help.'

'I don't need extra help, Mabel,' snapped Alice. 'I can manage perfectly well.'

'Of course you can, Mam, but only with Mrs Finch's help. Come on, tell me, what are the problems?' But as Alice did so, Mabel demolished them one at a time.

If they were all going to eat together it made sense for one of them to take responsibility for the cooking and they already knew Mrs Finch was a good cook. She could be asked to keep her toiletries upstairs and have a set time to use the bathroom in the mornings and the evenings.

'It's only temporary, Mam, just till Mrs Finch finds a place of her own... and think, she'd be here to help Dada go to bed in the evenings sometimes so you and Eddie wouldn't have to.'

Alice was still unconvinced, but when she saw the look of silent hope in Andrew's eyes, reluctantly she gave in.

'Well,' she said, 'as it'll only be until she finds somewhere, I suppose it'll be all right.'

'So, when she comes again tomorrow,' Mabel said, 'we'll tell her what we're suggesting and see what she thinks.'

Later, as she lay in bed, Mabel considered the offer they were going to make. She was all in favour and she knew her father was; she, too, had seen his look of hope, and knew how desperate he was not to have to get used to someone new dealing with his useless legs and wasted lower body. They had made the right decision, she was sure, and eventually, Mam, though still with misgivings, had agreed to the trial.

Chapter Nineteen

The following morning when Mrs Finch arrived, with a brave smile on her face, Andrew said, 'You're bright and early. When I'm ready, we want to have a chat with you over a cup of tea, if that's all right with you.'

Mrs Finch said of course it was, and decided they were going to say they had already found someone to take her place.

That was quick, she thought sadly, but fighting not to let her disappointment show.

Half an hour later, she wheeled Andrew through to the kitchen where Alice and Mabel were already sitting at the table, with a pot of tea and a plate of flapjack between them.

Mrs Finch looked at them apprehensively but Alice waved her to a chair and said, 'Tea?'

When they all had fresh tea in front of them, Andrew said, 'Mrs Finch, Mabel has had an idea that we hope might interest you. Mabel?'

'When we heard you were going to be turned out of your home,' Mabel said, 'we wondered if you might like to come and live here with us for a while? Just while you find somewhere else, somewhere close enough to still come and look after my father.'

A look of incredulity crossed the nurse's face, but Mabel went on, 'We have two rooms at the top of the house which we don't use at present except for storage. If you'd like to come and live there, you'd be more than welcome.'

'I'm afraid there is no kitchen up there,' Alice put in, 'nor bathroom, but obviously you can use ours downstairs.'

'We do hope you like the idea,' Andrew said, keen to add his voice to the invitation, 'but of course, if it doesn't appeal to you, please don't hesitate to say.'

For a moment they looked expectantly at Mrs Finch, who found herself completely lost for words.

'Perhaps you'd like to think it over,' suggested Alice, trying to hide the relief she felt that Mrs Finch had not jumped at the invitation.

'No,' she murmured. 'No, thank you, I don't need to think it over. You're kind, so very kind, to think of it, and if you're sure, I'd be eternally grateful.' She looked up and, catching Alice's eye, added, 'Just temporary, till I can find somewhere nearby. I don't want to impose...'

'It's not imposing,' Andrew assured her. 'We're pleased to be able to help.'

'Not only help you,' Mabel put in. 'But ourselves as well.'

'I must pay you rent...' Mrs Finch began.

'And we must pay for your care of Dada,' said Mabel. 'Don't worry, Mrs Finch, we'll sort it all out to suit everyone. In the meantime, we must arrange for your belongings to be brought here. The rooms aren't furnished, but I expect you've got some things of your own you'll want to bring.'

'Not much,' Mrs Finch admitted, thinking back to what she had considered keeping last night. 'It would hardly be a cartload.'

'That's all right,' said Mabel, 'and now, I think you and I should go and see my solicitor to find out whether this eviction is quite legal and not just a landlord trying to pull a fast one.'

'Oh no, Mabel. I can't afford a solicitor...'

'Don't worry,' Mabel said, 'he's my trustee and he's told me I can go and see him at any time. We only want a little advice, don't we? I'm sure he'll be happy to give us that.'

Alice made a fresh pot of tea and they sat together round the kitchen table to work out the details. By the time Mrs Finch left, Mabel had agreed to try and borrow Mr Holman's cart on Thursday afternoon, his early closing day, to transport her few possessions from Noah's Path to Barnbury Street.

'Mr Oakley, Mrs Oakley, I don't know how to thank you,' she said. 'You've literally saved me from being put out on the street.'

'We'll get Eddie to come round when he's finished work on Thursday,' Mabel said. 'He can help carry things; Stephen too. I'm sure Mr Solomon would let him come if he explained.'

'One more thing I'd like to say,' announced Andrew. All three of them looked at him in surprise.

'What's that?' asked Alice anxiously. What was Andrew going to suggest, now that it had all been agreed?

'If we're all going to be living under one roof,' he said, 'I think we should drop the Mr and Mrs Oakley. I should like you to call me Andrew, and I'm sure Alice feels the same.'

He glanced across at his wife and it was only with the slightest hesitation that Alice nodded and said, 'Of course, much more sensible.'

'Then you must all call me Doreen,' said Mrs Finch.

'Well, Doreen,' said Mabel, 'I suggest that when you've finished with Dada tomorrow morning, we go to see Mr Morrell and see what he has to say about your notice to leave. He'll know if they can carry out the threat.'

The next morning Doreen put on her Sunday best dress and her Sunday hat. She wanted to look as if she were someone who called at a solicitor's office every day of the week. She and Mabel walked to the offices of Sheridan, Sheridan and Morrell in St John's Square, but as they paused outside beside the brass name plate Doreen stopped and caught Mabel by the hand.

'I can't,' she murmured. 'I can't go in there?'

'Of course you can,' replied Mabel in a rallying voice. 'Why ever not?'

'They don't deal with people like me.'

''Course they do,' Mabel encouraged her. 'You're like me and they deal with me. Or at least,' she corrected herself as she thought of Mr Sheridan, who resented the fact that due to Mr Clarke's will she was a client of his partner, Mr Morrell, 'they have to. Come on, Doreen, let's go in and discover the worst.'

She set off up the stairs to the solicitors' offices on the first floor, followed by a reluctant Doreen.

As they reached the landing Mr Sheridan's secretary, Miss Hermione Harper, emerged from her office and confronted them. She stared at the two women for a long moment before saying, 'Yes? Can I help you?'

Mabel, who had come across Miss Harper on a previous occasion, now answered briskly.

'Good morning, Miss Harper. Yes, indeed, we'd like to see Mr Morrell, please.'

Miss Harper, somewhat wrong-footed at being addressed by name by someone who could only be a schoolgirl and one whom she hadn't recognised, snapped, 'Certainly not…' adding, 'he's in a meeting and anyway he sees no one without an appointment.'

Mabel, undeterred by this rebuff, said, 'He has told me I may come to see him at any time if I need help with anything. If he's in a meeting now, we're happy to wait until he is no longer engaged.'

'There's nowhere for you to wait,' answered Miss Harper. 'You'll have to make an appointment and come back again another day.'

At that moment a door a little further along the narrow landing opened and a young man appeared, carrying a sheaf of papers. He paused when he saw the girl being confronted by Miss Harper, and asked, 'Is there anything I can do to help, Miss Harper?'

'No thank you, Mr Charles,' retorted the secretary. 'These persons are just leaving.'

'No, they aren't,' Mabel said. 'I have come to see Mr Morrell, my trustee. I admit I haven't an appointment, but I am more than happy to wait until he's free. I shan't take up much of his time.'

'Don't worry, miss,' said Mr Charles. 'I'm on my way to give him these papers, so I can tell him you're outside and hoping for a few minutes of his time.'

'Mr Morrell asked not to be disturbed this morning,'

maintained Miss Harper angrily, her face flushing a blotchy red. 'I am only following his instructions.'

'Did he?' replied the young man, 'Well, a quarter of an hour ago he asked me to look out these files for him, so I shall take them to him now.' Turning back to Mabel he asked, 'Who shall I tell him is waiting to see him?'

'Mabel,' answered Mabel. 'Mabel Oakley.'

Still clutching the document files in his arms, Mr Charles moved along the landing, pausing briefly as Miss Harper barred his way for a moment, before she stepped aside and allowed him to pass.

Two doors along, he knocked on a closed door and then entered, pulling the door to, behind him.

Miss Harper stayed firmly where she was and Mabel, too, remained unmoved. She had heard all about Miss Harper from her father.

'She's a bully,' he had said.

Well, thought Mabel, standing her ground, bullies are always cowards, you just have to stand up to them.

Horrified by the whole encounter, Doreen edged back to the top of the stairs, ready to flee back to the street.

Miss Harper said, 'You can wait downstairs in the square, but I can assure you, it'll be a long wait.'

'I have no intention of waiting outside in the street,' Mabel said. 'I am a client of this firm and I expect to be treated as one.'

Completely taken aback, Miss Harper shrugged and said, 'Then you'll have to wait here in the corridor, I have work to do.'

'I'm sure you have,' agreed Mabel smoothly. 'Please don't let us keep you from it.'

Before Miss Harper could reply, Mr Morrell's office door opened and Mr Charles came out, followed by the man himself.

'Mabel, my dear. What a lovely surprise. Come along in and bring your friend with you.' Turning next to Miss Harper he said, 'Thank you, Miss Harper, that'll be all for now.'

Mabel took Doreen's arm and said, 'Come on, Doreen, let me

introduce you to Mr Morrell.' As she passed Mr Charles, who was still standing in the corridor, she murmured 'Thank you, Mr Charles. I didn't think I was going to get past Miss Harper.'

Charles looked at her and smiled. What an attractive girl! And the way she stood up to the dreaded Hermione! He'd never seen anyone do that before. Even his father tended to walk on eggshells where she was concerned. Fancy old Morrell being trustee to a girl like that. Mabel Oakley. That was the name she'd given, but who was Mabel Oakley? His guv'nor would know; he'd ask him.

Once the door of Mr Morrell's office had shut behind his visitors, Charles went back to the office he shared with the other clerk, Arthur Bevis. Arthur was not much more than an office boy, a copy clerk, expected to keep paperwork in order and filed in the right place. He was pleasant and biddable, but Charles found him boring in the extreme. He himself had this summer just graduated as a Bachelor of Law from Oxford University and was now articled to Hugh Morrell, his father's partner, while he studied for his professional exams. Charles's father, John, was the senior partner just as his father had been before him, and Hugh Morrell was the last of his line which went back three generations. It was a well-known and prestigious firm, and Charles was delighted to be following the family tradition without competition from other branches of either family. So, who was this girl, Mabel Oakley, who claimed him as her trustee? A feisty girl and a looker, too. He'd have to find out a bit more about her.

In the room along the corridor the feisty girl was introducing her friend Doreen Finch to Hugh Morrell.

'The thing is, Mr Morrell,' Mabel explained, 'Doreen has received this letter and a notice to quit and we wondered if there was anything she can do about it.'

Hugh Morrell reached for his spectacles, took the letter and the notice to quit and read each through, twice.

'How long have you lived there, Mrs Finch?' he asked.

'Nigh on thirty years. Me and Edwin, my husband, we moved into it when we was married and we never moved out again. We got a rent book and as that got filled up, we got another one. Edwin worked for the council and I'd just trained as nurse and then I was working at the London Hospital in Whitechapel.'

'And you never discovered who the cottages in Noah's Path belonged to? Did your husband ever have any documents about the house? Things like who was responsible for the upkeep? The roof? The chimneys? Anything like that?'

Doreen looked dismayed. 'No, sir,' she said. 'I got our birth certificates and married lines, but nothing about the house. When our rent book was finished, they'd bring us another one with our name on it. Each time it had gone up a bit but then everything has, so we wasn't surprised.'

'What happened when your husband died?' asked Hugh setting the papers down on his desk. 'Wasn't anything said then?'

'No, I don't think so.' She thought for a minute. 'Of course I told old Jack Lunn, the rent collector, at the time, and the next week when he come round, he brought me a new rent book with just my name on it. He said they were happy for me to stay in the house because Edwin and me, we hadn't ever got into arrears, which was more than he could say for others round there. But he never said who "they" were, an' I didn't ask.'

'The problem is,' said Hugh, 'as you paid weekly, they don't have to give you more than a week's notice to leave. If you'd been paying once a month, they'd probably have given you a month to be out. But unless you have a written tenancy agreement, I doubt if they are obliged to do that.'

'And what happens if I can't move out in the time they say?' asked Doreen, with a quiver in her voice.

'Then I'm afraid they are probably within their rights to put you out on the street.'

'That's ridiculous!' cried Mabel.

'It's unfortunate,' Hugh agreed mildly, 'but there's no comeback I'm afraid.'

'Well, there should be!' stated Mabel.

Hugh smiled at her vehemence. 'You're probably right, but any landlord would fight against it, tooth and nail.'

'Well, luckily we're able to offer Mrs Finch a home with us for the time being,' Mabel said. 'Just until she finds somewhere else suitable.'

'That's a generous offer,' Hugh said. 'Your father, as your other trustee, approves, I assume?'

'Of course he does,' returned Mabel. 'It's for his benefit as well as Doreen's.'

'And do you want me to draw up terms of agreement?'

'No,' said Mabel. 'We've already agreed everything, haven't we, Doreen?'

'We have, sir,' Doreen said. 'The Oakleys couldn't have been more generous.'

'I see,' said Hugh. 'Well, I won't press you if you're all happy with what you've agreed on a temporary basis, but if it was to become permanent, it would be to the advantage of both parties to have something in writing.'

Once the two women had left the office, Hugh summoned Charles. 'Take a note, Charles, and get it written up yourself. I shall put it in the Oakley file in case of need in the future.'

'If you don't mind me asking, sir,' said Charles, 'who is Mabel Oakley?'

'I do mind you asking, Charles,' returned Hugh Morrell. 'It's no concern of yours. Now, take this down, and remember the usual terms of privacy attach to this note as to any other document of which you have sight. Every client of this firm is entitled to complete discretion. Understood?'

'Of course, sir,' replied Charles, thinking as he did so that there was more to Hugh Morrell than Charles's father, John Sheridan, gave him credit for. He was a man of complete integrity, a truly old-style lawyer.

By the end of the day the note had been dictated and written, and Charles had placed it in Mabel Oakley's file. The heading on the note gave her name and address, and Charles memorised it. Mabel Oakley of 27 Barnbury Street.

Chapter Twenty

David left the house in Sloane Square on Saturday 12th September soon after six in the morning. He had been up before five to prepare for his departure. Lucinda had sat on their bed watching as he dressed in his uniform and added a few last personal things to the portmanteau he would carry with him. Fenton had already travelled to Southampton with the horses, so David would be just one of many soldiers of all ranks catching the train that morning on the first leg of their journey to France to join the expeditionary force. Lucinda had suggested that she might go to Waterloo to see him off, but David had insisted their farewells should be made in the privacy of their own home.

'There'll be hundreds of soldiers catching that train, my love. Plenty of wives will be there and often children too; it tends to become very emotional. I'd rather say goodbye here, in the peace and quiet of our own place, where you and I belong.'

Lady Melcome had bidden David farewell the night before. Despite both her husband and her son being in the regular army, Lady Melcome had never really become used to difficult goodbyes and found them easier in private. Surely Lucinda, a bride of only seven days, would feel the same.

Somehow Lucinda had managed to hold herself together when the time came for David to leave. She'd been determined not to let him see her cry; she was a soldier's wife now, an officer's wife, and they did not cry when their menfolk left for the front.

'Remember, Lucy mine,' David murmured as he took her in

his arms for a final embrace, 'you are the love of my life. Every morning I shall wake to thoughts of you and every night shall see your face before I fall asleep.'

For a long moment, Lucy clung to him. Then she released him and stepped back to look up into his face and give him her simple farewell. 'I love you, David. Come home to me soon.'

With that he had given her one last kiss, then turned and without a backward glance walked out of the house, one more soldier on his way to fight for king and country.

At the sound of the front door closing, Lucinda sank down on the chair in their bedroom, a now lonely bedroom until he came back, and finally gave way to her tears. In the few days since their marriage, David had taught her the secrets of the marriage bed, and after the first night together, he had found her a willing pupil. Their pleasure in each other had been rekindled every night and not only at night for, as David had whispered into her ear as he led her up to their bedchamber on a damp afternoon, 'We don't have to wait until it's dark, you know!'

At last, her tears all shed, Lucinda lay down on their unmade bed and clutching his pillow in her arms, and breathing in his lingering scent, she fell into an exhausted sleep. When she finally awoke again, the sun was high in a bright September sky. While she'd been asleep, Clara had crept into the room and left a ewer full of hot water beside the bowl on the dresser, and though it was barely tepid now, Lucy got up, rinsed her cheeks and bathed her eyes. Opening her wardrobe, she looked through all her clothes. It must not seem as if, in her husband's absence, she had dressed to catch a man's eye as she had throughout the summer, but elegant and understated. After much thought she selected a comfortable day dress in pale sea-green silk that fell almost to her ankles. She didn't bother to call Clara; she wanted no chatter as she dressed herself, brushed her hair, and pinched her cheeks to raise some colour. With one last look in the mirror, she tucked an escaping tendril behind her ear and prepared to go downstairs to find her mother-in-law.

Lady Melcome was in the drawing room, and she smiled as Lucinda peeped tentatively round the half-open door.

'Come in, my dear,' she said, holding out her hand. 'I was about to ring for luncheon. Are you hungry? I am. Something light I thought for now, and then dinner this evening, if you have no other engagement.'

'That sounds like a splendid plan, Lady Melcome,' responded Lucinda. 'And I thought that tomorrow I should go to Chanynge Place to visit my parents.'

'Good idea,' replied her mother-in-law. 'They'll be so pleased to see you.'

That afternoon Lucinda sent Clara round to Chanynge Place to say Lady Melcome would be calling the next day and brought back the message that they would expect her for luncheon. The bright sky of the morning had faded to a dull pewter as the day had become overcast, with grey scudding clouds blowing in on a southerly wind.

Would David be on the ship now? Lucinda wondered. Would the persistent wind make the Channel crossing uncomfortable? Was David likely to be seasick? Lucy had never thought to ask.

The afternoon seemed to stretch for ever as the time crawled by. Not wanting company, Lucy had the fire lit in her private parlour, where she wasted no time in writing to David at the army post office address he had given her.

'I'll want to hear what you've been up to without me,' David had said on their last evening together, 'all the little daily things that are part of your life. I'll want to hear where you've been and who you've seen, and what you've had for dinner.'

'And will you write back to me?' asked Lucy.

'My darling girl! What an extraordinary thing to ask!' exclaimed David. 'Of course I shall write back to you!'

'I just thought you might not have time, when you're fighting the Germans.'

'The Germans can wait,' David said firmly, before he added with a smile, 'I shall write to you whenever I can, I promise, but you mustn't be anxious if you don't hear from me straight away. The army post office is notoriously unreliable. Mama will tell you that when my father was fighting in Africa, sometimes she heard nothing from him for weeks and then a whole bundle of letters would arrive from him, all at once.'

'Well,' she said, speaking to the man in the framed photograph beside her bed, 'how long will it be before you can write back?'

She kissed the bottom of her letter, before sealing it and addressing it, ready for Watson to post.

Luncheon at Chanynge Place the following day turned out to be with her mother alone. It seemed strange to be addressed as 'Lady Melcome' by Felstead when she arrived and to know that, since her marriage, she now outranked her mama.

'Your father sends his love,' her mother explained, 'but he was called unexpectedly to a meeting.'

They took their luncheon in the morning room, '… So much more comfortable when it's just the two of us,' and talked about the wedding.

'I thought it went very well,' said Lady McFarlane. 'You and David made such a dashing couple. Everyone said so, with him in dress uniform, and of course your gown was a triumph. I imagine Madame Chantal will have customers queuing up when your photograph appears in *The Tatler*.'

As they ate their lunch, and talked about the big day, Lady McFarlane was thinking about Sir Keir's news. Could she risk telling Lucinda? Surely she wouldn't mention it to anyone else. It was to be announced soon enough. Sir Keir and two others were to be elevated to the House of Lords sometime in November. She knew Sir Keir had told no one else, not even Iain, who would now be heir to the new barony. She, too, knew that Lucinda, as the wife of a baronet, now outranked her socially, but that the distinction was to be short-lived; it was on the tip of her tongue to tell Lucinda the amazing news, when Lucinda asked, 'Where's Iain?' And the moment passed. There was, after all, only a short while to wait, before the official announcement would be made.

'Oh, he's out somewhere,' answered Isabella. 'I can't keep up with his social life.'

As Lucinda was about to return to Sloane Square, the front door opened and Iain appeared in the hall.

'Hallo, sis,' he said. 'What are you doing here?'

'Having lunch with Mama,' replied Lucinda. 'But she's gone to some tea party or other now, so I was just going home.'

Home, no longer Chanynge Place, but Sloane Square. It sounded peculiar, even to her own ears. For a moment Iain pictured his sister returning to her new home with only her mother-in-law to welcome her, and with unusual sympathy said, 'Well, I'm going to have some tea and, with luck, some of Mrs Bellman's scones. Why don't you stay and have some with me?'

Felstead brought the tea to the drawing room and the two of them sat down at the table in the window and shared the scones with cream and strawberry jam.

'David's gone, hasn't he?' Iain said. 'That must be tough for you. Don't suppose you've heard from him yet?'

'No, but he only went yesterday morning. I'm hoping he'll have a chance to write before too long.'

There was no letter from David when Lucy got home, but she found a hand-delivered envelope waiting for her on the hall stand. She recognised the handwriting at once. It was from Muriel, now a countess married to Lord Frain, inviting her to call on Friday, when she would be At Home to a few close friends. With the printed card was a handwritten note from Muriel.

Dear Lucy,

I do hope you'll be able to come on Friday. I have invited a few of the girls who came out with us, but as you and

I are the only ones who are already married, I thought it would be pleasant to have luncheon together, before the others arrive. Francis will be in the country for a few days with his daughters, so we shall be on our own for a good gossip.

Yours sincerely, Muriel

Lucinda read the message twice and smiled. Muriel had been the first of the season's debutantes to catch a husband and she and Francis Frain had not been able to attend Lucinda and David's wedding as they were still away on their own honeymoon.

Lucinda knew it was generally thought that Muriel had made a brilliant match, but she would never have considered the middle-aged Lord Frain as a possible husband for herself. Probably, she thought now as she pondered the matter, the idea of becoming a duchess when Francis Frain inherited the dukedom from his uncle outweighed her new husband's age and the two stepdaughters she had now to take on.

Had Muriel enjoyed the duties of a wife in the bedroom? Lucinda wondered. Had she and Lord Frain crept upstairs in the afternoons like she and David had?

Not the sort of thing she could ask about, Lucy thought with a smile. But Muriel was lucky in a different way: her husband would not be going off to war only seven days after her wedding. She would almost certainly have a hectic social life, invited everywhere as the new Lady Frain.

Lucinda decided she would accept Muriel's invitation for lunch. If it were only for ladies, she would not feel an odd one out.

Lucinda was about to leave for Muriel's luncheon that Friday, when Watson knocked on her parlour door.

'The second post has just arrived, my lady,' he said presenting her with a letter on a silver tray. 'I thought you would want it at once.'

'Thank you, Watson,' Lucy replied, her heart racing as she took it.

Once the butler had withdrawn, she picked up her letter opener and carefully slit open the envelope. Her first letter from David. For a moment she held the paper against her cheek, knowing the last fingers to touch it were David's.

Dearest Lucy

Well, we are on French soil at last, and what a journey! The platform at Waterloo was much as I had expected as the whole train had been commandeered to take yet more reserves to Southampton. Talk about chaos! Three companies of reservists had been marched from their barracks to the station and all were expecting to travel on this troop train.

Women and children had come to cheer the departing troops and the excitement of those waiting to leave was running high. The platform was crammed with people trying to say goodbye, trying to find the right carriages, reporting to their officers. The train finally drew away from the platform nearly an hour later than it should.

I found Fenton in Southampton. He had managed to get our horses loaded onto the ship with very little trouble, which, he told me, had not always been the case. Several more skittish animals had baulked at being walked up the gangplank and had had to be placed in a sling and hoisted aboard by a crane on the dockside. Thank goodness not Hector and Lysander! The crossing was smooth enough, though some of the horses (and some of the men) were distressed by the motion of the ship. At least we're on dry land now!

Enough of other people and their woes. How are you, my dearest girl? I have been away from you scarcely 36 hours and yet I've missed you every minute of that time. Leaving you was the most difficult thing I've ever had to do.

Write to me soon, my beloved, as I long to hear how you are passing your time. Sleep tight in our big bed and dream of me.

David.

Chapter Twenty-One

Mrs Finch's move from Noah's Path to Barnbury Street was easily accomplished, with the help of Mr Holman's waggon. Between them, Eddie and Mabel managed to load the few pieces of furniture and two boxes of Mrs Finch's possessions, so that they only had to make one journey. Her bed and the other furniture were carried up the three flights of stairs to the attic rooms at the top and within a couple of hours, everything had been arranged and sorted, and Doreen had settled herself in.

She took on the extra care of Andrew in the evenings, so that Alice could have a few precious hours to herself, and within a few days it was as if she had always been there. Gradually they evolved a timetable for use of the facilities, a treat for Doreen, because she had never had an indoor privy and, until now, her weekly bath had been taken in a hipbath in front of the fire. Alice still did the shopping, but they shared the kitchen and the cooking, and ate together in the evenings.

It was nearly two weeks after the McFarlane wedding that William called again. He had been at Haverford Court for the week before. It was generally considered to have been a wonderful occasion, and Alice and Mabel were eager to hear all the details.

'Miss Lucinda was a beautiful bride,' William told them, 'and Sir David looked very gallant in his dress uniform.'

'What was her gown like?' asked Alice 'What was it made of? Silk?'

For a moment William was flummoxed. 'Well,' he said, 'it was, well you know, a wedding dress. So probably it was silk?'

'Oh, Will,' laughed Mabel, 'you're useless!'

'Well,' returned William defensively, 'she looked like a bride! All right? Anyhow,' he went on, 'Sir David's gone to France now and Miss Lucinda – Lady Melcome, I mean – came to Chanynge Place on Sunday. Very fine she looked. She had luncheon with Lady McFarlane.'

'It must be very lonely for her, with him having to leave so soon after the wedding,' remarked Alice. 'She can hardly go about socially.'

'Well, she don't need a chaperone no more,' pointed out William, 'so I don't see why not.'

'Imagine having to have a chaperone or a maid with you every time you wanted to leave the house!' said Mabel.

'It's a sign of class I suppose,' replied her mother. 'Status.'

'Yes, I suppose so,' agreed Mabel. 'But I'm glad we aren't gentry, or I'd never be able to run my business.' Or, she added silently to herself in her head, meet someone new, like today.

She had received a note from Hugh Morrell that morning asking her to drop into the office to see him. She had happily ridden her bicycle across to St John's Square in answer to his summons. She had to ask no one's permission to go out, nor even tell anyone where she was going. She was her own mistress, able to go wherever her business took her. She knew that made her unusual, but she loved the work and she loved the freedom it gave her.

When she reached St John's Square, she pushed her bike in through the street door and went up to the first floor. As a courtesy she rang the bell to announce her arrival and had to run the gauntlet of Miss Harper's gatekeeping.

'I'm here to see Mr Morrell,' she said.

'Mr Morrell isn't available,' replied Miss Harper, a note of triumph in her tone.

'He sent me a note and asked me to come,' replied Mabel politely. 'Perhaps you would let him know that I'm here.'

'He's not here,' stated Miss Harper.

'But he asked me to come,' repeated Mabel.

'He's not here. He was taken poorly, the poor gentleman, and he's gone home.'

'Oh dear, poor Mr Morrell,' said Mabel. 'Did he leave a message for me?'

'I already told you, he's gone home. He wasn't well enough to leave messages for people. You'll have to come again when he's back in the office… if he does come back.'

'I see.' And Mabel did see. Hugh Morrell is getting on in years, she thought, and though he's not the senior partner, he must be considerably older than Mr John Sheridan. Who would handle her affairs if he wasn't well enough to continue working? 'And you don't know why he wanted to see me?'

'Certainly not,' affirmed Miss Harper. 'His dealings with you are entirely confidential.'

At that moment, the door to Mr John Sheridan's office opened and the senior partner came out. He stopped short when he saw Mabel Oakley being confronted by Miss Harper.

'Good afternoon, Miss Oakley,' he said stiffly. 'Is there a problem?'

Mabel had never liked John Sheridan. It was he who had sacked her father at the behest of a client, angered over a mistake about some papers. The fault was not Andrew's, but it was after his sudden dismissal that he had walked out into the street and, in a moment's inattention, been run over by a brewer's dray and lost the use of his legs. There was no comeback against Mr Sheridan, because the accident had not been his fault, but the Oakley family felt that if Andrew Oakley had not been summarily dismissed, he would never have been in the street, but safely behind his desk in the offices of Sheridan, Sheridan and Morrell.

John Sheridan knew he had treated Andrew Oakley shabbily, and so was always aggressively defensive. To compound the bad feeling, Hugh Morrell had drawn up Thomas Clarke's will, which left everything to Mabel Oakley. After the funeral, when the elderly solicitor had been ill, it was John who had had to deal with the Oakleys, this time as unexpected clients.

'Not really, Mr Sheridan,' Miss Harper cut in before Mabel could answer. 'Mr Morrell apparently asked Miss Oakley to call on him today, but as you know poor Mr Morrell went home earlier this morning, unwell. Miss Oakley seems to think he should have left a message for her.'

'I think no such thing, Miss Harper, I simply asked if he had done so.'

'I see,' said John Sheridan. 'In that case, I fear you have had a wasted journey, Miss Oakley, and there seems little point in you remaining here. You can rely on us to send word when my partner has recovered his health and is available to see you.'

There was nothing more Mabel could say, except a curt, 'Thank you, Mr Sheridan. Good afternoon,' and withdraw with dignity. As she turned to go back down to the street, she saw the look of smug triumph on Miss Harper's face and wished she could think of something to wipe the expression away.

Downstairs she collected her bicycle and wheeled it out into the street. For a long moment she stood, soaking up the afternoon sun, breathing deeply to quell her anger.

How can Mr Morrell work with people like that? she wondered.

Then she heard a call. 'Miss Oakley, please wait!'

Mabel started to walk away, pushing her bike, but the call came again. 'Miss Oakley, please wait.'

She paused, but did not turn round.

A tall young man appeared at her side and she realised it was the clerk, Mr Charles.

'Oh,' she said flatly. 'It's you.'

'Sorry to shout at you,' he said, with a rueful smile, 'but when Mr Morrell left to go home today, he asked me to give you a message if you called.'

'He did?'

'He did. He apologised for not being there after all, and asked me to tell you he'd looked into the validity of the papers you'd shown him when you came last week and he thought there was little you could do about it. He asked me to find out who owns Noah's Path and it's a firm called Everette Enterprise. We used to act for them, well, Mr Morrell didn't, but my father did.'

'Your father?'

'Mr John Sheridan. I've only recently joined the firm and it would be confusing to have two Mr Sheridans in the office. My Christian name is Charles, so that's what I'm known as, Mr Charles.'

Another Sheridan! Mabel thought bitterly; but at least he'd given her Mr Morrell's message.

'I'm sorry you've had a wasted journey,' Mr Charles was saying, 'especially as the answer to your question isn't the one you wanted.'

'Never mind,' Mabel said, managing a smile. 'At least you passed on the message.'

'Perhaps I could buy you a cup of tea, before you ride all the way back to Barnbury Street.'

'You know where I live?' For the first time Mabel looked at the young man properly.

'Of course,' Mr Charles replied. 'It's in your file. And because I work with Mr Morrell, I do know a bit about you.' Not as much as I want to, he thought but did not say. 'So,' he went on, 'will you come and have a cup of tea with me? There's a little café round the corner which does delicious sticky buns, if you like those.'

'But I hardly know you,' protested Mabel.

'Well, you'll get to know me better if we have tea together, won't you?' He solemnly held out his hand and said, 'How do you do, Miss Oakley? My name is Charles Sheridan, but my friends call me Chas.'

Mabel took the offered hand and answered, 'How do you do, Chas? My friends call me Mabel.'

DINEY COSTELOE

'There you are,' he said, with a wide smile. 'Now we've been introduced there is nothing improper in having tea together.'

Mabel started to walk forward again, still pushing her bike. Chas looked at her determined expression and guessed it would be a mistake to offer to push the bike for her. He led her to a small café called Rosie's Tea Rooms, two streets away.

He pushed open the door and called to the woman behind the counter, 'Hallo, Rosie, anywhere we can put the bike?'

'No, Mr Sheridan, you'll have to leave it outside. Take the table in the window and you can keep your eye on it from there.'

'Don't worry, Chas,' Mabel said, and delving into her bag she pulled out a piece of chain and a padlock. 'I can lock it to a lamp post, that's what I usually do.'

A very resourceful girl, Chas thought, as he watched her secure her bike.

Moments later they were seated at the window table, watching the people passing in the street.

Rosie came over and took their order, tea for two and not just sticky buns, but a plate of cakes to choose from. While Chas was speaking to Rosie, Mabel took stock of the young man across the table. His height was the first thing she had noticed, at well over six foot tall he towered over her, but now she saw that his almost black hair was irrepressibly curly, despite the large dose of hair tonic that had been applied in an effort to make it smooth and straight. His dark brown eyes crinkled with laughter lines and his mouth seemed permanently curved into a smile. None of his features was particularly distinctive, but the combination presented him as striking, not handsome in a classical sense, but very attractive.

Yes, he is attractive, Mabel thought, as she turned her attention to the choice of cakes on offer. And I shouldn't be here having tea with him on my own.

Indeed, she felt quite nervous. She had never been entertained to tea alone by a young man before. William certainly hadn't the

148

cash to treat her to tea in a café, and there had been no one else. Suddenly she felt awkward and shy.

To cover her nervousness, she asked, 'Is Mr Morrell very ill?'

'I don't know,' Chas admitted. 'He didn't look very good when he left, sort of pale and shaky. We put him in a taxi and I went with him. He's a widower, you know, but he has a housekeeper who looks after him, a Mrs Parsons. I left him in her care and only just got back to the office before you arrived. I was in the clerks' room with Bevis when I heard your voice.'

'My voice? And you recognised it?' Mabel was incredulous.

'Not the voice so much as the fact that you were standing up to Horrible Hermione. Not many people do that and I've heard you doing it twice now!'

'My father always said she was a bully.'

'Your father? How does he know her?'

'You really don't know, do you?' Mabel had assumed that as soon as Chas heard the Oakley name, he would know who she was and who her father was, too.

Chas shook his head. 'No, so tell me.'

'My father used to be your father's senior clerk.'

'So why isn't he now, instead of that idiot, Bevis?'

Mabel gave him a brief account of what had happened, an account with a definite Oakley slant.

'Right,' said Chas when she fell silent. 'That concludes any mention of our fathers. Now let's talk about us!'

'Us?' echoed Mabel. 'There isn't an "us".'

'No,' Chas agreed cheerfully, 'but don't you think there might be?'

'We don't know anything about each other,' Mabel said.

'You said that before,' Chas reminded her. 'And I thought it might be fun to discover. Why don't we meet up for tea here again? Next Monday.'

'Why next Monday?'

'Because today is Monday, so it will be our weeklyversary.'

'Weeklyversary?' Mabel looked at him quizzically 'What's that, when it's at home?'

'Well, we can't have an anniversary when we've only known each other for a week, can we? So, we'll have to have weeklyversaries, and they'll come round much more often!'

Mabel burst out laughing. 'You are ridiculous, Chas! You know that?'

Chas frowned for a moment, as if thinking, before he grinned and said, 'A feeling I've been told that before.' And they both laughed

'Thank you for my tea,' Mabel said as they stood outside on the pavement.

'My pleasure,' answered Chas, adding, as he watched her unchain her bike, 'same time next week?'

'Maybe,' she said as she mounted the bike. 'If I can.'

When William took his farewell that evening, Mabel saw him to the front door as usual.

'You was very quiet tonight,' he said as he put his arms around her. 'Something on your mind?'

'No, Will, nothing on my mind.' She let him kiss her gently and then pulled away. Not something on her mind, but someone? Yes, someone.

She watched William as he walked down the street to catch his bus. He turned at the corner to wave and she waved back, before closing the front door.

Dear Will. She was very fond of him, but there was a big world out there, other people to meet, and she was anxious not to find herself tied to someone she was just fond of, dear as he might be.

Chapter Twenty-Two

In his first letter home, David told Lucinda that the crossing to Le Havre had been relatively easy, but compared with the confusion that had greeted them as they disembarked at Le Havre, the remembered chaos at Waterloo station seemed like a picnic. The noise and the bustle were intense. The stentorian voices of the NCOs boomed as the incoming infantry battalions were assembled, numbered off in companies and finally marched away to their temporary billets. The cavalry remained at the port waiting for their horses to be brought ashore, and the French officials were furiously vocal as they threatened to be overwhelmed by the arrival of the British reinforcements.

David had reported his arrival to Brigadier Marsh at Brigade HQ as ordered; and then with instructions to find their horses a suitable stable and themselves a comfortable billet, he and Fenton had continued to wait for the horses to be unloaded. It was a slow process, with horses, nervous and unsettled from the voyage, whinnying and squealing in fear if their hooves slithered on the decking before they were brought ashore.

As David returned to the dockside to find Fenton, he found himself swallowed by the noise and chaos of the disembarkation. How could order possibly be restored from all this? he wondered, as he watched the seething mass of men and horses, but even as he watched he knew that it could be and would be, because that's the way it always was. Discipline would be reestablished, men would react automatically to familiar orders bellowed by their sergeant majors, and the chaotic crowd of soldiers would coalesce into normal ranks. They would become recognisable again as the army their friends and family had waved off from Waterloo.

Everyone in England knew the Expeditionary Force had been met with fierce resistance at the Mons Canal, where they had been outnumbered and outflanked, particularly when the French army had retreated, leaving them exposed. But knowing this from reports in the press and being involved in the fourteen-day strategic retreat were two entirely different matters.

'We're to report to the Queen's Bays, who have withdrawn,' David told Fenton when he returned from Brigade HQ.

'They're still retreating?' exclaimed Fenton. 'Running away from a few bloody Krauts? Sounds like the French more than like us!'

'Not a thought to be expressed in mixed company,' David warned. 'The French are our allies, but they can be very touchy about being on the same side as the English.'

While they were still waiting for their horses to be disembarked, David despatched Fenton into the town to find some suitable lodgings. 'Won't be easy with so many officers looking for a bed,' he said, 'but it doesn't have to be anything flash. We'll be moving out again tomorrow.'

So many people back home in England had expected the Expeditionary Force to send the German army packing – out of France, out of Belgium and home with their tails between their legs. All would be over before Christmas had been the cry, but the allies had been in retreat for weeks before David had joined the army in France, driven back from Mons on the Belgian border, fighting skirmishes all the way, almost as far as Paris.

The German plan to capture the French capital and knock France out of the war was close to being successful, but the French and British retreat had finally been halted when the allied army reached the River Marne only thirty miles from Paris. The city was still in grave danger of being taken, but with the fate of Paris and her citizens in their hands, the allies turned, held their ground and mounted a counterattack.

Now it was the Germans' turn to retreat and retreat they did, more than fifty-six miles, losing ordnance and prisoners to the allies along the way, before, with the French and the British hot on their heels, they reached the high ground on the far side the River Aisne. Here they dug in, to maintain an advantage and prevent further allied advances.

David and his company were drawn up below on the open flat land through which the waters of the River Aisne flowed, cutting them off from the enemy now established on the distant escarpment. David looked across the mile of low-lying land on either side of the river towards the plateau atop the hill that rose steeply in the distance.

It's not going to be easy to dislodge them from up there, he thought, as he scanned the ridge with his binoculars.

Moments later, Fenton was at his side, staring across the water towards the steep outcrop. He whistled through his teeth. 'Blimey!' he said. 'Goin' to take sommat to shift 'em off of there!'

The River Aisne lay between the two armies, with many of its bridges already destroyed by the retreating Germans, but the order to advance across the river came before the dawn. Under cover of darkness and amid swathes of thick fog, the allies began to cross the water. The Germans might have demolished some bridges, but, undeterred, the British and French struggled across those that had survived and on temporary floating pontoons where they had not. As the sun rose to burn off the fog, the enemy, high on the ridge, pounded them from above, raining shells on those still crossing the river and the land beyond. The infantry, crossing the open flatlands to reach the foot of the escarpment, were at the mercy of the shells, and those who had made it across to the foot of the bluff and begun to climb were strafed with fire from above. Men lay dead and dying, some crying out in pain, some calling on their mothers, some praying, as their lives ebbed away.

The allied armies were spread along the line of the ridge and after too many abortive attacks on the escarpment, the officers had to recognise such attempts simply left their men at the mercy of the German artillery entrenched on the hilltop.

The battle continued for several days, with neither army giving ground, but with relentless artillery exchanges there were heavy casualties on both sides. It became clear to all concerned that throwing more lives into futile attacks could no longer be sustained, and the order for the British to dig defensive trenches was eventually given by the Commander-in-Chief, Sir John French. An army on the move doesn't dig trenches, doesn't carry entrenching tools.

'Dig trenches, the man says,' Fenton grumbled as he scrabbled to remove earth from the small pit he'd been working on. 'What with? Me bare hands?'

Fenton wasn't the only one to complain, but working in relays, with whatever tools they could lay hands on or could borrow from the local population, the allies began to dig shallow pits in which they might hide.

'It's stalemate,' muttered Fenton as, despite the grumbling, the British continued to dig in. 'We can't get at them and they can't get at us. Looks like we're going to be here forever! An' what's more,' he went on, 'them holes ain't big enough to hide a rabbit! They need to be deeper, so's you can get down inside, for a bit of protection, like.'

David couldn't help agreeing, though he knew better than to do so out loud. Tommies grumbling at their lot was part and parcel of being in the army, but officers needed to maintain a distance, even with their own soldier servants.

Once the trenches had been dug, they had to be kept in good order, and men risked their lives building and repairing those damaged by shellfire. Even so, there was quite a lot of time when the artillery engaged each other across the divide, but the man in the trench had little to do except keep his head down. David used these quieter times to write to Lucy. He had received several letters from her, which he numbered in date order so they made sense. Apart from the very first letter he had written on landing at

Le Havre, he'd had almost no time to write; all he had managed to send was one hurried postcard from the Marne, before he'd been drafted into the pursuit to Aisne. And now, what could he say? Describe the bloody battle they had all been fighting? Those first days at Aisne had been harrowing enough to sicken him as he saw the lives of more and more men were wasted in attempted attacks on the higher ground. He didn't want to terrify Lucy or his mother with mention of the men in his company whom he had already lost, dead or wounded; nor describe how the battle was rumbling on with neither side possessing or conceding the few hundred yards that lay between them. He could, with a clear conscience, mention a little of trench life, but he kept it as light-hearted as he could, thinking as he wrote asking Lucy to send some biscuits and some tins of jam to brighten his army rations, that's hardly going to give anything away to an enemy who was probably asking for a similar parcel from home.

And some more socks, my darling, he wrote. Not much chance of doing the laundry here… despite the French promising that they're '… gonna hang out the washing on the Siegfried Line'. Maybe they are, but I regret to say I've been wearing these same socks for days now! I'm sorry it has been so long between this and my last letter, but the Germans have kept us pretty busy one way and another. The mail came up to the front yesterday, and lucky me was handed three from you. You have no idea what a boost they gave me. I keep them folded into my breast pocket next to my photo of you, close to my heart! There, you didn't know I was such a romantic, did you? Please will you ask Mrs Watson to make me one of her famous fruit cakes. Well, that's certainly not romantic, but it would be very well received in my dugout, that's what we call an enlarged part of the trench… room for more than one!

Well, I must turn in for some sleep now, as we seem to have a few moments' peace. Good of Fritz, perhaps their gunners have turned in, too! We have to take the chance of sleep whenever it comes as the bombardment from both sides is head-batteringly noisy!

Please give my love to Mama and thank her for her letters. Tell her I am safe and well and will write to her when I can.

And of course, my best love to you, my Lucy, remembering those precious days at Crayne.

David.

Chapter Twenty-Three

The Monday afternoon following her encounter with Charles Sheridan, Mabel returned to Rosie's Tea Room. She didn't approach the door straight away. She didn't want to arrive before Chas did; she wasn't at all sure she should arrive at all. It was all very well for him to say that as they had introduced themselves to each other, it constituted an 'introduction' and so it was perfectly proper for them to take tea together. She was fairly sure her mother wouldn't think so. She would have wanted Mabel to have been introduced by a mutual acquaintance.

But Mr Morrell is a mutual acquaintance, Mabel told herself. He would have introduced us if we had met in his office, wouldn't he? He might have introduced them, her inner voice warned her, but he might not have expected her to be seen in public alone with Chas afterwards. The thought of Mr Morrell made her wonder yet again how he was, whether he was better and back at the office; Mr Sheridan had promised to let her know when he returned, but she had heard nothing. Surely Chas would have told her. Which brought her back to Chas again. He'd probably tell her how Mr Morrell was this afternoon.

The clock on the tower of nearby St James's Church struck four. Mabel walked casually past the tea room and glanced in through the window. She could see that three tables were occupied, including the one where she and Chas had sat in the window last week, but all the customers seemed to be women. There was no sign of a tall, good-looking young man waiting inside. Mabel walked on past and went round the corner. She turned into the churchyard of St James's Church from where, perched on a tombstone, she could see the front of Rosie's, but could remain out of sight herself. The street wasn't busy and though there were a few pedestrians going about their afternoon business, there was no sign of Chas Sheridan. Mabel continued to wait in the churchyard, not wanting to be seen waiting, but loath to turn away and leave; he might still come. The church clock struck the quarter hour and then the half. Various people entered the tea rooms, but there was still no sign of Chas.

'I am in the right place,' Mabel said aloud, beginning to doubt her memory. 'There's the lamp post I chained my bike to!' Even as she watched, she saw customers leaving, walking off down the street. Not long afterwards the lights in the tea room went out and Rosie herself came out of the front door, carefully locking it behind her. A chilly autumn breeze had sprung up and Mabel shivered.

What on earth am I doing here, sitting on a gravestone? she thought, with a sudden burst of anger. It was time to go home. She should have done so ages ago instead of hanging about in the hope that Chas might yet turn up. What was he to her, anyway? Nothing. She slid down from the stone and pushed her bike out onto the street. Now she really felt the chill of the autumn wind, and getting onto her bicycle, she pedalled energetically all the way home.

As she rode, she held a conversation with herself. Fancy thinking Chas had really intended to meet you. How could you have been so gullible? Let's face it, you only met the man once. He must have thought you an easy pick-up!

Angrier with herself than she was with him, she made herself a promise: she wouldn't get caught out that way again.

'You're late home, Mabel,' said her father when she'd put her bike into the basement and gone up the outside staircase into the kitchen.

'Yes,' she replied vaguely, giving no explanation. 'Sorry, Dada, I had some things to do.'

Mrs Finch was peeling potatoes at the sink. 'There should be some tea in the pot,' she said over her shoulder. 'Probably a bit stewed.'

Chapter Twenty-Four

John Sheridan had called his son into his office that Monday afternoon and said, 'Charles, I need you to deliver this, this afternoon, to a client in Finchley. Mr Preston.'

'This afternoon?'

His son's dismay wasn't lost on John and he answered with heavy sarcasm, 'If it's not too much trouble, Charles?'

When Charles did not immediately reply, his father said, 'I doubt if you have much actual work to do with Mr Morrell still being away and this package needs to be delivered today... this afternoon. You understand?'

Charles drew a deep breath and began, 'Well, guv'nor...' But was immediately interrupted.

'In the office, Charles, you address me as "sir". Did I not make that abundantly clear?'

'Yes, sir,' Charles acknowledged. 'But,' he went on, thinking quickly, 'it's just that I had planned to visit Mr Morrell this afternoon, to see how he was going on, you know?'

'Very commendable,' remarked his father dryly. 'But not on the firm's time. This delivery is important, Charles, and promised for this afternoon.' He paused for a moment before saying, 'However, on your way back, it would be a courtesy to look in on Mr Morrell. You can discover when he thinks he might be coming back... if at all.'

There was nothing for it but to take the package, a thick brown envelope tied up with string, to Mr Preston in Finchley and deliver it as ordered.

When he arrived, he found the address was a private house,

not an office as he'd assumed. A woman he guessed was the housekeeper opened the door and showed him into a sitting room, where Mr Preston was seated at a desk.

'Thank you for making a special journey,' he said, as he accepted the parcel. 'If I could trespass on your time for another few minutes, you can witness my signature.'

Charles sighed. No point in saying no. Mr Preston opened the package and studied the enclosed papers, before saying, 'Yes, that's fine. I'll just call Mrs Grant.'

Moments later the housekeeper came in answer to his summons, hovering in the doorway.

'You rang, sir?'

'Yes, Grant, come in.'

She edged into the room and waited. Mr Preston selected three sheets of paper and, sitting down at his desk, signed each one with a flourish. Dutifully Charles and Mrs Grant stepped forward and signed as witnesses.

Mr Preston stacked the pages neatly together and, replacing them in the envelope, handed them back to Charles.

'Good of you to come so promptly,' Mr Preston said. 'Now, if you can return these to Mr Sheridan...'

Charles put them into his briefcase and took his leave.

Once outside, he looked at his watch. It was almost half past three. It might just be possible to get to Rosie's before four o'clock if he did not visit Mr Morrell on the way. He had used the old man as an excuse not to go out to Finchley, and had been caught out by his father. He'd have to go and see him tomorrow.

He reached the office just after four and ran up the stairs to leave Mr Preston's papers on his father's desk. He found the office empty, so he opened one of the unlocked desk drawers and tucked the package inside. He was about to leave again, when Miss Harper emerged from her office and came along the passage.

'Ah, Mr Charles. I'm glad you're back. I've had to wait to lock up behind you.'

'I'm sorry,' said Charles, 'but it's not yet five. Surely Bevis is still here.'

'No. Mr Sheridan sent him off on some errand and told him there was no need for him to come back this evening. He also told me that I might lock up and leave early, once you were back.'

'Well, I'm back now and have an appointment elsewhere, so if you'll excuse me...' He edged towards the top of the stairs. It struck him that if Mr Preston hadn't asked him to return the papers to the office, he wouldn't have come back this evening either, in which case Horrible Hermione could have been waiting for him all night. It was a thought that made him grin; he'd share it with Mabel.

'Good evening, Miss Harper,' he said. Polite enough in its way, but there was an insouciance about the way he said it which infuriated Miss Harper. She never quite knew where she was with Charles Sheridan... a lowly articled clerk, but at the same time, the senior partner's son.

As he reached the street, Chas heard the church clock strike the half hour and realised it was half past four; he began to run. When he arrived at Rosie's he was dismayed to find the little teashop locked up, with a closed sign in its window. He looked along the street. It wasn't deserted, there were people about, but there was no sign of Mabel Oakley. He paced up and down, hoping that she had been delayed as well. He peered in through the teashop window, a pointless act. If the teashop was shut, then it was shut, and she was hardly likely to be inside. It wasn't like Rosie to close this early. Perhaps there had been no customers and she'd decided to go home early. Had Mabel been waiting for him inside the shop until it closed?

Miserably he took one more walk around the area, but there was no one to see. He'd been too late, and he might as well go home. He'd have to make it up to Mabel as soon as he could... somehow.

The next morning Mabel went down into her workshop. She

had very little work to do, some simple record sheets for one of the local schools, and she found the thought of working on such a banal order very depressing.

She wondered how Mr Morrell was. Previously, she would have arrived at his office without invitation, but now she couldn't do that. Suppose he wasn't back? Worse, suppose she bumped into Chas? He would think that asking for Mr Morrell was simply an excuse to see him. No, she would steer clear of Sheridan, Sheridan and Morrell's offices until she was informed that Mr Morrell had returned.

'Pull yourself together,' she told herself. 'Not to trust a man you don't know is a lesson well-learned. Remember it!'

Chapter Twenty-Five

Over the last months, Mabel had been building up a list of regular customers. It never hurt, she thought, to make each of her clients feel valued and special, and from time to time she delivered one of her new advertising flyers to those who had stayed with her after the death of Thomas Clarke. With these occasional visits she had built a rapport with her customers, and nowadays when she pedalled up to their offices, she was often offered a cup of tea, a biscuit and a chat.

One of the oldest firms that used her services for their printing needs was Topperly and Co, the builders' merchants. Mr Topperly had been impressed with how she handled herself when he tried to insist that a thirty-day payment was normal. The terms had actually been cash on delivery. Mabel had stood her ground and it was Mr Topperly who had given way and paid up.

Mr Topperly admired her spunk and continued to use her for invoices and for locally delivered flyers, which, as she had suggested, really did bring him new customers.

Another of her regular customers was the furniture makers, Carter's. This was where Eddie had taken up his apprenticeship once Mabel was able to pay Mr Carter the required premium. The old man had been impressed by her forthright manner, and the upfront way she did business. He had agreed to reinstate Eddie's apprenticeship. He was old-fashioned enough to think Mabel would be better off at home as a wife and mother, but was nevertheless pleased to see her making a success of her printing business.

'Keeps her out of mischief until she finds herself a husband,' he had confided to his wife, after Mabel's last visit.

The following Monday, determined to put Chas Sheridan and weeklyversaries firmly out of her head, Mabel decided to take a trip up to the West End. East End corner shops like Grangers were not the only places Mabel advertised her business. Once a month or so Mabel went to the West End and walked the streets of Belgravia and Mayfair, of Knightsbridge and Kensington. Here she did not leave flyers, but smart business cards. The actual card she used was expensive, the font, the wording and the layout designed to appeal to a more discerning clientele who might want invitations for smart parties, business cards for men's wallets or visiting cards for ladies' reticules. She placed each card in a plain white envelope addressed in copperplate script that read: 'To the Occupier'.

This beautiful Monday morning was not one to spend in the workshop, turning out more invoices for Mr Carter, Mabel thought, as she looked out at the golden autumn day. The invoices could wait until tomorrow. She had little other work on hand and she decided it was just the day to take one of her occasional trips up west. And while she was there, she might take a walk along Chanynge Place. She had no intention of visiting number 11 where, for a while, she had worked as a housemaid for Lady McFarlane. She would be welcome neither at the front door, nor round the back at the servants' entrance. There was, however, a slim chance of some more work coming her way. Though her ladyship still did not know it was Mabel who had produced the invitations for Lucinda's wedding, her son, Iain, had been impressed not only by the quality of Mabel's work but also by her no-nonsense approach to a rush job at short notice. He had said so and Mabel thought, as she prepared for her day up west, you never know when further stationery might be required.

After careful thought, Mabel decided one of her cards, addressed to him personally, might remind him where she was, in case the family required any further printing. When she reached Chanynge Place she walked past the house before turning back and pausing for a moment on the pavement outside.

For goodness' sake, she told herself, get on with it!

With sudden resolution she walked up the steps to the glossy black door to slip the white vellum envelope, addressed to Iain McFarlane Esq., through the gleaming brass letterbox. The card inside was the same as all the others she was delivering that morning, advertising the business of Thomas Clarke, Printer and the contact address. Only Iain would know that it was Mabel Oakley who was now Thomas Clarke, Printer, and with luck he might keep the card.

Chapter Twenty-Six

Mabel did not know that on this particular Monday morning, in the Court section of *The Times*, there had been the announcement that Sir Keir McFarlane KC had been elevated to the House of Lords. Along with Mr Henley Travers, and Mr Arthur Moot, two other similarly elevated supporters of the Prime Minister, Baron McFarlane of Haverford would take his seat on the government benches in the House of Lords as soon as Parliament reconvened.

The night before this announcement was to be made, Lucinda had been invited back to Chanynge Place for a private family dinner, just the four of them, she and Iain and their parents. The dining room was laid up as if for a banquet, making it clear this was a special occasion. The occasion itself had not been announced, causing much speculation below stairs.

'Mr Felstead's been ordered to have champagne ready on ice,' William told Lizzie, 'so there's definitely something going on.'

'Do you know what?' Ada asked. 'Stands to reason it must be really special. D'you think Mr Iain's got engaged or something?'

'Hardly,' laughed Lizzie, ''cos if he had, his new fiancée would be at the dinner as well, wouldn't she?'

'Perhaps Lady Melcome's... you know,' Mrs Bellman murmured to Mrs Kilby. When Mrs Kilby looked blank, Mrs Bellman nodded. 'You know?'

The housekeeper looked startled. 'Most unlikely, Mrs Bellman,' she replied. 'Sir David's away at the war, so she can't be, can she?'

'I wouldn't be so sure,' returned the cook. 'They did have a honeymoon before he went.'

'But only a few days. Really, Mrs Bellman, I do hope you won't say such things in front of Lizzie and Ada.'

A few days is plenty of time if you're keen to get on with things, thought Mrs Bellman with a rueful smile. It only takes once! But she had enough sense to keep such thoughts to herself.

In the dining room the family chatted as they usually did while they drank their soup, but once the entrée had been served and William and Lizzie had withdrawn, Sir Keir told them of the honour he was to receive. The news was greeted with cries of delight by his children.

'That's fantastic news, guv'nor,' cried Iain. 'How long have you known?'

'Did you know, Mama?'

'Did you have to meet the king?'

'Did Mr Asquith send for you?'

'Have you been to 10 Downing Street?'

'What does he want you to do?'

'Will Iain inherit the title? Is this the beginning of a dynasty?'

'Have you known all along, Mama?'

'So *that's* what the Moët's for!' cried Iain. 'I did wonder!' He got to his feet and poured them each a glass. 'A toast!' he said. 'To you, guv'nor, to Lord McFarlane of Haverford!'

His mother and sister raised their glasses and echoed the toast.

Sir Keir raised his own glass in salute. 'To all of us,' he said and touched his glass to Isabella's. 'It will be announced tomorrow in *The Times*,' he said, 'but I thought we should celebrate as a family, before the rest of the world get to hear.'

'So it's official from tomorrow?' Lucinda asked. 'Did you know before, Mama?'

'I told your mother on the evening of your wedding day,' said Sir Keir, 'but it had to remain between the two of us until the public announcement. There's a great deal of paperwork to be done when a new peer is created. The king has to issue a warrant and direct the Crown Office to draw up the letters patent which actually create the appointment and title. If the information became public before these are approved and sealed, it could mean the whole process would be cancelled and no appointment would be made.' He smiled across at his wife and said, 'I had to swear your mother to secrecy, and give no inkling to anyone else, not even you two.'

'But now it's all right?' Lucinda asked anxiously.

Sir Keir reached for his daughter's hand and said, 'Yes, now it's quite all right. I'm so sorry David isn't here to celebrate with us, Lucy, but you can certainly tell him when you next write. Once the word is out,' he continued, 'I imagine there may be a fair amount of speculation in the press about why three new peers have been created just now. We need to be prepared for that, I think.' He smiled round at them, the family of which he was so proud, and said, 'But we can deal with that when it comes.'

The following morning, Sir Keir called his household together before the newspaper arrived, to ensure he broke the news himself: they were now working for a peer of the realm.

Felstead, having been warned half an hour beforehand, had quickly composed a speech of congratulation on behalf of all those below stairs. The news was greeted with exclamations of excitement and when the household had dispersed, there was a great deal of discussion in the servants' hall as to what this might mean for all of them. Certainly, it was considered a step up to be working for a lord with a hereditary title.

Felstead allowed half an hour for the staff to celebrate the news below stairs and then it was everyone back to normal duties. When the newspapers did arrive, Felstead took them into the library himself, leaving them on the oak corner table for Sir Keir to peruse later at his leisure.

It was William who found it in the letterbox, the plain white envelope addressed to Iain McFarlane Esq. It had not arrived with the first post, that had all been on the breakfast table; but as he took it from the inside letterbox, he noticed it had been hand delivered. He stared at it for a long time; surely he knew the flowing handwriting on that envelope, didn't he? Surely that was Mabel's educated hand. Why was his girl writing to Iain McFarlane? William remembered the day he'd seen Mr Iain leaving 27 Barnbury Street, just as he himself turned the corner. When he had taxed Mabel with the visit, she told him it was strictly business, but here she was, actually writing to Mr Iain at the Chanynge Place address. William was strongly tempted to take the letter and destroy it. Was a reply expected? he wondered. If no reply came, Mabel might well assume Mr Iain had not received the letter, or better still, had simply thrown it away.

For a long moment William stood with the letter in his hand... too long. Before he summoned up the courage to put it into his own pocket, the baize door leading to below stairs opened and Felstead came through. It was too late to hide it and so all William could do was place it on the silver salver on the hall stand for Mr Iain to find.

'What's that, William?' demanded Felstead, pausing on his way to the drawing room.

'A letter for Mr Iain,' answered William reluctantly, 'just come by hand.'

'Give it here,' said Felstead, 'and I'll take it in to him. If it's been hand delivered it's probably important.'

William watched as Felstead entered the drawing room, Mabel's letter in his hand.

Why, he thought angrily, did there always seem to be a link between his Mabel and Iain McFarlane, son of the house and now, William suddenly realised, heir to the new barony? From now on until he inherited the title, he would be styled The Honourable Iain McFarlane.

This latest thought actually gave William a glimmer of hope. If Mr Iain was one day going to be Lord McFarlane, he would be way beyond Mabel's reach and she would have to put him out of her mind. William knew Iain had been captivated by Mabel, but he also knew Iain had made no declaration, accepting there could be no future for them together. Mabel herself had always been ambivalent, never showing Iain any partiality, often dealing with him sharply, but treating him as an equal, calling him by his Christian name. 'Because,' she had said to William when he questioned this, 'I don't work for him and so I don't have to call him "Mr" as a sign of respect. After all, he addresses me as plain "Mabel", not "Miss Oakley" or even "Miss Mabel".'

'But that's because he's Quality,' William said in frustration.

'Well, I'm Quality too,' retorted Mabel, tired of the discussion. 'Just a different sort. Now will you stop worrying about Iain McFarlane, William, and help me wrap these record cards.'

Thinking of that conversation now, William wished, all the more, that he'd put the letter in his pocket before Felstead had seen it.

While those below stairs discussed the unexpected news over cups of tea and slices of Mrs Bellman's fruit cake, the family above stairs were beginning to make plans. The announcement was there to be seen in *The Times* this morning; Iain had fetched the paper from the library and read it out to them with great solemnity.

'We must hold a reception,' Isabella said. 'We must invite the other two who are to be honoured and their sponsors as well as your own... and the Prime Minister, of course.'

'I believe I am the first to be introduced to the House of Lords,' Sir Keir said. 'They only introduce one new peer at a time.'

'Are we able to come and watch the ceremony?' asked Lucinda.

'You are, from the public gallery,' replied her father. 'The date will be set very soon because the Prime Minister wants our support for two of his bills which the Commons are making a fuss about.'

'Then we must begin organising your reception straight away,' said Isabella. 'We must make a comprehensive guest list to ensure no one of importance is left out.'

'You never stop, Mama,' Iain said with a smile. 'You've only just finished organising Lucy's wedding!'

'Maybe,' agreed his mother, 'but this is an entirely different thing, and we must be seen to be active politically as well as socially. Your father will be part of the government.'

'Not part of the government,' Sir Keir corrected her gently, 'but sitting on the government benches in the upper house.'

Chapter Twenty-Seven

After the family celebration the previous evening and the excitement of the announcement, Lucinda was quite ready to go home. She would break the news to her mother-in-law and then write to tell David. How surprised he would be!

With Clara in attendance, Lucy had fully intended to walk home. The day was a bright one, the autumnal sun striking brilliance from the trees in the parks and gardens. Emerging from the house, Lucinda paused on the front step and drew a deep breath of fresh autumn air, but as she stepped out into the street, she was almost mown down by a passing motor. Clara made a grab for her mistress's coat, dragging her back onto the pavement as the driver blasted an angry warning on his horn.

'Look out, Miss Lucinda!' the girl cried, forgetting in her panic that she should now be addressing her as 'my lady'. 'You was nearly killed!'

Lucinda had been so absorbed in an idea which had just come to her, she had been paying no attention to the passing mid-morning traffic and might indeed have been knocked down but for Clara's quick reaction. Even now her mind was clearly elsewhere.

Perhaps, she thought with a stab of excitement, David might be able to come home for her father's introduction to the House of Lords. Perhaps he could put in for a few days' leave. After all, as a member of that august body himself, he ought to be there for the introduction of a new peer and one of the family to boot. And then there was the reception her mother was already planning, surely he should be there; how could she, Lucy, attend that without him?

All at once, she was longing to get home to write to David and all thoughts of a bracing walk in the autumn sunshine were set aside as a black taxi swung into the street and she held up an imperious hand to flag it down. Clara, astonished at her mistress's bravado, paused awkwardly on the pavement as the driver came round to open the door of the cab.

The driver had been surprised it was a lady who had hailed him, but he recognised quality when he saw it and paused before closing the door to ask, 'Where to, madam?'

Lucinda, sitting back in her seat, replied easily, 'Sloane Square,' as if she took taxis, only accompanied by her maid, every day of her life.

When they got home, Clara paid off the cabby with a half crown Lucinda had given her, and they went inside.

'Her ladyship has already gone out, my lady,' Watson informed her. 'I believe she's attending a luncheon given by Lady Charlton.'

So, she would have to wait for her mother-in-law to come home before she could share the exciting news. Suddenly, Lucinda felt exhausted and longed to sit down. She would go to her own little parlour and take a rest on the chaise longue before she settled to writing her letter.

'May I bring you anything?' Watson asked.

'A cup of tea,' Lucinda replied, as she turned to go upstairs, 'and some of Mrs Watson's almond biscuits, I feel like something sweet.'

When Watson followed her ten minutes later with the tea tray, he found her lying on the chaise longue, fast asleep.

It was over an hour later that Lucinda awoke again, and found cold tea and the almond biscuits on the table beside her. She ignored the tea, but ate two of the biscuits, before opening her writing desk and beginning her letter to David.

Dearest David,

You'll never believe the news! Papa has been elevated to the House of Lords! He's now Baron McFarlane of Haverford. We're all very excited. He says it's official now that the letters patent have been signed and sealed. Mama is already planning a grand reception to celebrate his new status. It sounds as if all the world and his wife will be there.

Lucy paused for a moment, chewing the end of her pen. Could she really suggest the idea that had come to her on her way home this morning? If she consulted Iain, she knew he would say, 'If you don't ask, sis, you don't get.' Well, she decided, I will ask, and maybe, just maybe, he'll be able to come home. Decision made, she turned her attention back to her letter.

I don't suppose there's any chance of you getting leave so you can come home for it, is there? We don't know a definite date for Papa's introduction, but he says it will be soon when Parliament reconvenes. I don't know how these things work, but it's going to be an incredibly important time for him. He says we shall be able to watch the actual introduction ceremony from the public gallery. Of course, all this means that Iain will be the heir to the barony, which will make him an extraordinarily good catch for some lucky girl in the next year or so. The husband-hunting mamas will be after him in a flash.

Do see if you can secure a few days' leave, my darling David, if only to join in the celebration party. You've been away more than a month already and I miss you so much.

Mrs Watson has made you another cake and I'll enclose that with this letter and some more socks I got from the Army and Navy Store. They're more likely to fit than any I could knit for you!

With these extras I'm sending you all my love and praying you'll be able to get some leave. There are lists of casualties in the papers now, and we hear of more fighting every day. Stay safe, my David. Stay safe and come home to me. Your Lucy

Felstead had given Iain McFarlane his hand-delivered letter in the presence of his parents and Lucinda. Iain had glanced at it and pushed it into his pocket, simply saying, 'Thanks, Felstead.' He didn't know who it was from, but whoever it was could wait. Indeed with all the drama of the morning, he didn't remember it was there at all until he'd been in the office for over half an hour, receiving congratulations on behalf of his father.

When he did remember and pulled it out, he was surprised to discover it only contained a printed card:

```
Thomas Clarke, Printer, for all your printing
needs: -

Invitations

Calling Cards

Headed Notepaper

Office Stationery

Swift, efficient service at reasonable prices

27 Barnbury Street London
```

Iain couldn't help smiling as he read the words. How like Mabel to remind her customers where she was and what she offered. Turning the card over he saw there was a handwritten message on the reverse in the same flowing hand that had addressed the envelope.

Can always manage a rush job for regular customers!

Mabel

Iain gave a rueful smile. Nothing to offer you just now, he thought. But he would keep the card. Stupid, but it was the only thing he had of hers, and it showed she had actually thought of him, even if it were simply as a paying customer. It was only when he got home again and found his mother compiling a guest list that he realised that they might have some work for her... for Thomas Clarke, Printer.

'When will you be sending out the invitations, Mama?' he asked.

'As soon as we can get them printed,' replied his mother. 'The thing is,' she went on, 'we need to have the date of the ceremony at the House of Lords confirmed. Your father thought we should hear that today. I have already been in touch with the Waldorf and have a provisional date for an evening banquet in the Palm Court.'

'Would you like me to arrange the printing when you're ready? I thought we might use the printer who did that excellent work for Lucy's invitations.'

'Perhaps,' his mother said, though he could see her mind was elsewhere. 'We'll need the new coat of arms at the top. I doubt if your man could deal with that. I have a firm in mind recommended by the College of Arms, so unless there's a problem, I think we'll commission them.'

Iain felt a stab of disappointment at this: it would have made the perfect opening for him to see Mabel again, but he could see his mother's reasoning, and he was fairly sure that Mabel wouldn't be able to acquire the requisite template for the coat of arms. He transferred the card in its neat white envelope into his wallet and put it back in his pocket.

When William came to see them on his next night off, he was full of the news.

'It's a great step up for the family,' he said. 'Lady McFarlane's in her element. Once he's been introduced to the House, they're going to hold a huge reception.'

'That all sounds very exciting,' Alice remarked, as they sat down to supper.

'It's a step up for all of us,' William told her, 'in case we want to move on. To have worked in a baron's household.'

'But you don't want to move on, do you?' asked Alice. 'To work somewhere else, I mean? You seem suited where you are, and Mr Felstead must be nearly retiring, isn't he? You'd surely be in the running for his job.'

'Not sure I want to stay much longer with the McFarlanes, anyway,' William said carelessly, not catching Mabel's eye.

'Really?' persisted Alice. 'I thought you were happy there.'

'Sometimes it's good to move on with your life,' murmured Doreen Finch. 'Doesn't do to get in a rut. Now, I made an apple crumble for dessert. Can I tempt anyone?'

A chorus of 'yes please' ran round the table and William, thankful for the change of subject, smiled at her gratefully.

Later, when Mabel went with William to say good night at the front door, she felt a sudden flood of affection for him. Dear William, so steady, so reliable; she reached out and gave him a hug. Holding her close in his arms, William forced the letter addressed to Iain McFarlane to the back of his mind. It was stupid to be jealous of someone like Mr Iain. He may have been infatuated with Mabel months ago, but surely that was a thing of the past. He bent his head and kissed Mabel gently, brushing her lips with his own before reluctantly letting her go. She had said more than once that she wasn't ready for any commitment just yet. William knew Andrew and Alice would readily accept him as a son-in-law, but he also knew he had to be patient. Mabel was no ordinary girl, with no present ambition to secure a husband and start a family. William knew he might lose her altogether if he tried to alter the direction of her life before she was ready to do so of her own accord.

Later, sleepless, Mabel lay in bed trying not to think of Chas; William tossed and turned, unable to forget the letter addressed to Iain McFarlane in Mabel's distinctive handwriting; and Iain sighed at the missed opportunity to see Mabel just once more, to wish her luck.

Chapter Twenty-Eight

The date for Sir Keir's introduction to the House of Lords was set for Thursday 12th November. There had been some idea that it might be Friday 13th, but the date was moved back one day to the Thursday.

'Superstitious nonsense really, Mac,' Asquith said to him, 'but there are folk who are superstitious enough to be anxious. No point in upsetting them.'

Sir Keir agreed, saying of course he wasn't superstitious, but secretly pleased the date had been changed.

The day dawned blue-skyed, but sharp with an overnight frost. Sir Keir, leaving the house early to go to the House of Lords robing room, needed his overcoat, scarf and hat to brave the cold November morning.

'Good luck, my darling,' Isabella said, demonstrating an unusual burst of affection as she gave him a hug in the privacy of their bedroom. 'I know it will all go very well. You'll look truly noble in your robes, and we shall be so proud of you, watching from the gallery.'

'We've rehearsed it,' Keir reminded her. 'I know what I'm supposed to do... all I have to do is remember.'

'You will, Baron McFarlane of Haverford.'

They'd had their breakfast together in the morning room, though neither of them felt like eating, and then there was Croxton, waiting with the car outside the house.

Later, when he had returned to drive Isabella and Iain to Sloane Square to collect Lucinda and thence to the Houses of

Parliament, a pale winter sun was making a valiant effort to warm the air.

Both women had been to consult Madame Chantal about what they should wear, and were dressed as befitted ladies of the aristocracy. Bearing in mind the low temperature of a normal November day in London, a long, navy coat fitted at the waist was added to Isabella's heavy, navy silk day dress; her hat and gloves were a paler shade of blue, complementing her outfit perfectly.

Lucinda, under Madame Chantal's guidance, had chosen a more modern style, a close-fitting suit of pale green wool worn over a simple, high-necked, white silk blouse. Her burnished hair was swept high upon her head; her hat, Lucinda's particular delight, matched the dark green of her gloves and was set at a jaunty angle and topped with a single dark green feather. Her mother smiled with satisfaction when she saw her walk out of the house; Madame Chantal had surpassed herself.

Mother and daughter sat side by side in the back of the car, a fur blanket across their knees, while Iain rode in the front passenger seat next to Croxton. The big day had come: they were on their way to the House of Lords to watch husband and father become a peer of the realm. Such was the nervous tension in the car that for a while they drove in silence. It was unlike Lucinda to remain silent for any length of time and Isabella glanced across at her daughter. Despite the fur rug, she looked pale and cold.

'You look chilly, Lucinda,' she said. 'Perhaps you should have worn the mink tippet David gave you.'

'I'm perfectly comfortable, Mama,' maintained Lucinda, though in truth she wished she were more warmly dressed. 'I'm sure it will be warm when we get there.'

Croxton drew up opposite St Margaret's, Westminster, the choice for many society weddings. The three McFarlanes stepped out of the Rolls and, giving his mother his arm, Iain led the way through the Cromwell Green Entrance into the Palace of Westminster. They had arrived.

Once in the Central Lobby where Martin Mayhew, Sir Keir's junior, was supposed to meet them, they paused on the threshold to marvel at the opulence of their surroundings. None of them had been to the Houses of Parliament before; none of them quite expected the grandeur of the lobby with its heavily patterned floor, or its tall gothic windows, flanked by the statues of earlier sovereigns gazing down on the business of the twentieth century.

Moments later their attention was claimed by Martin Mayhew coming forward to greet them.

'Lady McFarlane, Lady Melcome, good day to you. Mr McFarlane, what an auspicious day.'

Isabella inclined her head and Lucinda briefly touched his hand with hers. Iain, who knew him well from his father's chambers, shook hands and said, 'Indeed it is, Mr Mayhew.'

'Lord McFarlane has asked me to conduct you to the public gallery, so, if you'd care to come this way…'

They followed Mayhew out of the Central Lobby, passing beneath an arch and along the beautifully decorated corridor leading to the Peers' Lobby. From there they could enter the House of Lords Chamber, the magnificent hall where the peers sat to conduct their business.

'It's this way, my lady.' Mayhew led them to a flight of stairs off the lobby and ushered them up to the gallery above. The view, when they emerged from the staircase, was enough to take their breath away. The entire Chamber below was lavishly decorated in red and gold.

'I doubt if there will be many in the gallery today,' Mayhew told them, 'so please, take the seats in the front row.'

Lady McFarlane descended the steps to the front, but Lucinda came to a standstill as she looked along the length of the Chamber to the Woolsack and the sovereign's throne at the far end. The view from that height made her feel suddenly giddy, she was unable to focus and, afraid she was going to fall, she caught hold of the nearest seat to steady herself, gripping it so tightly her knuckles showed white. Iain, right behind her, took her arm, murmuring, 'Are you all right, sis?'

'Yes, of course I am,' retorted Lucinda, though she still gripped the back of the seat. 'I simply stopped to look at the Chamber from here. You have to agree it is extremely impressive. All that red and gold.'

Neither Lady McFarlane nor Mayhew had seen Lucinda pause, so to her relief, there were no awkward questions.

She had woken that morning feeling tired and unrested, and had it not been the day of her father's introduction to the Lords, she might well have stayed in bed, but today was far too important to them all and she was determined not to spoil it. How could she stay at home and later say to her father that she'd been too tired to come? Dutifully she had eaten the poached egg Mrs Watson had prepared after she turned down the food that lay in the chafing dishes on the sideboard.

'I'm sorry, Mrs Watson,' she'd said. 'I'm not very hungry this morning.'

The housekeeper eyed her with interest and said, 'Then I shall poach you an egg, my lady. You can't go out on such an important day with nothing inside you.'

Lucinda had not wanted the egg either, but when it arrived, perfectly cooked on a piece of golden toast, she found she could eat it after all.

The food had given her the energy she needed to dress, and with Clara's help, she had been ready and waiting when Mama and Iain arrived in the Rolls to collect her.

Carefully now, she made her way down the steps and once she was seated beside her mother, the vertigo diminished. Feeling a little better, Lucinda began to take in her surroundings. Though they were seated at one end of the huge Chamber, they were directly opposite the throne, where, resplendent on its gilded dais, the king would sit for the state opening of Parliament. In front of this was the famous Woolsack, seat of the Lord Chancellor.

'Isn't this an amazing place, Mama?' Lucinda whispered. There was no one but Mayhew to hear her, but somehow she felt the Chamber demanded whispered respect. Her mother agreed, but immediately returned her attention to the floor of the house, scrutinising those peers already seated. Was there anyone she knew? She recognised several gentlemen and was pleased to see them there.

Iain, sitting on the other side of his mother, was also looking down at those assembled below, and thinking about his father, now Baron McFarlane of Haverford. Within the hour he would be an accepted part of the upper house, part of its history. This thought brought Iain to consider his own position: next in line. When, sometime in the future, his father passed away, the honour of being Baron McFarlane would be his and later his own son after him; part of this Chamber. His own son. That idea brought him up short. He had no son, no wife either for that matter. Now with a style and title to pass on perhaps he should be getting married. He was only twenty-three, so time was on his side. Briefly he thought of Mabel, but pushed her back into the recesses of his mind where she belonged.

He surveyed the hall, marvelling at its magnificent ceiling, at the stained-glass windows admitting patterned light from the winter sun. Beneath the windows another gallery ran the length of each wall and below this were the coats of arms of earlier sovereigns; a piece of history of which his father, he and his heirs were about to become an integral part. He wondered if his father were nervous, worried about the ceremony ahead of him. Surely not, not the guv'nor, so used to being centre stage at the Old Bailey.

Though he had remained in the gallery, Mayhew had not seated himself beside the family, it was not his place, but he had positioned himself in one of the smaller balconies to the side. Three other people had come into the gallery, two women who sat together at the back, and an elderly man who took a place in another of the side balconies, but none of them acknowledged the family already in the front row.

They sat and watched as the benches below them began to fill. Lucinda stared down at the men taking their seats, some on the government side of the house, others opposite and one or two gentlemen on the crossbenches, owing no allegiance to either. Their morning dress was a sort of uniform, irrespective of which side of the house they supported.

How I wish David could be here, Lucinda thought with a sigh, but his answer to her letter had been quite unequivocal.

My Darling Girl

What exciting news about your father. You must all be delighted that he has been recognised in this way. He will be an excellent addition to the House of Lords. It was a lovely idea that I should come home on leave and join in the celebrations, but I'm afraid it's absolutely impossible. The fighting here has been ongoing for days and no leave will be granted for the foreseeable future. I certainly couldn't ask at such a time. I will be thinking of you all and wishing I was with you. Don't be too disappointed that I can't be there.

Please give my congratulations to Baron McFarlane and my regards to her ladyship. I look forward to hearing all about it.

Keep your letters coming, Lucy, love of my life, they are what keep me going in this dreadful war.

David.

Lucy had this letter with her now, folded into her reticule, but it did little to ease the ache of his absence.

She was just wondering how much longer it would be before the proceedings began when the hum of conversation ceased, and the Lord Chancellor took his place on the Woolsack. In the ensuing silence, led by Black Rod and the Garter King of Arms, and accompanied by his two supporters, Baron Scott and Baron du Barry, her father entered the Chamber. All three of them, splendid in their parliamentary robes, approached the Lord Chancellor, and Sir Keir presented him with his writ of summons. At the table of the house, his letters patent were given to the Reading Clerk.

Isabella had her eyes fixed upon Sir Keir as he listened to these being read aloud to the House, conferring the Barony of Haverford on Keir McFarlane, his heirs.

Even as she stared down on the scene below, Lucinda felt her world began to spin just as it had earlier.

Don't you dare faint! she told herself firmly. You must not faint. Concentrate on what Papa is doing. You will not disgrace us all and faint!

She closed her eyes, but that only made the giddiness worse. Forcing them open again she tried again to concentrate on the reading, her father taking the oath of allegiance to the king, the signing of the Test Roll, but the Chamber continued to revolve about her and though she tried to focus, Lucinda knew she had lost the battle. Lady McFarlane, concentrating on her husband, was unaware Lucinda was in distress and it was only when she felt her daughter slump in her seat that she realised there was anything amiss. Turning to reprimand her, one look at Lucinda's ashen face told her that she had passed out and was about to slide onto the floor. It was only because she had slipped sideways against her mother that she had not already done so.

'Iain!' hissed his mother, supporting Lucinda as best she could. 'Help Lucinda! I can't move!'

A quick glance at his sister had Iain on his feet and at her side. Martin Mayhew, seeing what had happened, came quickly to his aid, and together the two men managed to lift the unconscious girl away from her mother's shoulder.

'Up the stairs,' Mayhew said to Iain. 'We need to get her out of the Chamber.'

It was not easy to carry Lucinda, still a dead weight, up the steps to the entrance of the gallery, but somehow they managed it.

'Where can we take her?' murmured Iain to Mayhew. 'She needs to lie down.'

'I think there's a powder room for the convenience of ladies a little further along,' replied Mayhew.

'But we can't go in there,' objected Iain, and glancing back down to the front of the gallery saw his mother still seated, watching his father make his bow to the Lord Chancellor. Surely she should come to Lucinda's aid. He wanted to call her but that would only draw unwelcome attention to Lucy's predicament.

It was the younger of the two ladies at the back of the gallery who now came forward and offered help.

'Is she all right? Can I help? I have Mama's smelling salts with me. If we take her to the powder room where she can lie down, they'll soon bring her round again.'

'You're very kind,' Mayhew said. 'It's this way.'

When they reached the powder room, the woman said, 'Just carry her inside, put her on the couch and I'll stay with her until you can get more help. There must be a doctor around here somewhere.'

Lucinda was laid gently on the chaise longue that stood against a wall, and Iain and Mayhew went in search of assistance. The good Samaritan produced the promised smelling salts and having wafted them under Lucinda's nose was relieved to see her charge was regaining consciousness. Lucinda tried to sit up, wondering where on earth she was and who this woman was. That lady rested a hand on her shoulder and said gently, 'Don't move, my dear. Not until you feel quite well again. I believe your brother has gone to fetch your mother.'

'But I must get up,' protested Lucinda. 'Papa...'

'Your father will understand when he hears you were unwell,' soothed the woman.

While Mayhew went in search of further help, Iain returned to his mother. 'Lucy's in the ladies' powder room,' he told her. 'She's being looked after by a stranger.' As he spoke, he glanced down at the floor of the Chamber and saw that his father had disappeared. 'Mama, Lucinda needs you.'

'I know,' sighed Isabella. 'I'm coming. Whatever is the matter with the child?'

'I don't know,' answered Iain, 'but she does look very pale.'

Having regained consciousness, Lucinda was anxious to get up, and when her mother arrived she tried again to sit up.

'Lucinda, what is the matter with you?' demanded Isabella. She turned to the woman who was holding Lucinda's hand. 'I thank you for your care...?' Her voice ended on a query, expecting the woman to give her name.

For a moment she did not, but then said, 'Diana Fosse-Bury.'

Isabella's eyes widened, but all she said was, 'You've been very kind, Miss Fosse-Bury. I think it's best if we get my daughter home as soon as possible.'

It wasn't an actual dismissal, but Lady Diana Fosse-Bury accepted it as such. She smiled down at Lucinda, propped up on the couch, and said, 'I hope you'll be better soon.'

Outside Iain was waiting to hear how his sister was faring.

'Don't worry about her,' Lady Diana said. 'She's still a bit shaky, but I expect she'll be back to herself directly.' She moved to rejoin her mother, who was still at the back of the gallery, but Iain put out his hand to stop her.

'It was kind of you to come to our rescue,' Iain said. 'I don't know what we'd have done if you hadn't been able to look after her in the powder room.'

'The lady's mother...?'

'My mother was watching my father being introduced to the

House as a new peer. She hadn't realised Lucinda had really been taken ill.'

At that moment Mayhew reappeared, bringing a man he introduced as Dr Brent, come, as he said, 'To take a look at the gel.'

Iain and Mayhew waited in the corridor while Dr Brent took Lucinda's pulse, listened to her heartbeat and peered into her eyes before announcing, 'Not much wrong with you, young lady. Nothing to worry about.'

Once he had pronounced her fit to travel home, they made their way down to the Central Lobby, where Lucinda and Isabella waited for Iain to summon Croxton.

'Why didn't you warn me you were feeling faint?' demanded Isabella.

'You were watching Papa,' replied Lucinda. 'I didn't want to disturb you.'

'Well, it was far more disturbing to have you faint on top of me,' retorted her mother. Then, in a more conciliatory tone, 'Has it happened to you before?'

'I've felt giddy several times recently, but I haven't actually fainted before.'

'Well, as soon as we get you home I shall send for Dr Tanner.'

'I don't need a doctor, Mama. I'm just a little tired, that's all...'

She didn't add, 'And I'm lonely, I miss David.' Her mother wouldn't understand.

'How can you be lonely?' her mother would have asked. 'You have invitations for every night of the week if you choose to accept them. Everything a young married girl could wish for.'

'Except my husband,' Lucinda would have replied.

But this exchange never took place. It wasn't the sort of conversation Lucinda and Isabella would ever have.

Chapter Twenty-Nine

Despite her mother suggesting she would be far better at Chanynge Place, Lucinda insisted on being taken home to Sloane Square.

'I shall be fine once I've had a rest,' she assured her. 'Mrs Watson and Clara can look after me perfectly well, and,' she went on, 'you're supposed to be meeting Papa for lunch.'

This did not stop Lady McFarlane from striding into the house and calling for Mrs Watson. 'Lady Melcome has had a fainting fit,' she announced, almost as if it was Mrs Watson's fault. 'She has refused to come home to Chanynge Place, so I am leaving her in your care. If there is any repetition of this, you must tell me and I shall ask Dr Tanner to call. He's known her from childhood.'

'I'm fine now, Mama,' insisted Lucinda. 'Give my love to Papa and tell him how splendid he looked.'

The relief Lucinda felt when her mother finally got back into the car was intense. She sank into an armchair and closed her eyes. Mrs Watson took one look at her wan face and said briskly, 'To bed with you, my lady. I'll send Clara up to you directly with a nice cup of tea.'

'I don't need the doctor,' Lucinda protested.

'No,' agreed Mrs Watson, 'not at the minute. Now, a letter came for you this morning after you'd gone. Watson put it in your parlour,' she added with a smile.

Lucinda needed no further incentive to go upstairs and, fatigue forgotten, moments later was opening David's letter.

Darling Lucy

I wonder if you will get this note before your father has been introduced into the House of Lords. I shall be thinking of you all on that day and can assure you I'd rather be there than here in what's turning into a sea of mud.

I can't wait to hear all about it. More in due course.

Miss you, Lucy-mine
All love, David xx

Mrs Watson was a practical person. She had noticed how peaky her young ladyship had been for the last week and had a clear idea of the cause. It was too early to make such suggestions to Lucinda herself – she could barely be eleven weeks along – but Mrs Watson was pretty sure young Lady Melcome was what polite society called *enceinte*. She was surprised Lady McFarlane hadn't noticed the signs.

It was Clara who finally spoke to Mrs Watson about her mistress's fatigue.

'I'm really worried about her ladyship,' she said when she had found Lucinda asleep over her luncheon. 'I'm sure she's expecting. It's not only that she's always tired, but she hasn't had her monthly since Sir David left. She ought to have had two, I reckon.'

Mrs Watson nodded. Clara would know, it was she who washed young Lady Melcome's more intimate garments. None of her delicate underwear would have been laundered by Mrs Drew, who came in twice a week to see to the household laundry.

'And I don't think she's realised,' Clara went on. 'I reckon these fainting fits is cos her corsets are laced too tight. It won't be long before she's at the stage where she needs to wear loose clothes, for decency's sake, as well as comfort.'

'I'm sure you're right, Clara,' agreed the housekeeper, 'I've been thinking the same thing. Perhaps we should mention something to her mother?'

'No,' answered Clara. 'It's not up to us to speak to her. It's her ladyship herself we should be talking to first. It's nobody's business but hers and Sir David's.'

'Yes, but he isn't here. I wish Lady Melcome Senior hadn't gone down to Crayne again. She'd know how to broach the subject.'

'I could tell her,' Clara said.

'Who? Lady Senior?'

'No, not her. I mean I could talk to her young ladyship about... you know...'

'You?' retorted Mrs Watson. 'It's not your place to discuss such things with your mistress unless she speaks of it first!'

'In the ordinary way, I'd agree,' replied Clara. 'But we have to face it, she's got no one else she can talk to, poor lady, and it's time she understood what's going on.'

'I hardly think you're the expert, Clara.' Mrs Watson's tone was chilly.

'I'm the eldest of five children, living in a small cottage. I do know how these things work,' Clara answered.

'I have no wish to hear of your family arrangements,' snapped Mrs Watson. She had no experience of pregnancy, never having had a child, but since she was unwilling to speak to young Lady Melcome on the subject herself, she simply shrugged and said, 'It's not up to you. I'm sure it won't be long before Lady McFarlane recognises the situation and takes over.'

Clara had a poor opinion of Lady McFarlane as a mother, but she made no comment. She knew that with all the excitement of Sir Keir's elevation and the banquet to celebrate it yet to come, Lady McFarlane was enjoying her new position in society, too wrapped up in herself to give thought to her daughter's health.

Warned off by Mrs Watson, Clara said nothing to Lucinda, until one morning, several days later, she found her mistress on her knees in the bathroom, being sick into the lavatory. Clara came to her aid at once, giving her a glass of water to rinse the foul taste from her mouth. She helped sponge Lucinda's face and wash her hands before leading her back to bed.

'It's so stupid of me,' Lucinda said, exhausted, as she lay back on her pillows. 'I'm never sick. It must be something I ate.'

'You just lie still and rest,' Clara said, 'and I'll bring you a nice cup of tea.'

When she returned with the tea tray, her mistress was still lying, just as she had left her, with her eyes closed.

Hearing Clara come into the room, Lucinda opened her eyes and said, 'I don't know what's the matter with me, Clara.'

It was the opening Clara had been waiting for. 'Let's sit you up so you can drink this tea, my lady, and you'll feel better. You ain't ill, I promise you.'

'How do you know? You're not a doctor.'

'No, my lady, but I can explain.'

Propped up on her pillows, Lucinda took a sip of her tea and it did make her feel better.

'Well,' she said. 'Explain.'

'I think you're in the family way.'

Lucinda set down the cup with a jolt and stared at her. 'I'm what?'

'You're going to have a baby, my lady.'

'But I can't be,' cried Lucinda. 'Sir David's not here.'

'You have all the symptoms. Very tired, feeling faint, being sick.'

'How do you know all this?' demanded Lucinda.

'How do you *not*?' would have been Clara's reply if she had dared. Instead she settled for, 'I seen my ma when she's been expecting. The same things.'

'I don't want to hear about your mother.'

'No, my lady. But it strikes me you're carrying a honeymoon baby, an heir for Sir David.' She waited for this to sink in before adding, 'You surely know babies take nine months to grow, don't you?'

'Of course,' retorted Lucinda, 'I'm not stupid!'

'Well, 'specially if it's a first baby, the mother doesn't always realise she's expecting.'

'A baby!' breathed Lucinda in wonder. 'How can I be sure?'

'Excuse me for asking, my lady, but when was your last monthly?'

For a moment Lucinda looked blank and then said, 'I don't know. In the summer. Mid-August?'

When Lucinda had started her monthlies last year, her mother had explained briefly that all women had them and they were necessary to conceive a child. Lucinda had found the whole subject embarrassingly awful. She didn't know why they were called 'monthlies' either; she certainly didn't have one every month, for which she was extremely grateful.

Did men know about them? she wondered. Did David know? She supposed he must.

Knowing exactly when Sir David had been with his wife, Clara did a quick calculation. 'Then I think your baby will be born next summer, in June.'

'Next June!' It seemed so long away.

When she was alone again, Lucinda lay on the bed, her hand resting on her stomach.

A baby! Here, inside *me*. Half me and half David! Perhaps he'd have David's beautiful navy blue eyes.

She did hope so.

She had sworn Clara to secrecy. She wanted David to be the first person to know. He'd want a boy, she supposed, and gave a thought to Muriel Frain, now stepmother to two little girls, with a husband expecting her to present him with an heir. Would David really mind if they had a daughter first?

Feeling much better later in the day, she was about to write to him to tell him he was going to be a father, when she was suddenly beset with doubts. Suppose Clara was wrong? It would be dreadful to tell David before she was certain.

When she awoke the next morning, she discovered her brain

had been working during the night and she had made a decision in her sleep. She would ask Dr Tanner to call at the house and she would consult him. As the doctor of her childhood, she knew him well and though Clara would have to remain in the room with them, she was comfortable in his presence.

His confirmation that she was indeed expecting a child delighted her, but she said, 'You won't tell Mama, will you? I so want my husband to be the first to know.'

'My dear Lady Melcome, I can assure you, any consultation I have with you will always be entirely confidential. Unless you choose to tell her, Lady McFarlane will not even know I have been to see you, let alone the reason.'

The moment the doctor left, Lucinda went into her parlour to write to David.

David, dearest David.

I can't wait to tell you! Dr Tanner has just left and he has confirmed what I'd begun to suspect. You're going to be a father! What I'm told is called a 'Honeymoon Baby'! He'll be born in June. I say 'he' because I expect you'd like a son and heir first, but I know you'll be as excited as I am.

Clara knows of course, because she's seen me being sick in the mornings. I'm glad you haven't; it's not a pretty sight. I'm sure Mrs Watson has guessed as well. Difficult to keep such a thing secret, living in the same house. Your mother is away at Crayne at present, but I'll let her into the secret when she comes back before Christmas, unless of course you want to write to tell her yourself. I think you should. My parents are still celebrating my father's peerage, but when things have calmed down a bit, I'll tell them too. There's the banquet at the Waldorf still to come. I just hope I shall be feeling less tired that evening. I nearly disgraced myself at the House of Lords when I fainted and would hate to do something like that at the Waldorf, with so many important people there. Perhaps I won't go!

I'm going to post this letter straight away so you have the news as quickly as I can get it to you.

Darling David, a bit of you and a bit of me, mixed together into a new person. Goodness knows what he will turn out like!

All my love, Lucy.

Chapter Thirty

Mabel was at work, setting type in the print room, when there was a knock on the door. She wasn't expecting anyone so she set aside her tray and went to see. And there he was. Chas Sheridan, smiling his lopsided smile. For a moment she almost slammed the door again, but he was too quick for her.

'Mabel,' he said, 'I've got a message from Mr Morrell.'

'Have you?' She didn't sound particularly interested, but she held out her hand. 'Then you'd better give it here.'

'Mabel, I'm so sorry.'

'Sorry? What for?'

'Not meeting you at Rosie's.'

Mabel gave a brief laugh, 'Oh that! Doesn't matter, I didn't really expect you. What's the message from Mr Morrell?'

'Mabel, can I come in?'

'Come in? Why?'

'Because I have a message for you and it's very cold standing on your doorstep.'

'I'm working,' Mabel said, still blocking his way.

'And I won't keep you long.'

Reluctantly she moved aside and he stepped into the room. Looking round, he could see that though he was definitely in a workshop and not an office, it belonged to someone organised with a tidy mind; everything had its place, ready for use.

'Well?' Mabel wasted no time. 'What's the message?'

On his way over, Chas had thought about what he would say. 'He wants some headed notepaper for the firm.'

'Headed paper? Surely he has plenty of that. Any letter that comes from him is always on the firm's headed paper.' She glared at him. 'I don't think you've come from Mr Morrell, at all.'

Chas had the grace to look embarrassed. 'Well, I have and I haven't. He's back in the office now and he would like to see you if you can spare the time. Nothing urgent, he said, but something he'd like to discuss with you. It was me that thought of the headed paper. I think what we have is a bit old-fashioned and you could produce something in a more modern style.'

'Oh come on, Chas,' Mabel said half laughing and still angry. 'I told you about your father and my family. He wouldn't come within a mile of me and my business. What do you really want?'

'To say I'm so sorry I got chickenpox and I promise I won't do it again.' His words came out in a rush, but there was a gleam of amusement in his eye.

'Chickenpox! Chas, what are you talking about?'

'Not being there to meet you at Rosie's that Monday. I was coming, of course I was, but my father suddenly sent me on an errand to Finchley and I wasn't back in time. When I got there the teashop was closed and Rosie had gone. I did wait round for a while in case you'd been delayed as well, but no luck.'

'Chickenpox?' prompted Mabel, sounding sceptical.

'That evening I began to feel ill. I thought I was just tired, but by the morning I was feverish, with a pounding headache and no energy. I couldn't even get out of bed. Then a rash appeared and I was covered in spots. My mother was terrified it might be smallpox and she sent for the doctor.'

Mabel blanched. 'But it wasn't, was it?'

'No, Dr Sanders said it was chickenpox, but a nasty dose. He said it's often far worse in adults than it is in children.'

'But where did you catch it?'

Chas shrugged. 'Don't know. Could have been anywhere, the doctor said. He says there's a lot of it about just now, and I was to stay in quarantine.'

'And that's where you've been all this time?'

'Yes, just allowed back to the office today. I was going to write to you, but I'd have had to ask someone to post the letter and after what you had told me, I didn't want anyone at home seeing your name and asking questions; you're my secret. Anyway,' he went on, 'I'm quite better now, I promise you, so you won't catch it from me.'

'I certainly won't,' agreed Mabel. 'Because I shan't be anywhere near you.'

'Oh come on Mabel, I didn't stand you up on purpose.' He glanced at his watch and said, 'I'd better get going, I have got other messages to deliver. I'm quicker around London than the post and I can sometimes bring back a reply.'

He crossed to the door and then turned back and smiled. 'See you next Monday,' he said. 'At about four, but don't worry if you get held up. I'll wait.'

'You might be waiting a long time,' replied Mabel.

'Worth the risk,' said Chas, and with that he was gone.

She heard his footsteps on the gravel path and then silence. Closing the door carefully, she went and curled up in Mr Clarke's chair. The typesetting could wait. The workshop seemed suddenly empty and a little cold, as if Chas had taken his warmth with him. She thought of putting the kettle on, but a solitary cup of tea wasn't that appealing and so she locked the door and climbed the outside stairs to join her parents for elevenses.

'Had a visitor, did you?' asked Doreen, when she came in to join them. 'Thought I saw some bloke outside.'

About to deny it and then realising her mother might have seen Chas, too, she said, 'Mr Morrell's articled clerk. Came with a message asking me to drop in and see Mr Morrell when I'm able. You remember I told you he'd been taken ill? Well, he's back in the office now.' She turned to Doreen. 'He may have some more information about you being evicted, Doreen.'

'I don't have to come there again, do I?' Doreen asked anxiously.

'No,' Mabel reassured her. 'I'll go and see what he wants. Don't worry, it might be something completely different.'

The following day Mabel went to St John's Square to see Hugh Morrell. He was sitting at his desk when she was shown in by Miss Harper.

'Miss Oakley, Mr Morrell. She says you asked her to call in to see you.'

'Indeed I did, Miss Harper. Come in, Mabel.' For a moment the secretary stood, tight-lipped, by the door. As if surprised to see her still there, Mr Morrell said dismissively, 'That'll be all. Thank you, Miss Harper.'

Mabel knew that her trustee had not been well, but she was shaken by how ill he looked now. He had never been a large man, but the weight had fallen off him and the skin of his face and neck, now far too large for him, was the colour of parchment.

'Come and sit down, my dear,' he said, waving her to the chair opposite his desk. 'I apologise for not getting up, but I find I have little energy these days.'

Mabel sat down, and hardly knowing what to say, managed, 'Good morning, Mr Morrell. It's good to see you back in the office.'

'But not for long, I'm afraid,' he replied with a wry smile. 'I shall be retiring as a partner in this firm at the end of the month, and I wanted to talk to you about your trust fund. It wouldn't be right for me to remain as one of your trustees when the trust has several years to run, with no provision made for a replacement. Of course your father will remain as one trustee, but I think Mr Clarke wanted you to have legal advice easily available, and so I'm going to suggest that my place is taken by my partner, John Sheridan.'

'Mr Sheridan!' Mabel looked at him in horror. 'Oh no! That's impossible. My father couldn't possibly work with him.'

Hugh Morrell was taken aback by her outburst. 'I believe there was some difficulty between them some time ago, but surely they can work together if it is to look after your interests.'

'No.' Mabel spoke firmly. 'No they couldn't, and I couldn't ask my father even to try.'

'Well, I shall have to be replaced. The idea of two trustees is to have a check and balance in the administration of the trust.'

'I know that,' Mabel said. 'Mr Clarke said as much in the letter he left me...'

'Well, there you are then,' said Mr Morrell.

'But he knew the situation between my father and Mr Sheridan. He would never have asked them to work together. Can't you stay on as my trustee? Surely there's no reason for you to stand down, just because you've retired from the firm, is there?'

'There is, because I know I'm not long for this world.' He smiled at her and added, 'You are an intelligent woman, Mabel, and I think you can see that for yourself.'

'Yes,' she admitted, 'I can.'

'Well done,' he said. 'Honest as ever. You've always been straightforward in your dealings.'

'Mr Morrell, please can I be straightforward with you now?' she asked gently.

'Why not,' he replied, 'we both know the score.'

'What would happen if you didn't stand down?'

'I would continue to act as your trustee, but your father would be left on his own when I was no longer there.'

'Can't we do it that way?' pleaded Mabel. 'You just called me a woman, and that's what I am, but Mr Sheridan regards me as a girl, who doesn't know what she's doing. He would never have let me continue running Mr Clarke's printing business on my own. If he had been named as the other trustee instead of you, he and my father would have disagreed on every decision. Is it legal to have only one trustee? If my father was the only one, could he allow me to use my trust money if I asked?'

'Technically, the trust was set up to be administered by two people.'

'Mr Morrell, to put it bluntly, my father and Mr Sheridan actively dislike each other. If they were made joint trustees as you suggest, it would be setting the trust up to fail, and unless I got married, I would have to wait until I'm twenty-one to have access to my own money.'

Hugh Morrell sighed. He knew his partner well enough to know that he could be difficult to work with. If he and Mabel's father disagreed over the administration of the trust it would make Mabel's life impossible. He'd known there was some history between the two men, but he hadn't realised the depth of the antipathy.

'Please, Mr Morrell, couldn't you reconsider?'

'If the situation is as you describe it, Mabel, well, I'll think about it.'

'Thank you, oh, thank you,' Mabel said fervently.

'I'll sleep on it,' said the old man, 'but I make no promises.'

Chapter Thirty-One

The following Monday, Mabel followed her normal routine, visiting her most important clients. There was no message from Mr Morrell and nothing further from Chas. As morning became afternoon, she had still not made up her mind whether or not to go to Rosie's to meet him; one minute she was going to and the next, not. She had to admit she did want to see Chas again, and after all, he had not caught chickenpox on purpose. She had been angry with him for long enough. Finally, she made up her mind. She would go as soon as she'd tidied up in the workshop. She never left it untidy, even if she were in the middle of a job: Mr Clarke never had so she wouldn't either.

As she wheeled her bike up the path to the side gate, she heard someone knocking on the front door, no not knocking, banging with all their might. Mabel came out into the street to find a young woman standing on the step with a suitcase at her feet. Mabel was about to ask who she was and what she wanted, when the front door opened and Doreen Finch appeared.

Her eyes widened when she saw it was her daughter, Mavis.

'Mavis? What's happened? Are you all right?'

At which the young woman cried, 'Mum!' and burst into tears.

Clearly things were not all right, as Mabel saw when Mavis turned her head, revealing dried blood from a cut on her left cheek and a bruise turning her right eye purple.

Seeing Mabel at the gate Doreen said, 'Oh, Mabel, this is my daughter, Mavis. May I bring her into the house?'

'Of course you can,' Mabel said at once. 'I'll just put my

bike away.' She pushed her bike back behind the side gate and followed Mavis indoors.

'Shall we all go into the kitchen?' she suggested, closing the front door behind them. 'It looks as if Mavis could do with a cuppa and some first aid.'

Doreen had been on the point of ushering Mavis upstairs to her own rooms, but now she hesitated. Clearly Mavis's face needed attention, and she could only assume it was Sidney who had inflicted the damage. She would have liked to talk to Mavis alone first, but Mabel took things into her own hands and said, 'It's through this way, Mavis.'

In the kitchen Alice was preparing some vegetables for their evening meal. She glanced up as they came in and, seeing Mavis's face, she cried, 'Oh my goodness! Have you been in an accident? Come and sit down.'

'This is my daughter, Mavis,' Doreen said. 'Mavis, this is Mrs Oakley.'

Mabel put the kettle on and Alice took down the first aid box she kept on a shelf.

'Come along now, Mavis, dry your tears,' said her mother, and pulling a clean hankie out of her sleeve, she passed it across.

Mavis made an effort to blow her nose, but the wound on her cheek, which had already crusted over, broke open and began to bleed again. While Mabel made the tea, Alice and Doreen got a bowl of warm water and bathed the cut with cotton wool and then attended to the bruise with witch hazel.

'Now, then,' Doreen said, as Mabel handed them their tea, 'what's happened? Did Sidney do this?'

'Yes, this morning. I ain't going back to him, Mum, an' you can't make me.'

'Does he know where you are?'

'No, and he don't care.'

'But did you have a fight? Why did he hit you? What had you done?'

'I hadn't done nothing,' Mavis cried. 'I had his breakfast ready when he come in after the morning local train. Porridge. I'd made it good and thick to warm him up, but he come in later than usual and when I dished it up, he said it were cold. Said he weren't going to eat cold sludge, an' he wanted bacon and eggs. An' I told him he'd have to put up with it cos I ain't got no eggs or bacon till I went to the grocer's later and that's when he grabbed me and shook me till I was getting giddy. I tried to pull free, screaming at him to remember the baby, not to hurt the baby and that's when he backhanded me. He was shouting that I was a slut who didn't look after him properly and he didn't want the baby. So, I've left.'

'But didn't he try and stop you?' asked Doreen.

'He goes down the pub most lunchtimes when there ain't no branch-line trains due. So I just packed my case and walked back up the line to the mainline station and caught the next London train. All he wanted was a housekeeper, to look after him,' she said bleakly. 'He don't want the baby, he said it was a mistake an' I should have been more careful... as if it was my fault. Anyhow, I've left him and I ain't going back, so I've come to you, Mum. I ain't got nowhere else to go.'

If the irony of this statement was lost on Mavis, it wasn't on Doreen. When she had gone to Mavis for help, she had come away empty handed. However, she wasn't to going to do the same to her daughter or, more important, her grandchild.

Alice and Mabel had been listening in dismay to Mavis's dismal tale, and when she made her final remark, it was Mabel who came to her rescue.

'I suppose you could stay here,' Mabel said and turning to her mother she asked, 'What do you think, Mam?'

Used to her daughter's spontaneous generosity Alice said cautiously, 'It'll be very close quarters, but if it's only temporary, I suppose it'd be all right.'

'Well, Stephen won't be coming home to sleep much, will he? Mavis could have his room until all this is sorted out.'

'You said he doesn't know where you've gone.' Alice turned to Mavis. 'Won't he guess that you'll go to your mother?'

'Maybe,' Mavis conceded, 'but he's only known the Noah's Path address, not this one. She did let me know where she'd moved to, but I never told him about it.'

'As long as he doesn't know where you've gone,' Mabel said, 'you can stay here for a while. If Stephen needs to come home while you're here, you'll have to move up to Doreen's rooms. Mam's right, it will be a bit close quarters, but we'll find you a mattress to sleep on and at least you'll have a roof over your head. That'll be all right, won't it, Mam?'

Put on the spot, Alice agreed, reluctantly, that she thought it would, but only for a short while. 'As long as your father agrees.'

At that moment Andrew, who had been having his afternoon nap, called from the bedroom and Doreen went to him. By the time he came into the kitchen, it was all agreed.

'Why don't you show Mavis Stephen's room, Mabel,' suggested her mother. 'The bed's always made up ready, so you'll just have to find her a towel.'

While the two young women went upstairs, Alice and Doreen put Andrew in the picture.

'I knew he was a bad lot,' Doreen said. 'But they won't be told, will they, these young girls?' She didn't wait for confirmation, but went on, 'They always know best.'

'The problem is going to be space,' Andrew pointed out. 'It is going to have to be a short-term solution, because I'm not sure we could accommodate a baby here for more than a few days.'

'As to that,' Doreen responded, 'the wee mite isn't due for another four months, and we shall be long gone by then.'

'The trouble is,' Alice said to Andrew later, 'it's Mabel's house, so ultimately she has the final say.'

When Mabel and Mavis came back down, Mabel caught sight of the kitchen clock.

The hands were showing five minutes past four. Mabel stared

at it in horror. Having made the decision that she would go and have tea with Chas, she suddenly realised that if she didn't hurry, she might miss him: her fault this time. Promising to be back before in time for supper, she ran down the front steps, grabbed her bike and set off as fast as she could pedal.

St James's clock had just finished chiming the half hour as she arrived outside the café. Leaning her bike against the lamp post, she peered in through the steamed-up window. No Chas.

Well, she decided, that was it. Though he said he'd wait if she was late, Chas must already have given up. She turned back to pick up her bike and walked straight into Chas's arms.

'You're late,' he scolded, as he released her. 'What's your excuse? Have you got chickenpox?'

'No,' she said, giving him a warning look.

Chas laughed. 'Just decided to make me wait.'

'Not at all,' replied Mabel hotly. 'I was just leaving and...'

'Tell me over the tea and cakes,' Chas interrupted taking her hand, 'where it's nice and warm. Otherwise Rosie might think she hasn't any more customers and close up early again.'

The teashop was pleasantly warm after the raw winter air outside, and this time they didn't sit at the window table, but at a smaller table in the corner beside the fire. Once they were settled, Rosie herself came over to take their order.

'Your usual?' she asked with a twinkle in her eye.

As they drank their tea and ate their cake, Mabel told Chas about Mrs Finch's daughter appearing on their doorstep. Not the story of her hurried departure from her marital home, that was too personal, but said that she had arrived unexpectedly and was hoping to spend a few days with her mother.

Chas brought news from Sheridan, Sheridan and Morrell.

'Mr Morrell's still coming into the office each day but only for a couple hours in the morning. He's determined to clear his desk before he actually retires,' Chas said, 'but it really does exhaust him. Miss Harper fusses about him, always telling him what he should and shouldn't be doing, which doesn't help. I don't know why she does it, she's an interfering busybody, always poking her nose where it isn't wanted.'

While Chas was talking, Mabel considered telling him about the question of a replacement trustee, but decided against it. Much as she disliked John Sheridan, he was Chas's father and she knew if it was her own father who was being criticised, rightly or wrongly, she would be resentful and stand up for him. No point in upsetting Chas for no reason.

Dusk was beginning to fall outside and Rosie was clearing the last tables, encouraging them to finish their tea, pay up and go home.

'I must go,' Mabel said suddenly.

'Well, let's unlock your bike and then I'll walk you back.'

'But the station is in the other direction,' Mabel pointed out.

'So it is,' agreed Chas, 'but it'll still be there when I've escorted you safely to your front door. You shouldn't be out alone when it's getting dark.'

'Very spooky,' Mabel said, 'but you don't scare me. I often walk home by myself at this time of night.'

'That's fine if you have to,' agreed Chas, 'but tonight you don't; tonight I shall be your squire.'

It took them nearly half an hour to walk back to Barnbury Street, by which time the street lamps had been lit. When Mabel pushed her bicycle in through the side gate, Chas stepped through behind her. As the gate swung shut, he put his arms round her and held her close against him. Mabel could feel the warmth of his breath on her cheek and felt her own body relax against his.

'Have you forgiven me for catching chickenpox?' he murmured into her hair.

'No,' she replied, as she raised her face to his.

Chapter Thirty-Two

John Sheridan had left the office early that Monday evening. He had an appointment with an elderly lady who was rewriting her will. It was something she did on a regular basis and he knew he would not be back in the office that evening.

'I shall go straight home from Miss Sparrow's,' he told Miss Harper. 'If you'll just lock up when everyone else goes, I'll see you in the morning.'

'Of course, Mr Sheridan,' replied his secretary. 'Good night, sir.'

Once all the staff had left for the evening, Miss Harper made her usual tour of the office. She always liked having the place to herself, looking in the various offices.

Not snooping, she told herself, simply checking to be sure there were no important documents left out. This evening there was nothing to find, not even in Mr Morrell's office and so, reluctantly, she closed up and stepped out into the square to walk the half mile to her small flat. As she passed St James's Church, she paused to check her watch and then as she turned away, she saw two people coming out of a teashop, a man and a woman. There was something familiar about the man, and in the light from the café's window, she suddenly realised it was Mr Sheridan's son, Charles. What was he doing in a teashop with a young woman? She stepped back into the shelter of a shop doorway and watched. At first she didn't recognise his companion, the young woman unlocking a bicycle, but as she glanced up at Mr Charles and the light from the tea room caught her face, Miss Harper was amazed to see that it was that tiresome young woman, Mabel Oakley. What was she doing coming out of a teashop with young Mr Charles? Indeed, what was either of them doing, coming out of a teashop? She remembered that Mr Charles had left the office early, saying he had an errand to run for Mr Morrell. Clearly a lie, thought Miss Harper as, from the shadow of her doorway, she watched them walking down the street together, clearly on good terms. The girl was pushing her bicycle, but Mr Charles had his arm though hers. Definitely on friendly terms.

What'll Mr Sheridan have to say about this when I tell him? she wondered.

And tell him she would; it was her duty. Mr Charles might be the senior partner's son, but he was also the most junior clerk in the office and he had no right to tell lies and leave the office early, to go into teashops with a young woman. A most unsuitable young woman at that and one of Mr Morrell's clients into the bargain, it was most unprofessional. Miss Harper knew all Mr Sheridan's dealings with the Oakleys were difficult and had been since the day the clerk Andrew Oakley was sacked. Mr Sheridan certainly wouldn't want his son mixed up with a family like that.

Full of righteous indignation on her boss's behalf, Miss Harper went home. She would get in early herself tomorrow, so that she could speak to Mr Sheridan the moment he arrived; she spent the evening planning exactly what she was going to say.

The telephone in Miss Harper's office was ringing as she climbed the stairs the next morning. It was not yet half past eight, the official office opening time. At first she thought the caller could wait until office hours, but as it was still ringing when she reached her desk, she decided she'd better answer. Whoever it was seemed determined to speak to someone.

Miss Harper snatched the receiver from its stand and answered in her trilling telephone voice, 'Good morning! Sheridan and Morrell.' She had long since dispensed with the second 'Sheridan' and if Mr Sheridan had noticed, he didn't seem to care.

'Ah, Miss Harper, glad I caught you.'

Miss Harper sighed. She knew that voice all too well. 'Good morning, sir.'

'Good morning. Is Charles in the office?'

'Not yet,' Miss Harper replied. 'But I'm sure he won't be long.'

'I shan't be in, today,' said Mr Morrell, 'but please ask Charles to come and see me as soon as he gets in, will you?'

Charles Sheridan arrived less than five minutes later. Miss Harper heard him go into the office he shared with Arthur Bevis, but she did not pass the message on straight away. There was another ten minutes until half past eight, and she busied herself tidying her already tidy desk. On the dot of the half hour, she crossed the corridor to the clerks' office. Bevis was not in yet, a fact which didn't surprise her but of which she made a mental note for another day.

She walked into the office unannounced, to find Mr Charles sitting at his desk reading through some paperwork. He looked up as she came in and gave her a brief 'good morning'.

She did not return the greeting, but said with a glance at her wrist watch, 'Mr Morrell telephoned just now asking for you. I told him you weren't in the office yet.'

Charles's expression stiffened to a frown, so reminiscent of his father, that Miss Harper hurried on, 'He asked that you go and see him as soon as you arrived.'

'Thank you, Miss Harper, I'll just collect some papers which I think he might need and go at once.'

'He didn't *say* anything about papers,' sniffed Miss Harper.

'Nevertheless,' Charles replied as he got to his feet, 'I shall take them with me.'

There was no sign of the deference Miss Harper felt was due, and with tightened lips, she turned on her heel and went back to her office.

Just you wait until your father comes in, she thought with fierce satisfaction. When he hears who you've been associating with, he'll cut you down to size. You won't be so arrogant then!

At that moment the telephone rang again. This time, although it was a voice she knew, she was surprised to hear it.

'Miss Harper? This is Mrs Sheridan. I'm just telephoning to let you know that my husband won't be in the office today. He's unwell. He's asked me to let you know, and asks that you cancel his appointments for the rest of the week.'

When she put the receiver down, Miss Harper sighed. Her news about Charles and that Mabel Oakley girl would have to wait.

Once she had cancelled her boss's appointments, she checked on the two typists in their cupboard of an office to make sure they were getting on with their work, before making herself a cup of tea and taking it into her own office. There were things she could be doing, but none of them was urgent, so with neither partner in the building, she could afford to relax a little.

She considered tackling Charles herself, threatening to tell his father what she had seen, but if she spoke to him before speaking to his father, the element of surprise would be lost and young Mr Charles would have time to dream up some explanation. On balance, she decided, it would be better to wait.

She finished her tea and turned to her typewriter and the documents Mr Sheridan had dictated before leaving the office the previous afternoon. They would be ready for his scrutiny when he came back next week.

Charles had no idea if Mr Morrell wanted the file he'd been working on or not, but he wasn't prepared to knuckle down to Horrible Hermione. What a poisonous woman she was! He didn't know how his father put up with her. All right, she'd been his grandfather's secretary when he was senior partner, but that didn't justify her self-importance.

Thank goodness she'll be dead and buried before I get to be senior partner, he thought... if I ever do!

When he reached Hugh Morrell's house the door was opened by Mrs Parsons.

'Oh, Mr Charles,' she cried, the relief at his arrival clear on her face. 'Thank goodness you've come. Mr Morrell is in bed and he's been so anxious to see you.' She led the way upstairs to Mr Morrell's bedroom.

'Mr Charles to see you, sir.'

Charles paused in the doorway. The room smelled of sickness, a musty smell made worse by windows closed against the dank winter air.

The solicitor, propped up with pillows in an old-fashioned bed and looking even smaller and more frail than before, greeted Charles with a weak smile. 'Charles, my boy, come in, come in.'

Charles proffered the two folders he had brought from the office. 'These are the two cases you were working on when you were last in the office,' he said. 'I thought you might need them here.'

'And so I might,' agreed Mr Morrell, 'but first things first. Mrs Parsons, please will you bring a fresh pot of tea and then I'll need you both to witness my signature on a document.'

The housekeeper bustled away to make the tea. Mr Morrell had woken in some agitation this morning and insisted that Charles should be sent for. He had struggled downstairs to make the call himself, and when he'd rung off, it had been a worse struggle getting him upstairs and back into bed. He had lain exhausted, his breathing ragged and his eyes closed. She had waited on the landing, listening until he seemed to be asleep, and then hurried down to the kitchen, where she heated some beef broth and made him some toast. The old man thanked her but he had only taken two bites of the toast and the broth had cooled in the bowl on his bedside table.

Now she soon returned with the tea and some slices of her homemade fruit cake on a tray. She knew that Mr Morrell wouldn't eat the cake, but Mr Charles might and it seemed a pity to waste it.

'Don't go, Mrs Parsons,' Hugh Morrell said as she turned back towards the door. 'I need you for a moment.' He told Charles to bring him a folder from the chest of drawers and suggested they might use the tray to lean on. Extracting a sheet of paper from the folder, he laid it on the tray, covering most of it with another blank sheet of paper, leaving only the signature lines visible.

'I'm just going to sign and date this document,' he said, 'and I'd be grateful if the two of you would witness my signature.' Picking up a fountain pen from his bedside table he scrawled his signature, wrote the date and then printed his name underneath.

'Now if you two would do the same.' Seeing that Mrs Parsons looked uncertain, he handed the pen to Charles and said, 'You first, Charles.' Charles did as he was asked, before passing the pen to the housekeeper. 'Just the same,' instructed Mr Morrell.

When it was done, and the ink carefully blotted, he picked up the document and slid it into an envelope, which he sealed and placed in the folder from which he'd taken it.

'I'll keep it in the top drawer of the chest, for now,' he said. 'It'll be safe there.' And exhausted by his efforts, he closed his eyes.

Mrs Parsons disappeared as soon as she'd signed the document, but Charles waited for several long moments, listening to Mr Morrell's regular breathing. When he was sure the old man was asleep, he left the room, closing the door quietly behind him. Downstairs he found Mrs Parsons busy in the kitchen.

'I'm so glad you came,' she said. 'He'll rest more easy now he's signed whatever it was. I know he thinks well of you, Mr Charles. He trusts you.'

'He and my father have been partners for years, so he's known me since I was a child,' Charles said. 'Anyway, he's asleep now, so I'll be getting back. If he needs me again, just ring the office and I'll come straight away.'

Chapter Thirty-Three

As had happened once before, Lucinda received two letters from David on the same day. Delighted, she carried them to her parlour where she could enjoy reading them undisturbed. Looking at the post marks she opened them in date order.

Darling Lucy

What absolutely wonderful news! I couldn't be more thrilled to think that we shall soon be a family of three! Aren't you a clever girl! If the baby isn't due until June, depending on what's going on over here, I might possibly be able to get some leave and come home to be with you at Crayne when he's born. Well, I don't expect they'll let me actually be with you, but I shall pace up and down the landing while you do the hard work. Tough being a father! Never mind, there will be armies of people looking after you and you must take great care of yourself in the meanwhile. It will be wonderful to have another Melcome baby born at Crayne. Imagine! I was the last one. Never mind if he turns out to be a she, as long as she's as beautiful as her mother.

Longer letter when more time. Boche are keeping us busy just now!

All my love to you both... wish I could deliver the kisses myself.

Proud father David.
X X

David's delight at her news poured off the page. Lucinda could hear his voice in every word. Did all new parents feel like this? she wondered, as she kissed the kisses at the bottom of the letter. She slid it back into its envelope and turned her attention to the second letter.

It couldn't have been more different. It was scrawled in pencil on a piece of lined paper torn from a notebook and was dated just six days later.

Dear Lucy

Bad news. Fenton has been wounded, a nasty shoulder wound from flying shrapnel. He's lucky to be alive. He's been patched up in the hospital in Étaples but with so many wounded coming in, he's being shipped back to England. Not sure which hospital he'll be sent to, but will try and find out. I've heard most of the wounded are sent to Netley hospital near Southampton to begin with. He's a single man with no family to return to. Please can you find him and visit him in the hospital and see what can be done? Netley sounds a likely place so perhaps that is where to start looking.

Leslie Fenton, Corporal 4837 1st (King's) Dragoon Guards

I know you'll do your best.

Bless you my darling,
David.

Lucy read the letter through twice. Fenton badly wounded. Her first thought was that it could have been David. Fenton wouldn't have been far from David in the heat of battle; an exploding shell could have killed them both. Though they were officer and man, they had fought side by side in India, and there was a stronger bond than that of master and servant between them. Lucy had met Fenton only once and found him rather gruff. A no-nonsense man who knew what was expected of him, he was the perfect match for David, who always treated those who served him with fairness and respect. Of course she would go and visit Fenton in hospital if David wanted her to, but first she had to find him.

She decided the person to talk to was Iain. He would know how to discover the whereabouts of a repatriated soldier, and if he didn't, he would know who to ask. She called at Chanynge Place the next evening and found him about to go out.

'I need to pick your brain, Iain,' she said.

'My brain?' Iain laughed. 'Not sure how far that will get you.'

Lucinda explained her mission. 'David is keen for me to find Fenton, but really I don't even know how to set about it.' She handed him David's letter.

'Well,' he said when he had read it through, 'I suppose the best place to start is this Netley hospital place David mentions. I'll see what I can find out about it. Gerry Bloom might know. He's working in the War Office at present.'

'And if Fenton might be there, we could go and find out, couldn't we? You could come with me.'

Iain sighed. 'I expect so. Let's wait and see what Gerry says.'

Despite his apparent reluctance, Iain realised how important it was to Lucy to find Fenton for David, and the following morning, he told Martin Mayhew he was dealing with some private family business and might be out until noon. Mayhew accepted this without question, assuming it was business for Lord McFarlane, and Iain left Lincoln's Inn and headed for Horse Guards Avenue and the War Office. Arriving outside the building and being allowed entry were two very different things and it was nearly an hour before he was finally admitted to Gerry Bloom's box room of an office. Even then he had to wait at the door, for Gerry himself to approve his identity.

'Mac!' Gerry exclaimed as he rose to shake hands. 'What brings you here? No, wait a minute,' he spoke to the secretary who had escorted Iain through the building. 'Any chance you could rustle up some tea, Miss Perks?'

Miss Perks turned a deep shade of pink and replied that she thought she could and disappeared.

Gerry waved Iain to the only other chair in the room. 'Good to see you, Mac,' he said. 'Great news about your father's elevation to the Lords, and how's the married Lucy?'

'She's well,' Iain replied, 'and she's the reason I'm here.'

'Lucy is? What's she got to do with the War Office?'

'Not her exactly. It's about her husband, Sir David Melcome. His servant, Fenton, was wounded in the recent fighting round Ypres and has been shipped back to a hospital here at home, perhaps Netley? David's keen for Lucy to find him and visit him in the hospital. He's no family of his own, apparently, and David wants to be certain he wants for nothing.'

'Very commendable,' remarked Gerry, 'but not sure why you've come to me, old boy. I deal with outward armaments, nothing to do with the placement of the wounded, you know.'

'Yes... no. We didn't know what you did, but we hoped you would know someone who might be able to help us.'

'You say Lucy's husband thinks he might have been sent to Netley. Well, he could be. I do know that it's the largest military hospital in the country. It was built half a century ago and many of the wounded from the Boer war were brought there, so its reputation as a military hospital goes back a long way.'

'But now?' prompted Iain.

'Well, same again. Being not far from Southampton, the wounded brought home from France in the hospital ships can be landed there and taken by train to Netley. It's easier to sort the men out this side of the Channel. It also ensures all the names of the wounded are recorded.'

'So, if Lucy and I went down to this hospital, they would be able to tell us if Fenton was there, or, if he had been moved on, where he had been sent?'

Gerry looked doubtful. 'I suppose so, but really Mac, it ain't a place you should be taking a girl like your sister. Never been in one of these hospitals myself, I'm glad to say, but from what one hears, they're pretty awful: overcrowded, with more and more wounded pouring in every day. Look at the casualty lists in the papers. Seems to be no end to them.' Gerry gave a shudder. 'Many of those arriving are stretcher cases, hardly conscious, men who have simply come home to die. Not something a gently brought up girl like Lucinda should have to see.'

'I take your point,' Iain said, 'and I agree with you, but you've known my sister nearly as long as I have, so you know that if she's determined to do something, I won't be able to stop her.'

'Yes, I know she's always been strong-headed, but all I'm saying is, I wouldn't take *my* sister to a place like that.'

'You haven't got a sister,' pointed out Iain.

'No, I haven't,' agreed Gerry, 'but you know what I mean.'

'So, we can simply turn up at the hospital and ask for him by name and number? There'll be a record?'

'I imagine so,' replied Gerry, 'but as I said, it really isn't my province. You need a medical man who knows how these places are run.'

'Can you introduce me to one?'

'Not here,' answered Gerry. 'You need someone at Netley itself, and I don't know anyone to suggest. There must be admin offices where all the records are kept. They should be able to find your man, Fenton, is it? In their records, dead or alive. And if he's been moved on somewhere else, they will be able to tell where.'

At that moment Miss Perks reappeared with a tea tray on which were a large teapot, two cups and saucers and a plate with several slices of cake.

'Your tea, sir,' she murmured as she set the tray on Gerry's desk. 'It's the best I could do.'

'It looks splendid, Miss Perks,' said Gerry, 'You've taken a lot of trouble.'

At these words, Miss Perks blushed an even deeper pink, if possible, and murmuring, 'No trouble, sir,' she scurried out of the room.

'You're well looked after, Gerry,' grinned Iain, as the door closed behind her.

'She's only been here four weeks,' Gerry replied. 'It won't last, so might as well make the most of it.'

Between them they finished the cake and then, as Gerry seemed to be unable to supply any more information, Iain thanked him and stood up to leave.

'Sorry I can't be more help, Mac,' Gerry said, getting up to shake his hand. 'Regards to Lucy. Hope she finds her man.'

'Her *man's* man,' Iain corrected him firmly.

Lucinda was disappointed with the result of Iain's visit to the War Office. 'Didn't he know anything?'

'Big hospital, first stop for the ambulance trains coming in from Southampton,' summarised Iain. 'Names of the wounded recorded and if moved elsewhere, their destination.' He did not add, as Gerry had, 'dead or alive'.

'We must go down there at once,' stated Lucy. 'I want to be able to tell David in my next letter where he is and how he's doing.'

'I do have to work, you know,' Iain told her. 'We'll go on Saturday and not before.'

'I could go without you,' said Lucy.

'No,' replied Iain firmly, 'you could not!'

Lucy knew he was right. She shouldn't turn up unescorted at a military base, for that was what Netley hospital was, but it frustrated her to think that, in the four days until Saturday, Fenton might be moved on somewhere. Or die. She forced that thought to the back of her mind, but it didn't quite leave her.

Saturday morning found them at Waterloo station. Lucinda,

wearing a heavy overcoat, was plainly dressed, with only the smallest of hats perched on her abundant hair. She had arrived in a taxi to meet Iain. She had sworn him to secrecy about the proposed visit, determined her mother should not hear of where they were going and why. She knew Mama would not approve and might even try to forbid her to go.

Not that she can, Lucy thought. I'm a married woman now and answerable only to my husband.

At least that was what she told herself, bolstering her argument with the thought that it was David who had asked her to find Fenton. Even so she was pleased, when she saw Iain waiting by the taxi rank to meet her, that she did not have to walk into the station alone. It was far colder than she had realised and she was glad of her thick winter coat. Pulling it closely about her, she followed Iain into the station.

'I've bought us return tickets,' Iain said as he led the way to the platform. 'I'm hoping we shall be able to find the information we need fairly quickly.'

From Southampton they secured a taxi and were driven to Netley.

'Shall I wait for you, guv?' enquired the taxi driver.

'No,' answered Iain, 'we don't know how long we'll be. We'll get a taxi back.'

'Might not be that easy,' said the driver, 'not out here. Still, if you're sure...'

'Oh do come on, Iain,' cried Lucy, turning her back and gazing up at the incredibly ornate building that was the hospital. It stretched along the waterfront for more than four hundred yards, its frontage an imposing line of arched doors and windows topped with crenelations.

'Surely this must be the best hospital in the country,' Lucy said, in awe.

There was a wide path leading up to a pillared doorway which was clearly the main entrance, but the hospital extended into two wide wings, facing the water.

'It certainly looks impressive, but what it's like inside?' Iain wondered, as he remembered how Gerry had described it.

'Well, let's go and find out,' said Lucy and set off up the path to the front entrance.

Despite the chilly weather outside, the front door was not locked and opened to her touch. Inside was a large and busy reception area. Corridors led off in both directions, clearly running the length of the building. Cold winter light filtered through the arched windows, showing doors on the inner side of each passageway.

Presumably, Lucinda thought, leading into wards where the patients would be being nursed. Everyone seemed to be very busy, nurses in starched aprons with fly-away veils confining their hair, men in short white coats over uniform trousers, orderlies in the corridors pushing patients on uncomfortable-looking trolleys. A wide staircase swept upward to the floor above and beside it a lift clattered its way down to the hall, where it gathered up a patient on a trolley and carried him up to a ward on the next floor. No one took any notice of the pair standing just inside the door.

'Who do we ask?' wondered Lucy, looking round her in bewilderment at all the activity. Then she caught sight of a grey-haired woman working on some papers at a desk tucked in beneath the sweep of the stairs. 'What about her?'

'You wait here,' Iain said, 'and I'll go and ask.'

Leaving Lucinda in an alcove off the hallway, he crossed the hall and approached the desk. The woman did not look up straight away and he saw she was working on some columns of figures. Lucy, in the meantime, drifted down one of the front corridors and peeped through one of the open doors. She had been right. Beyond the door was a room lined with metal beds, packed as closely as was possible without making them inaccessible. She stared in dismay at the men lying in the beds. Nearly all of them had some sort of bandage; heads with eyes bound against the light, arms strapped; legs buried beneath cradles to protect limbs that were no longer there. The ward, only lit by high windows that let in little light, was stuffy and gloomy and completely depressing. How can these men get better in here? she wondered. One man cried out and a nurse appeared at his bedside, taking his hand in hers and speaking gently. Lucy couldn't hear what she said, and took a step forward.

'And just what do you think you're doing?' The voice was angry and abrupt. 'These men aren't peepshows for nosy women to gawp at!'

'I'm not gawping,' retorted Lucinda. 'I heard a man call out and I came to see if I could help.'

'And you're a nurse, are you?' The woman who had snapped at her was in nurse's uniform, her name, Sister Armstrong, on a badge on her chest. She was also much older than the other nurses Lucy had seen earlier.

'No, but I can...'

'You can do nothing helpful. You're just a child, nosing about among the wounded.'

'I am no such thing,' snapped Lucinda. 'I am Lady Melcome, wife of Sir David Melcome.'

'Are you indeed!' sniffed the woman. 'And who is he, when he's at home?'

'When he is at home,' replied Lucinda, 'he's a baronet and a major in the Dragoon Guards. When he's away, he's in France fighting for his king and country... as a major in the Dragoon Guards.'

'Is he indeed?' The words were still brisk, but the tone had softened. 'So, what are you doing here at Netley? If you've come to nurse, you'll be no good until you're properly trained.'

'I've come at the request of my husband,' Lucinda replied. 'He's asked me to try and find his soldier servant, Corporal Fenton, who's been wounded and possibly sent here.'

'Along with hundreds more,' said Sister Armstrong, 'and I can tell you there are over a thousand beds in the hospital and every one of them is full.'

'But surely there is a register of all the men who have been sent here,' said Lucinda. 'And if they've been sent somewhere else, that will have been recorded as well.'

'There is,' answered Sister Armstrong calmly, 'including those who were sent to the graveyard.'

This simple remark was nearly Lucinda's undoing, but she swallowed hard and replied, 'I thought there must be, it's only common sense. If I were running a hospital, especially one this size, I'd insist that every man who arrived, dead or alive, was accounted for. How else could anyone find what had happened to their father, or brother, or son?'

For a moment there was an awkward silence between them, Lucinda regarding Sister Armstrong with a challenging look, before the nurse said, 'Pardon me for speaking plain, madam, but you should train as a nurse. Hospitals all over the country are looking for trained nurses. This war is not going to be a short one, and the casualties will keep coming. Get yourself a training and do your bit, just as your husband is doing his.'

'I'm doing my bit for us,' answered Lucinda a little defensively. 'I'm expecting our child.'

'Are you now?' said Sister Armstrong. 'I should have realised. You have that look about you.' She shook her head in disapproval. 'Well then, you shouldn't be here in this hospital, where infection and disease are rife. Go home and protect your baby.'

At that moment Iain appeared at the door to the ward.

'There you are, Lucy!' he cried in relief. 'I couldn't find you.'

'I was just talking to Sister Armstrong about finding Fenton.'

'I thought you said your husband was in France,' the nurse accused.

'He is,' put in Iain before Lucy could explain. 'I'm her brother.'

'Well, sir, in her condition you shouldn't be bringing her to a military hospital like this.'

'No, well we're leaving now. I've found out what we came to discover.'

As soon as they were outside the hospital, Lucy said, 'Well, what *did* you discover?'

'The woman at the desk under the stairs has a huge card index and she looked him up. He was here, but only for a few days. He's been moved to Charing Cross Hospital for treatment.'

'Oh Iain. That's good news, isn't it?'

'The woman didn't know, all she had a record of was his name, number and destination. You should be able to find him there.'

Suddenly recollecting Sister Armstrong's remark, Iain said, 'Wait a minute, Lucy. What did that nurse mean by "in your condition"?'

'I'm expecting, Iain.'

'Expecting? Expecting what?'

'A baby, you idiot. What else should I expect?'

Iain stopped in his tracks and caught hold of her arm. 'I didn't know that!' he exclaimed. 'Or I certainly wouldn't have allowed you to come here.'

'No one knows except David, and now you.'

'You haven't told Mama?'

'No, she's got other things on her mind and there isn't any need to tell her the news until she's less fraught. So, I'll thank you to keep it under your hat until I say.'

Iain looked uncertain. 'Well,' he said, 'if you're sure. But I don't think Mama will be very pleased to be kept in the dark.'

Chapter Thirty-Four

It turned out that John Sheridan now had chickenpox, and had taken to his bed. Charles still lived at home with his parents and sister, but having already succumbed to the disease, he was able to continue going into the office where he acted as a conduit between his father and Miss Harper, who had taken charge of the office.

'Any news of Hugh?' John Sheridan asked Charles one day, when he felt better enough to think of anyone else.

'No, guv'nor,' answered Charles. 'I did go and see him recently and he didn't look at all well. To be honest, I doubt if he'll ever be able to come back to the office. I know his housekeeper is extremely concerned about him.'

'What made you go and see him?' asked his father.

'He telephoned the office and asked me to call at his house.'

'I see. What did he want you for? Anything I can help you with?'

'No,' replied Charles. 'Just some private business.'

'I see,' repeated his father. And though he said nothing more, it was clear from his tone that he didn't like being excluded from whatever it was.

It was Monday and Chas was looking forward to meeting Mabel again. As four o'clock approached, he gathered together the papers he had been working on and locked them away in Hugh Morrell's desk. He was sure Miss Harper went snooping after most people had left. He collected his coat from the stand in the corner of the room and was about to put on his hat, when Miss Harper appeared at the door.

'There's a telephone call for you, Mr Charles,' she said and, seeing he was dressed to leave the office, added, 'Shall I tell the caller to ring back? Say you're out of the office?'

Charles had been considering just such a message, but as soon as Horrible Hermione suggested it, he changed his mind.

'Certainly not,' he replied brusquely. 'Please put the call through here.'

'Well, if you're sure it won't make you late,' sniffed the secretary.

Moments later the phone on Hugh Morrell's desk rang. Chas lifted the receiver.

'Charles Sheridan.'

'Oh, Mr Sheridan thank goodness you're there. It's Mr...'

Recognising Mrs Parsons' voice, Chas interrupted. 'One moment, please.' Before he spoke to her again, he continued, 'Thank you, Miss Harper, the caller is through now, you may replace your receiver.' A loud click told him Miss Harper had rung off at last and the call was now private.

'Mrs Parsons, good afternoon. What can I do for you?'

'Oh, Mr Charles.' The woman's voice broke on a sob. 'It's... it's Mr Morrell. He's gone. I don't know what to do.'

'I'll come,' Chas said at once. 'You put the kettle on and make yourself a cup of tea. I'll be there as soon as I can.'

Miss Harper was back in her office with the door pulled to, pretending she had not been trying to eavesdrop. It had been a woman on the line, of that she was sure, but she had heard nothing more than an anxious voice, before Charles cut her off. Was it that pest, Mabel Oakley? Who else would be telephoning a lowly clerk during office hours?

Now, when he pushed open her door, she refused to look up. She had work to do, even if he hadn't. However, he didn't wait for her attention, he simply said, 'I have to go out, Miss Harper, and I won't be back today.'

'You're leaving very early, Mr Charles,' she said sharply. 'It's only just four o'clock.'

3RYINEY

'I have an appointment, Miss Harper, after which I shall be going home to report to my father. I trust that will be in order.'

Again she saw the steel in his expression and simply said, 'I understand.'

Oh yes, I understand, she thought when he had disappeared down the stairs. I understand all right. That little minx rings him at the office and he jumps to his feet to go and meet her. It's more serious than I thought.

Chas was indeed going to meet Mabel, but only on his way to Hugh Morrell's house. There would be no tea and cakes this Monday. Their meetings seemed to be fated.

He reached the teashop and found Mabel outside, about to chain her bike to the lamp post. She looked up as he approached and her face broke into a smile.

'Chas, good timing.'

'I'm glad you're here,' Chas replied. 'I can't stay. Mr Morrell's housekeeper's just telephoned to say that he has passed away. I have to go, she sounds in great distress.'

'Then I'll come with you,' said Mabel at once.

'Of course, if you want to, but what about your bike? I'm going on the train.'

'Perhaps Rosie would let me put it inside?' Mabel said doubtfully.

'Unlikely, and then you wouldn't be able to get it back until tomorrow.'

'Then I'll just leave it chained up here,' answered Mabel. 'And hope for the best. I'm definitely coming with you. He was my trustee and I am... was... very fond of him.' Moments later, with her bike secured to the lamp post, they were hurrying to the station.

'Poor Mrs Parsons is very upset,' Chas said. 'She's looked after him ever since his wife died more than ten years ago and is devoted to him.'

'I only met her once, when I delivered some papers to him for my dad,' Mabel said, 'but she seemed very nice.'

'She is,' agreed Chas. 'A bit shy, but once she gets to know you, she's fine. She's a great cake maker,' he added approvingly.

When they reached Hugh Morrell's house, they saw that all the curtains were pulled across, and the door knocker tied up in black crepe, indicating that there had been a death in the house.

Mrs Parsons must have watching from the window, because she had the front door open before Chas was able to knock.

'Oh Mr Charles, thank you for coming so quick,' she cried, pulling the door wide to usher them in.

'I said I would come if you needed me,' replied Chas, 'and here I am.' He stood aside to allow Mabel to precede him. 'I think you've met Miss Mabel Oakley before. Mr Morrell is her trustee and when I told her what had happened, she said she would like to come with me.'

Mrs Parsons looked a little doubtful, but said, 'Well I s'pose it's all right if she's with you, Mr Charles.'

The housekeeper led them into the sitting room. 'I put the kettle on like you said, Mr Charles, so if you'll excuse me, I'll just make the tea.'

'She doesn't like me being here,' Mabel said in a hushed voice. 'Perhaps I shouldn't have come.'

'You've every right to come,' Chas assured her. 'Mrs Parsons is obviously upset and she doesn't know you yet.'

It wasn't long before Mrs Parsons returned with the tea tray laid with two cups.

'Won't you join us, Mrs Parsons?' suggested Chas.

'Oh no, Mr Charles,' she replied, 'that wouldn't be at all proper, not with Mr Morrell lying upstairs.'

'Would you prefer it if I went up to see him now?' Chas asked gently.

Mrs Parsons looked relieved. It was what she had expected him to do as soon as he'd walked in through the front door, but because he'd brought this young lady with him, she'd thought it proper to defer the viewing of Mr Morrell's body until after the social niceties had been observed.

'Oh, yes sir, if you will.'

'Will you come up too, Mabel?' Chas asked.

Mabel's mind flashed back to the morning she had found Mr Clarke, lying dead on his kitchen floor. That image had stayed with her for months: the stillness of his body, the staring eyes, the cold stiffness of his outflung hand. No, she would not go and see the lifeless Mr Morrell.

'No,' she murmured, 'no, you go, Chas. I'll wait down here.'

If she had looked at Mrs Parsons at that moment, she would have seen the profound relief on her face, but she was looking at Chas and willing him to understand that the idea filled her with dread.

Chas simply nodded and said, 'I'll be down again in a minute or two. Why don't you pour some tea and wait for me here.'

While Mabel poured the tea, Mrs Parsons and Chas went upstairs to the bedroom where Hugh Morrell lay, eyes closed, peacefully in his bed. There was a stillness in the room, the indefinable stillness of death. The curtains were drawn across the window and the room was lit by a small bedside lamp.

'I come into him this morning, and he was awake and a bit fretful, like. He said he wanted some papers from the top drawer of his chest over there.' She pointed to the chest of drawers where Charles had placed the document they had witnessed last time he was there.

'He told me to look in the top drawer and bring him all the papers what were in there.'

'And you did?'

'Of course I did. The old gentleman was anxious about them.'

'So, where are they now?' A quick glance around the room showed Chas that there were no documents lying about anywhere.

'I left him looking through them, and when I come back up again with his tea and toast, he had gathered them all together and put them into just the one folder. He told me to put them back in the drawer, an' when he died I was to give them to you and nobody else. He said you'd know what to do with them. Once they were safely back in the drawer, he closed his eyes and I left him to sleep. I looked in on him several times during the morning, but he seemed peaceful, so I didn't disturb him. It was only when I took him some broth for his lunch that I saw he hadn't moved a muscle and realised he had stopped breathing.' Her voice broke on a sob. 'I shoulda noticed earlier. I shouldn't a left him cold in his bed. I shoulda been with him when he passed.'

'Did you call the doctor?' Chas asked.

'No.' She sounded surprised. 'Why would I? Nothink he can do for the poor old gentleman now, is there?'

'No, there isn't, but you have to call him because there has to be a death certificate.' Charles saw her sobs were going to break out again and he laid a hand on her arm, and led her out of the room.

'Why don't you go downstairs and see about that cup of tea? I'll collect the folder of papers from the drawer and bring it down with me. Then we can see about getting the doctor to call.'

The housekeeper mopped her eyes with a handkerchief. 'Thank you, Mr Charles. I didn't know what to do.'

'Don't worry, Mrs Parsons,' Chas said. 'I'll get things sorted out.' He didn't doubt the doctor would be able sign the death certificate, as he had been attending Hugh Morrell for several months. Hugh was a widower and had no children, so he supposed whoever was the executor of his will would make all the arrangements. Quietly he went back into the bedroom and retrieved the folder from the chest of drawers. He stood by the bed and, looking down at the silent old man, bade him a silent farewell before going back down the stairs himself.

When Mabel got home from their visit to Hugh Morrell's house later that evening, she found her parents had been really worried. It was long after dark and though the street lamps shed pools of light on the pavements, there were too many dark corners and backstreet alleyways for Mabel to have been out alone; a young girl could well be a target for a thief, or worse.

In fact, Chas had walked all the way home with her, so she was not alone at all, but her parents, waiting for the sound of the front door, were not to know that.

'Mabel!' exclaimed her mother, when she finally walked into the kitchen. 'Where on earth have you been? Your father's been worried sick, you're so late. You always get home before this.'

'I'm sorry, Mam, Dada, if you've been worried but I got delayed. I've all sorts of things to tell you.'

Mrs Finch, coming into the kitchen, was in time to hear this and she raised an eyebrow at Mabel's remark. Was she going to tell them about the young man who had left her at the gate with a hug and a kiss on the cheek? Doreen had seen them from her third-floor window as they'd stopped beneath a street lamp and wondered who he was. Not William, for certain. He was much taller than William for a start. Well, if not, it was none of her business. She was fond of Mabel, but she hoped Mabel knew what she was doing, hugging strange men in the street for everyone to see.

'I'm late because I heard some sad news,' Mabel said. 'Mr Morrell died today.'

'Mr Morrell?' echoed her mother.

'How do you know?' asked her father. 'Who told you?'

Mabel was ready for these questions and she had prepared answers that stretched the truth, but weren't outright lies.

'From his articled clerk, Mr Charles. He was on his way to Mr Morrell's house when we met in the street. When he said where he was going, I asked if I could go with him. I wanted to pay my respects to the old man.'

'I know you had grown to like Mr Morrell these last few months,' said her father, 'but I don't like you wandering about alone in these streets after dark. And he wouldn't either.'

'Oh, I didn't, Dada. When we got back into town, Mr Charles said the same and he insisted on walking me home. He brought me to the front door.'

'Oh, Mabel!' cried her mother. 'You should have invited him in.'

'I think he was wanting to get on home, Mam. I'm sure you'll meet him another day.'

Chapter Thirty-Five

O nce Chas had walked Mabel home on their return from Hugh Morrell's house, he went back to the office and took out the folder he had been given. He had opened it in the quiet of the empty office and found that it contained not only Hugh's will in a sealed envelope, and labelled as such, but another sealed envelope marked PRIVATE AND CONFIDENTIAL with his own name upon it.

Remembering the document Hugh had signed in his presence, Chas returned both items, unopened, to the folder and placed it in Hugh's office safe. Though this was addressed to him, it was clear from its bulk that it contained several documents and Chas wanted it to be opened in the office, in the presence of a witness. This done, he went home to break the news of Hugh's death to his father.

'Why did the housekeeper telephone you, Charles?' John Sheridan demanded.

'I assume she had been instructed to do so,' replied Chas.

'Well, never mind,' said his father. 'I'll be back in the office tomorrow morning and we can deal with everything then.'

The two Sheridans travelled to the office together the following morning, to be greeted by a surprised Miss Harper, who had not been expecting her boss until the beginning of the next week.

'Good morning, sir,' she said, coming out of her office to greet him. 'I hope you have quite recovered. I must say I wasn't expecting you this morning, so perhaps I could have a private word with you.' She glanced across at Chas as she added, 'I'm sure Mr Charles has plenty to be getting on with, seeing as he had to leave early yesterday evening.'

'We shall all have plenty to be getting on with,' said John Sheridan firmly. 'We have had some sad news, Miss Harper. Mr Morrell passed away yesterday afternoon, and we shall have to notify all his clients. Perhaps you'd be so good as to prepare a list. When you've made the list, bring it in to me and I'll decide who needs a personal letter and who can simply be informed with a general notification.'

He turned his attention back to Chas. 'You fetch the documents you brought home last night, Charles, and bring them into my office.'

Miss Harper glanced at Chas, but he was already turning away into Hugh Morrell's office, so she waited, wanting her private word before he came back. John Sheridan went towards his own office, but seeing her still hovering, dismissed her with a casual, 'Thank you, Miss Harper. That'll be all for now.'

It was now or never. 'I'm sorry, sir, but I'm afraid I do need a private word. It's about Mabel Oakley.'

For a moment Sheridan stared at her and then he said reluctantly, 'You'd better come into my office.'

Miss Harper followed him and carefully closed the door behind her. She wanted no chance that Charles Sheridan would walk straight in. He would surely knock on his father's office door first.

John Sheridan took off his coat and took his seat behind the desk.

'Well, what is it? We've a lot to do, so you'd better make it quick. What's the wretched girl been up to now?' Even as he spoke the words, he realised that his own irritation had made him speak unwisely about one of the firm's clients. Backtracking a little he said, 'Of course she may well be affected by Mr Morrell's death.'

'It wasn't about him being her trustee, sir,' said Miss Harper, in a hurry to get to the point. 'It's about her and Mr Charles. She seems to have gotten her claws into him.'

'She's what?' Sheridan was incredulous. 'What are you talking about, Miss Harper?'

'About seeing them coming out of a teashop together... and it wasn't the first time.'

'Coming out of a teashop? What has that to say to anything? They probably met inside.'

'No, sir,' maintained his secretary. 'They were walking together and that little minx had her arm through his.'

'And you are telling me this because...?' His tone was icy, but his secretary didn't recognise the danger signal and answered with a note of self-righteousness.

'Because, sir, I knew you'd want to know what was going on between Mr Charles and the Oakley girl.'

There was a moment's silence before John Sheridan quelled his anger and said, 'When I wish you to spy on my family, or on one of my clients, or anyone else, Miss Harper, I will ask you to do so. Should I find that you were making the same mistake again, I would have no option but to dismiss you.' Another silence before he continued. 'Is that quite clear, Miss Harper?'

His secretary was so astounded at his words that for a moment she made no reply and he asked again, 'Do I make myself clear, Miss Harper?'

Her 'Yes sir,' was almost a whisper.

'Then I'll expect that list of clients in the next half hour.'

Once his secretary had left the room, John Sheridan sat back in his chair, scowling. He didn't condone one member of staff spying on another... or on one of the firm's clients, but the information was useful, even though he wouldn't ever admit that to anyone else. Now Hugh was dead, Mabel Oakley would receive a formal notice of his demise... no need for a personal one in her case... and all connection with the firm would be severed. He would never have to deal with the Oakleys ever again. And nor would Charles, he would see to that. What had

THE GIRLS WHO DARED TO LOVE

he been thinking of, consorting with a tiresome girl like that, and a client? It was most unprofessional and he would nip it in the bud. Unlikely the friendship, if that was what it was, had progressed beyond a pot of tea and a plateful of cakes. Once he had seen the documents Charles had collected from Hugh Morrell's home yesterday, he would clear the air and get it over with. He wasn't expecting anything untoward: he already knew he was Hugh's executor, and expected a few small bequests, and the rest, he assumed, would be left to some charity or other; after all Hugh had no family. His wife had predeceased him and they'd had no children. Then he'd speak to Charles about what Miss Harper had said. There was no real need to disclose its source, though no doubt Charles would guess.

Chas had waited until he had seen Horrible Hermione come out of his father's office. He didn't know what she wanted to speak to his father about, but he didn't want to be involved. He gave her a couple of moments to get settled in her office, and then walked silently past her half-closed door to tap lightly on his father's.

His father was sitting behind his desk. He waved Chas to the chair opposite and held out his hand for the file.

'Now then, Charles, let's see what you've got.'

Chas opened the folder and handed the will across the desk. His father set it aside and held out his hand for the other, bulky, envelope.

'This one's actually addressed to me, guv'nor,' Chas said. 'I haven't opened it, because I don't know what it contains, but I thought I ought to have someone with me when I did.'

His father nodded his approval. 'Sensible,' he said. 'Well, I'm here now, so let's see what it's all about, shall we?'

Chas slid his finger under the flap and extracted several separate letters, each sealed and addressed in Hugh's copperplate handwriting.

Chas laid them on the desk in front of him. John Sheridan picked up each one and stared at them.

Mr Andrew Oakley.

Miss Mabel Oakley.

Mrs Millicent Parsons.

Mr Charles Sheridan.

Mr John Sheridan.

Dropping them all back onto the table except for the one addressed to him, John Sheridan tore his open.

Chas began to open his, almost afraid of what he would find. In the next moment his father tossed his letter aside and snatched up the still-sealed envelope containing the will. Ripping it open he pulled out the will and another, separate, sheet of paper.

Chas watched his father skim through the contents of the will, which was just as he expected it to be: one hundred pounds to Mrs Parsons, a fortune to that lady; twenty pounds to his gardener, Jack Pope; ten pounds to Edith Brown the laundry lady; and the residue to St Paul's Children's Home in Wood Green.

Setting it aside he reached for the extra piece of paper, and found himself holding a codicil. Dated just two weeks ago, it was written in Hugh Morrell's own hand. It reiterated the bequests in the main will with one exception. The signature was firm and definitely Hugh Morrell's. The codicil was witnessed by none other than his own son, Charles Sheridan, and Mrs Millicent Parsons, the housekeeper.

As he read and reread the document, John Sheridan's anger rose like a furnace within him. Mabel Oakley. She had played on the old man's feelings over the year he had been her trustee, until he had changed his will to favour her in this extravagant way, and Charles, his son, Charles, an articled clerk in his firm, had facilitated the bequest.

'How could you?' he breathed, his hand shaking, gripping the paper so tightly that it began to crumple. 'How could you do such a stupid, stupid thing? I shall contest this. Advantage has been taken of a frail old man, and you, Charles, you not only let it happen, but you encouraged that greedy little bitch.'

'Hold on, sir, hold on. I have absolutely no idea what is written on that paper. Mrs Parsons and I were summoned to his room and asked to witness his signature. The body of the document was covered up. All either of us saw was his signature line and then the witnesses' line. He signed his in our presence and then each of us signed as witnesses. He immediately took the paper away. I certainly had no clue as to what was in it, and sir, I still haven't.'

'Mabel Oakley!' John Sheridan almost spat the name out.

'What about her?' demanded Charles. 'He was her trustee, it shouldn't surprise you if he's left her something in his will.'

'Something in his will! And you let him!'

'I don't know what he put in the codicil,' reiterated Chas. 'I still don't. I just witnessed his signature.'

'"I just witnessed his signature"!' mimicked his father. 'That girl's been winding him round her finger, reeling him in, and you, Hugh Morrell's clerk, didn't even notice. Are you blind?'

'No sir, but even if I had known, it was none of my business.'

'Was it not?' sneered his father. 'You seem to have as special "friendship" with her. What's that all about then? You've been cosying up to her for weeks. You must have known her plan! Two stupid old men! She's making a habit of it, this sneaking her way into their wills. Well, as his executor, I shall contest it, that I promise you. He can't have been of sound mind at the time. It's a ludicrous bequest.'

Chas finally gave up explaining and turned to face his father, a remarkably similar expression of anger on his own face, and snapped, 'Since you haven't yet told me what the bequest is exactly, I couldn't possibly comment. All I can say is that Hugh was determined to write the codicil himself and to keep the contents of it from *you*. He wanted the enclosed letters to be delivered to their recipients, that's why he gave them all into my keeping. He didn't trust you, sir, and having seen your reaction, I can see why. But this I can tell you. Whatever Hugh has left Mabel, it's what he wanted her to have, and if you really do decide to contest the will, I will swear that he was of sound mind both when he wrote the codicil and when he signed it; and I imagine Mrs Parsons will too.'

'How dare you speak to me like this!' exclaimed his father, his cheeks ablaze with rage.

'I dare, Father, because it's true. If he'd sent the will, the codicil, and these letters to you, they might never have seen the light of day. I don't know what he has left Mabel, but I shall do my damnedest to make certain she gets it.'

'Get out of my sight,' snarled his father.

'Certainly, sir.' And with that he scooped up the letters from the desk and shoved them back into the envelope. When he opened the door, Miss Harper almost fell into the room.

'I thought I heard raised voices, Mr Sheridan. Is everything all right?'

Ignoring her entirely, Chas swept past her, stalked into the office that had been Hugh Morrell's and flung himself down in the chair that had been the old man's.

Had Hugh Morrell realised what fury he was going unleash when his partner read the letter addressed to him? Chas wasn't sure, but he had a sneaking suspicion.

For some time he simply stared into space, cooling down, then he realised he hadn't finished reading his own letter. He retrieved it from the large envelope and started again.

My dear Charles

If you are reading this, I have passed over to the other side. First of all, thank you for coming out to see me the other day and for witnessing my signature for the codicil at the same time. I have not redrafted the rest of my will as there was nothing else I wanted to change, so John will not know anything about my bequest to Mabel Oakley. With regard to her trust fund, I told her she really should have two trustees, so that there is a check and balance on everything decided in her name. I suggested your father could be a possibility. I know he and Andrew Oakley do not get on well, but think I can rely on them to keep Mabel's interests at the heart of things.

However, it crossed my mind that it wouldn't hurt for Mabel to have some assets outside Mr Clarke's original bequest. She is an enterprising young lady, and I think she will make the most of her bequest. Your father will probably disagree, but I hope he will accept that the bequest is not an aberration due to senility; it is, being completely of sound mind, a bequest I wish to make.

Please can you also ensure that the other letters reach their destination safely. They simply explain my motives.

I think I can trust you to stand a good friend to Mabel in the days to come.

Your mentor and friend,
Hugh Morrell.

Ten minutes later Chas walked out of the office on his way to deliver the other letters Hugh Morrell had left in his care: to Millicent Parsons, to Andrew Oakley, to Mabel Oakley.

Chapter Thirty-Six

After his dismissal from the firm, Andrew had not visited Hugh Morrell in his office and had never met his articled clerk. Most of their joint business was carried on by letter and their occasional meeting had always been held in the Oakleys' house. The two men had got on well and Hugh had never minded coming to visit Andrew if there was business to be decided.

One of the important things that might have been discussed in Barnbury Street was the approaching need for a second trustee to replace Hugh. However, since he had mentioned it to Mabel, Hugh had been either too busy tying up business or too ill for a face-to-face discussion before his death and to Mabel's relief the matter had not been broached again. Perhaps, she thought now, her father didn't know she was supposed to have two. Well, she had decided, she wasn't going to bring the subject up herself, and if it was introduced by someone else, she'd deal with it then. After all, Dada knew all about John Sheridan and he'd probably be as against him as she was.

The following day Mabel was working in her printworks when a call from her mother brought her out into the garden.

'Come on up, Mabel. We've got a visitor.'

Mabel washed her hands at the small sink in the corner and, wondering who it could be, went up the outside stairs and into the kitchen. There, standing awkwardly by the door, holding a briefcase, was Chas.

'Good morning, Miss Oakley,' he said.

Taking the lead from him she replied, 'Good morning, Mr Charles. Won't you come and sit down?'

Her parents had been sharing a pot of tea and some biscuits for a late elevenses at the kitchen table.

'Mam, Dada, I don't think you've met Mr Charles, Mr Morrell's articled clerk. You remember, he was the one who told me poor Mr Morrell had died? When I met him in the street he recognised me and told me the sad news.'

There, she thought, that should have warned Chas as to what she had already told her parents.

'And you went with him to Mr Morrell's house.' Andrew spoke in a neutral tone, but his disapproval was there by implication. He turned to Chas. 'Is it usual to take a young lady to the home of a deceased gentleman without her parents' approval?'

'No, sir,' Chas answered, 'but this wasn't a normal occasion. Of course, Miss Oakley and I have met on several occasions in Mr Morrell's office, so we have been properly introduced.'

'I see,' said Andrew.

'And when she said she would like to come to the house to pay her respects to a valued friend,' he went on smoothly, 'I agreed to take her. I'm sorry if that was inappropriate.'

'And why are you here now?' asked Alice, to change the subject and diffuse the situation.

'When I was at Mr Morrell's house, I collected some documents which he had left for me. I took them back to the office and locked them in the safe overnight, to be opened today in the presence of our senior partner.' He had remembered not to admit to being John Sheridan's son.

'In among the documents were some letters. One was addressed to you, sir.' Chas opened his briefcase and handed Andrew his letter. 'And this one is for you, Miss Oakley.'

Mabel took the envelope and saw it was addressed in Hugh's unmistakeable copperplate handwriting.

'What's it about, Mr Charles?'

'I have no idea, Miss Oakley. Something to do with your trust, I imagine.'

Andrew reached for a knife and slit open the envelope. He, too, recognised Hugh Morrell's handwriting.

The letter was short, but to the point.

Andrew skimmed through it and then said, 'I must read this properly in my own time,' and he slid it back into its envelope.

Mabel had also opened her envelope, but not yet extracted the letter. As with her letter from Thomas Clarke, she wanted to be alone when she read it, feeling more able to hear his voice, explaining what he wanted. She didn't want to read that he had put John Sheridan, Chas's father, as a suggested trustee. Not only was she worried that her father and John Sheridan would immediately be at loggerheads, but she was also terrified it would come between her and Chas.

'Aren't you going to read your letter, Mabel?' asked her mother.

'Later,' she said and turning to Chas, she said, 'Thank you for bringing it, Mr Charles. I'll see you out.' She led him to the front door. With the kitchen door still open behind them, they could only exchange a few words, and a private smile.

'I'll let you know the funeral arrangements as soon as I do,' murmured Chas. 'My father is the executor, so he will be sorting out things like that.' He reached out and shook her hand, a perfectly proper farewell, and murmured, 'I think you should read your letter sooner rather than later. See you on Monday.'

Mabel nodded. 'I'll come if I can.'

Chapter Thirty-Seven

Having learned where Fenton had been sent, Lucinda wasted no time in going to find him. She and Clara arrived at Charing Cross Hospital and were given directions to the ward where Corporal Leslie Fenton was recovering from surgery on his chest and his arm. They paused for a moment outside the ward.

'You can wait out here, Clara,' Lucinda said. 'I shan't be long. Just make sure you're not in the way.' And with that she went into the ward.

'Good morning,' she said to the portly nurse who sat behind a desk at the nurses' station.

The woman's expression was less than welcoming. 'Yes,' she said wearily, 'can I help you?'

'I wondered if I might speak to a doctor?' Lucinda said. 'It's about Corporal Fenton. I was told downstairs that he's in this ward, bed seventeen?'

The nurse looked doubtful. 'Dr Vincent should be doing his rounds shortly, but I doubt if he'll have time to stop and chat.'

'Oh, I won't take up much of his time,' replied Lucinda, making no effort to move. 'Just a couple of questions. I'll wait.'

With a sigh, the nurse found her a chair and Lucinda sat down. The business of the ward went on round her, with nurses coming and going. Curtains were drawn round beds, behind which dressings were changed, and blanket baths administered, to the accompaniment of murmured voices, or occasional cries of pain. Thinking about Netley and the desperate numbers of patients crammed into its wards, Lucinda felt this at least was a place where the future looked more hopeful.

Time ticked on and there was no sign of Dr Vincent, or indeed any other doctor. Lucinda was beginning to wonder if this Dr Vincent was really on his round. The nurses were clearly extremely busy and Lucinda was about to speak to the nurse at the desk again when a man in a white coat came into the ward. He was about thirty, small with dark cropped hair and a toothbrush moustache. Lucinda noticed he walked with a limp and she wondered if he had been wounded at the front as well. When the nurse who had been waiting to catch him murmured something, he turned to look at Lucinda and at once she got to her feet.

'Good morning, madam,' he said as he limped towards her. 'I am Dr Vincent. I understand you wish to speak to me about Corporal Fenton. Are you his next of kin?'

'No, Doctor,' Lucinda replied. 'My husband, Sir David Melcome, is his employer. They were side by side in the battle when Corporal Fenton was injured. Sir David has asked me to visit Fenton and find out how he is doing. All we've heard is that he had shrapnel wounds to his chest and arm. My husband wondered if there was anything we could do to aid his recovery.'

'I see, well, he is making a steady if slow recovery. His chest wound is healing nicely and we've managed to save his left arm, where the muscle was ripped away. He probably won't have the full use of it again, but at least in time he should learn to use it to some extent.'

'So, I suppose he'll have to stay here in hospital for some time.'

'Not necessarily,' replied the doctor. 'As soon as he's ready, in a couple of weeks he'll be moved on to a convalescent home somewhere, to complete his recovery, before being discharged and invalided out of the army. Has he any family? Sister Page,' he nodded back to the nurse, 'says he has no next of kin listed.'

'So Sir David understood. They have been together some

years, first in India and now in France. I'm sure he could come home to us, when he is discharged from here.'

'He would still need some nursing care. The best place would be a convalescent home. Perhaps in time he could return to your household, but he will never be as able-bodied as he was before. Certainly not active enough to be sent back to France.'

'Sent back to France!' Lucinda exclaimed. 'Surely not!'

'Many of those who have recovered from their injuries are returning to active service,' replied the doctor, adding with a faint smile, 'but not Corporal Fenton.'

'I see, about two weeks?'

'Not more,' said the doctor. 'We need the bed.'

Lucinda nodded. 'I understand. I'll come and see him again before then.'

It was clear to Lucinda that she had had her time with Dr Vincent, so she approached the figure in bed number 17. She stood for a moment looking down at him.

Leslie Fenton was lying with his eyes closed and apparently asleep. He had spent several days at Netley hospital outside Southampton, listening to his comrades dying around him. He himself was in constant pain which the morphine they gave him did little to subdue, but at least the wounds in his chest and upper arm had been cleaned and packed. With constant care and attention, the likelihood of losing his arm had been reduced. The nurses had done all they could for those men who had a chance of recovery, but the wounds of all too many had been neglected on the journey home and infection had set in. Those they could only give comfort as they waited for the release of death.

When Fenton heard he was being moved to Charing Cross Hospital in London, he had not been sure he wanted to go. Another move to another place, and all the effort and energy that would entail. He was told that he was lucky to be moving on, that what they had been able to do for him at Netley had only really been first aid. The treatment in London would be restorative, there would be specialists who had experience with such wounds. Of course, in the end, the decision hadn't been his to make. He was taken to the station with several of his comrades and put on the train. As they waited to be boarded, he watched the stretcher cases being loaded first. Then it was his turn. He was able to walk with help, his arm tightly bandaged and bound close against his body, his shoulder supported.

'You may not get the full use of your arm back,' one of the doctors had told him when he had been X-rayed, 'but if you follow the treatment and do as you're told, you should be able to regain some use. Are you right-handed?'

'No,' answered Fenton.

'Pity,' said the doctor. 'You'll just have to learn to be, like the rest of us!'

Now Fenton had been at Charing Cross for nearly a week. Progress was slow, but two small pieces of shrapnel had been removed from the deep gash in his chest below his shoulder and that wound was on the mend. His arm, with the muscle torn away, would take quite a while longer. However, he knew that as soon as possible, he would be sent to a convalescent hospital or nursing home. What with the constant stream of injured men arriving in the hospital trains, they needed every available bed.

Another move to God knows where, he thought. And what would be his future after that? He'd be invalided out of the army, with nowhere to go, no job to go to, even if he had the ability to hold one down. Sir David would have had to find another as his servant in the field.

'Good morning, Fenton.'

Fenton's eyes started open and he found himself staring up at a young woman standing at his bedside. He knew her face, but for a moment he couldn't place her.

'How are you feeling?' she asked with a smile.

'All right.' His speech was slow. 'Better, anyhow.'

'Sir David asked me to come and see you, to see if you needed anything.'

The mention of Sir David helped him to focus and his face creased into a confused frown.

'We've only met once before, Fenton,' said Lucinda, 'so I don't suppose you recognise me. I'm Lady Melcome, Sir David's wife. He was anxious about you and asked me to come and find you. And now that I have,' she went on, 'I shall be able to tell him how you're going on. He'll be relieved to know you're being well looked after and are on the mend.'

Fenton closed his eyes, but when he opened them again, Lady Melcome was still there. A nurse brought up a chair and Lucinda sat down at the bedside.

'They tell me you're doing really well,' she said. 'And it won't be long before you're able to come out of hospital. A couple of weeks at most.'

'Do they?' There was no missing the despondency in his voice. 'I know they need the bed.'

'So, where will you go?'

'I expect they'll tell me,' he replied. 'Convalescent place or some such.'

'Well, before you leave here, I'll come back and see you again. See how you're getting along. Now,' she said, getting to her feet, 'is there anything I can bring you?'

'Cigarettes,' he replied. 'And matches.'

'I'll remember,' she said with a smile. 'And you remember I'll be back to visit you again.'

'I might not be here,' said Fenton flatly.

'In which case I shall find you in the next place. In the meantime, Sir David will be delighted to know you're out of danger.'

When she left his bedside, Fenton closed his eyes again, and drifted off into an exhausted sleep.

While she had been sitting, waiting for Dr Vincent to put in an appearance, Lucinda had had the glimmerings of an idea and her brief conversation with the doctor had given it impetus. Now she knew the score, she wanted to get back to Sloane Square and see what arrangement could be made, in the two weeks before Fenton was to move on yet again. It would take a great deal of organisation, but she was certain it could be done, provided, of course, David agreed to it.

Both Dr Vincent and Sister Page were busy with other patients, so Lucinda simply walked out of the ward, gathered up Clara, who was waiting patiently in the corridor, and left the hospital.

As soon as she got home again, Lucinda went up to her parlour and started to make notes. Once she had sorted everything out in her own mind, she would write to David and explain it all.

It was simple really. Crayne. What about Crayne? The idea that had come to her began to take real shape in her mind. There must be hundreds of men who no longer needed expert nursing given in a large London hospital, men who were well enough to leave its care, but who had no one to look after them when it was time to leave. So, what about Crayne? Surely she could arrange for Fenton to go to Crayne for a few weeks, until he had recovered properly. David wouldn't mind. Indeed, she thought, he would applaud the idea. What use was a large empty country house with all those bedrooms, which was only used when his mother chose to spend time in the country? And what about the Crofts? Surely they were under-employed when none of the family was in residence. They had a daughter who was a nurse. Perhaps she could come to give Fenton the care he still needed. And if Fenton, why not more? There must be others who would otherwise be discharged into an unwelcoming world.

But what about her mother-in-law? Would she agree to the idea? Maybe for Fenton, but for other, unknown soldiers?

She drew a piece of paper towards her and ruled a line down the middle. 'Pros' on the left, 'Cons' on the right.

One of the main 'cons' was that her mother-in-law might well object. Not to Fenton being looked after at Crayne, but probably to anyone else. But Lady Melcome Senior had not been to Netley hospital, had not seen the rows and rows of wounded, lying in beds in overflowing wards; men who, despite the dedication of the doctors and nurses who laboured ceaselessly, really only had a future if they moved away from the overcrowded misery of the place. Another was not only her own lack of experience, Lucinda could only guess at what would be needed for the care of recovering soldiers, but that of the Crofts. Their daughter, Ivy, was training as a nurse, but at best was newly qualified, so would lack the necessary experience. More staff would be needed, with the whole house in use.

Lucinda thought of Sister Armstrong, whom she had met at Netley, experienced and determined. Someone like Sister Armstrong would know how to set up a convalescent hospital in a place like Crayne.

There were fewer things in the 'pros' column, but one of them was that the house itself was large enough for several men. There was a big kitchen garden, which with another gardener could provide fresh vegetables. The kitchens could be brought back into full use, and Lady Melcome Senior could have her own private suite of rooms for when she came to Crayne.

That night Lucinda went to bed with all her ideas circling in her brain. Tomorrow, she decided, tomorrow she would write to David outlining her plans.

Chapter Thirty-Eight

Closing the door on Chas, Mabel returned to the kitchen to see her father putting on his glasses, about to read his letter again, properly this time.

'Aren't you going to read your letter?' her mother asked Mabel.

'Yes, I'm just going downstairs to read it now.'

'Good idea,' said her mother. 'Read it in peace.'

'That Mr Charles seemed a nice lad,' Alice remarked to Andrew, as she poured them each another cup of tea. 'Good of him to bring the letters, don't you think? They could have just sent them in the post.'

'They had to ensure we had received them,' Andrew said. He took his letter out again to read more carefully.

'What does it say?' Alice asked.

'It's about Mabel's trust fund,' Andrew replied, passing it over to her. 'Here, read it for yourself.'

Alice took the letter and began to read it aloud.

Dear Mr Oakley,

Due to my ill health, I regret I can no longer act as a trustee for Mabel's trust fund. She is an enterprising young lady with a good business head on her shoulders. Indeed I think she no longer needs anyone to manage her affairs, but by the terms of the trust she must have two trustees to oversee her use of the trust money until she is twenty-one, or marries.

It would seem to me that John Sheridan would make an excellent replacement for me, already being au fait with the terms of the trust, but when I mentioned that idea to Mabel, she was absolutely against it, saying it would be an unworkable partnership. Anyway, I think such an approach should come from you. However, should you feel as Mabel does, that it would be impossible for you to work with Mr Sheridan, I do urge you to find someone else to fill my shoes. By the terms of the trust, it is necessary that there are two trustees to act together, and that way there can be no suspicion of impropriety.

I have great faith in Mabel and would not like her enterprises restricted by disagreement between her trustees, so I have left her something in my will which should give her the freedom to make some decisions of her own, without oversight from anyone.

However, it is important you select a new trustee, John Sheridan or someone else of good standing, with whom you can look after Mabel's legacy from Thomas Clarke, until she is able to assume control of her inheritance, as planned.

Yours sincerely,
Hugh Morrell.

'What do you think he's left her?' wondered Alice.

'I don't know,' said Andrew with a shrug. 'I imagine it's some money to allow her to make decisions without reference to her trustees, whoever Hugh Morrell's replacement turns out to be.'

Down in the print workshop, Mabel settled herself in Mr Clarke's chair and took out her letter.

My dearest Mabel.

If you are reading this letter, you will know I have gone to meet my maker. I had already told you that I would be unable to continue as a trustee for your trust fund. My death means that you must now approach someone of good character and integrity to replace me. You know I consider John Sheridan a good choice, for the reasons already outlined, but I also know you feel strongly against him so, if you and your father come to the conclusion that this would be unworkable, it will be incumbent upon you to find a person of suitable standing to take my place. I have explained this to your father in a separate letter.

I have always admired your courage and determination, Mabel, the way you stepped forward to help support your family after your father's accident, and so I have left you £250 to be for your use entirely as you choose to spend it.

This bequest is conditional on you finding a suitable replacement for me to act as trustee with your father, as per the terms of the Thomas Clarke trust.

I wish you all the best for your future, wherever it may take you. It is women of your calibre who will change the future and make their mark upon the world.

God bless you, Mabel.

Signed,
Hugh Morrell.

Mabel read the note through twice to make sure she had understood properly, but it was all there. Provided she fulfilled

Mr Morrell's condition, he had left her £250, to use without reference to anyone else.

Did Chas really not know, or had he known all along and that was why he had started befriending her?

She sat in silence for a long time, thinking about the old man. She had grown fond of him over the year, and she'd thought her affection was returned, but never, never in a million years would she have expected anything in his will, let alone as major as this. What was his thinking behind it? What had he expected her to do? Had he had some special project in his mind?

At last, growing cold in the print workshop, she got to her feet and slowly made her way back up the stairs to the kitchen.

Her parents were still sitting at the table and both looked up expectantly as she came in. They didn't ask what Hugh Morrell had written in his letter to her, but in the expectant silence, Mabel eventually said, 'Mr Morrell has left me some money.' She paused for a moment before adding, 'Two hundred and fifty pounds.'

Andrew and Alice could hardly believe their ears.

'But there is a condition,' she said, and explained exactly what it was.

'But it's outside your trust,' pointed out Andrew. 'If it becomes necessary to appoint John Sheridan as a replacement trustee, he won't be able to stand in the way of something you want to do, something he doesn't approve of.'

'I *told* Mr Morrell that you would never be able to work with Mr Sheridan,' said Mabel, frustration clear in her voice. 'It's all very well for him to say that man's the obvious choice, but I told him that it would never work!'

'If it's for your benefit, Mabel, I'm sure we can work something out.'

'It would make us beholden to him,' cried Mabel. 'And that's the last thing we want.'

'Well,' said Andrew. 'Mr Morrell obviously still thought it should be John Sheridan.'

'Mabel, it's a lot of money,' Alice said gently. 'Obviously Mr Morrell wanted you to have some money of your own, but he also knew you had to stay within the terms of Mr Clarke's trust.'

'But he didn't say it *had* to be John Sheridan,' said Mabel. 'Just a right and proper person of sufficient standing.'

'But who else could we ask?' wondered Alice. 'It can't just be anybody. Surely we must know someone who would be suitable.'

'Maybe,' agreed Mabel. 'But then who's to decide who is a person of sufficient standing?'

They could have discussed the matter all day and all night but in the end they decided to sleep on it and look at it with fresh eyes the next morning.

All very well to say sleep on it, Mabel thought as she lay, sleepless, into the small hours. Of course she wanted to accept the inheritance, it was a lot of money, but she still hated the idea of inviting John Sheridan to be her trustee. What about Chas? Would he be considered a suitable candidate? Unlikely. Although he had a law degree, he still had to pass his professional exams. She finally drifted off into an uneasy sleep and awoke unrefreshed and short tempered.

After breakfast, they reconvened in Andrew's room where they could discuss the problem in private. There was no need for Doreen or Mavis to know Mabel's latest piece of good fortune, not yet, anyway.

'The whole bequest hangs on the question of the second trustee,' said Andrew. 'It doesn't have to be John Sheridan, but you do have to have someone.'

'I had a thought about that, last night in bed,' volunteered Alice.

'About who we might ask?' Mabel said eagerly. 'Who?'

'Well, I'm not sure you'll like my suggestion,' replied Alice. 'But before you automatically turn it down, at least give me the chance to explain why I think he would be a reasonable choice.'

Mabel picked up her tea cup and sat back in her chair, a veritable picture of reasonableness. Who had Mam come up with? Uncle Frank? He was respectable, honest as the day was long, but he didn't have a business brain. Mr Solomon, Stephen's mentor. He was a businessman, who knew what's what, but Mabel didn't think he would venture out of his own community. Thinking of Stephen's boss made her consider Mr Carter, the owner of the furniture factory where Eddie was apprenticed. He might be a possibility, she supposed; she had a good relationship with him on a business level, but it would take courage to approach him on a personal level.

Well,' she urged, 'go on. Tell us who you've thought of.'

Chapter Thirty-Nine

Iain had been right, Lady McFarlane was not best pleased when Lucinda finally announced to her parents that she was expecting a baby.

'My dear girl, is that what all that fainting in the Lords was about?' demanded her mother. 'Why on earth didn't you tell me?'

'I didn't know for sure.'

'Didn't know?' cried Lady McFarlane. 'How could you not know, when all the signs were there?'

'Because you had never told me the signs!' Lucinda almost retorted. But she bit back the words, while making a promise to herself and to her unborn child. If she had a daughter, she would not hold back when it came to discussing the facts of life. She would pass on everything she knew, rather than let her child suffer fear of the marriage bed, the act leading to conception, and the problems of pregnancy.

'Because,' she answered, 'David had to be the first to know. I wouldn't tell anyone else until he knew; not even his mother. Now he's written to tell her, I can tell you.'

'Well, I'm delighted about the baby, of course,' said Lady McFarlane, 'but it's most unfortunate timing. You won't be able to come to your father's banquet at the Waldorf on Friday.'

'Why ever not?' demanded Lucinda. She had been looking forward to telling her own friends, in confidence, of course. Muriel Charlton had married before her, but as far as Lucinda knew, she was the first to find herself expecting.

'My dear child, no respectable lady of our station would go into society once it was known that she was "enceinte". Your father will be most disappointed,' she went on, adding almost as an afterthought, 'and it will completely put my table out. I had placed you next to the Prime Minister.'

'But how will anyone know?'

'The *servants* my dear. They know everything and it will get about. No help for it, I'm afraid. We don't want to embarrass your father. Still,' she added, 'David must be pleased, and hoping for a boy, of course. Men always want a son first, don't they?'

'I don't think he minds,' replied Lucinda. 'He says he doesn't.'

'Well, he would,' remarked her mother. 'He wouldn't want you to think he'd be disappointed in a daughter. Anyway,' she went on, 'we're delighted you're expecting. Now you must take care of yourself and only go into the society of family and close friends until you are confined. You'll have to give some thought to where you will give birth and we must get an experienced midwife to attend you.'

'That's already decided, Mama,' Lucinda said firmly. 'The baby will be born at Crayne, as its father was.'

'In the country?' Lady McFarlane sounded shocked. 'Surely not. David will want the best care for you, here in London.'

'David wants the child to be born at Crayne,' asserted Lucinda. 'He's already said so, and I am still in the care of Dr Tanner while I'm in town.'

'But has David given the matter proper thought?' wondered her mother. 'Giving birth in the country...'

'But I'm not ill, Mama. And Dr Tanner is not a country doctor. When I'm close to my time, I shall move to Crayne and a trained midwife will be there with me. It will all be properly arranged, I promise you.'

So, on the evening of her father's celebration, Lucinda remained discreetly at home. She didn't really mind. She had to admit, if only to herself, that she was very tired and the evening at the Waldorf would be a grand social affair. What a disgrace it would be if she fell asleep at the dinner table! Anyone who was anyone had been invited, even Lord Waldon and his daughter,

Lady Diana Fosse-Bury. It was Iain who insisted they be invited, in recognition of Lady Diana's kind attention to Lucinda at the House of Lords.

Lady McFarlane was against such an invitation. The Earl of Waldon was a well-known man about town with several acknowledged by-blows. His wife had long since retreated into social obscurity, seldom accepting invitations. Not so Lady Diana. She was a chip off the old block and already had a reputation not only for being a beauty, but for being extremely fast. Though her mother seldom came to town these days, her father had an apartment in Park Lane for when he was in London. However, most of the time Lady Diana lived there alone, attended by her devoted maid Frobisher, a footman named Henry, a couple of house maids and Wragge, an extremely aged butler. Isabella McFarlane had not recognised her at first, that day in the House of Lords, but as soon as the young lady mentioned her name, Lady McFarlane pretended not to know who she was.

'It's the least we can do, Mama,' Iain maintained. 'We owe them this courtesy. The whole of society will be there, what does it matter if there are three more, Mama?'

'It matters *who* they are,' retorted his mother, 'not the number of guests.' However, her husband took Iain's side, in what was fast becoming a real argument.

'You may not approve of Waldon's morals, my dear,' he said, 'but he is a man of power and influence; he has the ear of the PM, and is not a man to offend. He would expect to be invited.'

So against her own inclination, Isabella had had to give in; an invitation had been sent to Lord and Lady Waldon and Lady Diana Fosse-Bury and was accepted, surprisingly, by all three.

Iain was delighted. He had been truly grateful for Lady Diana's help when Lucinda needed her, but he had also been captivated by her beauty. Since then he hadn't been able to get her out of his mind and he wanted to get to know her better. His own station in life had improved with his father's elevation to the Lords, but even so he did not move in the same circles and so there was little chance of meeting and being properly introduced.

But, he thought, if she's the invited guest of my parents, I can speak to her without further introduction.

In the event, he did not have to approach her: it was she who made the approach. Iain was watching from across the room as she made her entrance, for it could be called nothing less. Dressed in a deceptively simple evening gown of peacock blue silk that emphasised her elegant figure, she followed her parents into the Palm Court, to be received by her host and hostess. Her hair, a mass of golden curls, was piled high on her head and held in place by a circlet of silver rosebuds, from which an artful curl escaped to tumble about her shoulders. She greeted her host with a wide smile, her eyes sparkling, and it was clear from the way he took her hand that she truly was welcome. Her hostess's reception differed entirely, polite but decidedly on the cool side of chilly; no more than a slight inclination of her head, and with no word spoken.

To Iain's surprise, once she had been received by his parents, Lady Diana walked boldly up to him, hand extended in greeting, and said, 'You're Iain McFarlane, aren't you? You may remember, we met in the House of Lords when your sister was taken ill.'

Remember? Lady Diana? How could he forget. He couldn't take his eyes off her. She was even more beautiful than he remembered: the curve of her cheek, soft and smooth; her wide mouth offering full, soft lips; and her eyes, reflecting the exact colour of her gown, were smiling up into his.

Slightly bemused, Iain took her hand, holding it a fraction longer than was necessary. 'Lady Diana. How could I forget? We were extremely grateful for your kindness.'

'Since we've met before,' she said, her head tilted to peep up at him from beneath incredibly long eyelashes, 'Diana will do. I don't stand on ceremony.'

'Diana,' repeated Iain. 'And it's Iain.'

'And is your sister not here?' asked Diana, glancing round the room. 'I was expecting to see her. Is she quite recovered?'

'She is well,' Iain said, 'but unfortunately today she is indisposed, and very much regrets she's unable to attend.'

'I thought that was probably it at the time,' remarked Diana. 'But "are you expecting?" isn't the kind of thing one can ask straight out, is it?'

'No,' agreed Iain, startled. 'I suppose not.'

What an extraordinary girl she is, he thought, as he noticed how, with the sparkle of mirth in her eyes, she seemed to be challenging him.

'She must be disappointed,' continued Diana. 'Such a special day for your father. I had hoped to renew my acquaintance with her this evening, but I suppose I shall have to make do with you.' She gave him a quizzical smile that made his heart beat double time. She really was the most beautiful woman he'd ever seen.

On arrival, Iain had glanced at the table plan, and discovered his mother had placed him next to Lady Waldon, punishment, he guessed, for insisting the Waldons be invited. Lady Diana had been placed at a different table, with some of the less important guests.

'I was wondering if you could tell me who else is sitting at my table,' Diana said now. 'I don't recognise any of the names.'

'In that case I think we should move one or two of the place cards,' suggested Iain, 'and put that right.' Iain knew his mother would be incandescent if he switched Diana to his table, but if it was done quietly she probably wouldn't realise until it was too late to do anything about it, certainly not without causing a scene, and that was the last thing she would want. He would have to deal with her fury later on, but to spend the meal at Diana's side would be worth a tongue lashing.

'If you wait here a moment,' he said to Diana, 'I'll see what I can do.'

Leaving her to accept a glass of champagne from a circulating waiter, he picked up her mother's place card and, casually strolling across to Diana's place, made the switch.

When dinner was announced and the guests began to take their seats, Diana slipped away to guide her mother to her altered place, before returning to her own, now next to Iain McFarlane. For some reason he intrigued her. He was an attractive man, perhaps a little younger than she, but what did age matter? They could have a bit of fun. She had plenty of experience to make up for any he lacked, and she thought, with a shaft of pleasure, she would enjoy teaching him.

By the end of the evening, Iain was entirely captivated by his dinner partner, leading him to pay little attention to young Maria Helford, Sir David's cousin and Lucinda's maid of honour, who had been placed on his left in the hope that an attraction might draw them together.

Diana had proved to be as entertaining as she was beautiful; she had the way of speaking to you as if you were the only person in the room. If Iain had been asked by the end of the evening what they had talked about, he would have been hard put to say, but the conversation had flowed, without any awkwardness or uncomfortable silences.

'I hope I shall be able to return such a delightful evening,' Diana said before she was rejoined by her parents to be driven home. 'Next Thursday I'm having a little soirée. Nothing as lavish as this banquet, of course, just a few friends spending time together. A hand of cards perhaps. If you would care to join us, you'd be more than welcome.' She slipped a card into his jacket pocket before her father claimed her saying the car was at the door. With a smile and the ghost of a wink, she allowed her parents to shepherd her away, leaving Iain to face his mother's rage.

As he lay in bed later, he decided the trouble he was in with his mother was a small price to pay for an invitation from the most beautiful girl in London. His mother's anger was in any case somewhat diluted by the success of the whole evening.

'I don't know how you could do such a thing,' she said. 'I especially put Lady Diana on that table because there were some people I wanted her to meet.'

'No, Mama,' replied Iain, 'you put her there because you didn't want her to sit near me.'

'Well, what if I did?' retorted his mother, entirely unrepentant. 'She has a reputation, and I wanted her nowhere near you. Don't you agree with me, Keir?'

'My dear, I think it hardly matters now, does it? Let's not spoil our memories of a wonderful evening over something so trivial. It was a triumph, my dear, and I think you'll find the invitations will come flooding in.'

Chapter Forty

David's mother had been delighted when she received his letter telling her about the baby. She had been at Crayne at the time, and she had hastened back to Sloane Square.

'My dear Lucinda,' her mother-in-law had cried. 'How wonderfully exciting! Why didn't you tell me sooner?'

'David wanted to be the one to tell you,' replied Lucinda, though it was she who had suggested that he should. 'At present very few people know, just David, you, my parents and the servants here in London.' Even as she spoke, she remembered her mother's remark. 'But I imagine the news will come out before very long.'

'Well, you must take life easy from now,' Lady Melcome insisted. 'I expect you're tired. I know I was with David.'

'A bit,' Lucinda admitted. 'But I'm thinking of going down to Crayne for a short while myself. I want to see about setting up a nursery, for when the baby comes.'

Now that she'd been to Netley and Charing Cross Hospital, Lucinda also wanted to see how the house could be used as a convalescent home. She had outlined her plans in a long letter to David, but so far had received no reply. She had made no mention of her idea to anyone else. It would be a great undertaking setting such a thing up and she was keen to see what she thought could be done, before expressing her thoughts to anyone but David.

Iain was the only one who knew she had been to visit Fenton in the Charing Cross, and she was determined that, even if converting Crayne House into a convalescent home was really too impractical, Fenton should be able to live there and be looked after, until he was strong enough to find employment somewhere in the outside world.

The day before she left for Crayne, she returned to the Charing Cross Hospital to visit him again. Even in the few days since her last visit, he seemed to have improved. He had a better colour and the lines of pain etched into his face were less deeply carved. She had not forgotten the cigarettes and matches, and she handed them over as soon as she arrived.

'Any news of how much longer you'll be here?' she asked as she watched him struggling to open the packet and pull out a cigarette, but knowing instinctively she should not offer help.

'No, not for certain,' Fenton replied. 'But pretty sure it won't be much longer. I can already manage some things for meself now, and it can only get better, can't it?' He managed to light his cigarette and drew the smoke deep into his lungs with a sigh of content.

'What news of the Major?' he asked.

'Still in the thick of it,' answered Lucinda. 'The fighting seems to be very fierce just now.' She had seen the casualty lists in the newspapers, and been horrified at the numbers of men being shipped home from Flanders. Her heart knew David was indeed in the thick of it, but she wouldn't let her thoughts go beyond that, wouldn't allow her to consider the possible consequences.

Really, she and Fenton had nothing to say to each other in the present circumstances. Unless David agreed to Crayne House being used as she was suggesting, she could offer the man nothing more. Promising to come again soon, she took her leave.

'It's very good of you to come, my lady,' Fenton said as she stood up to go. 'Thank you for the cigarettes. Please tell the Major that I'm going along nicely. Sorry I ain't there to watch his back.'

Lucinda said she would pass his message on, thinking, as she did so, she too wished Fenton was still with David, watching his back.

It was several days later that she received a reply from David, but it was not the reply she had been hoping for.

Lucy Mine

I am so glad you managed to find Fenton at Charing X. I should have known you would search him out one way or another. It seems as if the wounds he sustained were not quite as dreadful as they looked on the battlefield, though they sound bad enough. I suppose he was lucky not to lose his arm. I can understand that the hospital want recuperating men out of the surgical wards, our losses have continued to rise, and the stream of men arriving at the casualty clearing stations seems never ending.

If Fenton is well enough when he is discharged from Charing X, of course send him to Crayne. I am sure the Crofts will be able to look after him adequately, especially if Ivy has finished her training and can be at home to help. I'm not so sure about your idea of making Crayne a proper convalescent home. How would that fit in with you or my mother visiting? You couldn't have strange men wandering about the place, especially in your present state. You would need to make a family suite of rooms for your private use, but you would always be sharing your home with men you don't know, without the overall presence of a man of the house to ensure the proprieties are maintained. Your heart is in the right place, my darling, but with the best will in the world, you haven't the experience to organise such an enterprise. I know you suggested employing this nurse you met at Netley, but what do you really know about her?

And what about the Crofts? Crayne is their home too. I know they don't own it, but they have lived there and looked after it for the last twenty or so years. How would they feel about an invasion of unknown men, men who still need some nursing care?

My darling, you have a heart of gold, offering to lend the house to the military as a hospital, but I see too many disadvantages, not the least being that you must take life easy for the next few months, as you carry our child. You mustn't overexert yourself, trying to follow up on your idea.

Do offer Fenton a place at Crayne, and do employ Ivy to give him any nursing care necessary, but think twice, three times or more, before you go any further. Crayne is your home too, and I have said you may decorate and furnish it as you wish. I want you to be comfortable there, not trying to share it with men suffering from physical disabilities, or, dare I say it, what we have started to call shell-shock, night terrors, and in some cases complete mental breakdown.

When Fenton has made the recovery we all hope for, despite his injured arm, we shall employ him at Crayne full time. There will be plenty of work to do there in the coming months as we give the house the attention it's been missing for far too long.

Don't be disappointed by my reply to your wonderfully generous idea; I'm not saying it might not be a possibility in the future. When they let me have some leave, we can discuss it together and see if there is something we might sort out. We have to accept now that this war is going to go on for a very long time.

I love you for your outgoing spirit, I love you for your kind heart, I love you for being the mother of my children, I love you simply for being you, my love.

David.

Lucinda read the letter through several times, her heart sinking, as she took in what David had written. She was not to offer Crayne as a convalescent home. That was what it boiled down to. She could bring Fenton to live there with appropriate care, but no one else.

She thought about the scenes she had witnessed at Netley, the men brought home too late. Charing Cross Hospital was much better, but even so there was nowhere for the patients to relax, to become used to their new lives, lives without a limb, with impaired sight, with nightmares that woke them, screaming, in the night.

Well, she decided, of course she wouldn't go against David's wishes in the matter, but she would work it all out for when he came home again and they could discuss it properly. She would visit other convalescent homes and see how they were run, what facilities they offered, what staff were needed to service such a place, nurses, kitchen staff, maids, cleaners, gardeners, handymen. She would, she decided, make copious notes as she visited other homes, about what appeared to work and what did not. She would keep an eye open for suitable candidates to care for the patients. She would try and work out the cost of providing what would be needed on a daily basis; the income that would have to be generated.

She would take care not to overdo things while she was expecting, but she was not ill, and she would continue to lead what she considered to be a perfectly ordinary life. The only other person she might tell about her idea was Iain. He had come with her to Netley and he had seen first-hand what the wounded were coming home to. If they survived to move on somewhere else, where would they go from there? They needed more, further down the line, and a large house in the country could be exactly that.

The next day she returned to Charing Cross only to find Fenton had indeed been moved on. The almoner provided her with an address, Merriment Hall, a convalescent home near Salisbury.

'It's a lovely old house which used to belong to an Irish family,' explained the almoner, 'but it was left deserted at the end of the last century. The government requisitioned it, refurbished it and are now running it as a convalescent home for other ranks.'

Lucinda wasted no time in visiting Merriment Hall and she and Clara took the train to Salisbury. Merriment Hall had once been a gracious country residence, fallen on hard times. The renovation had been practical rather than beautiful, the refurbishment utilitarian, but it clearly served its purpose. As she got out of the taxi and approached the front door, she saw several service men, all in uniform, playing croquet on a rather lumpy lawn. Once inside the house she asked after Corporal Fenton and was directed to a book-lined room which looked out over the croquet lawn. Fenton was not watching the game, but sitting in an old armchair in the bay window, reading.

He looked up as she walked in and got to his feet, saying, 'Lady Melcome.'

'Sit down, Fenton,' she said and sat down herself on a rather uncomfortable chair, the other side of the bay.

He listened carefully to what Sir David had suggested about his future.

'We understand that it is going to take some time for you to get used to being right-handed,' she said, 'but when you are as fit as we can make you, you will still have a place at Crayne House.'

Fenton stared at her. 'I don't know what to say.'

Lucinda gave him a brief smile and said, 'I should say yes, please.'

Chapter Forty-One

John Sheridan had also been deliberating on the condition under which Mabel Oakley might receive her bequest from Hugh Morrell. As the executor of Hugh's will he was bound to try and facilitate his wishes, but he considered the whole idea of the codicil ridiculous. Somehow, for the second time, that wretched girl had wormed her way into an old man's affections, and into his will. Two hundred and fifty pounds! Two hundred and fifty pounds! And one simple condition. A replacement for Hugh as a trustee. It was a condition of inheritance and in his letter to John, Hugh had hinted that John might take on this duty. He did not state it in so many words, but his meaning was clear. 'Perhaps it would be beneficial all round if we kept the trust entirely in-house.'

'Well,' John addressed himself to his office, 'I shall certainly have nothing to do with it. The sooner we get shot of this upstart family, the better. I shall not come running at their beck and call. They can find their own trustee and good luck to them.'

It was then that the idea occurred to him. Andrew Oakley would, of course, have a say in the choice, but he, John Sheridan, as executor of the will, had the power to refuse a suggested replacement as unsuitable. Without the approval of both trustees, it would be difficult for the condition to be met.

He summoned Miss Harper and dictated a letter to Andrew Oakley and told her to send a copy of this to Mabel.

Dear Mr Oakley

I am writing to you as the executor of Mr
Hugh Morrell's estate. Since the death of Mr
Hugh Morrell you are the single appointed
trustee for Miss Oakley's trust fund. By
the terms of Mr Morrell's will, Miss Oakley
will inherit £250 provided she fulfils one
condition, that a second, suitable trustee
should be appointed to replace him. I believe
Mr Morrell was hoping that I would take this
on, but unfortunately I am not in a position
to offer my services in this capacity. You
may wish to suggest someone suitable for
this, in which case the terms of the bequest
will be accomplished and I will be able to
ensure Miss Oakley receives her legacy, but
as the executor I feel it incumbent upon me
to ensure the suitability of the replacement
trustee before I can do so.

If there is any difficulty with this, and
knowing your incapacity makes leaving your
home difficult, I would be happy to call upon
you for further discussion.

I remain yours sincerely
John Sheridan.

Dictation finished, he said, 'Get those sent off today, and
please ask Mr Charles to step into my office.'

The formality of the request made Miss Harper give an inward
smile, but, maintaining a straight face, she said, 'Of course, sir. I
think he's in the office.'

When Chas presented himself, his father waved him to a chair, while remaining behind his desk.

'You know why I've called you in.' It was a statement, not a question.

'No, sir,' replied Chas.

'Oh, for goodness' sake, Charles. This business about Hugh's codicil and Mabel Oakley.'

'It's a perfectly valid codicil,' said Chas. 'Written in his own hand, signed and his signature witnessed by two independent witnesses.'

'Were you both independent? You seem to have begun a friendship with Miss Oakley which, as she is a client of this firm, I find inappropriate.'

Chas did not reply. He knew his father had a point, but there was nothing illegal in his friendship with Mabel, though perhaps in the circumstances, it was becoming unwise.

'And then,' continued his father, 'you set about distributing letters to various legatees without my agreement as executor, which could well lead to some embarrassment.'

Chas had been ready for this conversation and responded coolly enough.

'You may remember, sir, that those letters were in an envelope addressed to me. As requested, I passed them on to the addressees, but I still have no knowledge of what they contained, as none of them was opened in my presence. We've had this conversation before, sir, and I have nothing further to add. I was simply an intermediary.'

Realising he was going to get no further in this direction, John changed tack. 'I accept that, Charles, but this liaison with Miss Oakley must cease. There must be no room for suspicion that you influenced Hugh in the disposition of his estate.'

'Miss Oakley and I have become friends…' began Chas, but was interrupted by his father.

'A little more than friends, from what I've heard.'

'Oh? And who have you heard that from?' exclaimed Chas. 'No, no, don't tell me, let me guess! Horrible Hermione?'

'For goodness' sake, Charles, please have some respect.'

'For Horrible Hermione? Why? She deserves none. My private life is nothing to do with her. There is absolutely nothing improper with my friendship with Mabel. There may be some bad blood between you and her father, but it has nothing to do with Mabel or me.'

John sighed. 'Face up to it, Charles. She's not our class. She is the daughter of a failed clerk, and has no place in the circles of society in which we move. It's not fair to give the girl ideas above her station. Hugh was most misguided to leave her so much money, with or without a condition. Luckily, I can stop her receiving the legacy.'

Chas looked at him suspiciously. 'Luckily? Why luckily? Why would you want to?'

'I've just explained why.' John Sheridan fought to keep the edge of irritation from his voice. 'She will get ideas above her station, and that way leads to disaster.'

'Obviously Mr Morrell didn't think so,' Chas remarked. 'And surely that codicil, whatever it actually said, was watertight.'

John opened a drawer in his desk and handed Chas the will and the codicil. Chas read them through, studying the codicil in particular.

'It looks fairly straightforward to me,' he said. 'Yes, it's conditional, but it won't be a difficult condition to undertake.'

'She will need another trustee before I pass over that money,' answered his father, 'and I am not prepared to do it. Even if she does find someone, I will have to agree the selection, and I am most unlikely to approve anyone she can suggest. She lives in a different world.'

'What *you* forget,' said Chas, 'is that for the last year she has been running her own business, extremely successfully. She's an intelligent girl and is making her own way in the world.'

'In her own world, yes, but not in ours, Charles. Remember,

her trust can be wound up when she marries. You must have known that for some time, so forgive me if I wonder if she's aiming at marriage, and perhaps you've been encouraging her.'

'Marriage!' exclaimed Chas. 'Whatever gave you that idea?'

'As you said, she's intelligent, so could it be that she's been cultivating you so she has an early escape route from the trust and can get her hands on the money?'

Chas stared incredulously at his father. 'You're really suggesting that Mabel is trying to trap me into marriage?'

'It is one possibility, you know.'

'No, I don't know,' snapped Chas. 'You don't give either of us any credit, do you?'

'My dear boy, I want to save you from making a disastrous mistake, that's all. You'll thank me some day, I promise you.'

'*My dear boy*'! Had his father ever addressed him as that before? Chas doubted it.

'And if I decide I'd prefer to make my own mistakes?'

'I shall forbid you to see her,' replied John. 'I don't want to have to come the heavy-handed father. But if I have to, I will.'

'You can try,' said Chas, getting to his feet. 'You can try, guv'nor, but I am not a child to be forbidden. I'm twenty-three!' And with that he walked out of his father's office, closing the door quietly behind him.

He paused at Miss Harper's office and, without knocking, stuck his head round the door. 'Ah, Miss Harper,' he said, 'as you're the centre of information, perhaps you'd be good enough to report back to my father. I'm on my way to see Miss Oakley.'

It would have amazed John Sheridan to know that an hour later, when Chas had called on Mabel at home, to warn her about his father's determination to prevent her from receiving her legacy from Hugh Morrell, his welcome was lukewarm.

He had knocked unannounced on the front door and been admitted by Doreen Finch. Recognising him from when he had called the previous day, she led him through to the kitchen, where

Andrew was sitting at the kitchen table with Mabel, learning to set type.

'Chas!' Mabel was startled into calling him by his nickname. Correcting herself quickly she said, 'Mr Charles! We weren't expecting you.'

'And just who is Mr Charles?' demanded Andrew.

'He's Mr Morrell's articled clerk,' Mabel replied. 'Remember, Dada, he came before, with the letters Mr Morrell left us.'

'I remember perfectly well,' replied her father. 'But who is he? That's what I want to know. Is Charles your surname, young man, or do you have another… like Sheridan?'

For a split second Chas hesitated. Had Mabel told her father about his relationship with the senior partner?

His hesitation was enough.

'I see. So you are John Sheridan's son. My wife remembered that he had a son named Charles. Well, young man, you aren't welcome in this house, so you can take yourself off and stay away from my daughter.'

Chas seemed to have paid no attention to this; he simply went on with what he had come to say. 'I came to tell you the steps my father is taking to stop Mabel receiving her legacy. He is refusing to become the second trustee…'

'We had no intention of asking him,' interjected Andrew.

Again, as if Andrew hadn't spoken, Chas went on, 'And he's not going to accept anyone you may suggest as suitable, which means Mabel may not be able to fulfil that condition of inheritance.'

'But that's ridiculous,' interposed Alice, who until now had taken no part in the conversation. 'Surely he can't do that?'

'I don't know,' admitted Chas. 'But I'll try and find out.'

'Don't bother,' snapped Andrew. 'We can find out for ourselves. We don't need any help from a Sheridan, thank you very much.'

This time Chas *did* react. 'In that case, sir, I'll leave you to it.' He walked to the door but then turned and said, 'I may be a Sheridan, but I take no part in your disagreement with my father. All I am interested in is seeing that Mabel can claim her inheritance. Mr Morrell wanted her to have that money, and so it should be hers.'

Mabel followed him out of the kitchen and out of the house. Standing on the pavement he took her hand.

'I shouldn't have come,' he said. 'It's just that I wanted you to be aware of what my father is planning to do.'

'But he can't, can he?' Mabel asked.

'Not if you find someone who he couldn't dismiss as unsuitable. I'll tell you something else, though. There is one thing our fathers do agree on.'

Mabel looked up at him. 'Really? What's that?'

'That we should never see each other again. I've been forbidden by my father, not that he can as I'm an adult, and it sounds as if your father will soon be doing the same.' He tightened his grip on her hand and asked, 'Will you disobey him?'

'I don't know,' Mabel replied miserably. 'It'll be the first time, if I do.'

'Well, that's up to you to decide, but I shall be at Rosie's at the usual time every Monday for the next six weeks. That takes us up to Christmas and gives you time to think things through, and if you haven't come there by then I shall know that you aren't going to.' For a brief moment he enfolded her in his arms, before murmuring, 'But I do hope you will.'

As he released her, the front door opened behind them and Alice appeared on the top step.

'I'd better go now before I make things worse,' he said.

Mabel's eyes filled with tears as she watched him walk away, watched until he turned the corner and was gone.

'You'd better come in, Mabel,' said her mother. 'And explain yourself.'

Chapter Forty-Two

From the night of his father's celebration banquet, Iain's thoughts were filled with Diana. Her card inviting him for the following Thursday remained securely in his pocket. He had made no mention of it to anyone else, simply said on the evening concerned that he was spending the evening with some friends and wouldn't be in for dinner. What with everything else going on in their newly elevated lives, neither of his parents enquired further into his plans.

When he arrived at the apartment in Park Lane and rang the bell, the front door was opened by Wragge, the butler. He peered out at the visitor; his balding head on a thin and scrawny neck poked from his collar, looking, Iain thought, smothering a smile, like an elderly tortoise.

Iain offered the butler his card, but Wragge stood aside and said, 'Good evening, sir. Lady Diana is expecting you.'

Diana, alone in the drawing room, was sitting in an armchair at the fireside as Wragge announced, 'The Honourable Iain McFarlane, my lady.'

As the butler withdrew, she stood and, holding out her hand, said, 'Good evening, Iain. Are you really honourable? I do hope not!'

A little thrown by this Iain said, 'Lady Diana…'

'Oh, come now, Iain,' she said, with amusement in her eyes, 'I thought we'd already agreed not to stand on ceremony. Never mind,' she went on, 'come and sit by the fire. It's a miserable night out there.'

Iain tried to think of something intelligent to say, but somehow words deserted him. Were they really only going to talk about the weather? He was rescued by the return of Wragge, who reappeared with an open bottle of champagne and two cut-glass coupes.

'Champagne?' suggested Diana. 'Or would you prefer a cocktail? One of Wragge's specials? They're delicious, but lethal if you're not used to them!'

Concerned not to make a fool of himself, Iain opted for the champagne and was relieved when Diana did the same.

Diana led the conversation as they sipped their drinks, with Iain wondering who the other guests might be and when they might appear. His mother always expected her guests to arrive within a quarter of an hour of the appointed time. He had been careful to arrive within fifteen minutes of the time Diana had scrawled on her card. Was that a mistake? Perhaps her set always came much later.

Even as he was trying to phrase the question in his mind, Wragge reappeared and announced, 'Dinner is served, my lady.'

'Your other guests…' began Iain, as Diana got up.

'Oh they're coming later,' she replied airily. 'But I want to get to know you better and I thought it would be much cosier just to have dinner à deux.' And flashing him an impish smile, she added, 'Don't you agree?'

Iain could imagine what his mother would have to say, but he also guessed that Lady Diana was setting out to shock him.

Iain could feel the colour rising in his cheeks and his heart pounded so loudly, he was surprised Diana couldn't hear it; but perhaps she could, a thought that made it beat even faster.

She seemed to be expecting an answer and he managed to murmur, 'Most certainly.'

'Perfect!' she said, resting her hand lightly on his arm, and they followed Wragge into the dining room. Here a table set for two had been placed in front of a roaring fire. The candles on the mantelpiece were set in ornate silver candlesticks, their reflected flames flickering dancing light on the silver and the crystal laid upon the table.

The food was served by Henry, their glasses filled by Wragge, and then they were left alone in the candle light.

Again it was Diana who took the lead in the conversation, asking Iain how his sister did, and what place he had in his father's office now he was down from Cambridge with a first-class law degree.

'Will you enlist?' she asked in a sudden and complete change of subject. 'Will you volunteer for the army?'

Iain didn't know what to answer. He had not really given it any consideration, after all he was training to be a barrister not a soldier. Did she think he ought to? Why did she want to know?

'I'm not sure they'd want me,' he hedged. 'I doubt if I'd make a very good soldier. I mean, as we have a first-class, well-trained professional army, better to leave it to them, don't you think?'

'I'd go if I could,' declared Diana. 'Pity they don't let women volunteer for active service. I'd go like a shot.'

'You could be a nurse, I suppose,' Iain said. 'They're going across the Channel to the hospitals in Belgium, aren't they?'

'Oh, I'd be a useless nurse,' said Diana. 'I'd want to be in the fighting. You have no idea how utterly boring it is being a woman and expected to knit and bake cakes.'

'Is that what you do, Diana? I don't see you as a knitter or a baker.'

'Well, I'm not,' she agreed ruefully, 'that's my problem.'

'There must be other things you could do?' Iain felt awkward. The conversation had suddenly taken a serious turn and it made him uncomfortable. 'My sister Lucinda's husband is over there, fighting. His servant, a man called Fenton, has been badly wounded. Lucy went to the huge hospital called Netley, outside Southampton, to find him.'

'Did she? That was very brave.' Diana sounded impressed.

'She didn't go alone, I went with her. Couldn't let her go to a place like that on her own.'

'And did she find him?'

'He'd been moved on, but she found him at Charing Cross Hospital.'

Their conversation was interrupted by the arrival of two more guests, introduced as Marcus and Daphne Champion, swiftly followed by Jack Symons and a young lady called Clemmie, who was clearly not his wife. From then on the evening became much more relaxed, reminding Iain of evenings up at Cambridge, with a card table being produced and later dancing to music on the gramophone. Brandy was brought and Iain realised that he was well on the way to becoming stupidly foxed.

It was nearing midnight before the party broke up. Overseen by a stiffly correct Wragge, the other couples drifted off into the night, Clemmie clinging on to Jack's arm as if she was afraid he might disappear and Daphne giggling as she tried to walk in a straight line.

'Stay for one more dance,' Diana murmured, as the front door closed behind the others.

Alone together once more, Diana wound up the gramophone. The music she chose was slow and moody. As with everything, she took the lead and, pulling Iain close, slipped her arms around his neck, her breast soft against his chest, his cheek pressed against her hair. When the music stopped, he waited breathless for a moment, while she, still dancing as she moved about the room, put on another record before slipping back into his arms. Iain could feel her heart beating in time with his own, the sinuous movement of her body against him inviting more. He slipped his hand behind her head and loosened the two silver combs that held her hair, so that it tumbled down her back, a waterfall of golden silk. She turned her face to him offering the softness of her lips. Iain had always had an eye for an attractive girl, happy to steal a kiss when the chance occurred, had in fact kissed plenty of pretty girls before. He thought he knew about kissing, but nothing had prepared him for how Diana kissed him now, deep and long and unbelievably erotic. Nothing he had ever done or felt before had prepared him for the surge of desire she'd unloosed. He felt the length of her body against his own as her hands began to roam, caressing his back.

The music stopped again and gently she pulled away from him, laying a finger across his lips.

'It's late,' she said. 'You'd better go now.'

For a moment Iain stood, bereft in the middle of the room. He had initiated none of the intimacy and all of a sudden she had withdrawn. She had returned to the gramophone, where the needle was continuing to circle the final groove, and lifted the arm.

At that moment the door opened and the butler came in.

'Mr McFarlane's taxi is at the door, my lady.'

Iain was about to say that he hadn't ordered a taxi, when Diana said, 'Thank you, Wragge. He's just coming.'

The butler withdrew and Iain said, 'I didn't ask for a taxi, Diana.'

Diana looked at him in surprise. 'Then how were you going to get home?' She gave a gurgle of laughter. 'You weren't planning to stay the night, were you?'

'No, of course not,' replied Iain, which was true, but neither had he expected to be dancing in Diana's arms at midnight. 'I had planned to walk. It's not that far.'

'Better to go in a cab at this time of night,' she said as she walked to the door. There she paused, presenting him with her cheek, before leading the way into the hall, where Henry was waiting with his hat and coat.

Iain took her hand in his and raised it to his lips, thanking her for an entertaining evening as Henry opened the front door, and he was ushered out to where the taxi was waiting. Behind him, he heard the front door close with an emphatic clunk. He walked straight to the taxi, and was about to give his address when the driver lowered his window and said, 'Chanynge Place, sir?'

Iain had given up being surprised that evening and simply said, 'Yes please,' and climbed into the cab.

'Are you honourable?' Diana had asked when he first arrived.

Was he? He certainly didn't feel so after their last hour together, but then, he told himself, remembering the way she had kissed him, neither was she.

Chapter Forty-Three

It was into the small hours before Iain finally fell asleep, and as a result it was well past ten o'clock before he surfaced, looking for some breakfast. He met his father in the hall on his way to the House.

'You're up late, Iain,' he said. 'But I'm glad I've caught you because I have some documents for you to take to the office. I'll leave them on my desk in the library. Go in and collect them before you go.'

'Yes, sir, of course,' Iain answered.

'Eat your breakfast first,' said his father. 'I'm off to the House.'

Iain sat down at the table and picked up the post that lay beside his plate: a single vellum envelope, formally addressed to him, The Honourable Iain McFarlane, in a neat sloping hand. The writing looked vaguely familiar, but he couldn't immediately place it. The footman, William, could have told him who had written to him. He had recognised Mabel's handwriting as easily when the letter arrived this time as he had on the morning of Sir Keir's peerage announcement.

Opening the envelope with his father's paper knife, Iain glanced at the signature. Mabel Oakley. What on earth had she written to him about this time, he wondered. Little Mabel Oakley! Lady Diana had swept Mabel Oakley into the shadows of his mind.

Turning the letter over, he saw that she had addressed him as '*Dear Iain*' and found himself grinning at her cheek, but she had never called him anything else, not since she had left the

McFarlane household in disgrace two years earlier. So what did she want now?

He scanned the letter briefly and then read it again. She was asking for a meeting on a business matter, and what was more, she was expecting him to come to her, not the other way about.

Dear Iain

I am sorry to trouble you, but please could we meet up to discuss a business matter? It's quite important and I don't know who else to ask. Please could you come to my workshop sometime tomorrow, Friday, so I can explain?

I look forward to seeing you then.

Yours sincerely,
Mabel.

What on earth could Mabel want? he wondered. If he had received this letter two weeks ago, he would have been delighted to have a reason to visit her again, but beside Lady Diana, all other women faded into insignificance, and Mabel now seemed particularly childlike. However, he was intrigued to know what business she might have with him, so he decided he would slip away early from the office this afternoon and visit as she'd asked. There would be no problem, Mayhew always assumed he was out on his father's business when there were unexplained absences from the Lincoln's Inn chambers.

That afternoon he took a taxi to Barnbury Street and approached number 27 through the THOMAS CLARKE, PRINTER side gate, remembering his last visit to collect Lucinda's wedding invitations. It seemed an age away.

Mabel's workshop door had stood ajar all day, despite the cold weather, and when he tapped, she came to the door to greet him.

'Iain, come in. Thank you for coming.' Waving Iain to a bentwood chair that she had brought down from the house in the hope he would come, Mabel crossed to the kettle, and set it to boil.

Iain watched her as she made the tea, surprised that she was taking the trouble. She had never offered him any hospitality before, but here she was, pouring tea and offering biscuits. Normally she would have come to the point of the meeting straight away, but this time she did not. Iain waited and they drank their tea in silence.

It had been Alice's idea that they should approach Iain, insisting Mabel should listen carefully before objecting to the idea. Her parents had thought well of Iain. He had come to fetch Mabel in his father's car after she had been wrongly dismissed, and later helped William save her from an attempted rape.

'It won't hurt to ask him,' pointed out Alice. 'If he says no, well he says no, but he might just as easily say yes.'

Her father added his weight to the argument saying, 'You never know, Mabel. It's surely worth a try.'

At first she had stood out against the idea of approaching Iain, but the continued pressure from her parents had finally persuaded her to give in. Now here she was, facing him across the tea cups, and she wished with all her heart she had not agreed to ask him for help.

At last she sighed and said, 'I've a problem I need to talk to you about. I don't know if you'll be able to help me, but I would like your advice.'

'Fire away,' Iain said, 'and I'll help if I can.'

So Mabel told him all about Hugh Morrell's bequest with its condition and the difficulties they produced. Iain was a good listener and heard her out without interruption.

When she finally fell silent, he said, 'So what it boils down to is that you have to find another trustee before the money can be paid out.'

'Yes,' agreed Mabel. 'But as I said, Mr Sheridan has refused to take it on.'

'But I thought you said your father wouldn't be able to work with him anyway.'

'I did, and it would be extremely difficult for him, but *he* was prepared to try. Mr Sheridan wasn't. I think his plan is to prevent me from fulfilling the condition of the extra trustee so that the bequest becomes void and the money goes back into Mr Morrell's general estate.'

Iain looked sceptical. 'Oh come on, Mabel! I hardly think that's likely, you know. He's a professional man, bound by a professional code of practice.'

'It's what I've been told,' Mabel insisted.

'Told? Who by?'

For a moment Iain thought Mabel wasn't going to answer, and when she did, it was with obvious reluctance. 'Someone in his office.'

'Just office gossip, then.'

'No.' Mabel spoke firmly. 'Someone I trust absolutely.'

'Don't you think whoever it was might have overheard a snippet of conversation and misunderstood?'

'No. It was a friend who works there too, and Mr Sheridan actually told him what he was going to do.'

'A friend?' Iain looked at her quizzically. 'He sounds rather special.'

Mabel felt the colour rise in her cheeks and murmured, 'He is.'

'Not William, then?'

'No.'

'I thought you two were walking out. That it was settled between you.'

'I'm very fond of William,' Mabel snapped, '*if* it's any business of yours.'

'It's not,' answered Iain. 'I'm sorry. Now,' he went on in a more rallying voice, 'what is it you want me to do for you?'

'I need someone to be my second trustee.'

'And you're asking me?'

'No,' lied Mabel, who had been about to do just that. 'I'm asking what you think I can do about it. You're a lawyer, aren't you?'

Iain shook his head. 'Not fully qualified, no.' He saw her shoulders slump, and added, 'But I can take advice for you. I can ask my father...'

'Oh no!' cried Mabel. 'You can't tell Sir Keir... Lord McFarlane, I mean.'

'Tell you what,' said Iain. 'I'll talk to another man in our chambers, a Mr Mayhew. He'll know what to advise. Now then, Mabel, look at me.'

'Yes?'

'This friend of yours, you are sure about what he knows? I mean it's no small thing to accuse a solicitor, acting as an executor, of trying to manipulate a will. Are you sure he hasn't got things wrong?' He paused and asked again, 'Who is he, Mabel?'

Mabel did not reply.

'The thing is, Mabel,' continued Iain, 'I can't take this any further until I know who told you all this.'

'It's Mr Charles,' she whispered.

'Mr Charles?'

'Mr Sheridan's son. He was Mr Morrell's articled clerk.'

'He was the one who witnessed the signature,' said Iain. 'Am I right?'

Mabel nodded.

'So he knew about the bequest before you did?'

'No. All he did was witness Mr Morrell's signature on a document.'

'But he had no sight of the document itself?'

'No,' Mabel assured him. 'He didn't know what that document was, any more than the other witness, Mrs Parsons.'

'But it turns out that it was the codicil which leaves you two hundred and fifty pounds.'

'Yes.'

'Hmm, I see,' mused Iain. 'But what I don't understand is why Mr Sheridan Senior is so determined you should not receive the inheritance.'

'He thinks I have wormed my way into Mr Morrell's affection simply to receive something from his will. He thought the same with the bequest from Mr Clarke.'

'I see. Well, even if he was right and you had done exactly that, it seems clear that this Mr Morrell really intended you to have this money. He took the trouble to write and sign the codicil, and have it witnessed. However much his executor doesn't like it, he doesn't have the right to try and block it. It would seem to me the right way forward is not to challenge him. After all we may still be misjudging him.'

'But—' began Mabel, but Iain held up his hand to silence her.

'Far better to find someone Mr Sheridan cannot possibly take exception to, so then you will have fulfilled the conditions and the legacy will be yours.'

'Yes, but who?' murmured Mabel in despair.

'I'll try and find you someone,' Iain said and got to his feet. 'I'll take advice from someone who might know what to do and I'll let you know.'

When Iain had gone, Mabel sat for a long time, thinking about what he had said. She agreed there was no way they could challenge John Sheridan, even if Chas was right. All they could do was find a suitable trustee. They were, she decided, back to square one. Consulting Iain had been a waste of time.

She went upstairs to tell her parents that Iain would try and help, but she wasn't hopeful.

'You should have more faith in him,' her mother said. 'He's a good man and he's always been a friend to you. He'll think of something.'

Chapter Forty-Four

Annie Granger closed the shop door at the end of the day and, with a sigh, went upstairs to the flat where she lived with her parents-in-law. She had been on her feet all day; pregnant, and exhausted, she longed for nothing more than a cup of tea and to put her feet up.

Annie had realised she was expecting before she and Ron were married, and as soon as she told him he was going to be a father, they had been married hastily at the register office. Having no possibility of a home of their own, they'd had to move in with his parents but it did not make for a happy household. Ron's mother, Sadie, was certain Annie had tricked Ron into marrying her because she already knew she was carrying a child that needed a father, but Ron accepted that the child was his. With Ron as a buffer between the two women, things hadn't been too bad, but then war was declared on Germany.

Ron, tired of the humdrum life of a postman and a wife with morning sickness, had been lured by the idea of adventure abroad. Afraid that it might all be over before he got to join in, he'd immediately queued up at the Recruiting Depot at New Scotland Yard and volunteered for the army.

'What on earth did you do that for?' demanded his mother. 'We've got an army to do the fighting. They don't need you!'

'Got to do my bit for king and country, haven't I?' He turned to Annie. 'You can see that, can't you, love?'

'Of course,' she replied, a little shakily. ''Course you must go.'

'Got to report to some place in Lincolnshire to do some

training,' he said and had disappeared for several weeks, before being despatched across the Channel to join the British Expeditionary Force.

Annie had been proud of him, going off to fight for his country, but it had left her living alone with a mother-in-law who despised her and treated her like a servant and a father-in-law who mostly ignored her. She had written several times to Ron at the address he had given her, but he was no letter writer and she had only received one reply, offering little comfort and saying he was now in France.

Today when she reached the top of the stairs, she found her mother-in-law sitting, stony-faced, at the kitchen table. On the table beside her was an opened envelope and a short note on lined paper, torn from a notebook. Annie could see that the letter started 'Dear Mrs Granger...' She reached out to take it but Sadie snatched it away.

'Take your hands off that,' she snarled. 'Don't you dare to touch it.'

Annie jerked her hand away, but said, 'That letter is addressed to me.'

'*I* am Mrs Granger,' retorted her mother-in-law.

Annie made a dart for the envelope and shook it at Sadie. 'But on the envelope it says Mrs A. Granger, and that's me. I am Ron's wife. So give me the letter!'

For a long moment their eyes were locked, but it was Sadie who looked away first and Annie snatched the letter from her hand.

Dear Mrs Granger

I regret to inform you that Private Ronald Granger was killed in action today. His effects will be returned to you in due course.

Please accept my condolence.

It was signed by Captain somebody, but the signature was indecipherable.

Blinking back tears, Annie read it again and thought, this scrap of paper is all that's left of him, my Ron.

But, as if the baby had heard her, it gave her sharp kick in the abdomen and she put her hand to her stomach. No, she was wrong. The baby was still there and definitely part of Ron.

Sadie saw the movement and with a look of pure hatred said, 'And I ain't gonna let you foist that bastard on him no more, not now, not ever! You got yourself up the duff and made him believe it was his. But I know better. I know your sort. You saw a chance to get your feet under our table an' you took it.'

'No!' exclaimed Annie. 'Of course I didn't. The baby is his. I ain't never been with anyone else. I love Ron...' Her voice faltered as she corrected herself. '... loved Ron.'

'Well, there ain't no place for you here, not you, or your bastard. You can take yourself off, we don't want nothink more to do with you.'

'Take myself...?'

'Off! Pack your bags and go!'

'Go?' echoed Annie sinking onto a chair opposite Sadie. 'Go where?'

'I couldn't care less, but you ain't staying here.'

'You can't just turn me out! I'm Ron's wife! I live here!'

'Not no more, you don't. If you aren't out of here before we open tomorrow, I'll put your baggage out in the street! It was you what encouraged him to join up,' Sadie went on. 'You told him it was his duty to go, and now he's dead. He ain't coming back and it's all your fault!'

'I never...' began Annie but Sadie ignored her.

'You've got tonight to pack up and be gone in the morning.'

For a moment Annie sat where she was, then she slowly got to her feet. Her Ron was dead. He was never coming back to her, so she didn't have to stay here. She could walk out of the door without a backward glance. Where she would go, she didn't yet know, but she would leave this hated place and bring up her child, hers and Ron's, in a place where there was love. She thought of her parents. They hadn't much room, but they would surely take her in, until she found somewhere.

She went into the bedroom she had shared with Ron, and pulled the cardboard case she had brought with her out from under the bed. She wouldn't wait to be thrown out, she would leave at once, this very night.

She hadn't many possessions to take, just her few clothes, and some small baby clothes she'd made. There were some clothes of Ron's, including an old jacket and a pair of trousers still hanging in the cupboard waiting for him to come home. Well, might as well take those too, she thought. He won't be needing them now. She folded them into the case; after all, she could always sell them. She had very little money of her own, just the ten bob note Ron had given her before he left.

Annie had looked at it with interest, turning it over in her fingers. She had never seen one before. 'Just for emergencies,' Ron had said.

Well, she thought now, this is an emergency all right. And folding it carefully, she put it into her pocket. At least she now had some real money. Sadie had never paid wages for what she did in the shop, just gave her bed and board. She looked round the room. The only other thing she slipped into her case before she closed it was her precious photo of her and Ron outside the register office on their wedding day, both of them beaming into the camera.

As she took her coat off the hook on the back of the door, something crackled in its pocket: a piece of paper. She pulled it out and found herself looking at one of Mabel Oakley's flyers, and Mabel's voice echoed in her ear.

'It's got my new address on it. Now we can stay in touch.'

Mabel Oakley! She smoothed the paper out and read the address. 27 Barnbury Street. That's where she'd go. If Mabel was able to take her in, she would be safe. No one would know where to find her and she needn't involve her parents. Putting her coat on, she stuffed the flyer back into the pocket and picked up her case.

The kitchen door was still shut, but she could hear Sadie moving about inside. Usually Sadie went downstairs when she'd left Annie to lock up, just to empty the till and to ensure the padlock and bolts were properly fastened on the shop door. So far this evening, shocked by the news, she had not left the kitchen. There must be some money in the till, Annie thought. If she was quick and quiet about it, perhaps she could take the wages she was owed on her way out. Dared she?

There was still little sound coming from the kitchen when Annie emerged onto the landing carrying her suitcase. Hardly daring to breathe, she edged her way down into the shop, and with a sigh of relief, drew the curtain across the bottom and switched on the light. Next, she unlocked the front door and put her case outside. With her escape route secured, she went back to the counter and opened the till. It made its usual clank as the drawer slid out, and for a moment she froze, but could hear nothing from upstairs. Reaching into the till she scooped up the coins in its tray and shoved them into her pocket. Not as much as she'd hoped, but there were a few shillings and they might tide her over. A last glance round the shop showed her some packets of Woodbines stacked on a shelf behind the counter. A final bounty. Pity they aren't Players or Senior Service, she thought, as she made a grab for a couple of packets.

And then she heard them, footsteps in the room above, her bedroom. Sadie's voice shouting, Sadie's footsteps on the stairs. Almost too late, Annie made a bolt for the street and, grabbing the case containing her worldly possessions, ran for her life. She'd left the light on in the shop and the door open behind her and as she turned the corner, she heard Sadie's shriek of fury as she saw the empty till. Without a backward glance, Annie ducked into the narrow alleyway that led to Noah's Path, and by the time Sadie had lumbered out onto the pavement, the street was empty.

'I'll have the police on you,' Sadie screeched into the chilly twilight. 'Thief! I'll have the cops on you!'

Annie waited for several long minutes, straining to hear if Sadie was still out there, waiting for her, and it wasn't until she heard the shop door being slammed shut and locked that she dared emerge from the alley and make her way towards the city. She had no real idea where Barnbury Street was, so she decided she needed to find somewhere to spend the night and find Mabel's house in the morning.

Having always lived in the surrounding area, Annie considered her options. She thought again of going to her parents', but immediately discarded that idea. The first place Sadie would look. However, then she thought of her mother's brother, Uncle Ray, who kept the Ragged Staff pub just near the new secondary school, and decided to go there.

When she reached the pub, she could see the bar was busy so rather than advertise her arrival to the assembled company, she went round to the yard at the back and tapped on the kitchen window. It wasn't Ray who opened the door to her timid knock, but his wife, Madge.

'Annie! What are you doing here?' She took in the suitcase and asked, 'You going somewhere?'

'Ron's dead,' Annie blurted out. 'Killed in France. Sadie's kicked me out.'

'She's what?'

'She's kicked me out. Says the baby isn't his, and I can't live with them no more.'

'I see,' said Madge, warily. 'And you think you'll come here?'

'Only for tonight,' answered Annie. 'I got somewhere else to go tomorrow. I just need somewhere to stay tonight.' Seeing Madge wavering she said, 'I'll be gone in the morning, promise you.'

'And where will you go then? You got a fancy man?'

'No!' snapped Annie. 'But I ain't going to tell you where, so that if she comes looking for me, you won't be able to tell her nothink.'

Madge looked at her for a long moment and then sighed. 'Just for one night then,' she said. 'I'll go and tell Ray you're here, and in the meantime, you can take your coat off and get washing them glasses.'

That night Annie slept in a narrow iron bed in one of the rooms above the bar. She didn't undress, it was far too cold. She put her coat back on and simply lay down in her clothes, pulling the thin blanket Madge had given her up to her chin. She thought of Ron, lying in a cold grave somewhere in France, her Ron, the father of her baby. She would never see him again, the baby would never know its dad, and not for the last time, Annie cried herself to sleep.

When she woke up early the next morning, she lay in the darkness and thought about what she had to do. She sat up and lit the candle she'd brought up the previous night and, tipping the coins out of her pocket, counted her money. There was twenty-one shillings and threepence farthing from the till, a little over one pound. Annie didn't think she had ever held that much money in her hands before.

Ray and Madge were both in the kitchen when she came downstairs.

'Now then, Annie,' Ray said with a smile. 'How about some breakfast, eh? Scrambled egg and bacon suit you? Madge is just cooking.'

'Thank you, Uncle,' replied Annie. 'I'd love some.'

'What's this I hear about your poor Ron? Killed in action? He was a brave man, going off to the war. You should be proud of him.'

Annie managed a smile. 'I am, Uncle. Very proud of him.'

When she had eaten every mouthful of the bacon and egg, she stood up and said, 'Thank you both for letting me stay last night.'

'You're very welcome,' Ray said. 'You can stay longer if you want to. We can let your mum know where you are.'

Annie reached up and gave him a hug. 'No, thank you all the same, Uncle Ray. I'll be moving on.'

'But where are you going? Your mum'll want to know.'

'Better I don't say. Just give her my love and tell her I'll be in touch.'

Annie finally found her way to Barnbury Street, and was about to go up to the front door when she noticed a side gate, with the sign THOMAS CLARKE, PRINTER. That was who Mabel had said she worked for. If Mabel was at work this morning it might be better to go and see her there, rather than turn up on the front doorstep with a suitcase. She opened the gate and followed the path, down round the house and into the small garden. The door to the print workshop was closed, but she could hear the regular thump of machinery, and so she peeped through the small side window and saw Mabel working the press. After about five minutes the sound stopped and Annie knocked on the door.

'Who is it?' Mabel called. 'Come in.'

Annie opened the door and looked in. 'Hallo, Mabel. It's me, Annie.'

'Annie!' Mabel exclaimed. 'How lovely! What are you doing here? Come in and sit down.'

Mabel put the kettle on to boil and then stacked the cards she had just printed.

Annie looked round at the workshop. 'Won't your boss mind you just stopping for tea?'

'My boss?' questioned Mabel, amused.

'Yes, Mr Clarke. The one what sent you round with them flyers.'

'No,' replied Mabel. 'I used to work with him, but when he died, I took over the business. It's mine now.' She made the tea and then pointed at the suitcase and asked, 'Are you on your way somewhere?'

'No,' Annie murmured. 'I wondered if I could stay with you for a little while. It's Ron.'

'What's the matter with him?'

'He's dead. He volunteered for the army and he's been killed in action.' And at last the enormity of the last twenty-four hours hit her. She broke down and, sobbing, told Mabel, her oldest friend, the whole sorry story.

'She's turned me out and I ain't got nowhere to go. I found the paper you gave me with your address on it so, well, I hoped you might be able to give me a bed for a few days while I find somewhere, get another job an' that.'

'Of course you can stay,' Mabel said. 'You can share my room. Come on, I'll take you up there now.'

'What'll your mam say?'

'She'll understand,' replied Mabel cheerfully. 'You're my oldest friend. We can't leave you out in the street, you know. Come on.' She picked up Annie's case and led the way into the house.

Alice was in the kitchen. She stared at Annie for a moment and then she broke into a smile. 'Annie? Annie Ford?'

Annie nodded and Mabel said, 'She's just coming to stay with us for a few days. She's going to share my room. That's all right, isn't it, Mam?'

For a moment Alice was at a loss. How many more waifs and strays was Mabel going to invite to live with them?

Chapter Forty-Five

Lucinda had to accept David's decision about turning Crayne House into a convalescent home. She felt sure she could persuade him, if only they could discuss the idea, face to face; she had seen what the injured men had to put up with at Netley. Surely it was better to get convalescent men out of the crowded hospital wards that she had seen there; the risk of infection, the sounds of the dying.

Well, she knew a discussion of that sort was better left until some future leave. However, he had given her a free hand to make changes at Crayne and there were definitely changes she could make to turn Crayne House into a more comfortable family home and also make converting it into a convalescent home in the future much easier. First, they should have electricity installed, and perhaps the telephone. But one thing at a time, she decided, and in her next letter to David she wrote,

What do you think about having electricity put in at Crayne? I went down there the other day and it was freezing. It's a very cold house at this time of year, and lighting and maintaining fires in all the main rooms is time-consuming for the staff. If we want to bring up our children there, rather than London, it would be far more convenient for us and the staff if we had electricity. The house could be kept cosy and warm in the coldest of winters, and all at the flick of a switch. No more cleaning oil lamps or carrying candles up the stairs. So much safer with a child in the house.

When David read the letter, he smiled ruefully. His mother had already mentioned the idea to him before he'd left and he had said she and Lucy should find someone to look into the idea. Now it sounded as if the decision had already been made. He couldn't really complain; he knew it was the sensible thing to do and they must move with the times. Besides, having turned down her idea of a convalescent home, he could make it up to Lucy by agreeing to the scheme. In his next letter, he wrote back:

It sounds as if will be an enormous upheaval. Have you found anyone who can examine how it is to be done, causing the minimum disruption?

Lucinda had. She'd mentioned the idea to Fenton and he said he knew a 'sparks' who had been invalided out of the army. 'Not an officer and that, but he was trained up by the army and knows his stuff.'

'I'll be back next week,' she said. 'You'd better tell him to come and see me if you think he might seriously be interested in tackling such a job.'

'I'm sure he will be, my lady,' Fenton assured her. 'It's hard to get work when you've been invalided out and the army don't want you no more.'

'But is he physically fit?' asked Lucinda. 'I mean there must be quite a lot of heavy work involved. I don't want him to begin the job and then discover he can't manage it and leave it all half done.'

'Certainly not, my lady. He walks with a stick and always will, but he can still do his job.'

Lucinda looked sceptical and began to wish she had asked Iain to find her someone in London, but she held her peace. She was keen to show the world that, young as she was, she was well able to run her own establishment while David was away at the war. She would meet the man and then decide. If she didn't think he was up to it, she needn't employ him. She had made no promises to Fenton and she had been assured that he had made none on her behalf.

'I'll see him next week,' she said. 'What did you say his name was?'

'Lofty. Lofty Hanch.'

'What a peculiar name,' remarked Lucinda.

'It's an army nickname, my lady, because of his size. Everyone calls him Lofty... I've never heard his real name.'

The day after her return to London, she was expected for dinner at Chanynge Place with her parents. She arrived a little early and was surprised to see Iain coming down the stairs, dressed for an evening out.

'Hello, Iain,' she said as she handed her coat to William. 'I see you're off out? Somewhere nice?'

'Yes, I am,' he replied. 'An evening with friends.'

'Which include your lovely Diana, I suppose,' said Lucinda with a grin.

'How do you... I mean who...'

'My dear Iain, the whole town is talking about you. Mama isn't very... what shall I say... pleased about it? She does *not* approve.'

'There's nothing to disapprove,' returned Iain. 'We've been in the same company occasionally that's all.' Iain kept his voice casual, unwilling to let even his sister know the number of times they had been together.

'Of course you have,' laughed Lucinda, who had heard from several people that Iain and Diana were being seen together about town: the walks in the park, an evening at the theatre, and often invited to the same select parties.

'I'll thank you to remember that it was she who came to your aid when you fainted in the House of Lords,' Iain said sternly.

Lucinda was immediately contrite. 'You're right, she did and I am very grateful. But listen, forget about her for a minute, I want to ask you something.'

'Do you now?' replied Iain cautiously. 'What is it this time?'

He didn't really have time to stop and chat, but he was keen to leave the subject of Diana and turn Lucinda's mind in a different direction.

'We're planning to have electricity installed at Crayne,' she said. 'David is happy with the idea and says we can go ahead.'

'Sounds like a big undertaking,' said Iain.

'Yes, I'm sure it will be, that's why I have to find someone who knows what they're doing.'

'Well, surely that isn't difficult. You approach the local electricity company. Who else?'

'Well, I haven't spoken to them...' began Lucinda.

'That's your first port of call, then,' said Iain. 'I suppose you want me to come with you.'

'Certainly not,' retorted Lucinda. 'I'm perfectly capable of interviewing a tradesman.'

'I doubt if it'll be a tradesman,' said Iain. 'A big job like that you'll be speaking to the boss. Do you know the questions you'll need to ask? Can they supply you or will you have to have a generator? Where would you put that, I wonder?'

'A generator?'

'It'll have to be pretty powerful, if it's going to serve the whole house. I haven't seen Crayne, but I understand that it is quite large.'

Lucinda thought of her own dismay at her first sight of Crayne and said ruefully, 'You could say that. But I haven't got that far yet. Fenton, you know, David's man? He knows someone who might do the work. Ex-army, army trained, but invalided out.'

'For goodness' sake, Lucy.' Iain sounded horrified. 'You can't employ some injured soldier to do a job like that! It has to be done by a reputable company, a firm with experience of such things... not some Tom, Dick or Harry!'

'Lofty Hanch, actually,' retorted Lucinda.

'Some little Lofty Hanch...' began Iain, before he suddenly burst out laughing.

'What's so funny?' demanded his sister

'I bet he is little! Really short, about five foot nothing.'

'Don't be silly, Iain,' Lucinda said scornfully. 'If he's known as Lofty by his friends he must be really tall.'

'Army humour,' laughed Iain. 'Nickname given to anyone who's on the short side. But, seriously, Lucy, whatever he's called and however short or tall he is, you can't simply let him loose on a house the size of Crayne. You must approach an electricity company and you'll probably need to have some plans drawn up, explaining how they mean to go about it. They'll have to take up floors and run wires. How many rooms do you want done?'

Lucinda looked at him in astonishment. 'What do you mean, how many rooms do I want done? All of them of course.'

'That'll cost a pretty penny, Lucy. Have you any idea how much?'

'Well, we can hardly do just half of it, can we?'

'Of course you can. You electrify the part of the house that you use. There must be several rooms, unused, under holland covers, which could be left until later. Will you be including the servants' quarters? Their bedrooms? Croft and Mrs Croft's sitting room?'

'Oh, for goodness' sake, Iain,' said Lucinda in frustration, 'I don't know!'

'Which is why you must instruct an electricity supply company. I imagine they'll send a surveyor out to inspect the house and tell you what is and isn't possible. I hardly think David's going to let you loose on his country home without a detailed breakdown of how it will be done and, more important, how much it will cost. Indeed, I imagine he'll want to be there himself, to keep an eye on things as they go along.'

'How much what will cost?' demanded Lady McFarlane, overhearing the end of the conversation as she came into the room.

'We're going to put electricity into Crayne, Mama,' explained

Lucinda. 'Think how convenient that will be, just to be able turn a switch and the lights come on.'

'Got to fly,' Iain said, beating a hasty retreat to the door before his mother could ask him where he was going. 'I'll see you later, Mother. If you want me to come down to Crayne with you, Lucy, of course I will. Just ask.' And with that he was gone.

'Surely you'll wait until David is home again, to oversee such a project,' Lady McFarlane said, ignoring Iain's departure and speaking to Lucinda. 'That's not something you can organise yourself, it wouldn't do at all, especially in your condition.'

'I'm not ill, Mama,' sighed Lucy. How many times did she have to say it? She wasn't going to be sitting at home making baby clothes until the birth. 'Think of the difference having electricity has made to this house.'

'We'll see what your father thinks of the idea,' said her mother. 'He'll be home in minute, so it's time I went to dress.'

When Lucinda asked him what he thought that evening at dinner, her father said, 'It may not be so easy to install in an old house like Crayne, but it's a good idea in principle. It won't be long before everyone has electricity.'

Thus encouraged, a week later Lucinda sent a telegram to the Crofts to warn them she would be visiting again at the weekend. Iain, very interested to see the famous Crayne House, agreed to come with her to meet Lofty Hanch.

The following Saturday morning, they took David's car and Iain drove them to Crayne, with one short stop in Park Lane, to collect Lady Diana.

'She wants to meet you again, Lucy,' Iain said. 'So I said she might as well come with us to Crayne. Hope you don't mind. It'll all be perfectly proper, you know. You're a married lady and you can be her chaperone.'

Lucy greeted this remark with a hoot of laughter. 'Me? Chaperone her?'

'Well, between you, you can ensure decency.'

The outing was a tremendous success. Though Lucy was shy

at first, remembering the embarrassment of her fainting fit, Diana soon put her at her ease, and before long they were chatting like old friends, comfortable in each other's company.

Lucinda explained what she was hoping to do. 'Iain says I need to have someone come and look at the house, so it can be properly planned.'

'Well, he's right,' Diana replied. 'You need to deal with someone who's done it before.'

When they arrived at Crayne, Lucinda introduced them to the Crofts, and they were delighted to meet young Lady Melcome's brother and her friend Lady Diana. They, too, were in favour of bringing electricity to the house, realising how much work it could save.

While Mrs Croft provided them with tea and some of her homemade shortbread, Croft went to find Fenton.

'Lady Melcome's here with her brother and a friend,' Croft told him. 'She says she's come to see some man about the electric.'

'That's right,' replied Fenton. 'He's on his way.'

When Lofty Hanch arrived, he turned out to be as short as Iain had predicted, but he was a muscular man and there was no doubting his strength. There was no doubt, either, that he knew his job. He had been in touch with the local electricity company and discovered they already supplied power to two other places in Crayne Abbas, one the doctor's house and the other the post office.

'If you approach them, my lady, sir, they should be able to bring a mains power cable right to your door, and then I can take it from there. I'll need three other blokes to work under me, so that we don't take too long to lay the cables. I'll do you a fair job for a fair price.'

Despite his doubts, Iain took to the man, but even so he was worried about Lofty's abilities. 'It's a big house,' he pointed out. 'How will you manage on your own? There must be heavy work involved, too much for one man.'

'Well, like I said, we'll need four of us, but I know three other blokes I've worked with before. I've already had a look round the place. All I need from her ladyship is a note of which rooms she wants done first and we can get planning. We'll start work after Christmas and come the end of January, you won't know the place. Be like a lighthouse, it will.'

At midday, Mrs Croft provided a thick vegetable soup followed by a raised pie. 'Only a scratch luncheon, I'm afraid, my lady,' she said apologetically, 'but warm and filling to keep out the cold.'

When they had finished the meal with apple tart and cream, Diana announced that she could hardly move. 'I think if you don't mind, Lucy, I'll stay here by the fire, while you and Iain go and interview the electricity people. You won't need me.'

'We'll be as quick as we can,' Iain said. 'I want to be back in town before its quite dark, if we can.'

Within the hour they were back again and found Lady Diana fast asleep on the sofa before the drawing room fire.

'You back already?' she murmured, stretching like a cat and rubbing her eyes. 'You were quick.'

'The man at Bucks Electricity Company was half expecting us,' said Iain. 'He knows Hanch and had heard that we were looking to put power into Crayne House. He says his company can bring power to the house but that the rest would be down to Hanch. He's going to write to Lucy with all the details for David's approval.'

The afternoon was closing in as they approached London and drove into Park Lane. As Diana got out of the car, a taxi pulled up beside them and her father, Lord Waldon, got out.

'What's this?' he asked. 'Are we having a dinner party?'

'We weren't,' Diana replied, 'but we could.' She turned to Iain and Lucinda. 'Will you stay? No need to change, we'll eat *en famille* and simply sit round the table as we are. That all right with you, Pop?'

'Oh, I couldn't,' began Lucinda. 'I'm not supposed to go into company just now.'

'We're not company, Lucy, we met weeks ago and have become good friends. Isn't that right, Iain? Not company at all? Let's go in at least, it's freezing out here.' She reached to take Lucy by the hand, and saying, 'You'll catch your death,' led her into the building.

Lord Waldon turned to Iain. 'McFarlane, isn't it? Never forget a face. Heard you'd been squiring my daughter about.'

Iain felt the colour flood his cheeks, but managed to say, 'I have had that honour, sir.'

'Fair enough, provided you remember the proprieties.' He glanced at the car, parked at the roadside. 'Yours?'

'No, sir, it belongs to my brother-in-law. We just borrowed it for the day.'

Lord Waldon nodded and then said, 'Well, we'd better follow the ladies. Your sister, I assume? Lady Melcome?'

'Yes, sir.' Iain was surprised that Lord Waldon knew who his sister was and wondered if Diana's father had been doing some checking up on him. He couldn't blame him, he supposed.

Once they were upstairs in the apartment and Diana had made the formal introductions, Lord Waldon said he hoped Lady Melcome and Mr McFarlane would indeed stay for dinner, but that he had business to attend to if they would excuse him from joining them.

It was a convivial meal. Once Lucinda had been convinced that there was no impropriety in her staying, she dashed off a note to Sloane Square to say that she was dining with her brother, who would escort her home later on.

By the time she got home again, Lady Melcome had retired for the night, but Lucinda wanted to write to David before she went to bed. Her head was full of the day and what they had been able to discover and she went straight to her parlour.

Our trip to Crayne was well worth it. I will send you the details when I receive them from the Electricity Company who will supply the power to the house and from Mr Hanch, the electrician who, with three men under him, will do the wiring. Oh David, it will make all the difference. He says he'll start after Christmas, I didn't want him to disturb your mother's Christmas plans, and then he'll be finished by the end of January.

I think we'll have the telephone line put in at the same time, so much easier to keep in touch with those in London. By the time you get home on leave, whenever that is, Crayne will be the perfect family home. All my love, Lucy.

Chapter Forty-Six

Once Iain had dropped Lucinda home to Sloane Square, he returned David's car to its garage and took a taxi home. He had enjoyed his day out with Lucy and Diana immensely, and had been pleased at how easily the two of them had slipped into comfortable conversation. But now he was on his way home, unexpectedly his thoughts had returned to Mabel and the question of her trustee. He had said he would try to find someone suitable, but how on earth could he fulfil that promise? Who did he know, apart from his father and perhaps Martin Mayhew, who might be prepared to take on the responsibility for some unknown girl? Someone who would work well with the present trustee, Andrew Oakley? Mabel had told him not to discuss the matter with his father, but he had not actually agreed with her. The guv'nor knew Mabel well, knew that she was making her way in the world. Surely he might be prepared to stand as her trustee? His mother wouldn't be pleased. She had never forgiven Mabel for refusing to return to the McFarlane household as a maid. She regarded it as a personal insult to her, and would have nothing further to do with her. Would his mother's disapproval of Mabel's unusual business stop her husband from giving her a helping hand now?

Nothing for it, Iain thought as he paid off the taxi, I'll have to speak to the guv'nor privately, and explain the situation. Mabel had come to him because she trusted him, and he was anxious that trust should not be misplaced. He had always thought the McFarlane family had owed Mabel more than the offer of her old job back when she had been proved innocent of theft. Iain thought his father had felt the same. It was that slight guilt which might come to Mabel's aid now.

When Felstead opened the front door to admit him, Iain asked, 'Is my father still up?'

'Yes, sir,' replied the butler. 'He's working in his library.'

Iain shed his coat, knocked on the library door and went in. There was a fire still smouldering in the grate, and the room was warm and welcoming on this cold night, with the burning applewood scenting the air.

His father was sitting at his desk, a brandy balloon at his elbow, and some papers in front of him, making notes on a legal pad.

He smiled as Iain entered and said, 'Oh, it's you, Iain.'

'Am I interrupting something?' Iain asked.

'No, nothing that can't wait. Come and sit down. Brandy?'

'Yes, please.'

His father waved towards the decanter on the side table. Iain poured himself a generous measure and sat down beside the fire and, having topped up his own glass, his father took the chair opposite.

'Your mother's already gone up,' he said. 'She wears herself out with everything she's been doing.'

'She's anxious to support you as a peer of the realm,' Iain said with a grin.

'Yes, I know, but I don't want her to wear herself into an early grave.' He took a sip of his brandy and went on, 'Was it today you were driving Lucinda down to Crayne?'

'Yes. It's an amazing house, isn't it?'

'I'm sure it is,' replied his father. 'Never seen it myself, but I imagine electricity will improve it!' He looked at Iain for a long moment and then said, 'Anything special I can do for you?'

'Well,' replied Iain. 'There is something I'd like to discuss with you, guv'nor, if you have time.'

'I always have time for you, Iain,' said his father. 'Put another log on the fire and tell me what the problem is.'

Iain reached over and poked the glowing embers into life, then put on another log, watching for a moment or two to be certain it would catch.

I always have time for you, his father had said, and Iain realised it was true. If ever he had gone to his father with a problem, large or small, Keir had listened carefully before responding in some way that invariably helped.

Keir watched him tend the fire and wondered if Iain was going to speak of his interest in Lady Diana Fosse-Bury, an interest that infuriated his mother.

'Woman trouble?' he suggested tentatively, thinking it was probably a good thing Isabella had already gone to bed.

'Sort of. It's Mabel Oakley.'

'Mabel Oakley!' exclaimed Keir. He certainly hadn't been expecting her name to crop up. 'What about her?'

'She's asked me for some help,' began Iain.

'Money?'

'No, certainly not. She's far too proud to do that. No, it's advice she's asked for and I'm not sure what to say.'

'But why has she come to you?'

'Because she trusts me, I think. I know Mother wouldn't approve, but I've stayed in touch with her since she left. I always felt we'd sold her short, once it was clear that she had absolutely nothing to do with the theft of Lucy's brooch.'

'We offered her her job back,' his father reminded him. 'And your mother wrote an excellent character reference.'

'Yes, I know all that,' said Iain, 'but was it enough?'

'You'd better tell me what she's after,' said his father.

'I'll have to explain. It goes back quite a long way.'

'I'm listening,' replied Keir.

So Iain told the story of Mr Clarke the printer and how he had taken Mabel on as an apprentice. 'When he died, he left everything he had to Mabel, including his house, but the money was in trust with two trustees.' He further explained that Mabel had continued to run the printing business on her own.

'But she's only a girl!' objected Keir. 'Surely that didn't last long.'

'Oh, she's very much still in business, though she kept the name Thomas Clarke, Printer, which means many of customers don't realise she now *is* Thomas Clarke.'

'But is she any good?' demanded Keir.

'Yes, she works to a high standard,' answered Iain. 'You've seen some of her work.'

'Have I?' Keir looked startled. 'When?'

'She was the printer who did the rush job for Lucy's second wedding invitations.'

'Was she? I didn't know that. They looked all right, didn't they?'

'Very professional,' agreed Iain. 'And she worked late to make sure they were ready the same day.'

'So what does she want now, if it isn't money?'

'Well, one of her trustees has died...' And Iain went on to outline the problem she was facing now. His father listened in silence, but when Iain finally fell silent, he said, 'So, without a second trustee she can't inherit?'

'No, and the executor of the will has said he must approve the person she suggests, as fit.'

'It's a fair comment,' said Keir. 'He must be sure that it's a man of integrity, so that when the trust is finally wound up it is in good heart, her money intact.'

'I quite agree,' replied Iain, 'and Mabel is no fool. She knows it's important too, but she doesn't know anyone who this solicitor, John Sheridan, would accept. And that, guv'nor, is why she's asking for help.'

'What is she expecting *you* to do?'

'She's hoping I can think of someone suitable, and prepared to become her second trustee.'

'Does she think you are going to take it on?'

'No, she realises it should be someone older and more qualified.'

'And you thought of me?' There was a gleam of humour in Keir's eyes as he spoke. 'How very gratifying!'

'No, guv'nor, I didn't think of you, or at least I didn't think of you as a possible trustee, but I thought you might think of someone we could ask. I doubt if it will be a very onerous job. She runs her business efficiently and is keeping herself afloat, even in these turbulent times. I did wonder about approaching Mayhew. What do you think?'

'I think it would be putting him in an embarrassing position, Iain. Difficult for him to say no, but rather unfair to expect him to take on an unknown girl for another three or four years.'

'Yes,' agreed Iain reluctantly, 'I suppose it would. Well, I'm stuck then.'

'I'll give it some thought,' said his father. He downed the last of his brandy in one swallow and heaved himself out of his chair. 'Time to turn in,' he said as he set his glass aside. 'You coming up?'

'Yes,' replied Iain. 'Nothing else I can do tonight.'

Together the two men went upstairs, parting on the landing, both still thinking about Mabel Oakley, the girl who, against all the odds, was still running her own business, a woman daring to invade the world of men, taking them on as equals. Surely they could find somebody to act as trustee.

Iain knew there was a real possibility that John Sheridan was doing as Mabel had told him, deliberately blocking her inheritance while claiming due diligence.

Lord McFarlane of Haverford was also thinking about the case. Would it really matter to anyone, except young Mabel Oakley, if he actually offered to act as a second trustee for her? Iain had not actually accused this John Sheridan of dishonesty in his dealings as Hugh Morrell's executor, but he'd hinted at it. He'd suggested the only way to overcome the 'due diligence' argument was to provide a suitable candidate as the second trustee. Surely, if he, now a law lord, offered his services to Andrew Oakley, in a perfectly private capacity, he would be accepted, both by the Oakley family and John Sheridan.

Keir would need sight of the wills of both Thomas Clarke and Hugh Morrell, but if they were perfectly signed, sealed and executed, Mabel Oakley's problem might be solved and Hugh Morrell's wishes carried out as intended.

Keir decided to sleep on the idea and see what he thought in the morning. Iain obviously thought well of the girl, and thought they owed her a helping hand, and his father was inclined to agree.

Chapter Forty-Seven

Mabel was about to go down to her print workshop on Monday morning when there was a knock on the front door.

'I'll go,' she called and pulled back the bolts. For a moment she stared in astonishment. Outside in the street was the McFarlane Rolls Royce, with Croxton standing beside it, as if on guard, but even more astonishing was that Lord McFarlane himself was standing on the doorstep, his hand about to lift the knocker again.

'Good morning, Miss Oakley,' he said, raising his hat with a smile. 'I do hope this isn't an inconvenient time to call, but I wanted a word with you and your father.'

'No, no, not at all,' stammered Mabel, standing aside to allow him to enter. 'Please come in.'

'I know it's early, said his lordship, stepping inside, 'but I'm on the way to my chambers and need to be there by eleven.'

'Who is it, Mabel?' called her mother from the kitchen.

'It's Lord McFarlane, Mam, come to speak to me and Dada.'

'Who?' cried her mother emerging from the kitchen wiping flour off her hands with her apron.

'I'm sorry to come unannounced, Mrs Oakley,' Keir McFarlane apologised, 'but I was hoping for a word with your husband. I hope it's not inconvenient.'

'No, sir, not at all. Mabel, show his lordship into the parlour and then go and tell your father that he's got a visitor.'

For a moment Mabel hesitated and Alice said, 'Perhaps you'd like to wait in the parlour, my lord.' She opened the door beside

him and stood aside to usher him into the front room, hissing at
Mabel, 'Go and tell your father!'

As Lord McFarlane walked into the parlour, he saw at once
that it was not in use every day. The furniture was polished and
the cushions were plumped up in the armchairs, but though
there was a fire in the grate, the room was chilly and the fire
unlit; definitely a room for visitors.

'Please, do sit down, sir,' Alice said. 'I'm sure Mabel and my
husband will be with you in a moment. In the meantime, may I
get some refreshment? Some tea perhaps?'

'That's very kind, Mrs Oakley,' he replied, sitting down in one
of the armchairs. 'Just a cup of tea would be very welcome.' He
hadn't wanted tea, but realised it would be a snub to Mrs Oakley
to turn refreshment down

When Alice had made her excuses and disappeared to the
kitchen, Keir McFarlane sat back in the armchair and wondered
again exactly why he had come to visit the Oakley family.

He had slept on the idea that had been put to him, and when
he woke the following morning, he found his brain had made
the decision for him. He would go and visit Andrew Oakley,
Mabel's father, and find out a little more about both the wills
concerned, but if it was clear what had been intended by each
of the deceased, then he would discuss the situation with Oakley
and take it from there.

Iain was just leaving the breakfast table when his father came
down.

'Ah, Iain,' he said. 'I've been giving consideration to what you
said last night, and I've decided to look into the situation.'

'Really, guv'nor?'

'I'm not guaranteeing anything, mind you, but I'll go and see
Mabel's father and find out how things stand. Where do they
live?'

Iain gave him the address. 'You know that her father is a cripple
now, don't you?' he said. 'Paralysed after a traffic accident.'

'Yes, I remember.'

'I hope you can sort it out,' Iain said. 'It really is important to Mabel.'

'We'll see,' was all his father said.

Keir wondered now what kind of man Andrew Oakley was, and what Isabella would say if she knew that for some reason he was sitting in the Oakleys' front room. She certainly wouldn't approve, but he was committed to nothing yet.

Leaving her mother to deal with their unexpected visitor, Mabel hurried into her father's room, pulling the door to behind her.

'It's Lord McFarlane,' she hissed. 'He wants to talk to both of us.'

'You're about ready to go through to the kitchen, Andrew,' said Mrs Finch, straightening the bed covers. 'Do you want me to push you through?'

'No, not to the kitchen,' Mabel said. 'Mam's put him in the parlour. I'll take Dada in there. We need somewhere to talk uninterrupted.'

Grasping the handles of her father's wheelchair, she pushed him into the parlour, where Lord McFarlane was waiting.

His lordship immediately got to his feet and crossed the room, hand outstretched.

'Good morning, Mr Oakley. Please forgive this intrusion.'

'No intrusion, sir,' Andrew replied shaking the extended hand. 'I'm always glad to have visitors. Won't you take a seat? Mabel, ask your mother to come in, will you?'

At that moment, Alice appeared carrying a tray with teapot and cups, a milk jug and sugar basin. Keir McFarlane could see at once that the best china had been brought out in his honour. Following behind was Doreen Finch, with a plate of homemade biscuits.

'I'll just pour your tea,' Alice said, setting the tray down on a side table, 'and then we'll leave you to it.'

'I'd like you to stay, Mabel,' said Lord McFarlane, 'if you don't mind.'

Mind? Mabel had had every intention of staying to hear why Iain's father had arrived unannounced on their doorstep. She had asked Iain not to speak to his father, and although she was annoyed that he must have done so anyway, another part of her realised that this unexpected visit might offer a glimmer of hope.

'You sit down too, Mabel,' said her father, as the door closed behind Alice.

Turning to Lord McFarlane, he asked, 'What can we do for you, sir?'

'It's more what I may be able to do for you,' replied his lordship. 'Iain tells me that there is a legal matter troubling you, but it's not something he can deal with. Something about a bequest, Miss Oakley? Perhaps you, or your father, would like to explain what the problem is and how it has come about. Put me in the picture.'

Briefly Andrew outlined what had happened from the time when Mr Thomas Clarke had left everything he had in trust for Mabel, until she married or reached the age of twenty- one.

'I am one of the trustees and the other was Mr Clarke's solicitor, Mr Hugh Morrell. Unfortunately, Mr Morrell has recently died, leaving me as the sole trustee, and that is our problem.'

Lord McFarlane continued to listen without interruption while Andrew explained about the terms of Hugh Morrell's will. When Andrew finally fell silent, he asked, 'And do you have copies of these wills, and the codicil of course?'

'Yes, we do,' answered Andrew. 'Mabel, can you fetch them? They are in the drawer of my desk, next door.'

'Yes,' she said, getting up. 'I know where they are.'

Moments later she was back with the folder of the documents which had been reluctantly supplied by the solicitors and the letter for Andrew which Chas had delivered.

'I was left a letter by Mr Morrell, too,' Mabel said. 'I expect you'll want to see that as well. It's in the print room.' Leaving the two men together, she went down to fetch it.

'I understand from Iain that Mabel is running her own printing business,' Keir McFarlane said to Andrew. 'She seems an unusually resourceful girl.'

'Yes, she'd been working with Thomas Clarke for some months, when he died unexpectedly, and she was determined to keep the business going. Thomas Clarke, Printer.'

'And it's successful?'

'Oh yes,' Andrew said. 'She works very hard to keep her head above water, but she's built up a client list and she certainly contributes as much, if not more, to the family income as she would if she was in service,' adding with a wry smile, 'and she's her own boss. Nobody's telling her what she can and can't do.'

'Hmm, a very independent young lady,' said Lord McFarlane, and turned his attention to the documents Mabel had handed him.

First, Thomas Clarke's will, which set up the trust, and then Hugh Morrell's, with its separate codicil.

He was reading Hugh's letter to Andrew when Mabel came back into the room.

'Here is mine,' she said as she passed it over to him. 'Mr Morrell makes it very clear what he wants to happen, he was just concerned that my father might have problems acting as the sole trustee. I think he thought Mr Sheridan would replace him, but he has refused. Says he's not in a position to do so.'

Lord McFarlane had been a judge long enough to see there was another agenda here, and wondered what the problem really was. All the papers were in order, including the handwritten codicil, signed and witnessed. Provided a suitable second trustee was accepted by Andrew, he couldn't see why the will should not be proved.

He smiled at Mabel. 'I agree, it's pretty clear. I'm impressed you run your business on your own. I would be very interested in seeing your workshop. May I?'

Disappointed, Mabel said, 'Yes, of course.' And taking him out of the front door, past the Rolls Royce still waiting in the street, she led him through the Thomas Clarke side gate and down the path to the basement workshop.

Keir McFarlane wasn't sure what he'd been expecting, but he was impressed by the way the workshop was laid out, the printing press the dominant thing, but the organisation of the other tools of her trade, type, inks, paper, card, everything in its place, showed him how well she managed her business.

'What would you do with Mr Morrell's bequest, if the problem of fulfilling the condition was solved?' he asked casually. 'Any particular plans? Expanding your business perhaps?'

'I have got an idea or two,' replied Mabel, 'but,' she went on, looking her erstwhile employer in the eye, 'you might not approve of them.'

'What you choose to use it for is none of my business,' answered Lord Keir. 'Mr Morrell has made that quite clear both in the codicil and his letter to you. It will be your money, and how you use it is nobody's business but your own. If you squander it, well, so be it, but somehow, I don't think you will.'

When Mabel gave no indication of how she might use her bequest, Lord McFarlane smiled at her and said, 'Iain is right. You are a most unusual and enterprising young woman.'

'Did he say that?' Mabel sounded surprised.

'Words to that effect. He thinks very well of you... as do I. Let's go back up to your father now and discuss what we can do.'

Back in the front room once more, Keir McFarlane looked at the man in the wheelchair and tried to imagine living in a world so reduced. Surely the frustration must be unbearable, and yet he seemed calm and resigned to his lot.

'What a fascinating workshop she has,' he said, as he resumed his seat.

'She has, hasn't she,' agreed Andrew. 'I sometimes go down there for my lessons. She's teaching me to typeset. If I became really proficient, she could take on more work, doing the actual printing.'

It might have been the determination of Andrew Oakley not to be entirely side-lined by his paralysis which finally decided Lord McFarlane of Haverford to offer himself as Mabel's second trustee. One thing he was sure of was that executor, John Sheridan, could not dismiss him as unsuitable.

'How would it be,' he said casually, 'if I offered to stand as your second trustee, Mabel? Would you be happy for me to help look after your affairs? What do you think?'

For a long moment Mabel stared at him. 'You would take it on yourself?' she breathed. 'Really?'

'I think I could manage that, provided your father agrees as well.'

'When Iain said he'd try and help, I thought he meant he'd find someone suitable.'

'Well,' replied Lord McFarlane with a smile, 'I think he has, don't you?' He turned to Andrew. 'As long as you're happy, as well.'

The two Oakleys hardly knew what to say, so their new trustee said, 'I suggest you write to Mr Sheridan and name me as second trustee. You may refer him to me at my chambers.'

'Mr Morrell took a small remuneration for his work,' began Andrew, wondering how much a judge in chambers would expect.

'I think I must waive any fee,' replied Lord McFarlane. 'This will be pro bono.' He got to his feet, saying, 'Now that's all agreed, I've got a meeting to go to. I will leave it to you to inform the executor that you are now in a position to accept the condition laid down in the will.' Shaking hands with both Andrew and Mabel, he said, 'My compliments to your mother, Miss Oakley... or may I call you Mabel?'

'Please, Mabel.' She went with him to the front door.

As he paused on the step, he said, 'I wish you well, Mabel. I can see why two gentlemen trusted you as they have. They recognised you as a woman of the future.'

Chapter Forty-Eight

The letter lay on John Sheridan's desk with the other post, but it had been delivered by hand. He looked at it and then rang the bell for his secretary.

'When did this come, Miss Harper?' he asked.

'I don't know, sir,' she replied. 'It was through the letterbox with the other post when I arrived. Is there something wrong?'

'No, never mind, I just wondered if you'd seen who brought it.'

'No, sir, I'm afraid not.'

When Miss Harper seemed to be waiting for more, John Sheridan said, 'Thank you, Miss Harper. I'll ring when I need you again.'

Thus dismissed, Miss Harper left the room reluctantly and returned to her own office.

There was another letter lying on her desk, also hand delivered, addressed to Mr Charles Sheridan, and she was pretty sure she recognised the writing on that one. Not the same as on the one to Mr Sheridan, but familiar all the same. Mabel Oakley.

Mr Charles had been sent by his father to visit a client and didn't know a letter had come for him. Miss Harper picked it up by its corners and peered at the writing. She was almost certain the handwriting on the envelope was Mabel's. She'd seen it often enough on documents that had been typed for Mr Morrell. So what was she doing, writing letters to Mr Charles?

If I'm right, she thought now, it proves what I tried to tell Mr Sheridan before; there's definitely something going on between that little trollop and Mr Charles; something very unprofessional.

Surely, she decided, Mr Charles's father will want to know.

Before taking it through to the senior partner, Hermione Harper knew she must have proof. There was only one way to find out. She set the envelope aside and put a light to the gas ring under the kettle. She would have to be very careful how she steamed the envelope open, in case it wasn't from Mabel Oakley after all. Business letters were delivered by hand occasionally, and she might have to reseal it.

To ensure he wasn't disturbed, John Sheridan waited until Miss Harper had returned to her office before he picked up his letter and, with the blade he used as an opener, slit the envelope open. The enclosed letter was brief, written in what John Sheridan now remembered was Andrew Oakley's neat handwriting, addressed from 27 Barnbury Street, London and dated the previous day.

John Sheridan Esq
Messrs Sheridan, Sheridan and Morrell
St John's Square,
London

Dear Sir,

Reference the Will of Hugh Morrell deceased.

I write as a trustee of the trust set up by Mr Thomas Clarke for my daughter, Mabel Oakley. Since the death of Mr Morrell, the other trustee nominated by Mr Clarke, I have invited The Honourable Lord McFarlane of Haverford to take Mr Morrell's place and he has agreed to stand as the second trustee.

His offer of acting as her second trustee fulfils the condition required by Mr Morrell for Mabel to inherit the money he has left her. There being no further impediment to the

*bequest, I look forward to hearing that the execution of Mr
Morrell's will is proceeding in the normal way.*

*Should there be any queries about this agreement, I suggest
you contact Lord McFarlane at his Lincoln's Inn chambers.*

*I remain, sir, your obedient servant,
Andrew Oakley*

John Sheridan read the letter through twice and then dropped
it onto his desk in disgust.

'How does she do it?' he asked his office bitterly. 'How does
that girl manipulate any man she comes across?' There was
nothing more he could do, not even confirm what was in the
letter with Lord McFarlane. Not even the Oakleys could make
such a thing up. Still angry, he put the letter in his desk and
went out to see if Charles was back yet. As he walked along
the passage he could hear the kettle whistling in Miss Harper's
office. A bit early for a cup of tea, he thought, but if she's got the
kettle on, she might as well make me one as well. Her office door
was half open and as he pushed it wider, he saw that far from
making tea, she was standing beside the kettle with an envelope
in hand, easing it open. So intent was she on what she was doing,
Miss Harper did not realise he was in the doorway, watching in
disbelief as she pulled the letter from the envelope.

'Miss Harper.' John Sheridan's voice was icy cold. 'Kindly
bring that letter to me.'

Miss Harper spun round, the letter still clutched in her
hand, the kettle still whistling on the gas ring. She stared at her
employer in horror, a rabbit caught in the headlamps.

In one stride he was across the room and taking the letter
out of her hand; he picked up the envelope and saw that it was
addressed to his son.

'How dare you?' he demanded. 'How dare you spy on my

son? Did I not make myself clear when I warned you before that if there was any question of doing so, you would be dismissed?'

'It's from that wretched girl,' cried his secretary. 'I know her writing.'

'I don't care who it's from,' retorted John Sheridan, and as he spoke, it was true. 'I will not employ untrustworthy staff, so you may clear your desk, Miss Harper, and leave this office immediately. And do not apply to me for a reference, for I will not give you one.'

Hermione Harper stared at him dumbfounded for a moment, before stammering, 'But I was your father's secretary and...'

'And now you've been dismissed for dishonesty,' interrupted her boss. 'Please clear your desk immediately and I will pay you what you're owed for this week.'

'You aren't even half the man your father was,' she hissed. 'He would never have got himself into the mess you're in now. He was a match for anyone.' And with that she yanked her desk drawer open and stowed her few personal belongings in her capacious handbag. Snatching her coat and hat from the stand in the corner, she held out her hand. 'Two pounds ten shillings and sixpence,' she said.

Her shouting had alerted the girls in the typing pool next door that something interesting was going on in the corridor and they peered round their office door in time to see Mr John Sheridan hand the terror of the typing pool some money. Suddenly aware of their presence, Miss Harper spun round. 'What're you lot gawping at?' she snapped. 'I'm leaving, right, and you can all go to hell!'

There was a gasp at her language, but she put the money into her coat pocket and pushing her way past Arthur Bevis, who had just emerged into the corridor, she stamped down the stairs, cannoning into Chas as he came in from the street.

'Get out of my way,' she snarled. 'You're no better than your father.' And with that she disappeared.

Chas took the stairs two at a time and found the various office staff out on the landing.

'What on earth's going on?' he demanded.

'Mr Sheridan's just sacked Miss Harper,' Bevis told him. 'He's gone back to his office.'

'Well, nothing more to see,' Chas said firmly. 'Back to work, everyone.'

Chas put his briefcase into Mr Morrell's office, which he had been using since the old man's death, and went along the corridor to tap on his father's door.

He found his father at his desk, staring blankly at a letter in his hand.

'Guv'nor?' Chas said. 'What's going on? Have you really sacked Hermione?'

'Yes, for disloyalty. I'd warned her before. If I caught her spying on you, me or anyone else in this office she would be out.' He looked across at his son. 'Perhaps I should sack you too, for your disloyalty.'

'What on earth do you mean?' asked Chas with a show of bravado he didn't feel. 'What have I done?'

'What have you done? You've been carrying on a relationship with a client of this firm, which is entirely unprofessional. You've discussed confidential office business with her and God alone knows who else. If that isn't disloyalty, I don't know what is.'

'I've been... What—' Chas began, but his father cut him off.

'You'd better read this,' he said, holding out the letter. 'After all, it's addressed to you.'

Chas took it and, having read it through, sank onto the chair in front of the desk.

Oh Mabel! What have you done?

Dear Chas

The problem of the second trustee has been solved. Lord McFarlane, where I worked when I was in service, has offered to stand as my second trustee. Thank you for warning me that your father might try and block me, he can hardly say Lord McFarlane's not suitable, can he? I think that means that I should receive the money Mr Morrell left me in due course. I know our fathers truly dislike one another, and that has made things difficult for us too. I need to see you. Can we meet at the usual place on Monday?'

Mabel.

'Do you deny that you told her what I said to you, in confidence, Charles? Did you tell her, and her father as well, that I was going to use my appointment as executor to exclude her from Hugh's will?'

'I thought you were wrong to try and alter the terms of Mr Morrell's will,' replied Chas calmly. 'It was perfectly clear that he wanted Mabel to have something of her own, other than whatever is in Mr Clarke's trust. I still think it would be wrong to alter his expressed wish. Your job as an executor is to carry out his wishes, even if you think them mistaken.'

'Don't you dare to tell me how to do my job.' John Sheridan started to his feet and for a moment Chas thought he was going to strike him. 'You're here to learn, do you understand?'

'All I did was to warn Mabel and Mr Oakley that they really did need a replacement trustee... which was what Mr Morrell thought, too. Only he expected you to do it, because he asked you to, but you never intended to, did you? You blamed me for the codicil, but if I hadn't witnessed his signature, it would have made no real difference, he'd simply have got someone else.'

'You may not have approved of what I was suggesting,' answered his father a little more calmly, 'but you had no right to repeat our private conversation to anyone else. *You* were disloyal to me and to the firm. How can I trust you now, any more than I could trust Miss Harper?'

'What made you sack her this morning?' asked Chas. 'What had she done that merited instant dismissal?'

'Steaming open your letter, if you must know. I caught her with the letter in her hand and the kettle boiling fit to bust. There had been another letter delivered by hand, from Andrew Oakley, to inform me that Lord McFarlane was taking over as a trustee for Mabel. Yours must have been delivered at the same time.'

'At least you've got rid of Horrible Hermione,' said Chas, trying to lighten the mood. 'I think everyone in the office will be glad to see the back of her. I certainly will.'

His father did not smile, he simply said, 'You'd better get back to work. And from now on, I want to see every letter you write, before it is sent out in the firm's name. You will continue with your articles under my supervision. In the meantime, I shall have to get on and find a new partner and a new secretary.'

'And what about Mabel?'

'Get out of my sight,' spluttered his father, 'before I do something I regret.'

Chapter Forty-Nine

Mabel was early on the following Monday. She waited in the churchyard, her eyes never leaving the front door of Rosie's Tea Room. She knew Chas would come. He hadn't replied to the letter she had pushed through the solicitors' letterbox along with the one from her father, addressed to John Sheridan; but she was certain.

He arrived as the church clock was striking four. It was growing dark, even that early in the evening. Mabel had left her bike tucked behind a large tomb near the wall, so that it was not immediately visible from the street. As soon as Chas came round the corner, she went out to meet him, walking into his arms as naturally as if she had always been there. He held her close against him and she clung to him, afraid he might disappear if she let him go. For a long moment they stood, only aware of each other, and then, at last releasing her, Chas took her hand and led her into the tea room, wonderfully warm after the chill of the night outside.

There was only one other table taken, by two elderly ladies, sharing a pot of tea and a plate of crumpets.

'Where have you two been?' asked Rosie as she took their coats and sat them down at a corner table near the stove. 'We've missed you.'

'Pressure of work,' Chas replied. 'Have you got any more crumpets, Rosie? Or buttered toast?'

'Can manage buttered toast,' Rosie replied. 'Crumpets were very popular today. They're all gone, I'm afraid. I'll just bring your tea. Won't be long.'

'You got my note then?' Mabel said, as she held out her hands to the stove.

'Yes, but there's a story that goes with it,' Chas answered, and related what had happened. 'The best thing is that Horrible Hermione has gone, and you should feel the difference it makes to everyone in the office.'

'But your father blames you for telling me what he was hoping to do?'

'He thinks I betrayed his trust,' Chas said. 'And of course I did.'

'But you did it because he was wrong.'

'That, and because, if I'd let him go ahead, I would have had to live with the fact that I could have stopped him and didn't. Mr Morrell wrote me letter as well, you know, in which he wrote "I think I can trust you to stand a good friend to Mabel in the days to come". He trusted me to look after you.'

'I see,' said Mabel flatly. 'You mean you only became my friend because he told you to.'

'Oh, Mabel! Of course I didn't mean that.' Chas reached for her hands and, gently smoothing the soft skin between her fingers, said, 'Look at me. Mabel. You've got it all back to front. Hugh Morrell could see what you already meant to me, so he knew he could entrust you to me. He could have asked anyone to witness his signature, but he particularly asked me, in case the codicil was queried. But, as you can imagine, my father isn't best pleased.'

'What did he say?'

'Told me to get out of his sight, before he did something he'd regret.'

'And did you?'

'Yes, of course. He's still furious with me, three days later, but he'll calm down in the end. At least I hope he will.'

'And if he doesn't?'

'Well, he hasn't yet,' admitted Chas with a rueful smile.

'Oh Chas, I should never have sent that letter to you' cried

Mabel, stricken, 'but I was so excited that Lord McFarlane had agreed, I couldn't wait to tell you.'

'It's not your fault, Mabel,' insisted Chas, lifting her fingers to his lips. 'After all, your father had written to mine to inform him about Lord McFarlane, so he already knew that, without reading your letter to me. He wouldn't even have seen yours if he hadn't caught Horrible Hermione red-handed, steaming it open.'

'She was what?'

'Steaming your letter open. My father found her in her office, holding the letter over the boiling kettle.'

'You mean, because she thought it was from me?' Mabel was incredulous. 'But why? And what made her think so?'

'I'm not sure she did, but she was certainly trying to find out. She was determined to tell my father about having seen us together, but when he found her opening my post, well it caught *her* out.'

'So what happened?' Mabel asked. 'Did she accuse you to your face?'

'No, he didn't give her the chance. To give him his due, the guv'nor sacked her on the spot. It was just unfortunate that everything happened on the same morning. Since then, my father has refused to speak to me. We still work in the same office, we still live in the same house and sit at the same dinner table, but in all that time he hasn't addressed a single word to me. It's been extremely difficult for my mother and my sister, with so much tension in the house. Mother asked me what on earth had come between us and begged me to apologise to him, but on the one occasion I tried to clear the air, he simply got to his feet and stalked out of the room. 'My sister, Lavinia, told me she'd heard Mother trying to reason with him, but he told her I had been untrustworthy and disloyal and he wanted to hear no more about it. Anyway, one way and another, living at home has become impossible.'

'Oh Chas! What will you do?'

'I'm going to leave,' answered Chas. 'I'm twenty-three, Mabel, and I shouldn't still be living with my parents.'

'But where will you go?' Mabel's hand tightened on Chas's fingers as if to stop him standing up and walking away.

'That's what I've come to tell you, Mabel; I'm volunteering for France. I'm going to sign up for the army.'

'No! Oh, no!' The words erupted from her without conscious thought. 'No, you mustn't.'

They were followed by a sudden silence as if the whole tea room were holding its breath, waiting for Chas's answer. But when they looked round there was no one in the room, except Rosie, waiting to clear up; the elderly ladies had gone.

'Stay for a while, if you want to,' Rosie said, as she went to pull down the blinds and turn the sign on the door to closed. 'I've got some paperwork to do before I leave. Stay in the warm.' And with that she disappeared into the kitchen and closed the door.

'Will you really join up, Chas?' Mabel asked in a small voice.

'Yes, though I haven't told my parents yet. I wanted to tell you first, to explain.'

'To explain?'

'Yes.' Chas got to his feet and began to pace the floor. 'It isn't just the difficult situation with my parents,' he said. 'There's your family to consider. If we continue to meet, well, you'll be defying your father and that in itself may come between us.' Chas searched her face and said softly, 'I love you, Mabel, love you with all my heart and I don't want to lose you. But it's not fair to ask you to choose between me and your family.'

'You're not asking me,' Mabel told him, looking up into his face. 'I'm telling you that whatever my parents say, I will never give you up... ever.'

For a long moment he held her gaze, before pulling her up into his arms and holding her close against him, so that each could feel the other's heartbeat.

He had kissed her before, but only on her cheek, and once a

tantalising brush of his lips on hers, but now he lowered his head and his mouth found hers, kissing her as he'd longed to do ever since he first saw her in Hugh Morrell's office, and she, standing on tiptoe with her arms round his neck, her fingers among his dark curls, returned his kisses, until at last they broke apart, breathless.

'I told your parents that we'd been properly introduced by Mr Morrell,' Chas said, 'but that seals our introduction, don't you think?'

Mabel gave a quick glance to ensure the blinds were indeed lowered, protecting them from prying eyes, and said, 'Yes, but perhaps we should do it again... just to be sure?'

'Definitely,' agreed Chas.

Later, sitting together side by side, Mabel within the circle of Chas's arm, she said, 'I've been thinking I ought to be doing something towards the war effort. Perhaps I could use Mr Morrell's money in some way.'

'What sort of thing?' Chas asked.

'I'm not quite sure, but I have a friend who's been recently widowed, her husband killed in Belgium. She's expecting their child, but there is little in the way of help for such mothers, left to cope with a baby on their own, struggling to earn enough to support herself with the child needing her at home.'

'But what can you do about that?' wondered Chas.

'I'm not sure yet,' admitted Mabel, 'but perhaps Mr Morrell's money will help me find something.'

She had been thinking of Annie, but now she also thought of Mavis, hiding from her violent husband, and was about to mention her when Chas said, 'You can't put the world right on your own, Mabel.'

'I know that, but if there's something...' She looked up at him earnestly. 'Women without a man to protect them have a very rough time. Many men regard them as fair game.'

'Not all men, surely,' exclaimed Chas.

'No, of course not,' Mabel agreed, 'but you remember I told

you how I had been attacked last year in my workshop by a man who shut me in and tried to rape me?'

'Yes, I do remember,' replied Chas, 'but not in any detail. I assumed that you were trying to put it behind you.'

'I was. I am. But it's not as easy as all that. There are mental scars long after the cuts and bruises have healed.'

'Surely there aren't that many...' began Chas, but Mabel cut him off.

'There's one living with us in Barnbury Street. Mrs Finch, my father's nurse, she has a daughter called Mavis. She's married to a violent bloke called Sidney and she's expecting their baby. He smashed his fist into her face because he said his breakfast was cold. She arrived at our house, looking for her mother. Her face was covered in dried blood, she had a black eye and a deep gash on her cheek. He doesn't know where she is, but she's terrified he'll turn up on our doorstep and demand she goes back to him.'

'But if she's his wife...' Chas tried again.

'Even if she's his wife, he has no right to punch her in the face, especially if she's carrying his child. She says he doesn't want the baby and never has done, so both mother and unborn baby are at risk, unless she's somewhere safe.'

'But surely, she's not expecting you to hide her,' said Chas.

'She's safe with her mother in our house at present,' Mabel said. 'We moved house recently and Sid doesn't know where we live now. There's no link Sid can follow, even if he managed to find her mother living in with us.'

'Even so,' said Chas, still looking doubtful, 'don't you think women should live with their husbands? I mean, isn't that what marriage is about, for better or worse?'

'Not if for worse means being attacked by the very man who's supposed to protect you,' retorted Mabel. 'Does your father hit your mother?'

The moment the words were out of her mouth Mabel regretted them. She should have made no mention of John Sheridan. She had no idea whether he was violent to his wife or not, but he was still Chas's father.

'No,' Chas answered coldly. 'Of course not.'

'But if he did, on a regular basis, would you think your mother should stay with him and put up with it for the rest of her life?'

'Oh, Mabel, I don't know. How on earth did we come to be talking about this?'

'You asked me what I might do with Mr Morrell's money,' replied Mabel. 'And I trust you... so I told you. Perhaps I shouldn't have, but having been a victim myself, women's safety is very important to me.'

Chas tightened his arm about her again, saying, 'If it's important to you, my love, then it's important to me.' He turned her face to his and very gently kissed her lips.

'Will you wait for me, Mabel, while I'm away?' he asked softly.

'Yes,' she replied. 'Of course I will.'

'And marry me when I come back?'

'Yes, Chas. Of course I will.'

Once Rosie was ready to shut up shop, Mabel and Charles left the warmth of the teashop for the wintry darkness outside. Together, with Chas wheeling her bike, they walked hand in hand through the chilly city to Barnbury Street.

Chapter Fifty

'Where on earth can she be?' Andrew demanded angrily. 'It's pitch black out there. She should have been home ages ago.'

Why was Mabel so late? Had something happened to her?

Alice was equally anxious. The streets of London after dark were no place for a young woman alone.

'Haven't you noticed that it's Monday?' Doreen asked, as she refilled Andrew's tea cup.

'What difference does that make?' he snapped.

'It's the evening she's nearly always home late,' replied Doreen. 'It's the evening she meets up with her young man.'

'Her young man?' queried Andrew. 'You mean William?'

'No.' Doreen shook her head. 'Not William, her lawyer friend. The one what came with all them papers.'

'You mean Charles Sheridan?' Andrew sounded appalled. 'But I forbade her to see him again!'

'It don't mean she hasn't though, does it?'

'Mabel wouldn't defy me like that,' Andrew said irritably.

'And what about William?' demanded Alice.

'What about William?' came a voice from the door. Unnoticed, Mabel had come into the house and overheard their last remarks.

'Well,' said Alice, a little flustered. 'You're fond of William, aren't you? I thought you had an understanding with him. We both did, didn't we, Andrew? And we were pleased, he's a nice, steady chap. Very dependable.'

'I agree with you, Mam,' Mabel said gently, 'and you're right,

I'm very fond of him, but I don't love him, not now I know what love is… with Chas.'

'Mabel! You haven't…'

'But he's a Sheridan!'

Her parents spoke together, but Mabel answered them one at a time.

'No, Mam, of course I haven't,' she sighed, remembering their kisses even as she said it, and longing for more. 'His surname may be Sheridan, Dada, but he's *not* his father. Anyway,' she turned on them defiantly, 'you needn't worry. He's about to join up to fight for his king and will be going over to France before long. You never know, with any luck, he may be killed and then you'll never have to worry about him again, will you?' And before her threatening tears completely overcame her, she dashed upstairs to her bedroom, slammed the door and turned the key in the lock.

Below, all those gathered in the kitchen stared at each other in horror at her final words.

Annie, who had been working her way through a basket of ironing, set down the iron to cool, picked up the folded clothes and silently carried them up the stairs. She was followed swiftly by Doreen and Mavis, anxious to escape the tension in the kitchen.

'Well,' said Andrew, when he and Alice were left alone. 'What on earth was that all about?'

'For goodness' sake, Andrew,' snapped Alice. 'What do you think it was about? She thinks she's in love with Charles Sheridan.'

'But that's ridiculous,' snapped Andrew. 'In love! She hardly knows the fellow.'

'But the important thing is that she *thinks* she's in love with him.'

'But with Charles Sheridan! John Sheridan's son?' Andrew couldn't keep the incredulity out of his voice.

'You may not approve—' began Alice.

'Approve!' interrupted Andrew angrily. 'Of course I don't approve—'

'You may not approve,' repeated Alice patiently, 'but the more you stand in their way and try to keep them apart, the more determined she will become. Let them meet each other, and the whole thing may well blow over while he is away at war.'

'And if it doesn't?' demanded Andrew. 'What then?'

'Then we shall have to take it more seriously,' replied Alice. 'In the meantime, as I doubt if you can stop her meeting him anyway, you should make it clear you're not trying to.'

'I thought she and William had something...' grumbled Andrew. 'I thought they... well, you know, would make a match of it. He's a good, steady bloke, is young William.'

'So he is,' agreed Alice. 'But perhaps she's been finding him, well, rather dull?'

'Dull?'

'Yes. Maybe this Chas, as she calls him, is a more exciting, more romantic character than dear everyday William. Someone different, *outside* the everyday. Let's wait until she's calmed down a little and when she comes downstairs again, we can try and talk to her. Explain we have no objection to her seeing Charles Sheridan, just ask her to bring him here to introduce him to us properly, just as she would any other man.'

But Mabel did not come downstairs. When Alice called them all to the supper table, there was no sign of her, and though the others heard Alice clearly and came to the kitchen for their evening meal, there was no response from Mabel.

'Shall I go and see if she's all right?' asked Annie.

'Yes,' answered Alice. 'Please do.'

Mabel, lying on her bed, with her eyes red from weeping, and tears drying on her cheeks, heard Annie's steps upon the stairs, heard her pause on the landing and then gently tap on the door.

'Mabel? Mabel, are you all right?'

Mabel turned her face into the pillow and made no answer.

THE GIRLS WHO DARED TO LOVE

'Mabel, it's supper time, are you coming down?'

Silence.

'Mabel, can you hear me?'

Silence.

'Mabel, I'm going downstairs now, but if I come back after supper, will you let me in? We could talk.'

Mabel listened as Annie went back down the stairs. She didn't want supper, she didn't intend to come downstairs again and she didn't want to talk. She just wanted to be left alone.

When Chas had told her he was joining up, she had listened, had understood that he needed to get away for a while, but even as they talked of his plans, her heart was crying out, 'Don't go! Please don't go! Suppose you go... and suppose you don't come back?'

She thought of poor Annie, whose Ron hadn't come back. Annie, who was being so brave, expecting a baby, a child who was going to grow up with no knowledge of its father.

Perhaps, she thought, as she lay on her bed hugging her pillow, I should talk to Annie. She was brave when her Ron decided to join up, and if Annie can be, so can I.

Still determined not to go back downstairs, Mabel made herself comfortable on the bed. To one side, a mattress lay on the floor, on top of which were two neatly folded blankets and a pillow. Annie's temporary bed.

I'll have to let her in when she comes up after supper, thought Mabel. Otherwise she won't have anywhere to sleep. Accepting that as necessary, when she heard footsteps on the stairs followed by a tap on the door, Mabel crossed the room and unlocked the door. When she pulled it open she found not Annie as she had expected, but her mother with a plate of stew in one hand and a cup of tea in the other. Alice pushed the door wider with her foot and came into the room.

'I thought you might be hungry,' she said, setting the plate down.

Disconcerted by her mother's appearance on the landing,

Mabel had taken a step back into the room. Now she was tempted to say she wasn't hungry and didn't want anything, but the waft of savoury steam from the plate told her otherwise, so she said nothing.

Alice handed her the cup of tea and Mabel took it automatically, closing her hands around the warmth of the cup.

'Annie will be coming up in a little while,' said Alice, perching on the edge of the bed. 'Are you going to let her come in to sleep, or should she go in with Mavis?'

This sparked Mabel into saying, 'Of course she'll sleep in here as usual.' Suddenly she found she didn't want to be alone after all. 'Why wouldn't she?'

'Your dad and I would like to have a chat with you, in the morning,' ventured Alice. 'We've all said more than we meant to, in the heat of the moment. Better we sleep on it, and then talk calmly about things in the morning.'

About to pick up the plate of stew, Mabel put it down again and, fixing her mother with an unflinching stare, said, 'I'm not going to give up Chas, whatever you say.'

'I know,' replied her mother. 'I quite understand.'

'No, you don't,' Mabel spoke truculently. 'You have no idea.'

'I think you'll find I have,' said Alice, 'but let's talk about it in the morning when we've all had a good night's sleep.' She got to her feet and turned at the door. 'Sleep well, Mabel. Annie'll be up in a minute.'

As soon as she heard her mother's footsteps on the stairs, Mabel again picked up the plate of stew left on the bedside table. Since breakfast she had only had buttered toast with Chas at Rosie's and the moment the hot food was in her mouth she discovered she was ravenous.

Annie paused at the door, uncertain of her welcome.

'Come in, Annie,' said Mabel, looking up.

'You all right?' asked Annie, still standing on the threshold.

'No, not really,' admitted Mabel, 'but I will be.'

Her mother had suggested they sleep on it, but Mabel had

very little sleep that night. She had no idea what her parents were going to say, but she and Chas had arranged to meet again at the café early the next week, after Chas had told his parents of his decision.

When they had reached Barnbury Street, Mabel had pushed her bike through the side gate, and Chas, following her, took her in his arms for a final kiss, before she went indoors.

'Let's meet on Thursday,' he murmured into her hair. 'Christmas Eve. If I'm late, just wait for me. I promise I'll be there.'

And with that whispered promise in her ears, Mabel finally fell asleep.

The following morning, Mabel and Annie went downstairs to breakfast together. Doreen was in with Andrew, getting him ready for the day, but Alice and Mavis were both sitting at the table.

Mabel made no apology for her outburst the previous evening, but Mavis, uncomfortable with the tense atmosphere in the room, soon made herself scarce. She didn't like Annie, and was suspicious of her moving in to the already crowded house. Mavis knew she herself was sleeping in Stephen's room, that if Stephen came home for any reason she would have to move upstairs and share her mother's rooms, but now there was Annie, sleeping on a mattress in Mabel's room.

Suppose they decide to give Stephen's room to Annie instead, worried Mavis.

She had watched Annie sucking up to Mrs Oakley, doing the ironing, peeling the potatoes, cleaning Andrew's shoes. All of which Mavis could have done, would have done, she supposed, had she been asked, but Annie had simply seen what was needed and got on with it.

Doreen came into the kitchen and greeted both Mabel and Annie with a smile.

'Your dad says he's going to have his breakfast in his room and will you come through, Mabel, when you've finished yours.'

Ten minutes later, Alice carried a cup of tea in to Andrew, saying, 'Why not come in and bring your tea, Mabel?'

Mabel picked up her cup and with a glance at Annie, still seated at the kitchen table, followed her mother out of the kitchen.

Chapter Fifty-One

Mabel and Chas met up as planned on Christmas Eve. 'Did you go to the Recruiting Depot?' Mabel asked when they were seated by the fire in Rosie's Tea Room. For the previous three days she had been praying he would change his mind, that she would now hear that his parents had talked him out of the idea, but the moment she asked she could see from his expression that he had volunteered.

'Yes,' he said. 'I went to the depot at Scotland Yard.'

Remembering her promise to be as brave as Annie had been, encouraging her Ron to go and fight, Mabel swallowed hard and blinked back her tears.

'And they accepted you?'

'Yes, no problem with that.'

'When will you go?'

'Not until after Christmas. I have to report to a camp in Lincolnshire for basic training, but I told the recruiting sergeant that I'm hoping to join the Royal Flying Corps. Imagine, Mabel! Imagine being able to fly!'

Mabel could hear the excitement in his voice and knew that now he'd made this decision, he couldn't wait to leave.

'So,' she said, 'so, you won't be going straight over to France yet?'

'No,' Chas answered cheerfully. 'Probably not for months yet. You can't get rid of me that quickly.'

Perhaps the war will be over before he has to go, thought Mabel. A glimmer of hope. But she knew in her heart it wouldn't be. All the reports coming back from the front made it clear that it was going to be a war of attrition, fought from the trenches snaking down either side of the sea of mud that was no man's land. Thousands of men had already been killed, and the men joining up now were being trained to fill dead men's shoes.

Forcing her voice to sound casual, she asked, 'Have you told your parents?'

'Yes, I told them that same evening.'

The Sheridan family had been at the dinner table when Chas dropped his bombshell. His father was still refusing to speak to him and despite his mother Anne's efforts to ease the situation, what conversation there was round the dinner table was extremely strained.

'And what did they say?' asked Mabel.

'My mother was very upset. Because I've been working in the family firm, it never occurred to her that I might join up. My father, on the other hand, was just plain angry.'

Even as he told her of his family's reaction, he could hear his father's anger echoing in his head.

'For Christ's sake, boy what were you thinking of?' His taking of the Lord's name in vain had amazed them all. Never had they heard John Sheridan blaspheme in that way before.

'Did it never cross your mind to talk to us first?' he demanded. 'That we might have liked to be consulted, to discuss the idea with you? We are your parents, after all.'

'It did cross my mind,' Chas had replied. 'But since you have refused to address a single word to me for more than a week, even when Mother asked me to try to mend fences, I decided you wouldn't be interested.' He locked eyes with his father. 'After all, I am old enough to make my own decisions.'

'Can't you go back and tell them you've changed your mind?' asked his mother tremulously.

He could hear she was trying not to cry, but he said, 'No, Mother, I can't. I've signed on the dotted line and I'm under orders to report to a base in Lincolnshire for basic training on the Tuesday after Christmas.'

'But I don't understand why. You're not a soldier, you're training to be a lawyer! Oh Charles, what made you do it?'

'I'm sorry you're so upset, Mother—'

'Sorry to upset her!' his father scoffed. 'How did you expect her to feel, springing this decision on us like this?'

'I think it's very brave of him to volunteer,' said his sister, Lavinia, speaking for the first time.

'You stay out of this, miss,' snapped her father. 'It's nothing to do with you.'

'Of course it is,' returned Lavinia. 'He's my brother.' She opened her mouth to say more, but a glare from her father made her close it again.

'I'm sorry, Mother,' Chas repeated, 'but I'm tired of the guv'nor telling me what I can and can't do.'

'Oh! I see!' said his father. 'It's all my fault, is it?'

'No, not really, but it's time I took responsibility for my own life. We've had differences of opinion, both in the office and here at home, and they make things very difficult between us.'

'You seem to be forgetting, Charles, that in the office I am your boss, I expect you to take orders from me, to tell you what to do, and I expect your loyalty.'

'I haven't forgotten and I'm ready to listen to your advice, but I'm not prepared to ignore my conscience and watch you trying to circumvent a perfectly reasonable bequest in Mr Morrell's will. I have a loyalty to the firm, but that includes to Mr Morrell. I witnessed his signature on that codicil, and I know he wanted Mabel to have the money. You had no right to refuse her.'

'What are you talking about?' asked his mother, confused.

'It's that Oakley girl,' snapped John. 'She's been nothing but trouble since that old printer Thomas Clarke left her all his money. Trying to pretend she's running a business. Her! It's the second time she's taken in a gullible old man, hoping to get her hands on his money.'

'Stop!' snapped Chas. 'Stop right there. That's complete rubbish and you know it. You also know that Mabel and I have become close and you don't like it. Well, I won't have you speak about her like that. She's the girl I'm going to marry!'

'Marry! Mabel Oakley!' exploded his father. 'You'll do no such thing. I won't allow it.'

'I'm twenty-three,' retorted Chas, 'so you can't stop me.'

'Wait,' cried his mother. 'Wait, what are you talking about now? What has Mabel Oakley to do with anything? She's Andrew Oakley's daughter, isn't she?'

'She is,' agreed her husband, 'and for some reason the Oakleys blame me for a traffic accident that he had over a year ago now.'

'But you went to see his family at the time,' cried Anne. 'You helped them out with some money, I remember you telling me.'

'I did,' said John, 'even though I owed them nothing. Oakley had already left my employ before he had his accident. It wasn't my fault he walked under a brewer's dray.' He turned to Chas. 'I want nothing more to do with that family. I wish Hugh had not seen fit to make such a bequest, but as I said, that girl seems able to twist gullible men round her little finger, and that,' he said glaring at Chas, 'now appears to include you.'

'I shall not discuss Mabel with you, sir,' stated Chas. 'We have agreed to get married when she's of age and no one can stop us. I know her father is about as pleased with the idea as you are...'

'That must be the only thing we'd agree on,' snapped John.

'But since he is unlikely to give his consent to our marriage, we have both decided to wait until I come back from France...'

'And what happens if another rich man comes along? What makes you think she's going to hang about waiting for you then?' demanded his father.

'Because she loves me.'

'Because she *says* she loves you,' mocked his father.

'Suppose you don't come back, Charles?' whispered his mother. 'Look at the lists of casualties in the papers. Thousands dead and thousands more wounded. My dearest boy, you don't have to go.'

'Of course it's a risk, Mother,' Chas said gently, 'but if

something should happen to me, Mabel will be well looked after. I have named her as next of kin on my paybook.'

'In that case you're no son of mine,' retorted his father. 'I think you've finally lost your mind.'

'No, guv'nor, I've lost my heart.'

'I got up from the table then,' he now said to Mabel, 'and with an apology to my mother, I left the dining room and went upstairs to my bedroom to pack. I leave today.'

'But the army doesn't want you until after Christmas,' cried Mabel.

'I know, but there's no taking back what was said, and I really can't stay in the house and play happy families over Christmas.'

'But where will you go?'

'My mother's parents live in Hove, just outside Brighton,' said Chas. 'She's contacted them and I'm going to stay with them over Christmas. When my father's back in the office, I shall go home and say goodbye properly to my mother and Lavinia.'

'But will I see you again before you go? I was hoping you'd come and see my parents before you went.'

'Really? I doubt if they want to see me.'

'Dada was furious when he realised that I'd been meeting you, but Mam managed to calm him down and now they'd like you to come and meet them. I've told them you were joining up and whatever they say, I'll never give you up. I don't care who your father is and they shouldn't either. You know,' Mabel went on, 'I think it was the fact that I was meeting someone they didn't know behind their backs, rather than who it was, that upset my mother most.'

'But your father still minds I'm a Sheridan,' said Chas.

'He minds, but Mam's convinced him my happiness is more important. He loves me more than he hates your father.' She managed a rueful smile. 'At least I think he does, and I think he'll come round... eventually.'

Chas glanced at his watch and, picking up his bag from under the table, said 'I must go or I'll miss my train.'

They said goodbye in St James's churchyard away from prying eyes. As they stood in the shelter of a buttress, Chas dropped his valise to the ground, gathered Mabel into his arms and kissed her, his lips finding hers, and she willingly returning his kisses. For a long moment, they held each other, Mabel's head cradled against Chas's shoulder, each reluctant to break away. As she felt the steady beat of his heart, Mabel had to fight the tears that threatened to overcome her determination not to cry. And as Chas felt the trembling of her body against his own, his arms tightened yet more strongly around her. How could he leave her now? 'You mean everything to me,' he murmured into her hair. 'I love you, Mabel, darling Mabel. I'll come and find you in your workshop on Monday before I leave for Lincoln and you can introduce me to your parents.'

Together they left the churchyard, with Mabel pushing her bicycle, and walked through the busy streets to where Chas could catch an omnibus to Victoria station. They reached the stop just as an omnibus drew up and Chas climbed aboard. As it pulled away again, Mabel stood on the pavement, bereft. The Christmas shoppers ebbed and flowed around her as she watched the bus disappear round a corner, taking Chas away from her; leaving her behind.

Chapter Fifty-Two

When Mabel finally finished up in the workshop on Christmas Eve, she found the household in a cheerful bustle of preparations for Christmas. Doreen was standing at the kitchen table, her strong hands covered in flour as she made the pastry for a tray of mince pies. Alice was giving a final stir to the dried fruit she had been hoarding over the last few months, adding a measure of brandy bought specifically from the pub on the corner. The kitchen, smelling of spices and brandy, the scent of Christmas, was warm and welcoming.

'We've left icing the Christmas cake to you, Mabel,' Alice said, adding softly when she saw Mabel had arrived home alone, 'couldn't your friend come?'

'No, Mam,' Mabel replied. 'He's gone to his grandparents'. He'll be back on Monday and will be coming to meet you then. Now he's joined up he has to report to somewhere in Lincoln on Tuesday.'

Mabel wondered how she could enjoy Christmas with the thought of Chas going into the army so soon afterwards. She had never shared Christmas Day with him, but somehow the prospect of his absence brought her close to tears. She looked at Annie and Mavis sitting side by side, cutting coloured paper into strips and gluing them together for a paper chain, and it all felt pointless. With a sigh, she turned her attention to the large fruit cake Doreen had made some weeks ago, and set about making the icing.

Eddie and Stephen were coming home, and Alice was determined everyone should join in and make it a truly festive

Christmas. Mavis had to move upstairs to her mother's rooms, so that Stephen could use his old room. Because Christmas Day itself was a Friday, Mr Carter had closed the factory for the weekend, and Mr Solomon, being Jewish, was only keeping the Sabbath, so neither of her sons had to return to work until Monday. Alice was delighted that she would at last have her whole family round her, if only for a few days.

'It's going to be a bit of squash,' she said, 'but we'll have a lovely day.'

Mabel found that, despite herself, she really enjoyed the day as she and her family celebrated in their own traditional way. Exchange of presents in the morning; Christmas dinner of roast beef with roast potatoes and thick savoury gravy, followed by the mince pies made by Doreen and Alice's plum pudding.

The afternoon lengthened to dusk beyond the window as the women cleared away the meal and the menfolk went into the parlour to stoke the glowing embers of the fire to a crackling blaze.

With curtains drawn against the chill and darkness beyond the window, they all squeezed into the front room to play the games they always played on Christmas night: 'Who am I?', when with much laughter they tried to guess that a strutting Eddie was Kaiser Bill, then charades and consequences, and gambling with matchsticks on the colour of a drawn card.

'I think it's time for a cup of tea,' suggested Alice when Stephen had won all the matchsticks and to further hilarity had been made, as a forfeit, to act as an elephant.

'I'll put the kettle on,' said Doreen, heading for the kitchen while Stephen still wandered around the room, his arm out in front of him as a trunk and trumpeting through his nose. As Doreen filled the kettle and set it on the gas, she saw the Christmas cake Mabel had iced the previous evening. Returning to the parlour she asked, 'What about the Christmas cake? Are we going to cut that now.'

'Why don't we leave it until tomorrow?' suggested Alice with a quick glance at Mabel.

'Good idea,' said Andrew. 'We'll save it for when William comes.'

For a moment Mabel didn't take in what her father had said, but as the words echoed in her head she looked across to where he sat by the fire in his wheelchair.

'What did you say?'

'When William comes,' repeated Andrew. 'He looked in yesterday morning to wish us merry Christmas. When he said he'd been given the afternoon off on Boxing Day, I asked him here. Where else would he go?'

Lying in bed, when the house was at last quiet, Mabel thought over the day. It had been fun. Eddie and Stephen were always the life and soul of any party, and there had been moments when Chas had slipped from her mind, but now, in the darkness, where the only sound was Annie's peaceful breathing on the mattress beside her, Mabel's mind was invaded by thoughts of Chas. How had he spent his Christmas, she wondered? Had he missed her as much as she was missing him? Three more days, until he came back to her, to meet her parents... and to say goodbye.

And before that, tomorrow, there would be William. Why, oh why, had Dada asked William to come and see them tomorrow afternoon? Had he done it because he realised William would be lonely at Christmas with no family to visit? Or was it that he hoped the presence of William would make up for the absence of Chas? Did Dada really think that if she saw William, she would realise that she had made a mistake; that it was he, the friend who had stood by her through all her troubles and clearly loved her, was the one she really loved? Dear, dependable William, rather than new and exciting Chas?

Chas. As she lay sleepless, she wondered how it would feel to have him lying close beside her in the bed, to fall asleep in his arms and wake curled against him. She remembered the feel of his arms around her in the churchyard, the incredible sensations that ran through her when they kissed, the ache within her body when close against his, a yearning for something more.

As she finally drifted off to sleep, her dreams conjured neither Chas nor William. No, they were haunted by Annie, who lay alone in her makeshift bed and was, Mabel now realised, crying in her sleep.

Chapter Fifty-Three

Christmas Day had dawned grey and cold. When Clara came in and threw back Lucinda's curtains, there were already flakes of snow drifting past her window.

'Merry Christmas, my lady,' she said. 'It's begun to snow again.' She handed Lucinda her bedjacket and plumped the pillow behind her.

'I'll just bring your tea, now,' she said. 'No need to hurry, my lady. Plenty of time before Croxton comes to fetch you to Chanynge Place.'

Lucinda sipped her tea and stared out at the pewter sky. She had been absolved from going to church this Christmas morning, the weather had been so cold, wet and icy, it was feared that she might slip and fall. She was glad. An hour in a chilly church was something she was happy to avoid.

When her parents had tried to insist that she come to Chanynge Place for Christmas Eve as well as Christmas Day, she refused. She wanted to wake up in the bed she shared with David and was adamant that she would not go to Chanynge Place until Christmas morning.

Isabella had also invited Lucinda's mother-in-law, but Lady Melcome had politely refused the invitation saying, if they would excuse her, she preferred a quiet Christmas at Crayne these days, unless David was at home.

'Next year, when this dreadful war is over, and you're a family again,' she said to Lucinda, 'we shall have a wonderful Christmas all together at Crayne, as we did when David was young, but this year I shall be quite happy in the country with Croft and Mrs Croft to look after me.'

Lucinda had to admit to herself that it was quite a relief to be with her own family for the festive season. Though they would only be six – the four of them plus Papa's unmarried sisters, Aunt Gertie and Aunt Fay, who always came for Christmas – she knew it would be better, if she had to be without David, to be in the familiar surroundings of Chanynge Place than alone with her mother-in-law at Crayne, or completely alone in Sloane Square.

Keir had suggested that they might, for a change, spend the festive season at Haverford, but this idea had been swiftly dismissed by Isabella.

'It'd be pointless to have all the upheaval it entails to move the household to Haverford and then stay for only a couple of days,' she said. 'We've had so many invitations this year, we need to be in town. And,' she added as an afterthought, 'your sisters are always more comfortable here.'

Croxton arrived promptly, and Clara escorted her mistress safely across the icy pavement and into the car. Watson followed behind with Lucinda's luggage and a bag of presents, stowing them safely in the boot.

Lucinda had given Clara Christmas Day off. 'Denby can look after me perfectly well,' she said. 'There's no need for you to come with me this time.'

Clara and Watson stood on the pavement and watched until the car had turned the corner, and then hurried back into the warmth of the kitchen. Now that Lady Senior was away at Crayne and their mistress would not be back until the day after tomorrow, there was no one to wait on; the servants could relax and enjoy their own Christmas.

It had been snowing steadily all morning and the road was layered with the smooth, white icing sugar of untrampled snow. Croxton drove at walking pace and apart from a plodding horse pulling a waggon in the opposite direction, they seemed to be the only vehicle braving the wintry weather. Looking out of the car window, Lucinda could see the tyre tracks left by their wheels were already filling up behind them. The snow had changed the landscape: familiar buildings dressed in white, trees heavy-laden with snow, or stark against the sky when the snowy burden had become too great. The familiar became unfamiliar. The few pedestrians, returning from church to their Christmas dinners, were wrapped up in coats, hats, scarves and gloves against the bitter cold.

As the Rolls was forced to creep at a snail's pace, a group of children, delighting in the fresh snow, hurled snowballs at the passing car, shrieking with laughter as one found its target on the window beside Lucinda.

Lucinda wondered, as she always did, where David was and whether he too was struggling with the winter weather. She had still clung to the hope that he might be able to come home for Christmas, but fierce fighting had continued and that hope faded further away with every letter he wrote. The last one, written several days ago, had arrived just yesterday, Christmas Eve, and was in her pocket, to read and reread, today, Christmas Day itself.

My Darling.

I'm so glad you are going to spend Christmas Day with your family at Chanynge Place. I shall be able to picture you all round the dining table eating Christmas goose and plum pudding. I don't know what fare we shall have here but I know they will make an effort to mark the day. Some of the men on respite behind the lines are planning a carol concert for Christmas Eve. There is a promised extra tot of rum for every man to help us all keep warm. The weather is very unkind just now, incessant rain, and there is mud everywhere.

I expect your mother will have decorated a Christmas tree to stand in your hallway. One of my men came back to the lines yesterday and brought a small branch from a tree which we have stuck in the side of the trench and decorated with a twist of tinsel he received in a parcel from home.

Thank you for the Christmas parcel which arrived here for me. I'm saving the smaller parcels inside for Christmas morning so that you'll know when I'm opening them, but I'm afraid Mrs Watson's fruit cake has already been demolished.

I shall be thinking of you on Christmas Day, going to church with your parents and singing carols round the tree. I enclose a small present which was specially carved by one of the men. I hope you will like it. We shall have our own private Christmas if I can get leave in June.

Oh, darling Lucy, how I wish I could be with you now, hold you in my arms and kiss you forever!

Take care of yourself, Lucy mine and our little one growing inside.

I love you both with all my heart. David.

She had opened the enclosed parcel this morning in the privacy of her bedroom, before she had summoned Clara to draw her bath. Inside, wrapped in some cotton wool, was a carved lion. He was about six inches long, made of polished wood. Slightly crouched, he had one front paw off the ground as if stalking his prey. His luxuriant mane, a little darker than the rest of him, was intricately carved, and his eyes had been marked in with black ink. Lucinda ran her finger along the smooth curve of his back. He was beautiful and carved especially for her. Leo. It was one of the names she and David had been considering for the baby, should it be a boy. Was that why David had chosen it? She'd ask when she wrote to him before bed tonight. Very gently she placed the lion on her bedside table, ready to slip it into her case before she left.

When they arrived at Chanynge Place, Felstead and William were both at the front door to greet her. The steps had been cleared of snow and ice, but even so she was grateful for them being one on either side as she went up to the door.

As she came into the hall, she saw David had been right. The Christmas tree, tall and decorated with silver ornaments and tiny bows of silver ribbon, stood, as always, in one corner of the hall. When she was a child, it had been her job to help decorate the tree, and as Christmas had drawn nearer she couldn't wait for Christmas Eve, when the tree would be brought into the house by Paston and set in its tub. When she was small, her father had lifted her up to attach the decorations, and when she still couldn't reach, he would stand on a stepladder and place the ornaments at her direction. Candles were already attached to the ends of branches, ready for lighting when darkness fell. It had become a tradition: she and Papa would decorate the tree and light the candles as darkness fell on Christmas Day. Looking at it now, she realised that the angel who always adorned the topmost branch was not yet in situ.

At that moment, her father came down stairs. 'Merry Christmas, Lucy. How are you?' He gave her a hug, and kissed her on her cheek. He never failed to greet her like this, though her mother thought it was unnecessary behaviour in front of the servants.

Lucy hugged him back. 'Merry Christmas, Papa.' But glancing up at the tree, she asked, 'Where's the angel?'

'She's here,' replied her father, picking up the angel from the hall table and handing it to her. 'Waiting for you to do the honours, though your mother says you're not to climb the steps.'

'Certainly not. The very idea, in her condition!' Lady McFarlane had emerged from the morning room. 'And not you either,' she added. 'We don't want any accidents to spoil our Christmas. William can do it.' William, who was still waiting to take Lucinda's coat, hat and gloves, stepped forward at once. 'Not this minute, William, when we're out of your way.'

Secretly relieved that she was not expected to climb the ladder, Lucinda divested herself of her outdoor clothes.

'That's better,' said her mother, 'Come along upstairs and join your aunts, there's a lovely fire in the drawing room.'

'Just a minute, Mama,' Lucinda said, looking about her. 'What happened to the bag of presents I brought with me?'

'Here, my lady.' William picked up the bag that Croxton had put inside the front door. 'Where shall I put it?'

'I'll have it here,' replied Lucinda, 'so I can put the presents round the tree.'

'I thought we'd have presents upstairs,' said her mother. 'After all, there are just the six of us, no need to put them round the tree first. Much easier for your aunts in the drawing room. William can bring the bag up for you with your other luggage.'

Lucinda was about to protest, but at that moment Iain appeared at the top of the stairs.

'Lucy! Merry Christmas.' He came down the stairs two at a time, and gave her a hug. 'We weren't sure you'd get here through the snow.'

'Croxton did drive very slowly,' Lucinda said. 'Some little boys tried to pelt the car with snowballs, but they weren't a very good shot and only one hit the target!'

They all went up to the drawing room, where Aunt Gertie and Aunt Fay were sitting on either side of the fire.

'Oh, it's Lucinda,' cried Aunt Fay. 'Look, Gertie, look who's here!'

'I thought she was in France,' said Gertie. 'Isn't that what you said?'

'No, dearest, it's her husband who's in France. Remember, I told you?'

'I'm sure you did not, Fay. I would have remembered.'

Fay smiled at her sister and murmured, 'You don't always remember, you know.'

Seeing his sisters seemed about to start an argument, Keir asked cheerfully, 'Who's ready for a drink? A glass of champagne, Fay? You, Gertie?'

Felstead had already opened the champagne and Lord McFarlane said, 'Thank you, Felstead, I'll look after the ladies.'

'Very good, my lord,' Felstead replied. Iain acted as waiter and when they had all been served, Keir raised his glass.

'Merry Christmas, everyone. And a special toast to David.'

'David,' they all echoed, except for Aunt Gertie who asked, 'Who is David?'

'Lucinda's husband,' answered Fay.

'Is she married?'

'Yes, dearest, she is.'

'Why didn't we go to the wedding?'

'We did.'

'I didn't,' maintained Gertie.

'You were there, Auntie,' said Lucinda, 'but it was some time ago. I expect you've forgotten.'

Not long after, Felstead came into the room to announce luncheon, and to Lucinda's relief, the subject was dropped while the aunts found their places and were settled into their seats. It's so sad, she thought, Aunt Gertie, who had always been such fun, joining in games with them when they were children, was now the one who was so easily confused.

The family ate their Christmas goose and plum pudding, just as David had predicted, and after the meal they retired to the drawing room to exchange their presents.

Lucy had chosen carefully: a silver inkstand for her father's desk in the library; a silk scarf selected from Madame Chantal's latest arrivals for her mother; and gold cuff links for Iain. For Aunt Fay she had found a pale blue quilted bag to keep her embroidery and silks safely with her and for Aunt Gertie a similar one in pink.

It wasn't until they were taking afternoon tea in the drawing room that Lucinda had the chance to speak to Iain privately.

'Are you going to take Diana up on her invitation tomorrow?' she murmured, keeping her voice low so that her mother should not hear.

'How are you celebrating Christmas?' Diana had asked on the evening they had been down to Crayne. 'Are you going down to the country?'

'No,' replied Iain. 'My parents intend to stay in town this year.'

'Then you must come to us on Boxing Day,' cried Diana. 'We have Open House for all Pop's business people, and I invite anyone I choose. They all have invitations of course, but there are no set times. People just drop in and leave, very much as they please.'

'Sounds like fun,' said Iain, wondering what his mother would say if she knew he'd received such a casual invitation to Lord Waldon's house and on Boxing Day.

'I'll make sure you receive an invitation, both of you.'

'I'm afraid I would have to say no,' said Lucinda. 'In my current condition as my mother calls it.'

'Do you always do what your mother tells you, Lucy?' enquired Diana. 'Even though you're married and a mistress of your own establishment?'

'Mostly,' sighed Lucy. 'It makes life more comfortable.'

'And will you tell her where you've been today?'

'Oh, she knows that Iain has driven me down to Crayne and why. There's no need to tell her anything more.'

'Of course I'm going,' Iain said now in reply to Lucinda's question, adding with a grin, 'but I probably won't advertise the fact.'

'If you and Diana are going to get serious, Mama will have to know at some stage,' Lucy pointed out.

'I know,' agreed Iain, 'but sufficient unto the day and all that.'

'Time to light the candles on the tree,' announced Keir. 'Let's all go down and sing some carols. Will you play for us, as usual, Fay?'

When they all trooped downstairs, they discovered that

William had already lit the candles on the tree and pulled the small pianoforte out of the morning room. Once they had gathered, the baize door from the kitchen corridor opened and the servants joined the family in the hall.

Fay took her seat at the piano and Lord McFarlane nodded to Felstead, who doused the lights, leaving the flickering candles as the only illumination.

Fay played the introduction to 'Silent Night', the carol they always started with, and soon the assembled household joined together in song to celebrate Christmas night.

Lucinda's thoughts flew to David. Was he singing carols too? Most unlikely, she decided. Most unlikely.

Chapter Fifty-Four

Darkness was falling across no man's land. The guns had been strangely silent since midday as if both sides had declared a ceasefire, and to the men huddled in their dugouts, the unexpected silence, broken by the occasional sound of laughter, was eerie. Could it be the calm before a new attack? But from where? The allies had received no orders, no alerts had been given.

'What's Fritz up to?' wondered Corporal Daniels, Major David Melcome's new servant. 'What's he got to laugh at?'

'Celebrating Christmas?' suggested the major, ducking back into the shelter of the dugout. 'Just been on my rounds,' he said. 'All the sentries will be extra vigilant, but there's no sign of anything untoward.'

'But who called the ceasefire?' wondered Captain Spode, from his chair at the back of the dugout. 'Was it agreed, do you think, just for Christmas?'

'Unlikely,' replied the major. 'But I did hear some singing coming from somewhere. At first I thought it was our lot, further back. Remember, there'd been talk of a carol concert on Christmas Eve? They were singing "Silent Night", but then I realised it was coming from across no man's land, from the German trenches, same carol but sung in German.'

'Well,' said Spode, 'might as well take advantage of some blessed peace. Have we got any cocoa left, Daniels?'

'No, sir, but we could have a brew of tea.'

'Better than nothing I suppose,' Spode sighed.

The intermittent singing could be heard quite clearly now and voices drifted across the divide from the German trenches.

'Hey, sir, guess what!' Private Alton, Spode's servant, flung himself in from the trench outside. 'Fritz has only got Christmas trees... along the edge of his trench. Come and look, sir, you won't believe it.' He scurried back into the frontline trench.

'For Christ's sake, Alton,' bellowed Spode. 'Keep your head down. You want it blown off by a sniper?' But despite this warning, all four men left the dugout and edged their way along the trench to where Alton had looked across at the Christmas trees. The distance between the trenches was no more than a hundred yards, and it was quite easy to hear what was going on, calls and challenges from either side.

'Hey, Tommy,' called a voice. 'You coming out to play?'

'Nah, mate,' came the reply from further along the trench. 'We don't play with nasty boys like you!'

'OK, but I got chocolate when you like to fetch.'

Major Melcome heard a scuffling noise, as if someone was scrambling up from the fire step below the lip of trench.

'Keep your perishing head down!' he bellowed. 'You going to die for a piece of chocolate?'

The scuffling stopped, and there was a thud as the man dropped back under cover.

'Hey, Tommy,' called another voice from across the divide. 'Tomorrow... we no shoot and you no shoot!'

'Some hope,' growled Spode.

Using one of the homemade periscopes, the major raised it above the parapet and looked towards the enemy lines. By the light of the moon gleaming on the dusting of snow from the previous day, he could make out the line of the German trenches, so close across the frozen stretch of no man's land, and there they were, a row of tiny Christmas trees lit with lanterns, perched on the edge of the enemy trench. No one had left the German lines but there were lights, voices and laughter, the sounds of a party.

'Daniels, you go back and sort out that brew,' ordered the major. 'Spode, better check along the other way and make sure the sentries are still keeping a sharp lookout for any unusual activity. Tell them there'll be an extra tot for them when they come off duty. I'll go this way and do the same. Doesn't look as if Fritz is up to anything, but all this partying may be a planned distraction.'

The two officers separated and made their way slowly to either end of their section of the trench, exchanging quiet words with the sentries keeping watch across no man's land, but apart from the unusual sounds of merriment and the line of tiny Christmas trees, there seemed no cause for alarm.

'Keep your eyes skinned,' the major warned each man, 'in case they are up to something.'

But there seemed nothing to alarm those in the allied trenches, and when Major Melcome and Captain Spode returned to the dugout they found Daniels and Alton had made tea and were warming a tin of stew on the Tommy Cooker that Daniels carried in his pack, the tiny stove which was their only means of heating food.

'Well,' said David Melcome when he'd finished eating. 'If they really are going to give us a night's peace, I'm going to turn in and get some sleep. Wake me if I'm needed.' Wrapped in his army blanket, he curled up at the back of the dugout, his head pillowed on his arms, and was almost instantly asleep. His final thought, as slumber claimed him, was, as always, of Lucy. He would write to her tomorrow... Christmas Day.

It was unusual to wake to nothing louder than birdsong, but when David awoke in the early hours of the morning, the guns were still silent. He thought of the words he'd heard the German call across last night.

'Tomorrow we no shoot and you no shoot.'

Could that really happen, a single day of peace to celebrate the birth of Christ? He struggled out of his blanket, climbed over the sleeping Spode and went out into the trench. The morning was bitterly cold, but thankfully the rain of the previous weeks had stopped and given way to severe frost and a chilling mist rising from the earth with the rising sun. He found Daniels on the fire step, using the periscope.

'Morning,' he said. 'Did you get any sleep?'

'Morning, sir. Yes, I relieved Alton out here at five-thirty.'

'Any movement from the other side?'

'Yes, sir, a couple of Boche have been out of their lines. Not sure what they were doing. Looked as if they'd just stepped out for a smoke. Bold as brass.'

'Unlikely,' commented the major, taking the pericope and looking for himself. 'Still, I agree, that's what it looks like. They're taking a risk though, *we* haven't agreed not to shoot!'

Even as he watched, a third man joined the other two, ghostly shapes in the early morning mist. The third man turned towards the allied lines and, waving his arms in the air, called out.

'Hey, Tommy! Merry Christmas.'

To the major's surprise, a voice a little further along the trench returned the greeting, calling back, '*Frohe Weihnachten.*'

Which of his men spoke German? he wondered. It had certainly pleased the Germans and several more climbed from the safety of their trench, one or two even wandering a little way onto the no man's land that divided them. As the sun crept over the horizon other ghostly figures emerged, becoming substantial, but casual, unthreatening.

'This is madness,' the major said to Spode when he went back to the dugout. 'If someone gives the order to shoot it's going to be a massacre.'

'Maybe they won't,' Spode said. 'Look, they're streaming out now and some of our idiots have gone out to meet them.'

Major Melcome knew that it would be impossible to stop them now it was clear that the German troops were unarmed. He gave the order 'live and let live', which had come to mean 'do not open fire unless you are fired upon'. With the excitement of the unbelievable happening all around them, the soldiers from both sides moved out into no man's land and met with smiles on their faces, even exchanging small gifts, mostly cigarettes, food and drink.

Major Melcome took Captain Spode aside. 'While there's this amazing truce, we need to prepare for the inevitable resumption of the war. Take a burial party out into no man's land and retrieve the men we lost two days ago. Bring them back here and we'll get them sent down to the cemetery at HQ.'

When Spode set off to carry out this order, he found himself meeting similar parties from the German lines. Bodies that had been lying unretrieved in the frozen waste due to the constant shelling were now gathered and taken away for identification and burial.

David Melcome returned to their trench and gathered a working party to start repairs on the trench itself. The unrelenting bombardment had damaged a long section of the defences, and any but the most hasty repairs were almost impossible.

And all the time they worked, patching the damaged trench with whatever came to hand, David watched the growing interaction between men from both sides as they ambled out into no man's land.

What effect would this break in hostilities have? David wondered as he watched the unlikely camaraderie and heard the sound of laughter. Would they now be reluctant to open fire on men whom they had discovered were just like themselves, sharing the same miserable lives in constant cold and freezing mud? None of the rank and file of either army wanted to be living in such miserable conditions, and it would not be easy to start shooting at a man with whom you'd just shared a cigarette or raised a bottle of beer.

During the lull in hostilities, David returned to his corner of the dugout and pulled his haversack from under his camp bed. Inside, carefully wrapped, were three small packages Lucy had enclosed in a parcel which had arrived a few days earlier. David had saved them to open on Christmas Day. He hadn't held out much hope that there would be an opportunity, but even so he had kept them safely and told her in his last letter home that he would open them on Christmas morning and be thinking of her.

Well, he thought, as he put the packages onto his bed, it was past midday, but at least he was opening them on Christmas Day, as he'd promised. Picking up the first one, its softness wrapped in red paper and tied with green string, he squeezed it gently. Socks, he guessed. Just what he needed. To be really comfortable, he would need about three pairs a day to replace the sodden ones put on in the morning. Three pairs a day! He considered himself lucky if he had clean dry socks more than once a week. With nowhere to wash let alone dry them, clean, dry socks were a luxury few of his men had, and like them, David seldom took off his boots. Carefully removing the paper Lucy had used, he opened the package and found three pairs of beautiful, dry socks, rolled into pairs. 'Lucy,' he breathed, holding them to his face. 'You marvellous girl.'

The second package was wrapped in the same paper, a neat rectangle also tied with green string. Cigarettes? he wondered. Again he was right: four packs of Players. Though cigarettes were handed out each day with the rations, extras were always welcome, valuable to the non-smoker as an unofficial currency with which to trade or barter.

The third package, the smallest, contained a leatherbound notebook, and in a pocket in the back binding, two small pencils, sharpened to a fine point, with an India rubber on the other end. On the fly leaf Lucy had written, '*A place to record your thoughts. All my love, Lucy.*'

Diaries were frowned on within the ranks, so David immediately slipped Lucy's gift into his tunic pocket.

Darling Lucy, he thought with an affectionate smile. I barely have time to dash off my letters to you, let alone keep a diary!

When Spode and his party returned from their expedition into no man's land, they had retrieved five of their comrades' bodies, frozen and mud-encrusted from the battlefield of the previous week. These they loaded into the back of a horse-drawn ambulance, to be taken back for proper burial in the ever-expanding cemetery behind the allied lines.

Spode had made a note of each man's name, rank and number, but had left their identification 'dog tags' on them so that their resting places could be properly registered.

'I need a drink,' he groaned when he finally returned to the dugout.

Out in no man's land someone had produced a football and immediately a game was improvised, nothing to do with the rules of soccer, but a good-natured kick about, with much laughter and shouting, and anyone and everyone joining in.

Despite the freezing temperatures, few of those who had ventured out returned to their own trenches until the light began to fade.

Was the party over, David wondered, or would they all reconvene the following morning?

They would not. The order came down from headquarters that there was to be no further fraternisation. No one was to leave his trench, except under orders from his commanding officer. Alton and Daniels had joined in the football, but neither David nor Captain Spode made mention of the fact. There was no point in reprimanding them for celebrating Christmas.

David and his men were due to be relieved in two days' time. They would go back behind the lines to where their horses were being rested and where they themselves would get the chance of a bath and some clean clothes. There would be daily riding out but no cavalry manoeuvres while the rutted ground was as hard as iron. Being out of the front line, even if only for a short time, would be a relief, and he would be able to write a long letter to Lucy describing the amazing events of that Christmas Day. Would she be able to believe it? David could hardly believe them himself.

Before turning in, he opened the notebook she'd sent and reread what she had written. She had asked for his thoughts, and so beneath her words, he wrote in capital letters, I LOVE YOU, LUCY.

On the next page he scribbled an account of the day's improbable happenings, not because he thought he'd ever forget them, but writing them in the book she had sent him somehow brought her nearer.

Though the order of no further fraternisation was obeyed, the truce was not completely over and in some sections of the line it was another twenty-four hours before the war recommenced. When it did, it was as if the break in hostilities had been an aberration, to be erased, as once again the air exploded with the pounding of heavy artillery. An allied offensive was about to be launched, aimed at breaking the stalemate of the last weeks. There was no respite for those who had been manning the forward lines over Christmas. No relief had been sent, but reinforcements were brought up ready for an attack to clear the Germans from their trenches the other side of the narrow stretch of no man's land.

The signal to advance was given. Officers and men from the allied trenches scrambled over the top into a barrage of defensive fire from the enemy. Those that fell before the retreat was sounded were left in no man's land for snipers to pick off at leisure.

No ground had changed hands in the aborted advance, but men on both sides had died in the effort to take or defend.

The Christmas truce was over and Germany and the allies were again most definitely at war.

Chapter Fifty-Five

On Boxing Day morning Isabella and the aunts all had breakfast in their rooms. There was no rush to come downstairs to greet the day and Lady McFarlane lingered over her breakfast tray. She and Keir were invited to Lady Scott's Boxing Day Luncheon, but it was fashionably timed for one o'clock, giving her plenty of time to dress for the outing. She sat up in bed, staring through the window at the gathering clouds.

Not a day to venture forth unless you had to, but, thought Isabella, we do have to. Imagine allowing a little snow to keep us at home on such a special day!

Thank goodness it's not actually snowing, she thought, as she gave consideration as to what she might wear. Definitely the mink coat Keir had bought her, in celebration of his peerage, but obviously she would have to remove that once they arrived at the house. She contemplated her winter wardrobe. Since she had learned of Sir Keir's elevation, she had known she must visit Madame Chantal and discover the latest rage in Paris, for as she explained to her husband, she couldn't appear dressed in last year's rags.

'Of course you must refurbish your wardrobe,' Keir had said, when she applied to him for a larger allowance. 'You've a position to maintain. But please, my dearest love, remember we still have some financial restraints.'

With this in mind, she had not ordered the two evening gowns Madame Chantal held out for her perusal; nor the extra tea dress; and with some embarrassment had turned down two less formal gowns which would have been perfect for morning visits.

With her usual tact and delicacy, Madame Chantal had realised what was required and when Lady McFarlane had chosen and ordered four complete outfits which would allow her to appear at several functions without repeating herself, Madame Chantal showed her how each ensemble could be worn with an added scarf, a lace fichu, an exchangeable collar or different coloured gloves; add an enchanting hat and the look became entirely different.

The cream woollen day dress would be the one for today, she decided. Its soft wool would keep her warm when she removed the fur coat, and the copper-coloured leaves detailed at the dropped waist, the ankle-length hem and the ruched neckline would give enough colour to draw the eye to the emerald necklace and earrings she'd been left by her mother. The whole ensemble would be discreet, nothing ostentatious. Lady Scott, her hostess, would not want to be outshone at her own luncheon and Isabella McFarlane was determined not to put a foot wrong in her first foray into the highest echelons of London society. There had even been a whisper that the Prince of Wales might look in, and if he did, the McFarlanes would find themselves moving in royal circles.

Sliding her feet out of the bed, she slipped into her wrap and rang the bell for Denby.

Though the three older ladies were taking their time to emerge from their bedrooms, Iain and Lucy had come down in time to join their father for breakfast in the morning room, where a cheerful fire already snapped and crackled in the hearth.

'What are your plans for the day?' Keir asked after they had all helped themselves to hot porridge from the porridge pot on the sideboard.

'Nothing like porridge to warm you up,' Iain said, avoiding the question as he scooped some honey from a large jar on the table, twirling the spoon quickly in his hand to prevent it from trickling onto the tablecloth.

'I thought you and Mama were going to Lady Scott's luncheon,' said Lucinda, coming to his rescue.

'We are indeed,' said her father. 'It is, your mother tells me, *the* Boxing Day event. And of course Lord Scott was one of my sponsors in the Lords. Their invitation is one of the reasons we didn't go down the country, as I'd suggested.'

'Would you rather have gone to Haverford, Papa?' asked Lueinda.

'No, no, of course not,' replied her father, a little too hurriedly. 'We're extremely comfortable here in London, and the Christmas season is always delightful with card parties, luncheons, musical evenings and the like.'

'So you'll be out until evening, I suppose,' said Lucinda.

'Almost certainly,' replied her father. 'You can have a quiet day here at home, Lucy. I know your aunts will enjoy your company.'

Lucinda considered the quiet day here at home, which wasn't now her home, with dismay. She glanced across at Iain. Nobody expected him to stay at home and talk to his aunts, and an idea slipped into her mind.

When their father got up and left the room, Iain and Lucinda remained at the table.

'How will you get to the Waldons' party?' Lucinda asked as she refilled their coffee cups.

'Oh, I'll get William to go and find me a taxi,' Iain replied. 'Why?'

'I thought I might go home. You could drop me off.'

'Of course,' agreed Iain, 'if that's what you want.'

'It's not,' said Lucinda. 'But it's what I want them to think.'

'Who?' Iain gave his sister a suspicious look. 'What are you up to, Lucy?'

'Nothing. I'm not up to anything, I just sort of had an idea.'

'Come on then,' encouraged Iain with a grin, 'spit it out!'

'I get into a taxi with you, as if going home, but I come with you to Diana's party instead.' Adding defensively, as she saw the expression on Iain's face, 'After all, I was invited as well.' She reached into her pocket and pulled out the invitation card.

```
Lord Waldon requests the pleasure of your
                  company on


                  Boxing Day


                  Open House


                  1pm–3pm


              55 Park Lane


                  Mayfair
```

Lucinda's name in beautiful copperplate was inscribed at the top right-hand corner.

'You don't have to show me the invitation,' sighed Iain. 'I've got one too, remember?'

But when Lucinda turned it over, he saw an extra message on the back.

Come if you can!

There had been no such message on his invitation, but then there didn't need to be one; Diana knew he needed no extra bidding. Nothing would stop him from joining her party.

'Of course, I couldn't attend alone,' Lucinda was saying, 'but it would be perfectly proper for me to arrive escorted by my brother.'

'I thought you weren't allowed into company while you're... you know?'

'Who's to know?'

'Well, I don't think it's a secret that you're going to have a baby, you know.'

'It may be known in some circles,' Lucinda said, 'but it doesn't show yet and it'd never be mentioned in polite company.'

That made Iain laugh. 'Are the Waldons polite company?'

'Of course they are, though perhaps Mama wouldn't agree. But that makes it safe to go. She's hardly likely to mix with Lord Waldon's circle of friends.'

'Probably not,' Iain agreed, 'but you can be sure it will get back to her in the end.'

'I expect so,' Lucinda replied cheerfully, 'but by the time it does it will be too late. Mama'll be angry, but she won't be able to do anything about it and I'll have had an enjoyable afternoon.'

'What about your reputation?'

'No doubt it will come under discussion,' said Lucinda ruefully. 'Reputations always provide food for the gossips. But I assure you, my behaviour will be beyond reproach, and as I said, I shall be escorted by my brother.'

'You do realise that means Mama will discover I was there too, don't you?'

'I'm sure she won't be surprised,' retorted Lucinda. 'It's an open secret, after all. You and Diana are so often seen in each other's company. It has been noticed, you know.'

'I do know,' said Iain. 'Lord Waldon spoke to me the evening we'd been to Crayne.'

'Really?' Lucinda was surprised. 'What did he say?'

'He didn't seem to mind, just told me to be sure I remembered the proprieties. Despite what everyone thinks, he is very careful of Diana's reputation.'

'And are you?'

'Am I what?'

'Remembering the proprieties?'

'Of course. The only times we are alone together is in her own home.'

'Well, it sounds as if he thinks you trustworthy, anyway. So, can I come with you... to the party?'

'What about the aunts?'

'What about them? They'll be perfectly happy here, warm and comfortable doing their embroidery. They're so used to each other's company, they'll never miss me!'

Just before one o'clock, there was a flurry of activity as Lady McFarlane came down the stairs, pausing for a moment halfway down, to make her entrance and be admired.

Lord McFarlane, emerging from his library, looked up at his wife and wondered, as he had so often over the years, how he had managed to woo and wed such a beauty. The cream dress fitted her perfectly, showing off her still-girlish figure, its sleeves trimmed with cream lace from the elbow and the whole ensemble topped with a smart cream confection perched upon her abundant hair.

Keir held out his hand to her and taking it, she continued down the stairs to where William awaited her with her fur coat and Felstead held the front door.

Turning to Lucinda she said, 'You won't need Denby for anything will you? I've told her to take the afternoon off.'

Lucinda assured her mother that she would not, and once dressed for the cold December day outside, Lord and Lady McFarlane descended the steps, already cleared of snow, to Croxton and the Rolls. It was colder than Isabella had been expecting and she welcomed the travelling rug the chauffeur gave her to cover her legs. Glancing back to the house she saw that Felstead had already closed the front door against the chilly air.

'Give me a quarter of an hour,' Lucinda murmured to Iain, 'and I'll be ready to go.'

Knowing there was no way of dissuading her, Iain replied, 'Fifteen minutes and if you're not ready by then, I shall go without you. I'll wait in the library.'

Upstairs in her bedroom, Lucinda hurriedly changed the skirt and blouse she was wearing for the elegant tea gown she had worn the previous day. Apart from slightly enlarged breasts, easily disguised with a lace fichu, and a slightly thickened waist, her pregnancy hardly showed and Madame Chantal had designed the gown especially for her. Its long, flowing skirt, falling from just below her breasts, swept down to her ankles in a swathe of blue velvet, concealing without difficulty her burgeoning change of shape. Quickly plaiting her hair, she coiled it onto her head and, securing it with a matching velvet head band, was ready to join Iain in the library with three minutes to spare.

'That was quick,' he said.

'Well, I didn't trust you not to go without me.'

'What did Denby say when you said you wanted to change?'

'I didn't need Denby, and anyway, Mama has given her the rest of the day off.'

Iain summoned William and despatched him in search of a cab, before turning again to Lucinda and asking, 'Are you really sure this is a good idea, Lucy?'

Lucy, who had indeed been having second thoughts, nodded. She didn't want Diana to think that she was still ruled by her mother.

'Yes,' she said. 'Diana asked me and I want to go.'

It wasn't long before William returned with a motor taxi. Iain offered Lucinda his arm as she descended the steps and climbed into the cab, clutching a small bag containing her indoor shoes for when she changed out of her winter boots.

'Haven't you been given the afternoon off, William?' asked Iain as he waited for his sister to get settled.

'Yes, sir,' William replied. 'Once luncheon is cleared away, I shall be going to have Christmas tea with Mabel and her family.'

Iain stiffened and then said casually, 'Well, I hope you enjoy yourself. How is Mabel?'

'Very well, thank you, sir.'

There was a note of satisfaction in his voice which Iain didn't miss, but all he said was, 'Good to hear.'

'Do get in, Iain,' Lucinda called from the back seat of the cab. 'It's freezing in here.'

As the taxi pulled away from the kerb, Lucinda asked, 'Who were you talking about?'

'Just making sure William was getting some time off,' replied Iain casually.

'No you weren't,' replied Lucinda. 'You were asking about some girl.'

'If you must know, I was asking about Mabel Oakley.'

'Mabel Oakley?' The name was familiar to Lucinda but for a moment she couldn't place it. Then her expression cleared. 'The maid, Mabel Oakley?'

'Yes.'

'But why? Why did William mention her to you?'

'I believe she and William have an understanding.'

'But what's that to you?'

'Nothing,' replied Iain, knowing it was now true. All thoughts of Mabel had been swept aside by Diana. He would always have an affection for Mabel, admire her for her determination, her tenacity, and her strength of character, but what he'd thought was love had been consigned to the recesses of his memory by what he now felt for Diana.

'She's out in the world, running her own business.'

'Really? What does she do?'

'She's a printer.'

'Funny sort of job for a woman,' remarked Lucinda dismissively.

'Maybe, but she's very good at it. It was Mabel who printed the extra invitations for your wedding.'

'Mabel the maid did?'

'We needed them in a hurry and she was prepared to do them immediately,' adding with a sideways look at his sister, 'because they were for you.'

'Well, I never,' said Lucinda. And then with an abrupt change of subject she asked, 'Have you got a present for Diana?'

'If it's any business of yours, yes, I have,' answered Iain.

'What have you got?'

'Never you mind,' replied Iain, slipping his hand into his pocket where the small jewellery box nestled.

When they arrived in Park Lane their knock was answered by Wragge, who stepped aside to allow them entry before passing their coats to Henry.

'If your ladyship would like to visit the ladies' guest room,' said Wragge, 'Mrs Frobisher will direct you.'

'I would just like to change my shoes,' said Lucinda, as the housekeeper appeared beside her.

'This way, my lady.'

Leaving Iain in the hall, Mrs Frobisher led Lucinda along a short passage to a guest room set aside for the convenience of ladies.

Lucinda sat down on an upholstered chair and quickly replaced her boots for the indoor pumps she had brought with her. A quick glance in the mirror showed her that the secret of her pregnancy remained concealed by blue velvet and then she allowed Mrs Frobisher to take her back to Iain, waiting impatiently in the hall.

'You took your time,' he murmured as Wragge led them into the spacious drawing room and announced their arrival.

Diana was on the far side of the room, speaking to an elderly lady seated in an armchair by the fire, but on hearing Iain's name she turned round with such an expression of joy on her face that Iain could hardly breathe.

Lord Waldon left the group of guests he'd been talking to and stepped forward to greet them, hand outstretched.

'Lady Melcome, what a pleasure. And Mr McFarlane, good afternoon.'

Their arrival caused a momentary break in the general

conversation, but it soon revived and Diana came over to greet them.

'You came, both of you,' she murmured. 'I was beginning to give you up.'

'Iain had to wait for me to get ready,' Lucinda admitted. 'And I had to wait until Mama had left the house.'

'Never mind,' smiled Diana, 'you're here now, both of you.'

Lucinda had been looking round the room, where guests stood in convivial groups, while waiters topped up glasses and offered canapés. She recognised no one, but that didn't mean no one recognised her.

'Come and meet my grandmother,' said Diana and led them across to the old woman by the fire.

'Grandmama, may I introduce you to Lady Melcome and her brother, Mr McFarlane. My grandmother, the dowager Lady Waldon.'

Lady Waldon raised a lorgnette and after a cursory glance at Lucinda, gave her attention to Iain.

'So you're the one whose name is being connected to my granddaughter's. Are you respectable? Are your intentions honourable, I wonder, or are you just a gold-digger, simply after her money?'

'Grandmama, you're a disgrace,' scolded Diana.

Iain managed to smile at the old lady and said, 'My intentions are entirely honourable, Lady Waldon, but I don't know yet if they are acceptable.'

'Hhmm,' Lady Waldon scowled at him. 'Your father's a judge.'

'He is, Lady Waldon. A law lord, recently sponsored by Lord Scott.'

'That's why your parents aren't here, I suppose,' she replied. 'They'll be at the Scotts' Boxing Day luncheon. *Dreadful* squeeze.'

'I believe they have that honour,' Iain answered quietly, holding her gaze.

The old lady lowered her lorgnette and turned her attention

back to Diana. 'Tell a waiter to bring me some smoked salmon, child, and caviar, and tell Henry I require another glass of ratafia.'

'You mustn't mind Grandmama,' Diana said, as she signalled to one of the waiters to attend to her grandmother. 'She always speaks her mind.'

'You mean she's always rude?' commented Lucinda.

Diana laughed. 'Yes, I suppose I do. But we're all so used to her, we hardly notice.'

For the next half hour, they stood among the guests, eating from the apparently never-ending selection of canapés they were offered. Introductions were made, polite conversation exchanged, groups broke up and shifted; more guests arrived, others took their leave.

There were few other guests of their age, though Iain did recognise Marcus Champion and his wife, Daphne. He introduced Lucinda, but almost immediately the couple drifted away into the dining room, where yet more food was laid out.

Diana, as her father's hostess, had to attend to his guests, but she was never far from Iain and Lucinda, making sure they were always included in one group or another. Iain was despairing of a chance to have a private moment with her as the numbers gradually thinned out and three o'clock approached.

'We should go,' Lucinda murmured. 'I'd better go and change my shoes.'

Seeing Lucinda turning for the door, Diana hurried over.

'Don't go,' she said. 'Stay a little while. I've spoken to Pop and when everyone here has gone, he's happy for me to show you my Christmas present.'

'What is it?' asked Lucinda.

'Wait until you see!' exclaimed Diana, her eyes sparkling.

Gradually, the drawing room emptied. Apart from the dowager Lady Waldon, who sat snoring gently in her chair, only Iain and Lucinda were left sitting now, with Diana. Her father returned, bidding farewell to his last guests, and said, 'I'm glad you're able to stay a while, Lady Melcome. I know this party is always very boring for Diana, very few people from her own circle and few of those real friends. I know she would like to show you her Christmas present.' He smiled at Lucinda. 'It's outside in the cold, I'm afraid. You'll need your coat. Perhaps you'd prefer to wait for your brother in here by the fireside.'

Lucinda was about to say that she was happy to fetch her coat and brave the cold, when she caught the beseeching look in Iain's eyes, and she smiled back at her host.

'I must admit, it's very tempting to stay here by the fire,' she said, 'and I am a little tired.'

'Let me send for some tea,' said his lordship, 'and a slice of Mrs Dewer's Christmas cake.' Turning back to Diana, he went on, 'You can have yours when you come back in, Diana. Don't be too long. I think it's going to snow again.'

The tea and the cake arrived, the tray placed on a side table. Lucinda looked across at Lady Waldon and wondered if she should offer her some tea. There were three cups on the tray and a cake stand, with not only the promised Christmas cake with marzipan and white frosted icing, but chocolate cake and some shortbread.

Lord Waldon had excused himself for a moment, and the minute he walked out of the room, Lady Waldon's eyes opened and fixed themselves on Lucinda.

'In my day,' drawled the old lady, 'no refined lady would have appeared in public in your state.'

'What do you mean, "my state"?' Lucinda tried to keep her voice calm.

'*Enceinte*! Breeding!'

'And in my circles, no *lady* would have remarked upon it.'

'It's time you learned to respect your elders,' snapped the dowager.

'I already do,' said Lucinda. 'If they are worthy of respect. Now, would you like a cup of tea and some cake? Or are you going back to sleep?'

When Diana and Iain came back into the room, their cheeks pink from the cold, Diana rang for more tea and more cups.

'So, do tell me,' Lucinda said, now leaving the pouring to Diana, 'what was your Christmas present?'

Diana looked at Iain and grinned. 'You can tell her!'

'Only a car!' said Iain. 'A car of her own!'

'I've named her Little Elsie!' laughed Diana. 'She needed a name!'

'And do you know how to drive her?' asked Lucinda.

'Not yet,' replied Diana, 'but Chambers is going to teach me.'

At that moment Lord Waldon came back into the room.

'Ah, tea,' he said, holding his hands to the fire, 'and then I think you should go home. It's started to snow.'

'Perhaps, sir, Henry might be able to find us a taxi,' said Iain.

'No need,' replied his lordship. 'Chambers, my driver, will take you home. He's outside, waiting with the car.'

Five minutes later Iain and Lucinda were in the back of Lord Waldon's car, wrapped in rugs and being driven slowly through the snowy streets, back to Chanynge Place. As they pulled up outside number 11, they found themselves waiting behind the Rolls as Lord and Lady McFarlane got out and struggled through the increasingly heavy snow, up the steps and into the house. Seeing a second car waiting, Felstead did not close the door immediately, causing Isabella to look back. As Croxton pulled away from the kerb, she saw that both Iain and Lucinda were getting out of the unknown car.

'Where have you been?' she demanded, as Felstead finally closed the door behind them. When neither of them answered, she stood firmly in the way. 'Where have you been?' she repeated. 'Whose car was that?'

'Let them get their coats off, my dear,' said her husband. 'And then they can tell us all about it.'

Chapter Fifty-Six

By the time William arrived at the Oakleys', the parlour fire was again alight, the kettle was singing on the gas and the Christmas cake was ready for a ceremonial cutting.

Although Mabel's heart hadn't at first been in her task of icing the cake, it was a job that was always left to her, and the measuring and mixing of the icing sugar, the squeezing of a precious lemon discovered on a market stall, the smoothing of the icing, the choice of the sprig of holly for the top and the careful inscription of 'Merry Christmas' in tiny silver balls had soothed her, and by the time she had finished, she had been ready for the delicate frill Annie had made from tissue paper to circle it.

As beautifully done as always, Alice thought, as she put it on its plate in the middle of the kitchen table. Just then there was a loud rap on the door.

'William's here, Mabel,' called her mother.

'Try to sound normal,' Mabel told herself as she opened the door. 'You're always pleased to see him.'

'Merry Christmas, Mabel,' he cried, 'Or should it be merry Boxing Day.'

'Either will do,' answered Mabel with a smile, finding she was genuinely pleased to see him. 'And same to you. Come in, quickly, you must be frozen!'

She stood aside to let him in, and as he passed by, he reached across to kiss her on the cheek.

'It is very cold,' he agreed, as he set aside a bag he had been carrying to relinquish his coat, hat and scarf. 'But I got warm walking here.'

'Surely you didn't walk all the way from Chanynge Place, did you?'

'No, not quite, an omnibus came along and brought me halfway.'

'We're all in the kitchen,' said Mabel, and led him along to join the others.

Once everyone had greeted William, he sat down at the kitchen table. Doreen made the tea and Alice found the special knife for cutting the cake.

'We saved cutting the Christmas cake until you were here to share it with us,' Andrew told him.

'And we thought we'd have tea and cake in here first, as it's warmer,' added Alice. 'We can move into the parlour afterwards. The fire's alight, and it will have warmed up the room by then.'

'Did you have a busy time at Chanynge Place?' Mabel asked him, once everyone had been served with tea and cake.

'Much as usual, but fewer family. Just the six. Lady Melcome's husband is away in France, as you know, but she braved the snow and came yesterday morning. Lady M was afraid she might fall in her delicate state, but we'd cleared the steps of ice, so there was no fear of that. Of course, Lord and Lady McFarlane were there, and Mr Iain.' He glanced at Mabel as he spoke, but she didn't react. William was feeling quite cheerful. Having seen Iain and Lady Melcome on their way to Lord Waldon's Boxing Day party, he had finally come to accept that whatever Iain McFarlane's feelings might once have been for Mabel, they had, according to society gossip, been overtaken by a tendre for Lady Diana Fosse-Bury, a tendre which would either very soon end in tears, or at the altar.

No, he thought now as he looked fondly at Mabel cutting another piece of cake for her father, he really did have nothing to fear from Iain McFarlane.

'Lady McFarlane's two sisters have come as usual,' he went

on, 'but although Miss Fay is in good health and looks after Miss Gertie as best she can, sadly Miss Gertie is very childish now. She is happy enough in company, but she is very forgetful and can't really be left on her own.'

'Are you still happy working for the McFarlanes?' Alice asked. 'Weren't you talking of moving on?'

William looked a little embarrassed. 'I was considering it,' he said, 'but on further thought, I decided to wait a while and see how things go.'

Mabel wasn't sure how it happened, but after a while, Doreen and the two girls retired upstairs, Eddie and Stephen headed for the pub, and Alice and Andrew withdrew into Andrew's room to set up the draughts board, leaving Mabel and William to sit by the fire in the parlour.

'How's business?' William asked, knowing that Mabel was always pleased to talk about her printing works.

'Not too bad,' replied Mabel. 'Of course, things are more difficult what with war an' all. The materials I need are getting more expensive, and people want fewer printing jobs done. To be realistic, before very long I shall have to put up my prices, or I won't make ends meet.'

She considered telling William about her legacy from Mr Morrell, which should tide her over if things became really tight, but she did not want to mention how the McFarlanes had come to her aid. William always seemed very touchy if Iain McFarlane came into the conversation; and anyway, that business was particularly private.

So she was very surprised when William introduced him into the conversation now.

'I wouldn't be surprised if Mr Iain wasn't engaged to be married very soon,' he said. 'He's been seen with Lady Diana Fosse-Bury a good deal lately.'

'Has he?' Mabel didn't seem very interested. 'Who's she?'

'The Earl of Waldon's daughter.'

'An earl's daughter? Well, good for him.'

'Of course, if they do get married,' went on William, 'they'll be setting up their own establishment, and perhaps Mr Iain will be in need of a butler.'

'So he might,' agreed Mabel, seeing where this might be leading. 'And you'd apply?'

'It would be a step up for me,' said William. 'And he'd know I'd been properly trained, not like some of these jumped-up pipsqueaks.' He looked across at Mabel earnestly. 'Of course it might never happen, at least not with Mr Iain, but one way or another, I could soon be in a position to be married myself.'

All of a sudden he was kneeling beside her chair and grasping her hands. 'I know you don't want to be tied down yet, Mabel. I know you want to run your business as long as you can, but there may come a time when you can't.'

'William, please, stop.' Mabel tried to withdraw her hands, but he held them fast.

'Just hear me out, Mabel, please?' he begged. 'I know you don't want to get married yet, maybe not for some time, but when you do, well, I'll be waiting for you, I promise.'

'William, dear William.' She disentangled her hands and drew away from him. 'I'm sorry. I can't.'

'You can't what?'

'I can't marry you, I can't marry you now, or sometime in the future. Not ever.'

'Why not?' William sounded confused. 'I thought we had an understanding. I thought, well, I thought you loved me. Maybe not as much as I love you, but enough...'

'I do love you William, I love you as a very dear friend, but...' She drew a deep breath. She knew that she had to tell him the truth. To banish any hope that he might have that in time she would change her mind.

'But...?'

'But I can never marry you. I'm in love with someone else.' Adding for extra emphasis, 'I'm going to marry someone else.'

'Who? Who else are you going to marry? You aren't even

engaged.' He held up her hand as if to show her. 'See? You aren't wearing a ring!'

'No,' agreed Mabel, 'but I will be very soon.'

'You hope!' exclaimed William bitterly.

'I *know*,' insisted Mabel. 'I am promised, to someone else.'

'I thought you were promised to *me*,' said William angrily. 'See, I have a ring.' He plunged his hand into his pocket and produced a small leather jewellery box. 'I have ring for you.' He opened the box to reveal a small engagement ring glinting in the firelight. 'For when you say yes.'

'I'm sorry,' Mabel said helplessly, 'dear Will, I can't.'

'But I'm not "dear Will" am I?' retorted William. He snapped the box shut and stuffed it back into his pocket. 'Who is he? No, don't tell me, I don't want to know. I suppose I should just be grateful that it's not Mr Iain McFarlane.'

'Iain McFarlane?' Mabel looked startled. 'Iain? Why Iain?'

'Oh, he thought he was in love with you, but now the sensible man has passed you up for the daughter of an earl.'

Mabel stared at him. William was as angry as she'd ever seen him.

'I'm going home now,' William said, getting up and walking out into the hall to find his coat, hat and scarf. 'I'll just say goodnight to your parents. I assume they know about this man you're going to marry.'

'Yes, they do.'

'But they didn't think to tell me about him?' The bitterness was back in his voice.

'I asked them not to. I needed to tell you myself.'

'I shan't see you again, Mabel,' he said, 'but I shall always love you.'

Without going into Andrew's room, he opened the front door, letting a blast of frigid air force its way into the house, and stepping out onto the pavement, he turned away and, without a backward glance, walked off down the street.

Mabel watched him until he rounded the corner, and with a

chill in her heart that had nothing to do with the influx of winter air, she closed the door, and went into her father's room, where the draughts board was set up, ready for a game.

'Where's William?' asked her mother. 'Didn't I hear him in the hall?'

'Yes, Mam,' said Mabel. 'He had to go. He said goodbye.' And with that Mabel burst into tears.

Chapter Fifty-Seven

On Monday morning, Mabel was in her workshop early, far too early for Chas to be here yet, but she couldn't settle to anything in the house. Her parents were restless as well. They knew Charles Sheridan was coming to meet them properly, and Andrew, in particular, was on edge. How could he make John Sheridan's son welcome in his home with all the history there was between them?

'You have to give the man a chance,' Alice said to him more than once. 'You may not like him, but he's very important to Mabel and you don't want to lose her, do you?'

Andrew certainly didn't; he idolised his daughter. He could hardly believe his little girl was not really a little girl anymore. Could she really be bringing a strange young man to the house, saying they wanted to get married? A man from an entirely different background, the son of a man Andrew actively despised?

Had she been wanting to marry William, Andrew would have been full of approval of her choice and wouldn't have considered her too young to be married. But William was gone. The end of Boxing Day evening had seen to that. Everyone had managed to find some excuse to give the couple time alone together in the parlour. Surely, thought Andrew, Mabel would come to her senses. But she had not. Though she had refused his offer of an engagement ring and William had stormed out, she had been unhappy ever since, and the next day had been very difficult for everyone.

'Why couldn't it have been William?' he asked Alice in frustration. 'What made her change her mind?'

'I changed my mind,' Alice reminded him with a smile. 'I was walking out with Herbert Ash when I met you, but once we met, poor Herbert didn't have a chance!'

'That was quite different,' said Andrew. 'Herbert wasn't the man for you!'

'No, he wasn't. A perfectly amiable young man, but I knew he wasn't for me. Maybe Mabel feels the same about William, an agreeable young man, but not the one for her.'

'And Charles Sheridan is?'

'You have to think of him as just Charles,' Alice told him. 'Without the Sheridan.'

Mabel wasn't the only one who had woken early that Monday morning. Chas was awake long before it was light. Christmas with his Pearson grandparents had been rather a dull affair. Church was expected and lasted nearly two hours. The food, a turkey with all the trimmings prepared by Bridget, their elderly Irish cook, washed down with some homemade elderflower wine, had been the best part of the day. After the ample Christmas dinner, his grandfather spent the afternoon asleep in his chair in front of the fire and his grandmother tried, with what she thought was gentle questioning, to discover why dearest Charles had fallen out with his father so badly that he'd left the family home, over Christmas, of all times.

As he had grown up, it had gradually dawned on Chas that his mother's parents did not like his father very much, and in the last few years he had come to realise that the feeling was mutual. When he and Lavinia had been younger, very often his mother would visit her parents, taking the children with her for a seaside holiday. His father seldom accompanied them and if he did, he kept the visit short. His mother tried to smooth such meetings, but now Chas and Lavinia were grown up, these were few and far between.

Despite his grandmother's questions, all Charles would say was that they had not wanted him to volunteer for the army, and that his father was particularly angry because Chas had done it without discussing it with him first. He made no mention of Mabel.

Charles had always been fond of his maternal grandparents, who had tended to spoil both him and Lavinia as small children, but by the end of the third day, he'd had enough of the rather oppressive atmosphere in the house, and decided to take the five o'clock milk train back to town. He couldn't wait to get back to London, to Mabel.

Mabel was still in her workshop when she heard the click of the side gate and the sound of footsteps on the path. She looked at the clock above the printing press. Surely it was too early of it to be Chas? But it wasn't: with a brief tap, Chas pushed the door open and Mabel was in his arms, the remembered kisses renewed; all thoughts of William forgotten.

'How did you get here so early?' Mabel asked when she could say anything at all.

'Caught the milk train.'

'Did you go and see your mother?'

'Yes, but my father was home too… still angry. It was a rather short visit.'

'Did they know you were coming here? To see me and meet my parents?'

'No,' said Chas. 'No point in making things worse.'

'Do I make things worse?'

'No, you don't, you make things better, but my father doesn't see things that way. Anyhow, I collected all my kit and kissed my mother and Lavinia goodbye. My father had shut himself in his study, so I didn't stay.'

'Where is your kit?' asked Mabel, suddenly aware that he'd brought nothing with him.

'In the left luggage office at the station. I'll collect it later. I didn't want to be carrying it about with me when I came here.' He looked round the workshop. 'Were you working?'

Mabel shook her head. 'No, just trying to pass the time until you got here.' She put her arms round his neck, and felt his arms tighten around her once more. 'Oh, Chas, I have missed you.'

Sometime later they broke apart and Mabel said, 'You'd better arrive at the front door so that I can invite you in to the house properly.'

One final kiss and Chas returned to the street, while Mabel ran up the steps to the kitchen door.

Alice had wondered if they should meet in the parlour, but Mabel insisted on the kitchen. 'It's where we spend most of our time, after all, and the warmest place in the house... where we're a family.' She wanted no echoes of Boxing Day night.

Doreen had got Andrew ready for the day. He was sitting now at the kitchen table, with Alice on one side and Mabel on the other. The kettle was on the hob and the remains of the Christmas cake was ready to share. It looked like an informal gathering for tea and cake, but there was an almost tangible tension in the room, and a spare chair, waiting. Eddie and Stephen had left early to return to work and the other members of the household had made themselves scarce.

It was a relief when there was a knock at the front door and Mabel was able to open it and invite Charles Sheridan into their home.

He paused in the kitchen doorway, taking in the scene, and Mabel said, 'Mam, Dada, I'd like you to meet the man I'm going to marry. This is Chas. Chas... my parents, Mr and Mrs Oakley.'

Chas stepped forward, going first to Alice, his hand outstretched, and said, 'How do you do, Mrs Oakley? It's a pleasure to meet you.'

To which Alice murmured a 'How d'you do?' as she shook his hand.

Turning immediately to Andrew, Chas said, 'How d'you do, sir?'

Again, he extended his hand, and there was a moment's pause, when it seemed that Andrew might not take it, might not respond at all, but then, as if lifting his hand took enormous effort, he touched hands briefly with Chas, and with a nod said, 'Young man.'

Mabel indicated the chair next to her mother, saying, 'I'll make the tea.'

Andrew pushed his wheelchair back from the table and said, 'Alice, perhaps you would take me back to my room for a moment. I should like to speak to... Chas... in private.'

Mabel looked at her mother in dismay, but Alice said, 'Of course,' and taking the handles of the chair, manoeuvred her husband back to his room, the place where he always felt most comfortable, most in control of his restricted life. When Alice returned to the kitchen, Chas was still standing by the table.

'If you don't mind,' she said quietly, 'Andrew would like to speak to you.'

Chas nodded and, with a smile he hoped was reassuring to Mabel, went in to join her father.

'What's Dada going to say?' Mabel asked her mother. 'Did you know he was going to speak to him like that?'

'I guessed he would,' answered Alice. 'Most fathers do, when a young man comes to ask if he can marry their daughters, don't they? They want to know their prospects, to decide if they are suitable husbands.'

Andrew had been stationed by the window, so that the daylight fell on the younger man's face, while his own was in shadow.

'What does your father think of you wanting to marry Mabel?' Andrew went straight to the point. If he was going to allow Mabel to marry this... Sheridan... this Charles, he wanted to know what kind of welcome Mabel would get from Charles's family. Would she be snubbed? Ignored? Belittled?

'He is against the idea,' answered Chas, frankly. 'He has forbidden me to do so. Of course I am of age, so he can't prevent me from marrying anyone I want to.'

'Even against his express wishes.'

'That is why I have come to ask you if Mabel and I may

become engaged. I expect she has told you that I have signed up for the army. I knew you might feel as my father does, and I don't want Mabel to have to choose between me and her family. I shall be away for the foreseeable future, but I love her dearly, and as I believe she loves me, I have asked her to wait for me and she has given me her promise.'

'And if I don't sanction this engagement?'

'We will wait until she is also of age and needs no permission,' answered Chas, 'but in the meantime, I would like to correspond with her while I'm away, to assure you we are doing nothing behind your back.'

'You were though, weren't you? Meeting up unknown to us.'

'Yes, but initially I didn't know anything about you and your history with my father. Not until Mabel told me. If you decide against me, I will wait for Mabel, wait for as long as it takes.'

'I see.' Andrew looked at the young man, son of the man, John Sheridan. He thought of the love he felt for Alice. If her father had refused his blessing, he would have waited for her, for as long as it took.

Charles Sheridan sounded sincere. Chas... not Charles Sheridan... sounded sincere.

Andrew remained silent for a long time, before he finally said, 'I shan't withhold my blessing if Mabel has given her promise and you have given yours. But if you break your word to her... or allow any harm to come to her...' He left the sentence unfinished.

'Thank you, sir,' said Chas, hardly able to breathe. 'Thank you.'

'I think we've finished here.' Andrew drew a long, slow breath and said, 'Perhaps you'd be good enough to wheel me back into the kitchen... Chas.'

When the two men returned to the kitchen, Alice and Mabel were sitting at the table, a pot of tea between them and slices of Christmas cake on a plate.

'Charles...' Andrew corrected himself, 'Chas has asked if we

will allow Mabel and him to become engaged. I have agreed
to an engagement, so that they may correspond, but with Chas
going away to fight, there will be no thought of actual marriage
until he comes back.'

Mabel leaped to her feet and flung her arms around her
father's neck. 'Thank you, Dada, thank you!'

They drank the tea and ate the cake and then Chas said, 'May
I have your permission to take Mabel out this afternoon? I'll
bring her back in the early evening, as I have a train to catch to
Lincoln tonight. I have to report to the camp at seven o'clock
tomorrow morning.'

'As long as you bring her to the door,' said Andrew.

Within twenty minutes the two of them were walking down
the street, arm in arm.

'Where are we going?' asked Mabel, though she didn't really
care.

'It's too cold to be outside. Let's go to Rosie's first and then I
thought we could go to a picture house.'

Once in the familiar warmth of Rosie's Tea Room and seated
by the fire, Mabel asked what she had been dying to ask, 'What
did Dada say to you?'

'He told me to look after you, and I said I would.'

'Is that all?' Mabel sounded disappointed.

'No, he asked what my father thinks about us.'

'And what did you say?'

'I told him he had forbidden me to marry you, but that he
can't stop me because I'm of age. I said we were prepared to wait
until you were twenty-one if necessary, and your father believed
me.' He looked across at her and asked, 'Will you marry me?'

'You asked me that before,' replied Mabel with a smile. 'And
I said yes, remember?'

Chas took her hand. 'You did, but I just wanted to be sure you
haven't changed your mind.'

'Well, I haven't.'

'Good,' said Chas, with a smile, and taking a small leather

box from his pocket, he said. 'Darling Mabel, we're engaged now, so will you wear my ring?'

Mabel stared at the ring, nestling in the silk-lined box. A deep blue sapphire set with a diamond on either side. For a split second she thought of William, but she pushed the thought away and held out her left hand.

'Oh yes, Chas.' And there were tears in her eyes as he slipped it onto her finger.

Somehow the afternoon vanished and it was time for Chas to take her home. The weather was cold and growing colder as they hurried along the streets. Once again they slipped down the path at the side of the house and went into the workshop.

'I love you, Mabel,' Chas said again as he held her close. 'I'll write to you as soon as I have an address for you to use... and you will write back?' Suddenly Chas sounded unsure.

Mabel had been fighting back tears, but she gave him her promise.

'I must go now,' Chas said. 'If ever you doubt me, my darling, just look at your ring and know that you are mine.'

One final kiss and he was gone. Mabel heard his footsteps on the path and the click of the gate, but this time they told her he was leaving, not coming home.

As she lay in the darkness of their room later, she turned to Annie and asked, 'How do you make yourself get up every morning, now you're on your own?'

'I do it because I have to,' came the reply. 'What else can I do?'

'You can stay here with us... for as long as you like. And between us we'll make a difference, you'll see.'

Epilogue

June 1915

Lucinda was nearing her time and so she had moved from Sloane Square to Crayne House for her lying in. It had been David's wish that the baby should be born at Crayne as he had been.

Some weeks before the expected date, Fenton had come up to London, collected the two Lady Melcomes from Sloane Square and driven them down to Crayne in David's car. It spared Lucinda the discomfort of a train journey. It was now absolutely clear to anyone who looked at her that Lady Melcome was expecting a happy event.

When Fenton appeared at the door, Lady Melcome Senior looked at him in dismay. 'How will you drive, with only one arm, Fenton?' she asked.

Lucinda had been wondering the same thing, but hadn't liked to mention his injury. Fenton, however, seemed quite relaxed about it.

'With no difficulty, my lady,' he replied. 'I've been practising in the paddock. It's not hard, one-handed, once you get the hang of it.'

Watson came out with the luggage, which was piled into the boot. Then the two ladies were helped into the back seat of the car and made comfortable with cushions.

'I hope you have a comfortable journey, my lady,' said Watson, before he closed the doors.

As Fenton pulled away from the kerb, Lucinda found she was holding her breath, unobtrusively watching how he managed to drive with his damaged arm. And then it struck her. Much of the muscle in his upper left arm had been damaged, but his hand was strong, able to grip the steering wheel and change the gears. The journey was uneventful, but even so, both ladies were relieved to arrive at Crayne House without mishap.

Lady Melcome Senior was staying with Lucinda to be on hand when her grandchild was born. Dr Tanner, who had been looking after her in London, had recommended an experienced midwife, Sister Frances, and she too moved into the house, to be close by as the day drew nearer. They were all now comfortably established as they waited, with varying degrees of patience, for the new arrival.

There had been several improvements made at Crayne House while David had been away at the war, the main one being its electrification. Lofty Hanch, the ex-army electrician, had been as good as his word and by the end of January, there was electricity at the touch of a switch in every room. No question anymore of oil lamps and candles, the work was done and the convenience delighted everyone concerned, particularly the Crofts, who had lived in the large house without electricity or gas for nearly twenty years.

Mrs Croft was almost in tears when the lights were first switched on.

'Oh, my lady,' she said to Lady Senior, 'what a difference it'll make to all of us.'

'Well, you have Lady Melcome to thank,' replied Lady Senior. 'We should have done it years ago.'

The telephone had also been installed and connected to the local exchange, so there was now easy communication between Crayne and London, though Mrs Croft treated that with far more caution.

'You have to be careful what you say, my lady,' Mrs Croft

warned her, 'because I'm pretty sure that operator at the exchange listens to every word. That instrument's no good for secrets.'

Preparations had also been made for the arrival of the baby. Having discussed matters with David's mother, Lucinda had set up the nursery on the top floor. She wasn't sure she would want the baby so far away from her, but when Lady Senior pointed out that it had been the nursery for generations of Melcomes, including David, Lucinda acceded.

'Sister Frances will have the room next to the child,' Lady Melcome Senior said. 'There is a bathroom up there and plenty of room for a day nursery when the time comes.'

'How long will Sister Frances stay?' wondered Lucinda anxiously.

'As it's your first baby, she'll stay about four weeks, but she's a midwife, not a nanny.' replied her mother-in-law. 'We should be interviewing suitable nannies sooner rather than later. You will need someone experienced, to ensure the child is properly cared for.'

An advertisement was placed in *The Lady* magazine and there had been a procession of nannies applying for the job. The two Lady Melcomes had made a short list and then interviewed them together. It came down to two, both supplying glowing references, Freda Rush, Lady Senior's choice, and Gladys Moore, Lucinda's. Freda Rush was in her forties, and to Lucinda's eye as stiff and starched as the cap and apron she wore to her interview.

Her grey eyes are cold, thought Lucinda. They would miss nothing and would pardon no mistakes. Previously nanny to Sir Anthony Beacon's son Beverley, she was no longer required now that young master Beacon, aged seven, had gone away to prep school.

Gladys Moore was a little younger, but she had a ready smile and had only left her last place, with Mr and Mrs Vernon, because her charges, twin girls, now had a governess and there were no more babies expected in the nursery. She answered Lady Senior's questions in a gentle voice, and though it was clear she would stand no nonsense in her nursery, she displayed a warmth when speaking of her erstwhile charges that appealed to Lucinda.

'Of course it must be your decision,' Lady Senior said in a tone at odds with her words, 'but Nanny Rush is the more experienced and the Beacons are, of course, a well-known family.'

'I found her a little cold,' replied Lucinda, and intimidating she thought but did not say. 'Nanny Moore had a warmer personality, and her references were just as good, don't you think?'

'Yes, but you have to consider that standards in the Vernons' household may not have been quite as high as Sir Anthony's,' remarked her mother-in-law.

'Possibly,' conceded Lucinda. 'But I think Nanny Moore would fit in better in our household, and I think David would like her better.' And that made the decision. Gladys Moore was offered the position and would move in to Crayne House as soon as the baby was born.

Fenton had become a fixture on the staff, and though there were no hunters in the stables since David had taken his two cavalry horses, Hector and Lysander, with him, there were still two shire horses, Barley and Rye, who worked the fields of the home farm and needed looking after.

As her time drew ever nearer, Lucinda became increasingly anxious about the actual birth. When she applied to her mother for information, Isabella simply said, 'You will go into labour, the midwife will be there to help you and after a short while, you'll produce an heir for David.'

In light of this unhelpful advice, Lucinda turned to her maid, Clara, for more information. It was, after all, Clara who had explained things to her mistress before, when she had realised that Lucinda was expecting long before Lucinda had herself.

It amazed Clara how little her mistress had been told of what to expect. It was not considered genteel for a lady to know exactly how babies came into the world once the nine months of waiting were over. Clara, who had seen her mother give birth more than once, was able to give Lucinda an explanation of how the baby would be born.

'There will be pains, my lady, contractions that will be pushing your baby out, and your waters will break, but Sister Frances will be with you all the time and knows what to do.'

'Waters?'

'Your baby is protected in a sort of bag of water,' Clara explained. 'That has to pour out and the baby comes after. It's one of the signs the baby is coming. Then when the time is right you will give a final push and Sister Frances will ease the child from your body. The moment she does, the pain will stop. The baby will have to be washed clean, but then be put in your arms.'

'It doesn't sound very dignified,' said Lucinda doubtfully, trying not to sound too afraid. Dignified? It sounded awful.

'It isn't,' agreed Clara,' but I promise you, it's what every woman, from the queen to the scullery maid, goes through, before she can become a mother, and the minute you have the little mite in your arms you'll forget the pain.'

The last days of June were hot, and Lucinda became increasingly uncomfortable. Sister Frances insisted she stay in the house, keep her legs up to stop her ankles from swelling, and eat what she called 'gentle food' as well as drink copious draughts of water.

She did as she was told, but however she sat or lay, she couldn't get comfortable. Her back ached and she twisted and turned trying to ease it, but nothing seemed to help much and it settled into a dull ache. Sometimes she could feel the baby kicking as if trying to escape.

'You're tired of being in there, aren't you, little one?' she whispered. 'Never mind, it won't be long.'

It turned out to be sooner than she had expected. Feeling an urgent need to go to the bathroom, she heaved herself out of her chair and slowly negotiated the stairs to her room. As she went into the privacy of her bedroom she paused, horrified to realise she had wet herself before she could get to the lavatory. Suddenly afraid, she rang the bell for Clara. Only Clara should see how she had disgraced herself. As she stood waiting for her maid to appear, Lucinda had a sudden memory of the last time she had wet her drawers and of being smacked by her nanny.

'I won't allow Nanny Moore to smack you,' she told her baby and was rewarded by yet another kick in her stomach.

When Clara came to her mistress, arrived in answer to her ring, she took one look at her and said, 'I think we should call for Sister Frances now, my lady.' As they waited for the midwife to come up from the servants' hall, Clara helped Lucinda take off her damp clothes and eased her into the nightdress they had chosen for her lying in.

Sister Frances bustled into the room and immediately took over, ordering Clara to go downstairs at once and tell Mrs Croft to boil some water and have it carried upstairs to the master's bedroom. The bed she shared with David had already been prepared for the birth.

Lucinda looked at the bed with new eyes; the bed where she and David had lain together to make this new person about to be born. Sister Frances helped her into the bed, and as she did so, it seemed to Lucinda that someone had just plunged a knife into her stomach so that she cried out with the unexpected pain.

'Now then, my lady,' said the midwife. 'None of that, there's a way to go yet.'

Clara had been despatched to tell Lady Senior that her young ladyship was now in labour, but it would be some time yet.

David's mother had heard the scream and hoped that the labour would not be a long one. Going to the telephone, she rang the McFarlane house in Chanynge Place. The phone was answered by Felstead, who told her only Mr Iain was at home. Wondering if it would be proper to tell Lucinda's brother that she was in labour, and remembering Mrs Croft's warning about the operator at the exchange, she decided to let him know obliquely, without actually using the word and asked to speak to him.

THE GIRLS WHO DARED TO LOVE

'Good morning, Mr McFarlane,' she said when she he came on the line. 'This is Lady Melcome speaking.'

'Good morning, Lady Melcome,' replied Iain. 'I'm sorry, my mother isn't here to take your call.'

'That is no problem,' said her ladyship. 'I just wanted to inform her that the baby will be arriving very soon.'

'You mean Lucy's having the baby now?'

'Very soon,' confirmed Lady Melcome. 'Please will you pass the message on to your parents?' And before he could ask any more embarrassing questions, she replaced the receiver and the line went dead.

For a moment Iain stared at the telephone in his hand and wondered what to do. His parents would be out until late afternoon. It was Friday and Iain had decided to take the day off to be with Diana. He'd been invited to have dinner with her in Park Lane and it seemed to him too beautiful an afternoon to spend in the office, but less than half an hour ago there had been a ring at the doorbell and moments later Felstead had brought in a telegram, surprisingly addressed not to Iain's parents, but to him.

'Telegram for you, Mr Iain,' Felstead said, holding out a tray.

Surprised, Iain reached for the familiar buff envelope. Who on earth would be sending him a telegram? They were dreaded by every family with someone fighting in France, but Iain had no one at the front, and it was with some curiosity that he slit it open.

Felstead waited at the door while Iain read the message, not once but twice. It had been sent from a post office in Southampton earlier that morning.

ARRIVE WATERLOO 25 JUNE 3.30pm STOP PLEASE
MEET STOP SECRET STOP MELCOME

David. Of course it was David. He must be coming home on leave.

403

'Any reply, sir?' asked Felstead. 'The boy's waiting.'
'Yes,' replied Iain. 'That's the reply, Felstead.

YES STOP IAIN.

Felstead went back to the waiting telegraph boy to reply to
the message, while Iain looked again at the telegram.

Lucinda's husband was coming home on leave, coming
today, this afternoon and it was to be a surprise. Lucinda was
herself at Crayne and according to her mother-in-law, if Iain had
understood the rather cryptic message correctly, actually having
her baby right now.

She'll be overjoyed when she hears the news, thought Iain. But
then there was the instruction to keep it secret.

Iain immediately summoned Felstead.

'There must be no mention of this telegram, Felstead, you
understand? Its arrival must remain entirely between you and
me.' Felstead looked affronted and Iain went on hastily, 'I'm not
suggesting you gossip, Felstead, don't think that, but it is most
important that there is no speculation about it.'

'I understand, sir,' said Felstead, stiffly.

'What's the date today?' Iain asked.

'I believe it's Friday twenty-fifth of June, sir.'

'I was afraid it was,' murmured Iain. 'Thank you, Felstead.'

The butler, still stiff with umbrage, left the room and Iain had
an hour and a half to decide what to do.

David'll want to go drive down to Crayne immediately,
thought Iain, but his car is already there. Croxton is out with
the parents, so we can't take the Rolls. We'll have to go by train.
And I must send a message to Diana to say why I can't come to
dinner after all.

About to write a note to Diana, he had a better idea. As I've
got time to kill before his train gets in, I could go and see her
now and explain.

The secrecy wouldn't apply to Diana, only to those who might see Lucy and spoil the surprise.

Having made his plan, he wrote a note to his parents asking them to telephone Crayne House as soon as they got in, and then rang again for Felstead.

'I have to go out, Felstead,' he said when the butler came in. 'Please could you give this note to my parents as soon as they get in? It's most important.'

Felstead took the note and, laying it on the letter tray in the hall, said, 'Anything else, sir?'

'No, thank you,' replied Iain, 'not at present.' He was careful not to repeat the warning about the telegram.

Five minutes later he was in a taxi on the way to Park Lane.

Diana was sitting, reading, in the shade of a mulberry tree in the garden behind the apartment. She was dressed in a casual summer skirt and blouse, and had taken her shoes off, but to Iain she still looked as beautiful as ever. Wragge had sent him unannounced into the garden and for a moment he'd watched her unnoticed, enjoying her beauty, as if for the first time.

Sensing someone watching her, Diana looked up and saw him. 'Iain!' she exclaimed with a smile. 'What a lovely surprise! I didn't think you'd be here until much later.'

'Well, I'm afraid I'm not here at all really,' admitted Iain. 'And I can't stay.'

'Why ever not?' said Diana with a pout. 'Have you somewhere more important to be? With someone more important than me?'

'No. Well, not exactly,' Iain paused. The idea which had come to him in the taxi, and had seemed such a good one, now seemed crass.

'The thing is, well, Lucinda's having her baby now.'

'You mean now this very minute?' cried Diana, startled.

'Yes, I think so.' He explained about the telephone call from Lucy's mother-in-law.

'But that's not the problem,' and he pulled the telegram out of his pocket to show her. 'This arrived about an hour ago.'

'And it's from Lucy's husband?'

Iain nodded. 'Yes. He must be home on leave and going to surprise her. The problem is that he'll think his car is here in town and he can simply collect it and drive straight down to Crayne.'

'And isn't it?'

'No, David's man came up from Crayne to fetch Lucy and Lady Melcome a couple of weeks ago and the car is still down there. My parents are out with Croxton in our car until later this afternoon...'

'And so you want us to take him in Little Elsie!' exclaimed Diana.

'Well, not exactly,' admitted Iain. 'I was just wondering if I could borrow her to drive him down as quickly as possible.'

'No, you can't,' said Diana, so firmly that Iain stared at her in surprise.

'Well,' he stumbled, 'it was just a thought, you know. I doubt if he has much leave. Pity if he wasted any more of it, sitting on the slow train to Buckingham.'

'Of course it would,' agreed Diana.'

'So, why can't we take Little Elsie and get him there as fast as we can?'

'We can,' replied Diana, 'but I shall be driving!'

Iain sighed. He knew Diana had been taking driving lessons from Chambers, Lord Waldon's chauffeur, but he hadn't yet seen her behind the wheel.

'Oh, come on Di-dy,' he said using his private name for her. 'We'll need to get there as fast as possible.'

'I can drive fast,' retorted Diana. 'I often do with Chambers.'

'Look,' began Iain, 'perhaps we should suggest David drives.'

'He'll probably drive faster than I would,' pointed out Diana with a grin.

'Di-dy, are you going to take pity on the man,' said Iain, 'and let us use your car to get him to Crayne to be there when his son is born?'

Diana pulled a face and then suddenly smiled the smile that always made Iain's heart beat faster.

'Of course I am, but not for your sake, for Lucy's.'

'And David or I can drive?'

'You drive a hard bargain, Iain McFarlane,' said Diana, 'but you can drive if you want to. Now, give me time just to change into something more respectable and then we'll fetch the car.'

'Will Chambers let you take it without him?'

'Chambers is out with my father, so he can't object.'

Iain had only driven Diana's Little Elsie once, but they got her started and within fifteen minutes, they were on their way to Waterloo station.

The train from Southampton steamed in exactly on time, and Iain and Diana saw David hurrying across the concourse towards them.

'Iain!' he cried grasping Iain's outstretched hand. 'Thank you for coming.' Then he turned to Diana and, before Iain could introduce her, said, 'How do you do? You must be Lady Diana.'

'Yes,' replied Diana, holding out her hand. 'How do you do, David?'

David seemed entirely unmoved by her casual use of his Christian name, simply demanding, 'How's Lucy? Is she still at Crayne?'

'She is,' replied Iain, 'and we're on our way to see her now.'

'Where's the car?' asked David.

'Yours is already down at Crayne,' answered Iain.

'So we're going in mine,' said Diana, adding with a grin at Iain, 'but you can drive if you want to.'

However, David turned down that suggestion and so it was Iain after all who sat behind the steering wheel. Concentrating on the road and the traffic, Iain said, 'You'd better tell David what's been happening, Diana.'

So Diana told him about the short telephone call to the McFarlane household from his mother. 'She didn't exactly say Lucy was having the baby, but she said it would be arriving "very soon" and asked him to tell his parents.'

'She said "very soon" twice,' prompted Iain, 'and then abruptly she put the receiver down... or else there was a fault on the line. Whichever, the line went dead, so I wasn't able to ask anything else.'

'You really think that Lucy is actually having the baby, now this minute?' demanded David.

'As far as we know,' replied Iain.

'Then you'd better put your foot down,' said David, with a trace of panic in his voice. 'I need to be there.'

'Sorry, David, but I've got my foot to the floor as it is. Hills slow Elsie down, you know.'

'How much leave have you got?' Diana asked, hoping a change of subject might help alleviate the tension.

'Just a week. Then I have to go to the War Office for a couple of meetings, before I go back to France.'

'Lucy's going to be over the moon that you're here,' Diana said. 'Such a surprise!'

'Well, I didn't know until yesterday that I could definitely come,' David said. 'I'd applied for leave in June weeks ago, but you never know if promised leave will be cancelled for some reason or other and I didn't want her to get her hopes up and then be disappointed. I didn't want to tempt fate, so I didn't send the telegram until I was off the boat and on my way to the station.'

'Anyway, you're here now,' said Diana, 'and whether she is having the baby now or not, you'll be together in another hour or so.'

Lucinda was exhausted. She had been prepared for pain, but nothing like the pain of the contractions that stabbed her in the abdomen at regular intervals. The first pain that had surprised her into a scream was repeated over and over again, and though she tried not to cry out, the sweat poured off her and she moaned in anticipation of the next one. Clara sat beside the bed, bathing her forehead with rosewater, sponging her face and neck to try and soothe her.

Sister Frances wasn't concerned that Lucinda's baby was taking its time to make its entrance. It was a first baby after all, and they were notoriously slow. She checked that the infant was presenting the right way round; not a breach birth. Thankful for that anyway. She knew she could have turned it if necessary, she had done it several times before, but it was a process she hoped to avoid. On some occasions it was relatively simple, but on others it had been impossible and the baby had forced its way into the world feet first.

With a nod to Clara to keep bathing Lucinda's face, the midwife slipped out of the room, and went in search of Lady Melcome Senior, who was sitting in her private parlour.

'How much longer?' she demanded when Sister Frances came in.

'Hard to tell,' replied the midwife. 'It's a first baby...'

'Should we send for the doctor?' asked Lady Melcome.

'No need for that,' Sister Frances assured her. 'I just thought I'd let you know that it may be a while yet. Clara is with her and keeping her cool with rosewater. She seems a sensible girl.'

Sister Frances might not have been worried by the slow progress of Lucinda's labour, but Clara was. She looked at the mother-to-be, lying amid the crumpled bedclothes, her skin pale, her eyes closed. She was of delicate build, the bulge of her pregnancy standing out, and Clara wondered how much more her mistress could take.

When Sister Frances returned to the bedside, she examined her patient again and relaxed a little: the baby's head was now engaged, and though it was only the very top of the head she could see, at least it was progress.

As Little Elsie was finally approaching Crayne Abbas, the car began to splutter and lose power.

David, who had dozed off in the front seat, started awake. 'What's the matter?'

'I think we might be running out of petrol,' said Iain.

'There should be a can in the boot,' Diana said. 'Chambers never travels without one.'

'But Chambers didn't know we were travelling,' said Iain. He drew up at the side of the road, but kept the engine running. 'Look in the boot, David.'

David got out of the car and flung open the boot, in which he was relieved to see a large jerrycan. He grabbed it, but though he could feel petrol sloshing about inside, it felt ominously light.

'Where's the tank?' he called to Diana.

Diana climbed out of the car to show him. She had seen Chambers refuel the car on several occasions, and she pointed to the pipe leading to the fuel tank.

'You have to turn off the engine when you refuel,' Diana called to Iain.

'I daren't,' Iain called back. 'We might never get her started again.'

'If you don't, you might blow up Elsie and us with her.'

'She's right,' said David. 'You'll have to turn it off.'

As soon as the engine died, David removed the petrol cap and poured the contents of the jerrycan into the tank.

'It should be enough to get us there,' he said when they were on the road once more, and he was right... just. As they turned in through the gates of Crayne House, Little Elsie began to splutter again and despite careful nurturing, she finally came to a halt.

'You wait here,' David said as he sprang out onto the drive. 'I'll send Fenton to fetch you.' And with that he set off at a run towards the house.

Diana got into Elsie's passenger seat and heaved a sigh of relief. 'Well,' she said, turning to Iain, still sitting behind the wheel, 'we made it!'

'Let's hope David has as well.'

David reached the house and banged on the front door, and when it didn't open instantly banged again and again.

After what seemed an age, Croft, grumbling at the impatience of whoever it was demanding entry, opened the door to find his master on the step.

'Where's my wife?' David demanded.

'She's upstairs, sir, but…'

With no further ado David took the stairs two at a time only to find his way barred by a nurse when he tried to enter the room.

'Who are you?' she demanded. 'You can't come in here.'

'I can and I will. I'm her husband.'

'I don't care if you're the King of England,' snapped the nurse. 'Your wife is indisposed and will not want to see you.'

At that moment Lady Melcome, alerted by Croft that her son had arrived, hurried up the stairs to welcome him.

'David,' she cried. 'My dear boy, why didn't you let us know you were coming?'

'I didn't know myself,' David said as he kissed his mother on the cheek. 'Now, I want to see Lucy.'

'I don't think that's a good idea,' said his mother mildly. 'She's still…'

'I'm here in time?'

'In time for what? It'll be a while before the baby is actually born. Sister Frances will tell you when you may see her. Come downstairs and wait with me.'

Sister Frances was still bristling with indignation at the thought the husband had believed he could simply walk in to see his wife, before the baby was born.

'It's no place for a man,' she muttered. 'No place at all.'

A cry from within the room sent the midwife hurrying back to the bedside, and as the door swung closed behind her, David had a brief glimpse of Lucy, lying on the bed gripping Clara's hand.

Moments later the door opened again and Clara came out.

'Clara?'

'I have to get more towels, sir,' she said as she hurried to the linen cupboard.

As she came back, David caught her by the hand. 'Clara, will you tell Lucy I'm here?'

Clara looked at him anxiously. 'I don't think Sister Frances will like it if I do.'

'And I won't like it if you don't,' David said with a smile. 'I want her to know I'm here.'

Clara nodded and went back inside. This time the door did not immediately swing shut, and David had another sight of his beloved Lucy lying on the bed. At that very minute Lucy turned her head and saw him in the split second before the door was pushed shut by the midwife.

'David,' said his mother, who still stood on the landing. 'Leave her be.'

At least she knows I'm here, David thought, not, as I had hoped, a complete surprise, but she knows.

'I think David has forgotten us,' Diana said after they had waited a quarter of an hour. They had left Elsie and were sitting on a bench in the shade of one of the lime trees that lined the drive.

'Let's just walk up to the house, Fenton can bring some petrol and fetch Elsie any time.'

Together they walked hand in hand along the drive. The evening sun lay mellow on the garden and they paused to look out across to the stables, where they could see Fenton grooming one of the shire horses.

'Diana?'

'Hhmm?'

'Will you marry me?' The words were out before Iain had time to consider them. When the time came to ask her, when he'd asked permission of her father, when he'd bought the engagement ring he'd seen in Garrard's, when they were in a summer garden beneath a full moon, then he'd propose to her.

Diana froze, not looking at him, still staring out to the stables. 'What did you say?'

'I said will you marry me? But I shouldn't have.'

'Why not?'

'I haven't asked your father yet.'

'No,' agreed Diana, still not looking at him. 'But you have asked me, and I'm the one who needs to answer... don't you think?'

For a long moment Iain made no reply, and then he reached for both her hands and turning her towards him, he said, 'I love you very much, Di-dy. Will you marry me?'

Diana gave a gurgle of laughter and, looking up into his anxious eyes, said, 'I was beginning to think you'd never ask. And Pop was getting quite worried, you know.'

'Is that yes?' ventured Iain, and before she could answer he drew her into his arms.

'Yes, I suppose it is,' said Diana, when she was able to say anything at all. And they kissed again.

'Come on,' she said still gripping Iain's hand and leading him towards the house. 'We'd better go and see if there's a baby yet.'

They found David pacing up and down the landing like a caged lion.

'The bedroom door's closed and that battleaxe of a midwife won't let me in,' he said. 'I have only had a glimpse of Lucy through the door when the maid came out.'

'Well, she's probably right,' said Diana. 'Having a baby isn't a very dignified procedure. One's awfully exposed, you know.'

Both the men looked at her in amazement. Neither of them was a prude, but neither of them had ever heard such frankness from a lady, and certainly not from an unmarried one.

'Diana!' scolded Iain. 'You are a disgrace!'

'I think you've got your hands full there, Iain,' grinned David.

'Yes,' Iain looked across at his new fiancée, 'I think so too.'

From the bedroom Lucinda cold hear muffled voices on the landing, and could hardly believe what she was hearing. David. Her beloved David. She thought she had seen him as the door closed and was going to ask Sister Frances, but something in the woman's face deterred her. Clara had come over to her side, waiting for the midwife to move away so she could whisper Sir David's message. But Sister Frances did not move away. She examined Lucy again. The contractions were coming all the time now.

'In a moment you'll need to push,' she said to Lucy. 'But not until I tell you.'

The baby's head was beginning to emerge. Any moment now.

'On the next contraction, push,' said the midwife and Lucinda gathered her strength.

As Sister Frances put her hands out to hold the emerging baby's head, she suddenly gave a cry. 'Don't push. Don't push.'

It seemed impossible not to, but the urgency in the midwife's voice made Lucinda try to hold back. Clara watched as Sister Frances slipped her hands behind the baby's head.

'Don't push!'

It was then that Clara saw it too: the umbilical cord was round the baby's neck. She drew a sharp breath, watching as, with gentle fingers, the nurse gripped the cord and looped it forward over the infant's head, releasing the pressure it had been exerting and allowing her to say, 'Now push.'

Moments later, with the head clear and free, Sister Frances eased Lucinda's son into the world, giving him a smart smack on his backside, causing him to draw his first breath and protest at such indignity.

'A fine boy,' said the midwife as she passed him over to Clara. 'We'll get him tidied up,' she said, 'and you too,' she said to Lucinda, 'and then we can tell the father.'

Those on the landing had heard the cry and knew that another soul had been delivered safely into the world.

'She has to let me in now,' David said, moving towards the door.

'No,' said Diana firmly. 'You must wait until they're ready for you.'

'Quite right,' came a voice from the stairs.

'But I don't even know if I have a son or a daughter,' said David in frustration.

'Let Lucinda tell you herself,' suggested Lady Melcome as she reached the landing. 'Don't spoil it for her. She's done all the hard work, let her have a moment with her baby.'

It seemed an eternity to David, but at last the door opened and he was allowed in. Lucy was sitting propped up in bed, and in her arms she held a bundle wrapped up in a shawl. All David could see was the top of its head.

She beamed across at him. 'Oh, David,' she cried, tears of joy pouring down her cheeks. 'I can't believe you're here. Come and meet Leo.'

David crossed to the bedside and looked down at the scrap of humanity he and Lucy had produced. Leo.

'Here,' Lucy said holding the bundle out to him, 'you hold him.'

For a moment David hesitated and then, stepping closer, he reached and took his son in his arms. He looked down at the baby lying comfortably in the crook of his arm. Leo's eyes were open, gazing up unfocussed at his father, and in that moment David knew that he would do anything to protect the child.

Suddenly the door opened and Sister Frances bustled back in. She stopped in shock as she saw that it was David holding the baby.

'Now, now,' she scolded. 'Baby should be with his mother and then she needs to sleep. You should be outside giving the family the good news that you have a strong and healthy son.'

David passed Leo back to Lucinda, saying, 'I'll come and see you when you've had a rest, darling Lucy.'

Leaning down he kissed her gently on the lips, the first kiss they had shared since that day in September when he had walked out of their bedroom in Sloane Square and gone to war.

The next six days seemed to fly by. Lucinda was still tired, but she was anxious not to miss a precious minute of David's leave. Sister Frances had said she should be staying in bed for at least ten days, and then be allowed to get up in the afternoons.

'That's ridiculous,' cried Lucinda. 'I'm not ill.'

'No,' agreed the midwife,' but giving birth is a strain on your body, and you need to rest.'

Eventually they agreed on a compromise. Lucinda should stay in bed until after breakfast and Leo's ten o'clock feed. Then she could to get up and come downstairs. That was her favourite time of day. She and David spent those precious hours alone in the drawing room, where they could sit by the long windows and look out across the garden.

Against her better judgement, Sister Frances allowed Leo to be brought down in his crib and placed beside his father. She was then dismissed and was very much afraid that his father picked him up, holding him asleep in his arms, not what a father was supposed to do at all. But David was all too aware that he only had one short week in which to get to know his son, to feel the baby safely in his arms, relaxed against his shoulder. The next time he saw him... if there was a next time... the child might be several months, if not years, older. Who knew when the war might end? Though he kept a smile on his face, he was under no illusion as to the state of the war continuing in the trenches.

The news of Iain's and Diana's engagement had been greeted with delight by Lucy and communicated by an effervescent Diana to her parents, in excited telephone calls.

'And about time too,' laughed Lord Waldon.

'You must stay here for the Christening,' Lucy cried. 'Leo is being baptised on the day before David leaves and we'd love you both to be godparents.'

Lucinda's parents came down to attend the service. Lady McFarlane had initially been dismayed by the news of Iain's engagement, but as her husband pointed out before she was too outspoken about it, 'It's a very good match for Iain, you know; an earl's daughter, my dear.'

'It rather depends on which earl,' retorted Isabella. 'Waldon and his daughter are too fast for my liking.'

'A point you've made several times already,' remarked Keir, 'and since, like it or not, we are now going to be connected to the Waldons, it's something I don't wish to hear again.'

As always, when Keir spoke to her in that tone of voice, Isabella at last took heed.

The family and the godparents gathered round the font and watched as baby Leo David Randall Melcome, dressed in the starched lace of the Melcome family Christening robe, was baptised into the Church of England as a member of the aristocracy should be.

That night, to the private horror of Sister Frances, David and Lucy lay side by side in the big bridal bed. There was no question of them making love, but each drew comfort from the tender warmth of the other's body.

Both knew that tomorrow they would have to say goodbye with dignity and smiles. There could be no tears, or at least only in private.

First thing in the morning Fenton was going to drive David up to London for his meeting at the War Office. David went up to the nursery and seen only by Clara, sitting silently in the corner of the room, he gently lifted his son from his crib. Leo was awake and lay quietly in his father's arms, as if he knew that this was an important moment. David kissed the child on the top of his head and murmured, 'Goodbye, old son. Look after your mother.'

He and Lucy had said their private goodbyes in their bedroom, but determined to see him off properly, Lucy was dressed and downstairs when Fenton brought the car round to the front door. The whole household was lined up in the hall to wish the master God speed, and gentleman as always, David thanked them for their continued care of his family. Finally, David took Lucy's hand and raised it to his lips. 'Look after the heir,' he said with mock humour, before leaning close, so that only she should hear, and whispering, 'we'll make another one on my next leave.' Then he stepped into the car and was driven away.

'Now, my lady,' said Sister Frances. 'Back to bed with you. It's too early for you to be down here.' And for once Lucinda didn't protest, but allowed herself to be led upstairs to the bed she and David had just shared, where the pillows still carried his scent, and clutching one in her arms she wept until she fell into the sleep of exhaustion. When she awoke, he would still be gone, but she had a new treasury of memories to keep her going until she was back in his arms once more. And she had Leo. The greatest gift of all.

Acknowledgements

I was writing this book during a very difficult period in my life and would probably not have completed it without the support I received from the people around me, my family and friends. So my thanks go to everyone involved.

My editor Rosie de Courcy for her steady reassurance when I was struggling, allowing me to write at my own pace.

My agent, Judith Murdoch, always a calm voice of confidence, encouraging me to keep going, and not least my loyal following of readers.

It is done and I thank you all.

About the Author

DINEY COSTELOE is the author of twenty-four novels, several short stories, and many articles and poems. She has three children and seven grandchildren, so when she isn't writing, she's busy with her family. Find Diney online at dineycosteloe.co.uk, or on X @Dineycosteloe